Feldheym

Olden, Marc.

Kisaeng   c1991

DATE DUE

30✓ 6/97

KISAENG

A NOVEL

MARC OLDEN

DONALD I. FINE, INC.
NEW YORK

9/13/91
Feld

Library of Congress Cataloging-in-Publication Data

Olden, Marc.
Kisaeng / Marc Olden.
p.   cm.
ISBN 1-55611-247-5
I. Title.
PS3565.L29K5   1991
813'.54—dc20   90-56066
CIP

Manufactured in the United States of America

10   9   8   7   6   5   4   3   2   1

Designed by Irving Perkins Associates

For my beloved mother Courtenaye,
who told me to believe in the magic of my dreams.

Kisaeng: Korean Geishas.
Literal meaning: recreational creature

It is not beauty that traps a man, but himself.

Chinese

Use a thorn to draw a thorn.

Thai

ONE

Laughing Boy, the counterfeiter, flew home to Seoul on a cold December morning. He brought with him from Hong Kong a Sharpei puppy and ten million dollars cash.

The puppy, whose breed dated from China's second-century Han dynasty, was for his mistress, a fourteen-year-old Austrian named Elana whom he'd acquired in London eight months before in exchange for a Fabergé silver clock worth fifty thousand pounds.

The ten million was for Col. Cha Youngsam, the mournful-looking, forty-two-year-old head of South Korea's CIA. "The Razor" Youngsam was ruthless, manipulative and fanatical about squirreling away cash. Laughing Boy owed him thirty million dollars and had three weeks to pay it all or be killed.

Time had never been more valuable. In a week he would be off again, commencing a ten-day trip to Europe and America, where clients were waiting to pay him twenty-three million dollars for counterfeit bonds, securities and American currency. With luck he would have enough to pay Youngsam and turn a three-million-dollar profit.

There was the unexpected, of course. Like the flow of water, a man's future was uncertain. Everything was the will of heaven, and the world did not belong to any man. Still, Laughing Boy expected to reimburse Youngsam, then return to the world of those who were happy.

1

Laughing Boy's real name was Park Song. He was in his late thirties, a slim, sharp-chinned Korean with slick dark hair, small eyes and a white-toothed smile. He had acquired his nickname because of constant and often untimely giggling. Those who believed that laughter sprang from the mouths of fools were easily taken in by Song's cheery exterior, which hid a powerful ego and a ferocious cunning.

He counterfeited traveler's checks, foreign bonds, securities and passports. His preeminent product, however, was the American hundred-dollar bill. It was a work of art into which he'd put all his aspirations and dreams. He prided himself on being able to approximate the loops, crosshatching and intricate whorls that made American paper money the hardest currency to copy. Whatever else he did imperfectly, Song created dollars well.

His sizable profits had gone into such investments as Hong Kong real estate, Taiwanese flea markets, a small Bordeaux vineyard and a Manila shopping mall. He had also treated himself to a course at Le Cordon Bleu in Paris, where he had spent twelve weeks learning to prepare classic French cuisine. Money brought him freedom and luxury. It also allowed him to buy love.

It was snowing when he cleared customs at Kimpo Airport without a baggage inspection, found his waiting limousine and settled in the back seat. He ordered David Mitla, the bearded thirty-five-year-old former Israeli paratrooper who was his bodyguard, to put the Sharpei's traveling case in the front seat.

The Korean chauffeur, a Judo silver medalist at the 1984 Olympics and sometime bodyguard, stacked the luggage in the trunk. He received no help from Mitla. The Israeli positioned himself with his back to the car, a hand on the Uzi beneath his Burberry topcoat as he scanned crowds entering and leaving the terminal.

From Kimpo the limousine headed east along the Han River toward downtown Seoul. Song poured himself cognac from the bar, drinking while he stared through tinted glass at ginkgo and willow trees whose bare branches were chalky with snow. He finished his third drink as the limousine passed Nanji Island, and began to tap nervously on the empty glass with a thumbnail when the car neared the pine-forested mountains just outside the city.

The day before, in Hong Kong, he had sold four million dollars in fake American hundred-dollar bills to a gnomelike Irish provo with a ratty mustache who claimed to have planted the bomb that killed Lord Mountbatten and his grandson. Laughing Boy had remained indifferent to the mick's appeal for admiration. Any fool knew that boasting and lying were the same thing.

The hundreds had gone for thirty-two cents on the dollar, a good price, though the total was far short of what Laughing Boy needed to stay alive. With no time to quibble he had been forced to sell choice Hong Kong investments at bargain prices: his floating restaurant anchored off Aberdeen, a seat on the Hong Kong stock exchange, a twelve-story chalet on Chi Ma Wan Peninsula and the three Kowloon motels that catered to prostitutes. His once financially secure future had disappeared, leaving him bitchy and depressed.

The ordeal with Youngsam was beginning to consume Song. It disturbed him to discover that being clever was no guarantee against setbacks. His possessions were dwindling, which was awful, but not as awful as seeing the deadline approach full tilt. He could always buy more property; he could not buy another life.

Until recently he had enjoyed the Razor's protection. Youngsam had shielded him from arrest, prevented his extradition to the West, furnished him with a KCIA passport and found buyers for his fake money. He had also covered up crimes involving Song's sinister obsession with the domination and abuse of women.

In turn, Song had served Youngsam as forger, informant, money launderer and assassin. Two weeks earlier something had gone wrong with the money laundering, costing Youngsam millions and leaving Song facing extinction. Could anyone survive the Razor's ill will when it came to money? A fish had a better chance of climbing a tree.

"To assure me of your good intentions you will make a down payment on your debt," Youngsam had said. "An immediate down payment."

A pain started in the small of Song's back and moved to his groin. "Immediate? You gave me three weeks to raise the money—"

"I insist on a show of good faith. Ten million dollars at once."

"I don't understand."

"To indicate your seriousness about settling the debt. If you don't make this down payment you will lose one finger a day until you do."

A tingling sensation in Song's hands and feet began to spread along his limbs. When he spoke his voice was thick. "Immediate, you said."

"I'm not unreasonable. You have two days before the loss of your fingers is at issue. As for the rest of the money, you still have three weeks to settle your account in full."

Song clenched his fists to stop his hands from shaking. There was no running away from this new complication in his life. To leave Korea would only mean eventual extradition from his new home to face murder charges in America and Italy. That his potential executioner was also his protector was an irony that did not amuse Laughing Boy.

But if raising thirty million dollars in three weeks was difficult, coming up with ten million in forty-eight hours was near impossible. Passing counterfeit to Youngsam was out of the question. KCIA forgery experts examined every dollar Song paid Youngsam; anyone discovering a single phony bill stood to win a bonus of a year's salary. As for Youngsam, he had vowed to attach all counterfeit bills to Song's body with a staple gun.

Until this second ultimatum, with its threat to his fingers, Song had reason to be confident and upbeat. He was an excellent counterfeiter, running his affairs with a minimum of waste and a tenacity of purpose. The Youngsam episode, a costly one to be sure, marked that rare occasion when he and not someone else had been the sheep thrown to the wolves.

His troubles with the KCIA chief had originated with Song's desire to own a bank, an idea that had persisted in his head for years and remained a fixation he could not control. In the past the timing had not been right; either he had lacked the money or been unable to secure the proper locale and front man. But three months ago these elements had finally joined together and Song had rushed forward to realize his life's dream. At last he was going to own the rainbow.

In September he had opened a bank in the Cayman Islands. His partner was Gerard Petrus, a plump fifty-two-year-old Frenchman and fellow Bordeaux vineyard owner for whom he had twice counterfeited U.S. Treasury bearer bonds. A banker with years of experience in handling covert accounts, Petrus also knew the importance of keeping secret banking information to himself.

Song saw Petrus as being gifted with a calculating mind and no end of willpower. Both planned their moves well in advance, hid their true feelings and used people to their advantage. Petrus was the constant schemer, never allowing his brain to be at rest while being careful about what he said. Song admired these traits, although he sometimes found it difficult to predict the Frenchman's next move.

The two knew people in need of financial secrecy. Cocaine cowboys, tax evaders, gun runners, intelligence agents, businessmen dodging creditors, husbands dodging wives, Third World politicians foreseeing early retirement. The demand for financial secrecy had never been greater.

Both agreed that the Cayman Islands were an ideal home for hot money. Located 475 miles south of Miami in the Caribbean, the islands' secrecy laws were more protective than those of Switzerland. Bank employees who dared admit the existence of a secret account faced two years in prison. Access to account information or identities of depositors was forbidden without a court order, which was rarely granted. What one was not informed about one could not inquire about.

While Petrus had more banking experience, Song himself knew a thing or two about secret assets, bribery, tax evasion and shell companies, the usual fiscal skullduggery consistent with offshore banking. He was well prepared for the world of secret money, where those who were able to handle hidden assets and keep information to themselves could become very wealthy indeed. Song and Petrus, it seemed, had only to open shop, remain mute and grow rich.

They formed a company, TransOcean-Caribbean, and agreed that Petrus should be the front man. The Frenchman had the more acceptable business profile, so why not leave the day-to-day running of the bank to him. Song, hidden behind shell companies registered in Panama and Luxembourg, would be the silent partner. Both would recruit depositors.

In the bank's third week Petrus telexed Song about customers he had signed up; one had made a half-million-dollar deposit with a promise of more to come. Song himself had secured two impressive clients, one of them the head of a Philippine tear-gas company who had made millions thanks to a surge in violent protests against Corazón Aquino's government. The other was Cha Youngsam, in need of a hiding place for bribes received from drug dealers and corrupt military contractors. Youngsam also wanted to conceal funds embezzled from his rich and very trusting wife.

If Song was committed to keeping the Razor as his benefactor, then assisting the spymaster in his hour of need was only realistic and farsighted. Besides, it made one feel important to do favors for powerful men. Helping the penny-pinching Youngsam to hoard his wealth would always insure Song a kind welcome. Or so he thought.

Two weeks earlier Youngsam had telephoned him at his Seoul home to ask if he knew that TransOcean-Caribbean money was being invested in Petrus's private business endeavors. A Korean businessman who imported Russian furs and regularly briefed Youngsam on his foreign contacts had reported that Petrus was quietly financing oil and gas ventures in Russia. A Korean consul in Liverpool had reported that Petrus was behind a front company speculating in the London gold market. In both cases Petrus had lost a great deal of TransOcean's money. Youngsam no longer trusted the Frenchman's fiscal integrity. He wanted his money back at once.

He had never met Petrus and had taken Song's word that the Frenchman knew his business. Song had recruited Youngsam for the bank. Song needn't bother laying the blame for the bank's problems on someone else. Song himself would have to make good all losses or suffer the consequences. Unfair or not, he was the scapegoat.

In fact, Song had known nothing about Petrus's secret ventures. The news caught him completely by surprise, leaving him panicky and with abdominal pains as he envisioned Youngsam's reaction if his money was not returned.

The KCIA chief viewed humanity with distrust bordering on paranoia. It was no surprise when he charged Song as well as Petrus with conniving to rob him. He ordered that his money, all thirty million dollars, be returned, and threatened to kill both of them if it was not.

Song had been toughened by army service in South Vietnam and Korea. Given his natural amorality, he had taken to the intrigue, brutality and corruption of his military life as a duck to water. He also possessed considerable training in *taekwon do*, Korean karate, and *keupso chirigi*, the art of attacking vital points on the body.

A year earlier when an American Secret Service agent working undercover tried to penetrate his organization, Song had killed him with a kick to the throat. More recently a brashly cheerful Italian from Interpol had attempted the same ploy, only to be strangled to death by Song, who had then covered the corpse in concrete and added it to the floor of a Hong Kong warehouse.

But for all his savage ways, Song could never hope to match Youngsam. The KCIA chief was Korea's most powerful man after the president, allowing him to commit criminal acts on a grand scale. And since Youngsam was not inclined to wait out his enemies, this made him even more dangerous.

As suspected, Petrus's business ventures were in serious trouble, and so was the bank. The Frenchman, far off in the Caribbean, appeared to be beyond Youngsam's reach. Song, however, residing in Seoul, was near enough to be pulled in whenever the spymaster saw fit. And it was during one such encounter following disclosure of the bank fiasco that Song was told to make good Youngsam's losses or suffer the consequences.

The bank's failure was Song's worst nightmare come to life. All telexes and telephone calls to Petrus went unanswered. Youngsam had him under surveillance and no doubt was tapping his phones. Song was ready to charter a plane to the Caymans, confront Petrus and beat him to death, when he learned that the Frenchman was headed for Haiti on a Cessna jet packed with gold bullion.

That same afternoon TransOcean-Caribbean Bank closed its doors permanently.

More bad news from Youngsam, whose spies were always at work: Cayman authorities had requested Song's immediate extradition. Petrus had let slip Song's full criminal history, coloring it somewhat with the claim that Song had conceived the bank fraud. Petrus added that his felonious partner, as he now called Song, had grabbed the lion's share of bank proceeds for himself.

A congenital and unrepentant liar, Song was as straightforward as he had ever been when he told Youngsam he had never taken a penny from the bank. The KCIA chief had less interest in claims of righteousness than in getting his money back.

Laughing Boy the deceiver had himself been deceived. And by a goddamn Frenchman. He learned that Petrus had surfaced in Paris to meet with attorneys and influential government friends who were being asked to intercede with Cayman authorities on Petrus's behalf. Through Youngsam, Song also learned that Petrus and his supporters had cut a deal with Cayman authorities, one that amounted to little more than a wrist slap. Petrus would voluntarily return to the islands to face prosecution, with the understanding that he receive not more than four months in the local jail, an easy place to do time it was said.

Worst of all, Petrus would not have to make restitution of any kind. The Frenchman's intermediaries successfully repeated the argument that Song had walked off with almost all the money, so let him reimburse depositors. Because Cayman authorities wanted to protect their banks from public scrutiny, Petrus would be allowed to keep the insignificant sum he claimed to have pilfered. As for Laughing Boy, to whom could he complain? His sordid history had branded him a villain; any claim of innocence became laughable.

For the Frenchman it had all ended well. Song, on the other hand, was furious at, for once, being blamed for something he had not done.

At noon two days earlier he had received a telephone call ordering him to KCIA headquarters, where the spymaster handed him a telex.

Yesterday morning, according to the telex, caretakers had discovered two large suitcases in the Bois de Vincennes on the southeast edge of Paris. Because of nearby bloodstains, police were called to the scene. The suitcases were found to contain most of the remains of a middle-aged white male whose body had been cut into pieces and wrapped in plastic garbage bags. The skull had been crushed and the neck of a broken bottle shoved up the corpse's rectum. All of his fingers had been sliced off.

The remains were identified as those of one Gerard Petrus, who had been missing since leaving his attorney's office on Quai des Tuileries twenty-four hours before. Three Asians had been seen removing two large suitcases from a blue Toyota still parked near a Bois de Vincennes entrance. When police searched the car they found a bloodied length of pipe, apparently used to club Petrus to death. They also found his fingers, which had been wrapped in tinfoil and placed in the glove compartment.

Song's heartbeat was suddenly irregular and the abdominal pains started again. Youngsam sat poker-faced behind his desk.

The spymaster said, "Petrus, as you can see, will not repeat his crimes. His arrogance in thinking he could get away with what he had done needed punishment. He offered to return the money, but, of course, I no longer trusted him. And a man I can't trust is a man of no further use to me.

"He was surprised at how much we knew about him. We knew, for example, that he'd paid large sums to certain French officials to intercede for him with Cayman police. He'd also paid off several outstanding debts and been quite generous with his attorneys. Much of the stolen money was no longer in his possession, and the rest, I've learned, is sequestered in numbered accounts in four different countries. Recovering it would be difficult, if not impossible."

Youngsam's deep-set eyes seemed to bore into Song. "I want my money back, which is the only reason you are still alive. Now let us take up the matter of your down payment."

Fifteen minutes later Song left Youngsam's office, waved his chauffeur away and began walking Seoul's streets. There was a tightness in his chest. In spite of the December chill he was perspiring. He cupped his face in both hands; his skin was hot and sweaty. He removed his hat and topcoat, dropped them on the sidewalk behind him and pushed into the lunchtime crowds, knocking an old man to the pavement.

How was he going to give Youngsam a ten-million-dollar down payment in just forty-eight hours?

Forty minutes later a weary Song found himself in Chongmyo, a forested park located in the center of Seoul and the site of several traditional temples. Stopping in front of one shrine, he bent over, hands on his knees, and breathed deeply. Then using his right fist he massaged the area over his heart. In minutes his breathing and heartbeat became normal. He approached the temple, eyes on the evil-repelling symbols—dragon, tiger and phoenix—carved into the beams and doorways. The temple opened only on special ceremonial days, so worshippers had left offerings of wine, pigs' legs and an ox's head on the front steps. In the December chill Song's nostrils flared at the smell of still-warm rice cakes.

Eyes closed, he stood alone in front of the temple, arms outstretched and fingers extended, fingers that Youngsam had just threatened to cut off. He swayed from side to side, barely hearing the distant buzz of traffic.

Suddenly he opened his eyes.

He knew how to get the down payment. Simply sell off some of his Hong Kong property.

Another thought had come to him as he stood in front of the temple, namely how he might get back at Youngsam.

Song began to giggle.

TWO

Park Song lived in an exquisite pavilion within sight of Seoul's Kyongbok Palace, where, in 1895, Japanese assassins murdered Korea's Queen Min, stabbing her, then burning her with kerosene. An enthusiastic gardener, he had planted many of the flowering lilac trees, giant pink lotuses and miniature maples within the arabesque walls surrounding the low, one-story building.

Recently he had added a temperature-controlled wing to house a collection of Hollywood memorabilia that included costumes worn by the midgets in *The Wizard of Oz* and rocks from California's Mount Lee, site of the legendary fifty-foot-high "Hollywood" sign. He delighted in Hollywood movies of the thirties, musicals in particular. A boundless admiration for Fred Astaire had led him to embrace tap dancing as a hobby.

In fond imitation of Joan Crawford, his kitchen was carpeted in white and a bedroom paneled entirely in Viennese mirrors. His homage to the actress also included eating the breakfast she had consumed for years: soda crackers with mustard and a coddled egg, no salt, no butter.

Two hours after arriving home with money collected for Youngsam via partial liquidation of assets and the provo sale, Song stepped into a huge sunken bronze tub modeled after one in Tom Mix's Beverly Hills mansion. Placing a T-shaped straight razor on the tub's edge, he then lowered himself up to his neck into the jasmine-scented water and sighed. A hot bath was that rare innocent pleasure which didn't bore him.

He had just completed the last of several telephone calls, this one to a customer in New York, guaranteeing that $1.5 million in counterfeit Brazilian treasury bonds would be delivered on time. The first step toward becoming businesslike was to appear businesslike.

In other telephone calls Song had cracked down on associates in Seoul and abroad. Paper needed for the final currency printing hadn't arrived from America, and while Song's printers insisted they were blameless, he had made it clear he wasn't interested in excuses. He'd been even more abusive with his American paper suppliers, threatening to have them killed if the paper was not in Seoul tomorrow morning.

No sweat, they'd said in that loose American way he'd come to despise. The paper was absolutely, positively, on its way and should arrive at any moment. Song had never made such a large request before and it wasn't easy to come up with so much paper on short notice, know what I mean? Song was unforgiving; when you forgave people they took advantage of you. The paper was to be in Seoul no later than tomorrow morning or there would be hell to pay.

He had not explained why he needed such an enormous amount of paper this instant. But as he knew, nothing was harder to keep than a secret. One could bet the truth would emerge in short order. The best he could do was pay Youngsam as quickly as possible and close this nasty chapter in his life.

Some knew Youngsam was pressing Song, but the counterfeiter was too brutal for others to amuse themselves with jokes at his expense. He demanded and received respect from coworkers and associates, Youngsam being the one exception. The hand you cannot bite, you kiss. Committed to retaining his fingers, Song had telephoned Youngsam from Hong Kong, confirming that the down payment would be made on time.

Later this same evening Youngsam was having his men collect the ten million and bring it to him at the home of his mistress, a former beauty queen whose film career he was sponsoring at considerable cost. The KCIA chief was also investing heavily in copper shares, believing that the spread of AIDS in Zambia and Zaire, source of much of the world's copper, would devastate the skilled work force

and produce a global shortage. When it came to sniffing out profit
Youngsam moved faster than a scalded dog.

In the tub, Song now patted his face with a large damp sponge. He
had just left an exuberant Elana next door in the master bedroom,
where she was holding a one-sided conversation with the Shar-pei.
The beige, long-faced dog was nervous and moody, which Elana saw
as being sensitive. Song, somewhat more discerning, viewed the puppy's behavior differently; like any purebred the dog was simply inclined to follow its own selfish whims.

Older women tended to possess this same selfishness, which was
why Song preferred adolescents in whom he could infuse certain
knowledge and skills. He schooled each girl in the feelings, manners
and attitudes of a *kisaeng*, the most delightful lover a man could wish
for. Song's affairs abruptly ended as he decreed. Then he would
select another girl and begin training her. Emphasis was placed upon
sexual submissiveness.

Song revered Korea's ancient traditions, particularly the tradition
of the *kisaeng*. It had begun almost a thousand years ago when the
court of the Koryo kingdom chose adolescent girls for their beauty,
charm and talent, then trained them to be singers, painters, musi-
cians, dancers and storytellers. This training produced the most
highly educated women in the country, women who became the
companions of kings, nobles, scholars and artists.

They were known as *kisaeng,* "recreational creature."

They were also known as the "perfect woman."

Tourists and foreign businessmen visiting Korea still had the opportunity to attend a *kisaeng* party at luxury restaurants, where they
were attended by female escorts who sang, danced, played traditional
musical instruments and wrote calligraphy with brush and ink.

But as Song knew only too well, today's *kisaeng* was merely part of
a sex industry aimed at male tourists from America, Japan, Europe
and Australia. What else could one say about women who had under-
gone a state training course, the two main components of which were
a commitment to anti-communism and a study of the sexual positions
preferred by Japanese men.

He wasn't fooled by government attempts to pass these females off
as replicas of those highly cultivated artists of past centuries. Today's
kisaeng was, in fact, a whore hired to entertain tired businessmen,

each of whom paid generously for the privilege of being swindled. The favors of these pseudo *kisaeng* did not come cheap.

Song's knowledge of "the perfect woman" was far from shallow. He owned rare books and age-old records on the subject, including antique scrolls describing a sixth-century group called *wonhwa,* "Original Flowers." The group, which predated *kisaeng,* was composed of beautiful young women chosen to serve as role models for the country. It was disbanded when one of its two female leaders killed the other in a jealous rage.

To a great extent Song had succeeded in instilling much of the true *kisaeng* tradition in Elana, who was bright, manageable and eager to please. The best tutors had been hired to teach her poetry writing, storytelling and Korean music, which she considered out of tune because it was not based on the tempered scale of the Western tonal system.

Song himself had handled some of the training, teaching her calligraphy and the royal court dances, which he had her perform wearing the traditional costume and tiny flower crown. He had also taught her folk dancing, with its graceful uplifting shoulder movements and slow rising and sinking movements of the knees. And he had taught her how to pour his drinks and place morsels of food in his mouth as *kisaeng* had done for centuries.

She mastered *hangul*, the relatively simple Korean alphabet, which consisted of only ten vowels and fourteen consonants. However, she had trouble speaking Korean, often forgetting to put verbs at the end of a sentence as required in proper speech. But with English words frequently appearing in Korean conversation Song didn't demand that Elana perfect the language. She was young and inexperienced; to be too critical would dampen her enthusiasm for learning.

As an orphan Elana had come to him without a penny to her name and wearing only the clothes on her back. Security, therefore, was important to her. Because a stable homelife mattered more than an unknown future she submitted to Song's demands. She had been a virgin who had turned out to be marvelously sensual, and under his direction an excellent lover. Sexually, she did whatever he wished, although with her passion came a possessive streak that he sometimes found annoying. To avoid impregnating her, Song bathed his testicles in warm water before intercourse, inducing temporary infertility while giving himself an exciting pleasure-pain sensation.

He had created his own perfect woman, one who was not for sale to a foreign businessman with a fat wallet. She was Song's personal property, trained solely for his gratification and indulgence. In knowing that other men could never have Elana he had enjoyed her even more. When he had told her there would never be another man in her life, she'd thrown herself into his arms and wept with joy.

Song was generous. The return he got was a contented and joyful young lover. Each gift, he told Elana, was a portion of himself.

Last month he'd given her a ten-thousand-dollar Honda Gold Wing motorbike outfitted with AM/FM stereo, onboard trip computer and rider/passenger intercom. He treasured photographs of the slender, blonde teenager posed on the motorbike dressed in French bra and panties that left her nipples and genitals exposed.

On the trip to Hong Kong he had not forgotten Elana, left behind in Seoul to indulge in her favorite foods, Coca-Cola and chocolate cake. At the exclusive Landmark shopping mall he had bought her two Claude Montana leather jumpsuits with shoulders extending six inches on either side. She was now wearing one of the jumpsuits.

In the tub Song lifted a leg from the water and examined a calf muscle hardened by dancing and the martial arts. After soaping the leg he shaved it with the straight razor, using long, sure strokes. A leg like this could kick Youngsam's balls through the top of his head. But this was fantasy, and fantasy was the result of a weak mind. Song was far from weak. He'd get Youngsam in a more subtle way.

And just when would he do that?

Now was as good a time as any.

He was getting an erection. Looking over his shoulder at the master bedroom, he called out, "Elana, come here. Now."

The door opened and the teenager entered the bathroom, the puppy in her arms. She stopped several feet from the tub, kissed the dog's snout and waved one of its paws at Song.

He lifted a watery hand in greeting. "Leave him in the next room, then take off your jumpsuit and get in the tub. Lock the door so we won't be disturbed."

Face pressed against the dog's head, she left the bathroom humming "Born In The U.S.A." Two minutes later she returned, nude and smiling, a gold chain around her waist. She was slender and small-breasted, with green eyes and shoulder-length golden hair parted in the middle. Her nails were painted green, her pubic hair shaved off.

Elana climbed into the tub and slid into Song's embrace. Without a word she licked his nipples, gently pulling at each one with her full lips. One hand went between his legs. Then ducking her head under water she took his erect penis in her mouth. Her hair darkened as it floated on the water's surface. Eyes closed, Song leaned back in the tub.

Long seconds later she came up for air. Using both hands she pulled wet hair away from her face and smiled at Song. He returned her smile, remembering to nod his approval.

He said, "Are you happy with me, I mean really and truly happy? Please speak the truth. I'll know if you're lying."

Placing her head on his chest she gently circled his right nipple with a small forefinger. "I love you. I want to stay with you forever."

"That's not what I asked. I asked if you are happy, really and truly happy."

"I am. I have everything I could want. And I really do want to stay with you forever."

She looked at him, sodden hair framing her small face. Her full mouth produced a trusting smile. Song kissed her eyes, tasting the water and feeling her lashes flutter beneath his lips.

She tongued the outside of his ear and began to writhe against him. Her voice was a whisper. "I always want to be as happy as I am now."

Song brought a length of her hair to his lips and kissed it. His fingers massaged the back of her neck. It was time.

He picked up the straight razor and quickly slit both sides of her mouth, then sank his teeth in her right shoulder. Elana screamed. Song, leaning back in the water, locked his legs around her waist, squeezing until she couldn't breathe. Her shrieking was instantly reduced to a gasp, then nothing.

Opening his legs Song placed his right foot on Elana's stomach and contemptuously pushed her away from him. She landed face down in the water and began floating toward twin faucets fashioned in the shape of wild horses raised up on their hind legs. Still holding the razor, Song dived into the blood-darkened water after her.

He rose quickly, Elana's corpse in his arms. Rushing forward, he slammed her back against a wall, forced his penis into her and ejaculated.

He let the dead girl slip from his hands and fall into the water, then, eyes closed, stood with his forehead pressed against a bathroom wall made of paving stones taken from D.W. Griffith's driveway. The tension that had been with him earlier was gone. His mind was now clear and calm.

He could not fully satisfy his sexual instinct without killing. For this unique erotic experience he needed a woman without equal or equivalent, a woman surpassing what was common or usual. He needed one with recognized similarities to his mother yet formed with his distinctive needs in mind.

Song needed his own "perfect woman." He had often found her, and he had killed her each time.

Three hours later he was tap-dancing on the polished black granite floor of his living room in front of a fireplace flanked by bronze Art Deco lions, when a bowlegged, white-jacketed servant interrupted to tell him that three men had arrived for Youngsam's money. Song, dapper and white-tied, was dancing along with a Fred Astaire and Ginger Rogers video of *Swing Time* now airing on an oversized television screen.

He continued to dance while talking. "Tell the gentlemen the suitcases they want are sitting outside this room. They can just take the cases and go. No need for me to see anyone."

When the servant closed the door Song smiled, thinking, Youngsam, you're in for a surprise. On screen Astaire had just finished "Never Gonna Dance" and, with Ginger, was about to go into "The Way You Look Tonight," Song's favorite number in the movie. It gave him goosebumps every time he saw it.

Humming along with the music he smoothly duplicated Astaire's every move.

Youngsam was forgotten.

In the study of his villa behind Seoul's only Anglican cathedral, Cha Youngsam squatted in front of five leather suitcases on the carpet facing his desk, remembering the evil omen that had foreshadowed his loss of thirty million dollars. A heavily built man with deep-set eyes and an unpleasant nasal voice, he would never have admitted to being superstitious. But Korean spiritual traditions believed in prophecy, something he accepted without question.

The omen, a recent one, had appeared on Buddha's birthday, on the eighth day of the fourth lunar month. That night he had joined the crowds at Chogye-sa Buddhist temple in downtown Seoul, where he had purchased a paper lantern and a candle. After writing the names of his family on a tag beneath the lantern he inserted a candle in the lantern, lit it, then hung the lantern from one of several wires stretched across the temple courtyard.

In the darkness around him row upon row of flickering candles brightened the courtyard. Youngsam bowed and prayed that Buddha's grace be upon him and his family. He also prayed for continued help in stockpiling money. The process of accumulating wealth made him deeply happy and assured him of a pleasant life. Money would also allow him to make a timely exit from intelligence work rather than stay too long and fall victim to one more pushy military strongman. With money he could escape his enemies.

Suddenly a blast of wind tore at his lantern, sending it dancing wildly on the wire. A second later the lantern caught fire and burned. *An evil omen.* Youngsam knew it, and so did the horrified devotees around him. A burning lantern promised ill fortune for the year to come.

Misfortune sought him out immediately. Shortly after the lantern incident his wife suffered a mild stroke and his eldest daughter, now in her first year at a Boston medical school, lost a leg in a motorcycle accident. His twenty-four-year-old mistress, who lacked the patience to learn anything properly, had begun an affair with a Japanese film director in hopes of advancing her movie career.

Finally there had been the catastrophe with Park Song's bank and its threat to Youngsam's hopes for a cushy future. The loss of thirty million dollars made his other problems seem trivial by comparison. Even a government edict to crack down on student demonstrations favoring the unification of North and South Korea failed to command his full attention. He could give little thought to anything except recovering his money and, not interested in explanations or alibis, lost no time in pressuring Park Song. Song had talked him into making deposits at TransOcean-Caribbean, which made Song accountable for subsequent events. Youngsam, whose enemies claimed his pockets were sewn tight to make handing over cash a physical impossibility, was lethal when he felt cheated out of money rightfully his.

To hell with bad omens. He was going to squeeze his thirty million out of that bastard Laughing Boy. Forget what they may have done for one another in the past. It was the weight of the present, with its loss of his money, that was pressing down upon the KCIA chief.

In his study he pulled a suitcase toward him and stroked it. Cheap leather, broken clasps, a loose handle. Probably picked up in a Hong Kong flea market, but no matter. What mattered were the contents.

Opening the suitcase, Youngsam stared at the money and felt his chest tighten. His breathing became rapid and shallow. He was staring at a mass of American hundred-dollar bills, a wondrous sight. He patted the money. He would count it, of course. Trust only yourself and no one would ever betray you. When the count was complete, the money would be wired to banks in Macau, Hungary and Liechtenstein, banks checked out by Youngsam so there would be no repetition of the disaster he had just experienced with Song and the Frenchman.

Were there any counterfeit bills in these suitcases? Youngsam doubted it. Song knew the consequences for handing over a single bogus note. Youngsam had been wise to let him live. Scare him, yes, but keep him alive because if anyone could raise thirty million on short notice it was Song. Laughing Boy was so vain he probably enjoyed the smell of his own farts. He could also be as loony as a March hare. But few men were as clever and resourceful.

Scooping stacks of hundreds from the suitcases, Youngsam placed them on his desk. Minutes later he had emptied the suitcase and begun unloading a second. He had almost cleared this suitcase when he saw it. Tucked between two stacks of hundreds. A foil packet the size of a small envelope. Chances were that Song didn't even know it was missing.

Youngsam picked up the packet, peered at it through wire-rimmed spectacles, then weighed it in his hand. He unwrapped the packet, delighted at putting one over on Laughing Boy. And then he saw the contents. Stunned, he let the packet fall to the carpet. He stepped back, away from the tinfoil and the things it had contained. His neck muscles tightened; he had trouble breathing. He was close to vomiting.

Scattered at his feet were human fingers. Bloodstained fingers with green-tinted nails.

While brutal and coldblooded, Youngsam had an intense aversion to touching dead flesh. He avoided physical contact with his torture victims, particularly after their demise, preferring to leave such details to subordinates. It was a lifelong revulsion dating from that morning when as an eight-year-old in a dirt-poor family, he had awakened to find a younger brother lying in his arms dead from starvation.

Youngsam tiptoed around the fingers and stepped to his desk. Palms down on a spotless green blotter, he waited until his breathing returned to normal. Then with an unsteady hand he pulled the telephone toward him, picked up the receiver and began dialing.

In his living room an exhausted Song flopped down onto a shellback sofa, loosened his white tie and watched *Swing Time*'s end credits. Humming "The Way You Look Tonight," he dried his face with a small hand towel. On a low rattan table a telephone rang incessantly.

Song removed his tap shoes and made a mental note to have new taps put on the soles and heels. Closing his eyes, he massaged his feet. The telephone, which his servants had been told to ignore, continued ringing.

Finally he stood up and stretched, then walked over to the rattan table. Smiling at his reflection in a mirrored wall, he removed an opened bottle of Moët et Chandon from an ice bucket and filled a glass with the chilled champagne. One sip and he sighed with pleasure. A second sip, then he picked up the receiver. "Yes?"

"I'll see you dead for this."

Song held his champagne glass up to the light and eyed the bubbles. "Colonel Youngsam. Good of you to call. I trust the down payment's been delivered safely. Ten million dollars, as promised."

"You're a sick bastard and you're not getting away with this."

"Get away with what?" Song bit his lip to keep from laughing.

"You killed her, you fucking pervert—"

"Oh her? Elana, you mean? Well, yes, matter of fact, I did. How did you know? It only happened a couple of hours ago—"

"I said I would cut off your fingers if you didn't make the down payment. Well, you've made the down payment and I'm going to remove them anyway. Each and every one. Play your disgusting games with young girls if you will, but *not with me*."

Song couldn't stop smiling.

"Colonel, will you please tell me what you're talking about?"

Anger made Youngsam more nasal than usual. "You thought sending me that girl's fingers would be amusing. The joke is going to be on you."

"Ah, I see. You're saying I deliberately sent—" Abruptly Song's tone changed. "Colonel, forgive me. What happened was this, I wrapped the fingers in foil, then mislaid the package. I would never send you such a gift."

"You're a liar."

"I put the fingers on a table with the money. You see, I was transferring the money to less expensive suitcases and at the same time I wanted to save the fingers as a keepsake. One gets more sentimental about some girls than others."

Looking into the mirror Song used a forefinger to stroke his eyebrows. "I was in a hurry, your men were coming to pick up the money, and I wanted to be ready when they arrived. The fingers *accidentally* ended up in one of the suitcases. I'm truly sorry for any inconvenience. You weren't too upset, I hope . . ." *I hope you heaved your fucking guts out, you greedy scum.*

Youngsam said, "You expect me to believe such a fairytale?"

"By the way," Song said, "would you do me the usual good turn and send someone over to remove her body? I don't know what I'd do without your help at these times. She's upstairs in the bathtub. Tell your men to wear gloves and not to touch anything. The last time someone left bloody handprints on the doorjamb—"

"You're lying about the fingers and you know it." But this time there was doubt in Youngsam's voice.

"Colonel, why would I do such a thing?"

"Because you think you're clever. Because you know—"

Youngsam stopped, not wanting to admit that others might know of his distaste for corpses. How could Song have possibly learned about his little brother's death? In truth, the counterfeiter knew all about Youngsam's horror of touching dead flesh. This incident, among others, was in a detailed report on the spymaster that Song kept on file and updated periodically.

Youngsam said, "Now that you've proved you can raise the money you think you're free to do as you please."

Song said, "It's criminal the way these student riots are embarrassing our country. Who cares if one of their leaders died last week after your men took him in for questioning. What was the cause of his death? Oh yes, a heart attack."

Song finished his champagne and refilled the glass. The student hadn't died of a heart attack. He had died when one of Youngsam's men had placed the tip of a ballpoint pen in his ear and stomped on it.

News of the student leader's departure from life had only increased the rioting. At the same time his followers had accused Youngsam of the student's murder and demanded his resignation. The Razor might weather the storm and he might not. Should he be forced to resign, it was better to do so as a rich man. More than ever Youngsam needed Song, and the counterfeiter knew it.

"Colonel, believe me when I tell you it was an accident. I was so intent on having the money ready that I probably knocked the fingers into the suitcase and never noticed it."

"I say you're lying—"

"Colonel, I've got my printers coming over later. They're working around the clock to get our products ready for my trip. I'd really appreciate Elana's corpse being removed before they arrive."

Youngsam exhaled. "If you ever do anything like this again I'll personally put a bullet through your fucking head. I'll have the body picked up before your printers arrive."

After a brief silence he said, "Her fingers instead of yours. Was that it?"

"Colonel, really, I—"

"Well, my friend, you still owe twenty million. After you've repaid it, we'll see what sort of joke I can play on you."

He hung up.

Song burst out giggling. Look for Youngsam to have a few sleepless nights in the near future.

Song picked up a file folder lying beside the ice bucket and opened it. An eight-by-ten color photograph lay on top of several typed pages. It was a picture of his next perfect woman.

Song studied her face. A truly beautiful adolescent. Blonde hair, no physical imperfections and no history of mental illness.

He would pick her up in New York, his last stop, and bring her back with him to Seoul to begin her education as a *kisaeng*. She would want for nothing. Her short happy life with him would be a golden one.

He had reviewed her résumé and records every day for the past week.

She was thirteen years old.

THREE

On a cool April morning an eleven-year-old Park Song entered a bank in the trendy Myong-Dong district, holding his mother's hand and willing himself to resist a fear that had him nearly paralyzed. If you look frightened, his mother had warned, then the banker might become suspicious and her scheme to defraud him would surely fail.

Song's mother, Arang, was in her late thirties, a slim, dark-haired woman with a quiet elegance and dominant eyes. Once a popular *kisaeng* with important political and military patrons, she'd eventually lost the bloom of youth and been discarded. Utilizing her calligraphic skills, she had turned to forgery, supplementing this with prostitution and petty theft. Song adored her sense of adventure and the energy that drew people to her.

His father, Tae, was in his mid-thirties, a slight, handsome man with a friendly air and a trim mustache. Earlier in his life he had spent three years in Los Angeles trying to break into film musicals as a singer-dancer. Eventually he saw that Asians never appeared on American screens except as demonic villains or humble servants. Off-screen their occupations were generally limited to those of gardener, pool cleaner and houseboy.

A fascinated Song listened to his father's tales of stars he'd seen in

23

studio commissaries and restaurants where he'd waited tables; of glorious parties held at producers' mansions, where he'd cleaned pools; of being rewarded with a quick glimpse of the king Clark Gable after sitting for long rainy hours in crowded bleachers hastily erected for a film premiere. Tae's evocations of Hollywood left their mark on the boy, who came to share his father's love of film musicals and the belief that movie stars were gods come down to earth.

Nowadays his parents were confidence tricksters who used their considerable charm and intelligence to fleece marks in a dozen Asian cities. Together with Song, an only child, they lived in a world of fast money, smooth talk and constant excitement, a world where swindles were committed for pleasure as well as profit. Their cons: stock fraud, selling illegal leases on government buildings and schemes to return the personal effects of recent Korean war dead to their families.

Song had worked cons with his parents before but nothing like the one they were now seeking to pull off at the National Bank of Korea. This sting, a loan against forged securities, was a matter of life or death. Arang needed bribe money for a police detective who had learned that she and Tae were defrauding investors in a nonexistent Peruvian silver mine.

The detective, Chun Wonjong, was a chinless forty-year-old with an exaggerated opinion of his own importance and a hair-trigger temper. He enjoyed intimidating people and possessed an unlimited capacity for making them suffer. For the past three days he had held Tae prisoner in a flat belonging to a crony. If Chun was not paid off by noon today he had promised to kill Tae and arrest Arang for forgery. Song would be sent to an orphanage or left to fend for himself on the streets of Seoul.

Arang's forced good cheer couldn't stop Song from worrying about his father. Soft-spoken and quick to laugh, Park Song lived with his parents in a small flat in Tongdaemun Market near the ancient Great Eastern Gate, the largest market in South Korea. Pleasant and well mannered, he was also secretive and a liar with fantasies of wealth and power. He had a strong fear of his own death, which he acted out by killing animals in a substitute death.

On one occasion, on the grounds of Changdok, Seoul's best preserved royal palace, tourists wandering the wooded paths of its Secret Gardens encountered the adolescent Song and a caretaker's twelve-year-old dim-witted daughter having sex in a shaded grove. He had smeared himself and the girl with blood from a pigeon he had beheaded. Traces of the bird's blood were on his lips and teeth. He had also bitten the girl's face severely enough to draw blood. Song had the girl's consent, so it wasn't rape. He had even given her presents, among them a bathrobe and a cheap wristwatch. Police and family of the girl were paid off.

His parents knew of Song's strong sex drive. What they didn't know was how destructive it had become. There had been similar episodes in Song's past but none as ominous as this one. Lately he had begun to fantasize about killing young girls, whom he found most pliable and yielding, easily allowing him to exercise command over them. The more Song fantasized, the stronger became his desire to take a girl's life.

His parents, who had so often conned others, now conned themselves into regarding their only child as normal. A misplaced loyalty made them reject the idea that his behavior might be the forerunner of more violent sex crimes. To examine Song too closely meant questioning their permissiveness in raising him.

Without Arang to safeguard him, the delicate, sickly Song might not have enjoyed more than a few months of life. By the age of six he'd endured operations to correct a curved spine, remove a bowel obstruction and open his throat so that he could eat. His mother had placed his welfare before that of her own and Tae's, hiring the best surgeons. It was she who willingly spent long months at his bedside, reading and singing to him as he lay in heavy body casts. And it was she who pushed him into tap dancing and karate to strengthen his delicate physique.

As confidence tricksters, Arang, Tae and Song believed in taking as much as possible for as little in return. What set Song apart from his parents was a callousness coupled with a determination to let nothing stand in his way. Money was more than just bits of paper allowing you to buy tea kettles and jars of mustard. Money was power. Song felt it, knew it, believed it.

Money would save his father from the corrupt Chun. Money and his mother.

In the second-floor office of Mr. Khitan, first vice-president of National Korea Bank, Song sat at the banker's desk and toyed with a lacquered red cigarette box inlaid with sharkskin. His mother and the bowlegged Khitan stood out of earshot at a window overlooking a maze of narrow lanes crowded with boutiques, silk shops, beer halls and restaurants. Song couldn't hear their conversation, but he saw the banker touch Arang's hair. Gently brushing aside the hand she whispered into Khitan's ear. Her looks might have faded, but she still possessed the charm that had once made her a desirable *kisaeng*. In Song's eyes she'd never stopped being beautiful.

The boy eyed the packet of fake securities that lay on the large oak desk beside a silver-framed photograph of Khitan's wife, a chunky woman with a hard face. According to Arang, the banker had a fondness for the ladies, a weakness that could be used to cloud his judgment. Who best to trick such a man into advancing money on counterfeit stocks but a still-attractive *kisaeng*?

Tae, who'd met the banker two weeks earlier at a race track, had directed Arang to approach him on the Peruvian deal. While Khitan had shown interest he had been slow to commit himself. Now, with Tae's abduction, the banker's approval had suddenly become a matter of life or death.

A frantic Song looked at a small ceramic clock on Khitan's desk. Twenty to eleven. Less than ninety minutes left to save Tae's life. Closing his eyes, the boy clenched both fists and gritted his teeth. Rigid in Khitan's high-backed leather chair, he fought a stabbing pain in his stomach. Mustn't give in to his fears, not when his mother and father needed him so badly. When someone touched his shoulder Song opened his eyes and saw Arang standing at his side and smiling at Mr. Khitan, who was just leaving the room. A moment later mother and son were alone. Song began to cry. Khitan had turned down the loan. Tae was dead.

Song tried to stand, but Arang's slim hand kept him in the chair. She placed a finger to her lips. They remained behind the desk, neither one speaking or looking at the other as they listened to the tick of Khitan's small desk clock and traffic noises from the crowded street below. When the banker returned to the office he was slightly edgy. Leaning against the door, he mopped his brow with a monogrammed handkerchief, then crossed the room, removed an envelope from inside his jacket and handed it to Arang. An exhilarated Song leaped from the chair.

The boy watched his mother check the contents of the envelope. He had never seen so much money. Tae was going to live. This nightmare was going to pass and the three of them would be together again. Song had never been more proud of his beautiful mother. He wanted to hug her, to throw himself in her arms and tell her how wonderful she was. Instead he watched silently as she counted the cash.

Arang drew Song aside to the window, handed him the envelope and whispered in his ear, repeating earlier instructions. He was to leave the bank immediately and wait for her at a corner tea shop. She would be along shortly. She and Mr. Khitan had one more piece of business to complete, then she would meet Song and they would go get Tae.

The boy didn't ask questions; it was not necessary for his mother to elaborate. As he ran from the office the thought of his beautiful mother with the lecherous Khitan was enough to make the boy want to kill.

In a seedy apartment on the top floor of a high-rise facing Yongsan Garrison, the American army base, a frightened Song and his mother watched Detective Chun count the bank money. Tae was nowhere to be seen. Song had a premonition that something was wrong.

According to small, thin-lipped Chun, who sat on a windowsill holding the cash-filled envelope, Tae wasn't feeling well. He was presently in the back room having a snooze. Resting his eyes, you might say. Arang and Song could link up with him after Chun completed the count.

Chun's cronies were a bald man with a sightless right eye and a short bespectacled man with a narrow face. Song knew these two weren't cops. They were more scary than the amiable con men and petty thieves he'd met through his parents. Both smelled as bad as they looked.

Song glanced over his shoulder toward the back room as Arang tightened her grip on his hand. The boy stepped closer to his mother. They were powerless against Chun and his gorillas. Song and Arang could only hand over the money and hope for the best.

Money counted, Chun scratched his chin and eyed Song, giving the boy a cold smile. Song stayed close to his mother. Chun's stare frightened him so much it was all he could do not to run away. Finally Chun looked at Arang then jerked his head towards the back room. Song wondered if his mother had noticed the bald man whispering to his little companion. And did she see them smirk as people did when only they knew the joke?

Forcing a smile Arang bowed, respectfully thanked Chun for his kindness then led Song down a narrow hallway toward the back room. The boy clung tightly to his mother's hand; they were both scared but she was keeping up a brave front for his sake. Chun deserved to die. Was there any escape from his cruelty?

At the back room door mother and son exchanged looks. Both felt the ghostly silence in the room; it hit them with heart-stopping force. Song, with his sensitive stomach, was on the verge of throwing up. Why was his father so quiet? Song called out to him.

Silence. At the far end of the hallway Chun and his men stared at the boy and his mother with a quiet malevolence.

Arang opened the door.

She and Song saw a small room with unclean bedding on a filthy floor, litter strewn about, and a khaki blanket covering the lone window. A single dim bulb shone down from a cracked ceiling and the tepid air smelled of perspiration, beer and stale cigarette smoke. Pigeons cooed on the windowsill.

Song and his mother looked around for Tae.

Arang saw her husband first. She screamed.

Tae's bloodied head, barely visible in the half light, faced them from a low table near the filthy bedding. The eyes had been gouged out and a rolled playing card stuck in each empty socket. A cigar had been jammed into his mouth; his hair was parted neatly in the middle. Both feet had been severed from his legs. His body was nowhere to be seen.

Arang, hands covering her face, sagged against the doorjamb. Song vomited, dirtying his clothes and the floor. Stomach emptied, he stumbled to the window, clutched the blanket to avoid falling and continued to heave. As he clung to the blanket it came loose and dropped on him, covering the boy from head to waist.

Shrieking, he spun around in a panic, desperate to free himself from the suffocating darkness. Blanket thrown aside, he sank to the floor, weeping uncontrollably and curling into a fetal position beneath the window. Each second brought with it a thousand bitter and unbearable sorrows. It was impossible to hold back the tears. For the first time in his life he hated being alive.

Holding a cigarette Chun, followed by his grinning accomplices, strolled into the room and stood behind the grieving Arang. "You hooked yourself up with a zero," he said to her. "Your Tae was unessential, a little man who thought he was better than the rest of us because he'd gone to America."

Chun looked at the burning end of his cigarette. "Mr. Hollywood. Very popular with the ladies because he was a good dancer. I had him dance for us. Wet his pants. Very frightened man you had. That was his final performance. Since he wouldn't be dancing again I decided he wouldn't need his feet."

As his thugs roared with laughter the little detective crouched over the weeping Song, a hand on the boy's buttocks. A drag on his cigarette then he looked at Arang. "My men have heard you were once a highly desired *kisaeng*. I've promised them they could have you. You and the cash in exchange for your freedom."

He touched Song's tear-stained face then rose to face Arang. "Try to please my men. Should they find your charms less than enthralling, I promise it will go hard with you."

Licking his lips he stared at Song. "My joy lies in other pleasures. The young man and I will go next door and amuse ourselves."

He snapped his fingers at Song. "Here, boy."

A tearful Arang touched Chun's arm. "I beg you, a moment with my son. Please let me talk to him. The shock of his father's death has upset him. Let me calm him down, then I shall do your bidding."

Chun nodded. He could afford to be generous. Of course this tramp was going to obey him. When his men finished with her, she was going to die. Did she know it? Probably. So let her say goodbye to the boy. A brief moment of seedy passion with these two apes and this whore's life would be over. Chun's passion was for boys and the tramp's son filled the bill quite nicely.

He stepped back, leaving Arang and Song alone at the window. Arang, bending down, took her weeping son in her arms. *"Goodbye,"* she whispered. "I love you very much. Tae and I will always be with you. Now listen. Say nothing. Just do as I say. Get to your feet then stand to the left of the window. Say nothing. *I will save you."*

She kissed his cheek then helped him to his feet and watched him move from the window. Arang then faced Chun. "Please talk to the boy. He doesn't understand that he must leave me. Please talk to him."

Chun dropped his cigarette on the floor, crushed it under foot and stepped to the window. He'd talk to the boy. He'd slap the little bastard's teeth loose. A kick in the ass might also instill the right attitude.

Arang now had to give the performance of her life. She began with showing Chun the proper deference, averting her eyes and looking down at the floor. He ignored her, as she knew he would. Hand raised, the detective prepared to strike Song. That's when Arang rushed the detective, wrapped her arms firmly around him and hurled herself through the window, carrying Chun with her, the two plunging fifteen stories screaming to their deaths.

Cold air rushed into the room, tearing at the face of an hysterical Song. Pigeons, wings flapping loudly, sprang from the sill and flew wildly in all directions. Bits of glass glistened on Song's shoes. Newspapers and food wrappings swirled about the room. On the street below the harsh wail of police sirens blended with the blaring horns of cars caught in the sudden traffic stoppage.

For long seconds Chun's thugs stared open-mouthed at the broken window. Then the man with the sightless right eye caught his narrow-faced companion by the elbow and together they backed out of the room. A dazed Song was left alone to look down at the broken body of the mother who'd just given her life for him.

SAIGON/APRIL 1975

Late evening. Song, gripping a Fabrique Nationale 35DA pistol, followed a blood trail along the corridor of a squat office building on the edge of Cholon, Saigon's Chinatown.

Both he and the burly, thick-lipped Kim Shin, who was at his elbow, wore the uniform of army captains with the collar insignia of South Korea's crack Tiger Division. Close on their heels: three Korean enlisted men armed with AK-47 assault rifles. Their quarry: a man they had been tracking for twenty minutes, a man losing blood with every step.

Outside the building his blood had appeared dry. Inside it had appeared wetter and slightly frothy, indicating the bleeding was getting worse. Song was excited. He was closing in on Harrison Random, a dwarfish forty-two-year-old CIA agent who had stolen a certain item from the American embassy that Song now wanted for himself. Not for the Korean embassy, where he and his best friend, Shin, were attached to Intelligence, but for himself. Random had taken a set of currency plates capable of producing the most authentic-looking hundred-dollar bill imaginable. Song wanted those plates more than a drowning man wanted a breath of air.

He had endured life in orphanages and reformatories and supported himself by laboring in the stench of slaughterhouses and sewers. He had been imprisoned for petty theft and forgery. To avoid starving he had eaten out of garbage cans, slept in doorways, tap-danced in sleazy nightclubs and dealt drugs. Faced with a substantial prison term or a stint in the army for blackmailing a prominent gay cabinet minister, he had chosen the army, where he quickly manipulated his way to a commission. As a junior officer he played yes-man to his superiors, and ultimately his kowtowing had paid off with promotions. It also paid off when senior officers conceded him a small share in payoffs received from military contractors and drug dealers. Money didn't console him for the loss of his parents, but it did comfort him for having to endure a lifetime of suffering.

Which was why he wanted Random's plates. Bills from these plates looked real because the plates themselves were real. They belonged to the U.S. Treasury, which had quietly authorized their use by the CIA's Saigon station to fund covert operations in Southeast Asia. With a private source of cash the Saigon station was able to proceed with dubious operations while bypassing congressional probers, anti-war groups and a hostile media. This money didn't have to be justified, accounted for or listed in a budget. Nor did it leave a paper trail that could be followed. Officially it didn't exist. It was unknown, and what was unknown could not be inquired about.

To get these plates, Song was willing to kill a dozen Harrison Randoms. His desire to own them was like a madness inside him. Possessing them, he could return to Korea a wealthy man. The future had come, providing he found Harrison Random.

With Saigon surrounded by the North Vietnamese army and expected to fall within days, the CIA station chief had ordered the plates destroyed, along with intelligence reports, dossiers and stockpiles of cash. Under no circumstances were the plates to fall into Communist hands. And they couldn't be returned to Washington, where sticky questions might be raised about their function and purpose. They must be destroyed.

Working around the clock, the CIA incinerated mountains of classified material while evacuating Americans and locals who'd worked with the agency. In the resulting pandemonium Harrison Random was presented with an opportunity he finally proved equal to. Long envisioning life in Hawaii with a younger wife and beachfront property, he'd taken advantage of the chaos prompted by America's hasty retreat and stolen the plates. He had then approached Jean-Louis Nicolay, a baby-faced thirty-year-old French restaurateur to whom he'd occasionally sold stolen counterfeit hundreds from these plates. This time Random was playing for higher stakes. Did Jean-Louis, a known black-marketeer and dealer in contraband, want to buy the plates that made these exceptional hundreds? Price: five million dollars. Cash only, no haggling. Take it or leave it. Nicolay took it.

He acted on the orders of his silent partner in a trio of massage parlors on Tu Do Street, where "yellow fever"—the lust for Asian women—enticed Americans such as Harrison Random. The silent partner was Park Song, and as soon as he heard of the plates they became his obsession. Nicolay, who'd met Song when providing him with young Vietnamese and Eurasian girls, was ordered to accept Random's offer at once. He was to agree to the American's terms, then leave the rest to Song, who intended to get the plates without paying for them. Which meant conning Random or killing him.

The sting. Song began by making sure Random never saw him and Nicolay together. In dealing with Nicolay, let the American feel he was on familiar ground. A new face might make Random too cautious. He'd be more likely to let his guard down around someone he knew. On Song's orders Nicolay ingratiated himself further with Random by flattering the American's second-rate intelligence skills. The Frenchman also entertained Random at his beach house on Con Son island, where beautiful young Vietnamese women with eyes and noses surgically revamped Western style did things to Random in bed that his Quaker wife would have refused to do even had she known of them.

Nicolay never thought about keeping the plates for himself. He had only to remember that night at his beach house when he'd peeked into a guest bedroom and seen a naked, blood-smeared Song dancing alone, the head of a twelve-year-old Vietnamese girl dangling from his waist. The girl, a war orphan, had been purchased by Nicolay from her grandparents for twenty American dollars. He'd known she'd end up another blanket-wrapped corpse when Song finished with her. But he had never expected *this*. The incident at the beach house had inspired a black fear that would stay in Nicolay's mind forever. Fear remained the source of his awe and regard for the often giggling Song. Fear was a reminder that Nicolay's head could also be removed if he ever double-crossed the Korean.

Song baited his con with a good-faith payment of ten thousand dollars passed on to Random by Nicolay. He also forged a bank letter that Nicolay let Random read, then took back. It was on genuine bank stationery mailed from Hong Kong and credited Random's account there with five million dollars. The difference between Random and Song was—the American wanted to appear clever, while the Korean *was* clever.

A final meeting between Nicolay and Random to exchange the "letter of credit" for the plates was set up at Nicolay's Chinatown restaurant. Song, hidden in the kitchen, heard Random say, "To hell with it, I'm going to do this thing my way. There'll be a short delay while I get a second opinion. Got to make sure you're not blowing smoke up my ass."

Meaning he wanted additional confirmation that five million dollars had indeed been deposited in his numbered Hong Kong account. Until then the plates would remain in his possession. He punctuated this last remark by opening his jacket and allowing Nicolay to see the Colt .45 tucked in his belt. Song decided the next move was his.

Random's wire would expose the con; Song could then kiss those plates goodbye. Solution: Song would have to take the plates at once. Backed by four soldiers he rushed from the kitchen.

Random's .45 was forgotten. He'd never so much as test-fired the thing. He ran into the bathroom and dove through an open window, plates taped to his chest.

He was on the run and in pain; two of Song's bullets had struck him in the back. Song and his men pushed through crowds of Vietnamese, American soldiers, Europeans, following Random's blood trail five blocks to the National Police compound on Vo Tanh Street, where Saigon merged into the Chinese suburb of Cholon. Song thought: why had Random fled into the arms of the secret police? Random probably believed or hoped he'd lost Song on streets teeming with refugees, South Vietnamese army deserters and Viet Cong spies.

Nothing was going to save the tiny Mr. Random. The plates were instant wealth; Song intended to kill anyone who came between him and the plates. He'd have them if it meant tearing down the Vietnamese police compound brick by brick. The plates were payment for his parents' untimely deaths and his own harsh life. Acquiring them was his divine mission.

Home to intelligence agencies and the secret police, the National Police compound was a series of low office buildings and barracks connected by a network of alleys. Song and his soldiers saw just two plainclothes policemen and a handful of secretaries, none of whom wanted to tangle with the Koreans whose army was rated the most savage in Asia. Apparently everyone else at the compound had deserted, no surprise in a city under siege. Three days from now Song and all remaining Korean embassy personnel were due to be flown out of Saigon on American helicopters. If the normally bustling compound was empty it was to be expected. Looking out for number one was the only thing on everyone's mind these days.

The North Vietnamese had a noose around Saigon's neck; the city would fall within the week. Facing prison camps or execution, South Vietnamese police and intelligence agents had refused to remain at their posts and were deserting by the hundreds. Some hoped to catch an American flight out of Tan Son Nhut Airport or to evacuate by helicopter to an American aircraft carrier offshore. Some had fled to the harbor, seeking to bribe their way onto the first boat or barge leaving Saigon. Song had seen police throw away uniforms and weapons in an attempt to blend in with the city's civilian population. The Communists were known for punishing their enemies, for washing out blood with blood.

Not all South Vietnamese policemen were leaving Saigon empty-handed. On the pretext of collecting funds for a last-ditch defense of the city they were now looting banks, jewelry stores, wealthy homes and gold shops. Until now, fear of the police had kept thieves away from the almost empty compound. Song, however, knew it was only a matter of time before deserters, robbers, refugees and bands of murderous veterans appeared in the compound to begin carting off everything that wasn't nailed down. He had to find Harrison Random and those plates. *Quickly.*

Inside the compound, Song stood in the doorway of a large empty office, presumably that of a high-ranking officer. The blood trail had led here before moving on. Apparently Random had collapsed in the doorway, somehow gotten to his feet, then continued along the corridor. Song lifted a hand in a signal to Kim Shin and the soldiers. *Maintain silence, find the American.*

Song, as point man, came to a large empty area that had been partitioned into a dozen cubicles. He noted further indications of an abrupt departure: desk drawers pulled out, card cabinets upended, stationery cabinets and coat racks overturned. Sheets of paper were still in typewriters and the soil around houseplants was hard and dry. Empty screens flickered brightly on data-display terminals.

A sudden noise to his right and he spun around, terrified, ready to empty his pistol, until he realized it was a ringing telephone. The search of the cubicles yielded nothing. An impatient Song picked up the blood trail near a rear cubicle, the trail turning right into a fluorescent-lit gray corridor. Song took off after Random, his fellow soldiers forgotten.

Song's men caught up with him at the end of the corridor, where he was examining a glass-paneled door leading to a staircase. He was looking for wires leading to booby traps. Looking for indications that a grenade had been fastened to a tripwire, or that a shotgun had been wired to fire when the door opened. Something to suggest that when he opened the door the ceiling was rigged to collapse and bury him.

Booby traps were a way of life in a war which had started thirty years ago when the Vietnamese had begun fighting their French colonial rulers. The Viet Cong currently used eight hundred tons of booby trap explosives, courtesy of American bombs and artillery shells which had failed to explode. Song felt it ironic that America should braid the rope used to hang them. As for the retreating South Vietnamese, they were too fixed on saving their own skins to think of guerilla tactics. Since Random hadn't set off any explosions Song suspected the area was secure.

Without touching the door he peered through the glass at a rusted metal staircase leading down one flight to a steel door. Behind the steel door was a corridor lined with small offices and supply rooms. It also contained rest rooms, a small cafeteria and most important of all, two computer rooms. Song occasionally visited the computer rooms to exchange intelligence with the South Vietnamese.

He'd passed Random in the corridor a few times but neither had spoken to the other. Song suspected Random saw him as just another gook who should have been off somewhere ironing shirts or playing Ping-Pong. The Korean, in turn, viewed the CIA agent as thick-headed and dull.

Nor was Song any more impressed with South Vietnamese Intelligence which he saw as a reflection of the Vietnamese people themselves—incompetent, dishonest and self-serving. The South Vietnamese government was too crooked to be straightened out. Without American support it would have collapsed years ago. Even with American money and advisors the South had commanded very little loyalty outside of Saigon. It had been a case of the rooster wielding great influence over his own dunghill and nowhere else.

As for the American army it had been on the verge of collapse for months, suffering from massive desertions, drugs, and the systematic killing of hundreds of officers by their own men. One needn't be a military genius to conclude that such an army was self-defeating and of no use to anyone save whores, black marketeers and dope dealers. Song had worked on reports concluding that the United States had lost the war and its soul. The reports had also noted the negative effects of this disastrous adventure on the American people as a whole. In future dealings with the United States, Korea intended to rely heavily on this data.

At the door leading downstairs, Song ordered the enlisted men through first. True, Random hadn't set off an explosion, but why take chances? Should the door happen to be booby-trapped, let someone else's arms and legs be blown off. Just because Song wanted the plates didn't mean he had to be a fool. One needed discretion as well as judgment.

Rifles ready, the three enlisted men passed safely through the doorway. By the time Song and Kim Shin stepped onto the landing behind them a sergeant had picked up the blood trail on the narrow rusted iron staircase leading one flight down to the corridor. Eyes on the steel door, Song again signaled for quiet, stepped onto the staircase and took the lead. The idea of owning the plates was so electrifying that he felt like dancing.

Reaching the steel door he decided to go in first. Booby traps were no longer on his mind. The prize waiting in the corridor was his, to be claimed by him and him alone. He had no intention of losing it.

He gripped the doorknob, took a deep breath then slowly pushed it open.

Holding his breath he stepped into the quiet, humid corridor. The blood, still fresh, led halfway down the empty hall and into a computer room on the left side. Here an open door allowed Song to hear men speaking in Vietnamese. He also smelled cigarette smoke and heard a Vietnamese male singing phonetically with Aretha Franklin's "Respect." Song wrinkled his nose in disgust. With the exception of the great black performer James Brown, whom he admired more for his dancing than his singing, Song detested pop music, considering it commonplace, uninspired and vulgar.

Perspiring heavily he walked quietly alongside the blood on the stone corridor floor. Behind him the enlisted men peeked into empty rooms lining the passageway, a safety precaution born of years of caution. At the computer room Song stopped out of sight of the doorway and whispered to Kim Shin. *No witnesses were to be left behind. No one must know what happened to the plates.* Kim Shin nodded in agreement.

Then Song whispered, we'll go on my signal.

The signal. He raised his pistol overhead, holding it up for the men to see. A count of three, then he brought his arm down sharply and leaped through the doorway.

He rushed into a gray, windowless room bursting with computers, terminals, printers, card readers and disk control units. Song's men quickly trained their weapons on four Vietnamese males, two of whom were standing in front of a central processing unit. One had been singing along with a cassette player at his feet. Frightened by the sudden appearance of the Koreans he accidentally kicked over the cassette player, which continued to play. A third, who'd been walking towards a magnetic tape controller, was so taken by surprise that he stopped in the act of lighting a cigarette, allowing the match to singe his fingers.

The fourth man, whom Song recognized as a lieutenant in the secret police, had just placed the last of four suitcases in front of a printer at the far wall. He started to protest but was shouted down by the Koreans. One didn't argue with armed men pointing guns at you. Not in these chaotic times. The lieutenant shut up.

Random. Glassy-eyed and open-mouthed he sat on the floor, back against a disk control unit. Beside him a sad-faced young Eurasian woman in bell-bottom jeans and tie-dyed blouse knelt, holding his hand. Behind them the Koreans shouted and cursed as they used rifle butts to force the four Vietnamese males to their knees.

Song rushed over to Random, yanked the .45 from the American's belt and slid it across the black linoleum floor toward the Koreans. He jammed his pistol under Random's chin. "The plates," he said. "Where are they?"

As a silent Random stared at the ceiling the Eurasian woman pointed toward a nearby folded Vietnamese newspaper dotted with bloody fingerprints. Song reached down for it. Slowly, almost reverently, he unfolded the newspaper. The plates were inside. Two thin pieces of metal slightly larger than an actual hundred-dollar bill.

He refolded the newspaper, gripped it tightly and stood up. The biggest con of all and he'd pulled it off. If only his mother and father had lived to see this. He began to do a time step, right then and there, pistol in one hand, plates in the other. Song was ecstatic and didn't give a damn who knew it. Across the room a smiling Kim Shin hoisted his own pistol in triumph.

Song smiled at the woman. "Your name?"

She'd turned back to Random and now held him in her arms, her face mostly hidden in shoulder-length black hair. "Constanze Herail," she said in French-accented English. "I am his fiancée. He was going to take me to Hawaii. We planned to get married there and live by the ocean."

Miss Herail's account of a happy future struck Song as fiction, and not the most original fiction at that. Vietnamese and Eurasian women were always being hoodwinked by American soldiers out for a bit of nookie. Still, a desperate Harrison Random had turned to Miss Herail as the nearest point of refuge. Who else was he going to press into service? Not the American embassy, for sure. Song eyed the woman. Random had been her ticket out of Saigon, a ticket now canceled. Unless Miss Herail found another exit she'd end up in a Communist reeducation camp, cleaning toilets and chopping down trees when not listening to Marxist lectures and being abused by guards.

Song leaned in for a closer peek at Miss Herail or rather at the photo ID pinned to her blouse. The ID said she was employed at the National Police compound. It would have been more normal for her and these four to run off like their coworkers. Had Random told them about the plates? Song's gaze took in the four suitcases and the

Vietnamese now kneeling with hands locked behind their heads. Their American weaponry, M-16s and .45 automatics, had been confiscated by Song's men and placed on top of a printer. It bothered Song that these five were still here when everyone else had flown the coop.

"What sort of work do you do for the National Police?" he said to Miss Herail.

She stroked Random's forehead with long fingers tipped in orange nail polish. The American's eyes were closed, his breathing labored. "He's dying," she said.

"What is your job?"

She spat out the words. "Records. I work with computer records."

"And these gentlemen, what do they do besides travel around with suitcases?"

"They're policemen, they paid me to help them."

"Help them do *what?*"

"Gather tapes from the machines."

Song had the picture now. The policemen had come to the computer room to steal files. Not knowing how to work the computers, they'd brought her along to do it for them, to locate tapes and remove information from computers without destroying it. If Song was right, those four suitcases across the room were crammed full of tapes, dossiers and other information.

Aretha Franklin sang "Natural Woman" while Song considered his next move. With the war's end just days away the computer room had become a gold mine. If Song hadn't been so occupied with the plates he would have realized this sooner. And done what these policemen were trying to do.

The Special Police and the CIO, South Vietnam's Central Intelligence Organization, kept files on captured Communists who had turned informer, collaborator or defector. The files also held the names of spies within Viet Cong and Northern forces along with those Vietnamese agents the Americans hoped to leave in place after the evacuation. To Communists these were the names of traitors who had tortured, imprisoned and assassinated their comrades. Which was why Song knew that the People's Army would empty its purse, if necessary, to buy these files.

The four policemen kneeling in front of Song's men had to know the value of this information. Otherwise why return to the compound when they could have been escaping from the country? From experience Song knew that in a crisis the South Vietnamese were more likely to fly away than stick it out. For years the South Vietnamese army had been thinking with its feet. Why stop now?

Song guessed the four policemen had already made a deal to sell these files to the Communists. To protect those listed in the files they should have been destroyed days ago. But the South Vietnamese had run off and left the files intact. No surprise. If Song had learned one thing from army service it was that only cowards survived a war. Well, he would take the files and sell them to the Communists himself.

Everything happened in threes. As a boy he'd lost his mother, his father and his innocence in one terrible day. Today he had acquired the plates, had valuable files practically handed to him and received a commitment from the shrewd Kim Shin to assist in Song's counterfeiting. For the first time in his life he felt lucky. And with that feeling came the conviction that he could now have everything.

He walked to the far wall, placed the folded newspaper on top of the first suitcase, then went back to stand in front of the policemen. The one Song knew, a Lieutenant Dau, was a short thirty-year-old with a small gold crucifix hanging from his neck. Song knew him to be pigheaded and obstinate. He hadn't worked with Dau, who was a punisher rather than an intelligence gatherer. As an interrogator in the secret police he prided himself on breaking by any means needed important Viet Cong prisoners and sympathizers who'd proved too tough for other interrogators. Dau was always brought in at the end of the game. The Americans had named him Relief Pitcher.

Song stepped in front of the lieutenant. "Who are you selling these files to?"

Dau stared off into the distance, then abruptly spat on Song's neatly pressed trousers, hitting the Korean just above the left knee.

In the tense silence Song looked down at the offending stain and shook his head sadly. Then he shot Dau through the left eye.

One step to the right and Song was in front of the next Vietnamese. *"The name of your buyer."*

* * *

U.S. Marine Corporal Manny Decker, M-16 in hand, stood on a landing in the main building of Saigon's National Police compound, staring at the blood trail.

The .45 on his hip weighed a ton and he was hungry, not having eaten since lunch. At the moment what bugged the slim twenty-year-old Decker most was the blood. It meant he and the others could be walking into trouble. The blood led into a gray corridor. Decker and marines Ivan LaPorte and Maxey Twentyman, all armed and in civilian clothes, were escorting CIA agent Brian Schow to a computer room in the corridor where the marines were to assist Schow in destroying the computerized records of ten thousand Vietnamese who had worked with the South Vietnamese government and the Americans during the war.

The war was lost. Saigon was surrounded by a huge Communist force whose tanks were a mile away from the city and coming closer. First priority on American helicopter flights from Saigon to offshore aircraft carriers went to Americans and their families, Vietnamese VIPs and foreign embassy personnel. Of those who couldn't be flown out because their evacuation had been left too late, the ones at highest risk were Communists who had gone over to the CIA and South Vietnam's Special Police. These were the people described by Schow as pencil dicks who couldn't pick fly shit out of black pepper but shouldn't be hung out to dry.

Schow, a plump thirty-five-year-old Californian whose family owned an alligator farm in Orange County, was known for entertaining at CIA parties by spinning plates on long sticks while whistling "The Sabre Dance." He'd been picked to destroy the files because he'd been running an informant network of important Vietnamese contacts and knew what to look for in the computer room. Decker had escorted him on past hush-hush jobs and found him something of a busybody who meant well but wasn't too bright. Like many agents, Schow was in intelligence because he didn't want to be in combat.

"Piece of cake," he said of the mission to the abandoned National Police compound. "We go in," he told Decker, "destroy anything that can identify locals on our team, then split. We owe the gooks that much. The Commies get those files and anybody listed in them has run his last race."

Decker, a security guard at the American embassy, had his own thoughts on the matter. The blood on the corridor made him wonder if this mission was going to be a piece of cake like Schow said or the one that got him sent home in a body bag. For openers, whose blood was it? And was the wounded party dead or merely lying somewhere ready to shoot the first face that turned the corner. Seventy-two hours from now Decker expected to be evacuated from Saigon. He didn't want to return to the world having joined the body count.

LaPorte and Twentyman, also marine security guards, felt just as strongly about leaving Nam in one piece. Maxey Twentyman, a twenty-three-year-old Georgia farm boy called Buf, "big ugly fucker," after the nickname of the B-52 bomber, had told Decker, "If I get wasted make sure they send my redneck ass back to Macon County. Don't let them bury me in no country where you can blindfold the people with dental floss."

LaPorte didn't want to talk about dying. Talking brought it on, he said. So he just brooded about dying. A handsome Puerto Rican from Brooklyn, he'd joined the Marines the same time as Decker but ended up taking his basic training in California. Six months after LaPorte and Decker arrived in Nam, LaPorte's wife Lucette had given birth to Felix Raymond LaPorte in Brooklyn Hospital. The closer he came to leaving Nam the more LaPorte worried about dying before seeing his wife and son. As civilians, he and Decker had met at New York karate tournaments, where they'd competed as middleweights. LaPorte had guts and fairly quick hands but couldn't match Decker's hand speed and ability to put combinations together. In three matches Decker had easily defeated LaPorte every time.

After basic training both had turned up at Marine Security Guard School at Quantico, Virginia, each glad to see a familiar face. In those days LaPorte had been gung ho, a highly motivated marine, crazy for the Corps and hot to be a *mustang*, an enlisted man who becomes an officer. Decker had nicknamed him F.L. for Fearless Leader. Cut open his heart, everybody said, and you'd find the inside painted marine green.

Decker'd had one happy moment above all in the Corps and he owed much of it to Gail, his lady. She, not his parents, had flown down from New York to Parris Island, South Carolina to share the proudest day of his life, his graduation from Marine boot camp. The ceremony marked the end of eleven weeks of recruit training which had been as sadistic as drill instructors could make it short of flat-out killing you.

Goodbye to almost three months of backbreaking, ballbusting hell. Basic training over, drill instructors no longer called you slime, shithead, Communist faggot, or that lowest form of life, civilian. On Graduation Day they called you Marine, something they'd deliberately refused to do for almost three months. Marine meant you were top-drawer, foremost, and unequalled on God's earth.

On the parade ground, in front of a reviewing stand and bleachers packed with relatives and friends, the honor men from each platoon were announced. These were the top trainees, super marines of the future. While other graduating recruits wore khaki, honor men were outfitted in dress blues, a gift from the Marine Corps Association. Decker had been his platoon's honor man. It was something he'd wanted and had busted his buns to get.

Before joining the Corps, he'd made *nidan*, second-*dan* black belt in Shotokan karate, getting the rank by spilling blood, his and other people's. He'd racked up thirty trophies in competition against the best fighters in America, taking on all comers and in the process losing a few teeth and suffering his share of broken bones. Back then it had been enough for Decker to do one thing well and that thing had been karate.

Confidence had given him energy and he'd had confidence to spare. Decker believed he could beat anybody. He was king of the hill and if he swaggered through the streets in those days, who could blame him? But nothing had matched the emotion he'd felt when under a fiery sun he'd stood on the parade field with his company and heard his name called as a platoon honor man and he'd stepped forward as a *Marine* for the first time. The base band had played the Marine Hymn and "Auld Lang Syne" He'd blinked away tears and there'd been a catch in his throat and he'd never loved Gail more.

She'd known how important this day had been to him. When the Manhattan restaurant where she worked wouldn't give her time off from her waitressing job she'd quit and flown to South Carolina to be with him. Gail and the Corps. For Decker there'd never be another time when he'd feel so wholly satisfied with his life.

His mother, a so-so singer who'd never risen above Broadway understudy, and his stepfather, a talent agent obsessed with his glamorous clients, hadn't even considered making the trip. They regarded him as little more than a nuisance. The lives of his ferociously ambitious parents centered around show business. Decker wasn't in show business, which made him a nonperson, somewhere between a freak and troglodyte.

Observing his parents in action provided Decker with a firsthand look at how lies, trickery, and other forms of chicanery could be used to get your way. There were no more dangerous people in the world than cunning people. The lesson wasn't lost on him.

His natural father, a veteran of World War II, had been recalled when the Korean War broke out and died when a North Korean pulled the pin on a grenade, killing them both. Natural father aside, Decker eventually realized that his family were people he'd never have associated with if he didn't have to. They'd provided him with no emotional security and he'd grown up being on guard against them. Family life was Decker's first contact with the world's dark side.

The one person he'd trusted had been Ran Dobson, the skinny Marine recruiting sergeant from Oklahoma who'd been stationed in New York. Ran, no pretty boy, had been fond of saying that the man upstairs had created him ugly, then hit him in the face with a shovel. He'd been Decker's first karate instructor and his only friend, teaching him to conquer his loneliness by becoming good at something.

It was Ran who in five years turned him from a frightened adolescent into a disciplined fighter with the most important weapon of all, an unbendable will. Ran had been the reason Decker had joined the Corps. One of his most treasured possessions was Ran's leather-covered swagger stick which he'd given Decker before flying to a new assignment in Vietnam where he was to die, a victim of "friendly fire."

Ran's death left an empty space in Decker's heart that would never be filled.

After Parris Island Decker was scheduled for Marine Security Guard School where outstanding enlisted men were trained to guard American embassies and consulates. But first he had the two weeks' leave granted new marines. He spent every day of that leave with Gail in a Hell's Kitchen walk-up she shared with two girls who considerately found somewhere else to stay during that time. He called his mother only because Gail said to, but he avoided the family apartment, a Fifth Avenue duplex in the Village.

His mother telephoned once to say that she and his stepfather were moving to a house in Westchester with a pool, tennis court and a two-hundred-year-old oak tree. Decker said he'd write and he did, eventually sending two letters his first month in Saigon. Both went unanswered. Gail, meanwhile, wrote him over twenty letters a month. If she was thousands of miles away from Decker, she had let him know that her heart was with him every second.

But Vietnam had changed Decker and those changes weren't going to improve his relationship with Gail. He'd killed, the first time a year ago, when he'd helped beat back a Viet Cong attempt to infiltrate embassy grounds and, more recently, while a bodyguard for the American ambassador on a trip to inspect evacuation proceedings at Tan Son Nhut Airport. Killing had uncovered Decker's dark side, something he was afraid to bring home to Gail. The closer he came to leaving Saigon, the more he feared being unable to leave this part of him behind.

Over here he'd seen things that couldn't be described. How could he put into words what it was like to go to Graves Registration—the morgue—and see dead bodies of naked GIs sitting in fiberglass chairs, faces stitched after being blown apart, faces more hideous than any horror film ever made.

And there was the Saigon hospital visit two months ago when he'd gone to see Kevin Lee. Kevin was a cool black dude from New Jersey who at sixteen had lied his way into the Corps to become the youngest marine in Decker's Parris Island class. He was a music freak who dreamed of starting his own record company. Gonna be the next Berry Gordy, he said, but better looking. Much better looking.

During a Cong rocket attack on the airport Kevin had suffered back and leg wounds. However, his recovery was expected to be normal, with little aftereffects from his injuries. Which is why Decker was stunned when a bulky, full-faced American nurse, who'd been working three days without a break, wearily said he couldn't see Pvt. Kevin Lee because Pvt. Kevin Lee had died only minutes ago.

A crazed, wounded Viet Cong prisoner had left his bed, stolen a fork and gouged out the sleeping Kevin's throat. MPs had shot the Cong, but it had come too late to do Kevin Lee any good. Kevin Lee had died of a bad paper cut, as they say.

And there was the nine-year-old Vietnamese girl with no legs, a sweet little thing who'd put forth her best effort to kill Decker and nearly succeeded. It happened one night four months ago when Decker, LaPorte and Buf had left a bar near the CIA compound.

Decker and Buf had been reluctant to leave because the bar was one of the few joints in Saigon where for sure you could meet some round-eyed tail—white women like nurses, embassy personnel and U.S. dependants. But the homesick LaPorte, anxious to make an overseas Christmas call to his family, had insisted Decker and Buf accompany him. It would give them something to do besides get juiced and look at broads who'd rather do the wild thing with officers than enlisted men.

For Decker, leaving the bar also meant deciding whether or not to call Gail, a decision he didn't want to face at the moment. Somehow the war had come between them and he didn't know how to tell her. She was writing Decker about their future together, but since the present meant nothing to him why bother to think about the future?

As for Buf, round-eyed tail or not, he was quite willing to leave the bar. The food was so bad, he said, that pygmies came from miles around to dip their spears in it. He'd also pissed off a CIA guy by saying the guy had a dickfor on his shirt. When the guy said, what's a dickfor, Buf said, if you don't know, I ain't gonna tell you. The CIA guy, big enough to block out the sun, slid off his bar stool and said, "Hey, turd face, you calling me a queer?" It was left to Decker to step in and guide Buf away before he and the CIA guy tangled assholes.

As they were walking out of the bar, in rolled the legless girl on a small platform, holding a battered tin cup of faded flowers for sale and wearing a heartwarming smile on her little round face. LaPorte bought two flowers, saying they were for his Lucette and Felix. Decker said what the hell, and bought one each for himself and Buf. He'd read somewhere that flowers were the language of love. LaPorte loved Lucette and little Felix. Question was, did Decker still love Gail.

A block away from the bar, Buf, the drunkest of the three, proclaimed at the top of his lungs that he'd rather smear honey on his bare ass and sit on a beehive than spend another day in this Nam shithole. He playfully threw an arm around the necks of Decker and LaPorte, drew them close in and said that he, Maxey Byron Reynolds Twentyman, was a bona fide, certified, verified meteorologist, meaning he could look at a girl and tell *whether*.

That's when the three men heard the explosion.

And the screams. Turning, they saw one big fireball where the bar used to be. Later they learned that the legless girl's platform had been wired with plastique. *Hey, GI, my flowers come with a C-4 surprise.* The Viet Cong had fixed her up. She had killed herself and twelve Americans. When LaPorte said, I saved you guys, me and my family, he got no argument from a shaken Decker.

But that night and for nights to come, the legless girl came alive for Decker. In his dreams the explosion happened over and over, with the screams of the dying tearing at his brain. He saw his body being shredded by the C-4, saw pieces of his bloodied bones flying in all directions and felt the flames melting his eyeballs. From then on he was afraid of going to sleep. He knew he was terrorizing himself and couldn't stop. In dreams his fears crawled from the dark cave of his mind to haunt him, dreams that only increased his doubts about surviving Nam.

The nights turned Decker into a haunted man.

Following the blood trail.

In the corridor, a silent Decker, flanked by LaPorte and Buf, stood a dozen yards or so from the computer room. The blood had dripped its way straight to the computer room with no stops in between. The door was open and what was worrying Decker were the voices coming from the room. Until he knew who they were, it was safeties off and look alive.

He heard male voices but couldn't make out what they were saying. He also heard the voice of "the Queen" herself, Aretha, getting down and dirty.

Schow was nominally in charge of the detail but when things got hairy Decker would call the shots. No problem there. In a crisis Schow preferred that someone else make the hard decisions. As Buf told Decker, Schow is so unsure of himself he's probably got twelve-year-old kids he ain't named yet.

A fourth marine, Pvt. Al Jellicki, had also been assigned to the detail. At the moment he was in front of the building protecting their car, a secondhand Peugeot, from armed Vietnamese deserters who were grabbing everything that wasn't nailed down. Decker touched the hand radio hanging from his belt and thought about sending for Jellicki, the beefy twenty-two-year-old poker expert whose Saigon winnings were said to exceed fifty thousand dollars.

LaPorte could change places with him. Outside, LaPorte might worry less. Then again, maybe he wouldn't.

Decker looked at the Puerto Rican, who appeared calm enough and seemed to know what Decker was thinking because he whispered, "I'll be fine, bro'. Let's just do it, then get the fuck out of here and start packing."

Behind them Buf, a shotgun in his large hands, whispered, "Let's rock and roll."

Decker motioned an uneasy Schow to move further behind the marines and smiled when the CIA agent gingerly stepped around the blood. Schow, who wore a flak vest under a summer gabardine jacket, carried two .38s, one in each jacket pocket. When Decker told him to hold the guns in his hands, the CIA agent looked as if he were ready to shit his pants.

Marines through the doorway first. No argument from Schow, who was more than happy to stay outside until given the all clear. This assignment wasn't a piece of cake any more. Not with blood on the floor.

They inched towards the doorway in silence, Decker was the point man. LaPorte and Buf were spread out behind him, with everyone taking care to avoid anything on the floor that might make a sound. Near the computer room door, Decker halted and began his hand signals. He'd go through first, then Buf and LaPorte.

Once inside everybody knew the drill. *Spread out, keep low and take cover. Above all, watch your ass. The only way to go was home.*

Decker, heart beating frantically, exhaled. Using the palm of one hand he wiped sweat from his forehead then dried the hand on his jeans. He pushed dreams of the legless girl from his mind.

Showtime.

He charged through the door, dove to his right and came up in a crouch behind a metal desk, M-16 to his shoulder and pointing across the room, eyes taking in everything at once. He saw the Korean soldiers. Saw the Vietnamese kneeling with hands behind their heads. Saw two Vietnamese lying on the floor. Forget them. They were dead, asleep in Jesus. Decker had been in Nam long enough to recognize the lifeless grace that went with being deceased. He could also smell them clear across the room and see the telltale brown stain in their pants. With death your sphincter muscles loosened and you crapped in your pants.

Then there was the man sitting on the floor, back against a computer, a woman hovering over him. Decker couldn't see his face; the woman had her arms around him, sobbing as she slowly rocked back and forth. The man't hands were white, making him American or European. What the hell was going on here?

"Freeze! Nobody move! Guns on the floor. Now!"

The Koreans froze. Two uniformed soldiers, their backs to Decker, cautiously looked over their shoulders. Two officers faced him. None of the Koreans panicked, none of them did anything impulsive. They simply stood in place, eyeballing Decker as though he were a toy soldier and they were the real thing. They also didn't drop their guns. Decker didn't like that.

Three Korean enlisted men and two officers, all with enough fire-power to make things unpleasant if they so desired. Decker recognized the officers as Korean G-2, Intelligence, who often put in an appearance at the American embassy and CIA compound for intelligence briefings. Neither was what you'd call a nice guy.

One was Capt. Kim Shin, a stocky dude with a volatile temper and a reputation for throwing his rank around. The other was Capt. Park Song, the man everybody called Laughing Boy because of his stupid giggling. Song was big on buying stuff from the American PX, especially video cassettes of movie musicals. Decker had heard some weird shit about him and young girls. If just half of it was true, Song was a sick man.

Best buddies, Song and Shin were attached to the Republic of Korea's crack Tiger Division which had fought alongside American and South Vietnamese troops during the war. So vicious were the Koreans that the North Vietnamese had avoided taking them on. Faced with the prospect of fighting ROKs, the NVA often decided that discretion was the better part of valor.

Korean troops had long since left the country. Those few still around were attached to their Saigon embassy and working with the remaining American advisors. In their day ROKs had been the most feared soldiers in Nam and as tough on their South Vietnamese hosts as they were on the Viet Cong and North Vietnamese army. Nor had the relationship between Korean and American troops been a union of spirits and marriage of hearts. A mutual animosity had begun with the ROKs' heavy-handed tactics with South Vietnamese locals and the Korean commander's insistence on being treated as equal in rank to the overall U.S. commander. Nobody could accuse the Koreans of too much tact.

But for the best karate workout in Saigon, you had to go to them. Decker was a Japanese stylist but training with Koreans had kept him on his toes. They were aggressive, always in shape and forced you to concentrate every second. They were tough fighters, cold-blooded, belligerent and easily provoked. To disagree with them on anything —technique, strategy, conditioning—was a waste of time. Arguing with Koreans was like farting against thunder.

Having seen Song work out a few times Decker had been impressed, especially with his high kicks. The problem with Song was, he could dish it out but he couldn't take it. Hit him once, even accidentally, and he'd clean the floor with you. It was bully-boy stuff, like a spoiled child who constantly had to have his way.

He'd avoided working out with Decker. The coolness between the two had started with Song being afraid of him, then deciding he just didn't like having an American in the training hall. The relationship had really gone downhill after Decker had learned how Song had set him up for a bad beating.

Decker had more than held his own in competition against the Koreans and had managed to win the respect of a few Koreans who admired his fighting spirit. They were in the minority, however. Koreans resented Westerners training with them, especially one as good as Decker. Song encouraged that hostility.

The martial arts had taught Decker that Asians could be racists too. Some Asian instructors would keep certain techniques to themselves, teaching non-Asians only so much. Others gave you a hard time until you packed it in and quit. Deep down most Asian instructors believed Westerners to be physically and mentally incapable of learning the martial arts, no matter how long they trained. Decker had learned to be wide-awake around those Asians who detested Westerners enough to discourage them with dirty tricks.

Song may have been forced to smile at Westerners during intelligence briefings but he didn't have to smile at them during karate training. He damned sure didn't smile at Decker, who had made the mistake of being good at something that belonged to Asians. He had to be put in his place. By an Asian.

Six months earlier during a practice session Song urged a Korean fighter to challenge Decker in a "friendly" sparring. Given the bad vibes between Decker and Laughing Boy it came as no surprise when the fighter went upside Decker's head for real.

At stake in this fight for Decker was his pride, the honor of the Corps and, last but by no means least, his ass. So the fight between Decker and Hatchet Face went on as scheduled. Hatchet Face gave him two cracked ribs, a fat lip and a fractured cheekbone before Decker dropped him screaming to his knees with two kidney punches, then knocked him cold with a roundhouse kick to the head. When a bleeding and very belligerent Decker looked around for Laughing Boy, the Korean had split.

The next day Decker went searching for Song with payback in mind. But the Korean didn't show at the training hall or the embassy, not that day nor for some days afterward. With news of the fight making the rounds of the American community it remained for Paul Jason Meeks of the ambassador's staff to call Decker in for a verbal reaming. The gravel-voiced, square-built Meeks, who parted his hair above the left ear and combed it across a balding pate, laid down the law. Decker was a Marine Security guard, making him a representative of the U.S. government. Any negative conduct on his part could easily become an international incident. Decker could respect America's allies no matter how much they might provoke him or he could avoid all athletic contests with foreign nationals effective immediately. Since karate was important to Decker he bit the bullet and promised to behave himself. He'd stay away from Captain Park Song.

In the computer room Decker, still crouched behind the desk, peered along the barrel of his M-16 at Song and Kim Shin some twenty-five feet away. To Decker's left, Buf, hidden behind a printer, kept his shotgun on the Korean enlisted men. LaPorte was to the right, crouched near a second metal desk, his face almost hidden by the stock of his M-16. On the cassette player Aretha was cooking on "Chain of Fools." Decker was sweating.

Song, who was standing over the two dead Vietnamese, had a pistol in hand. Meaning he'd been the one who wasted the dead gooks who Decker figured to be Special Police or intelligence agents. Maybe he'd been settling old scores, a way of life over here.

Decker said to Song, "What are you people doing here?"

Smiling, Song returned his pistol to its holster then looked at his fellow officer. "Captain Shin had a scheduled meeting here to close out some business. Our embassy was worried about the captain's security, so I was assigned a detail and ordered to escort him back."

Buf said, "You people walk here from your embassy or you take a bus? We didn't see no automobile outside. Unless, of course, somebody relieved you of it."

Song's eyes lingered on Buf for a few seconds, then moved to the kneeling Vietnamese. "They shot one of your CIA agents. His name is Harrison Random. That's him on the floor with the woman. We were coming down the hall when we heard her arguing with Random. Apparently he'd changed his mind about taking her to America with him so she decided to get even with the help of these four. I'm afraid we arrived too late to save him. These men attacked us. We were, of course, forced to kill in self-defense."

Looking over her shoulder at Decker, Constanze Herail shouted, "No, no. It is not true. We shoot nobody." She pointed to Song. "He is the one who shoots because he wants Random's plates."

Somebody, Decker realized, was trying to run a game on him. He didn't know the girl, but he knew Laughing Boy. Which made Decker want to hear the rest of the girl's story.

He watched Song glare at her as though he wanted to pull out her heart and stomp on it. If looks could kill, the girl was dead. Song started to breathe heavily and Decker thought, the guy's hyperventilating. Then he decided no, the little gook's not having problems with his health. He's freaking out. What the hell for?

Suddenly Song took two quick steps, placing him directly over the seated Constanze Herail. Without a word he punched her in the face, then kicked her in the ribs, knocking the screaming woman onto her ,back. When he lifted his foot for a second kick, Decker fired into the ceiling over Song's head. The Korean dropped into a protective crouch, arms shielding his face and head from falling plaster. His men brought up their guns, ready to fire on the marines, and Decker thought, holy shit, it's happening for real. But Song barked an order in Korean and the guns came down at once. Coughing, he stepped forward, hands waving the tainted, smelly air away from his face.

Glaring at Decker, Song removed his hat and used it to brush a chalky powder from his uniform. One day he would kill Decker for this insult. He'd kill them all—the woman and the marines as well. Kill them for insulting him, for coming between him and the plates.

He refused to blame himself for this new complication. Refused to even consider that he should have taken the plates and left while he had the chance. No, he didn't blame himself for this unholy twist of fate. He blamed Decker.

He blamed Decker for making him afraid. The shot fired over Song's head had been horrifying. He didn't want to die in this stuffy, airless room with its infernal machines. Not when he was so close to being rich.

How near had he come to dying? He watched Decker rise from behind the desk, M-16 aimed at Song's chest. "Whatever happens," the marine said, "you get it first. Now do us both a favor and leave before somebody gets hurt."

Song looked over his shoulder at the suitcases and at the folded newspaper.

Decker shook his head. "Forget it. Nothing's leaving this room except you and your friends."

Song turned to face him. "I'm an officer. I outrank you. I want those suitcases."

"I don't think those suitcases are yours."

Hands massaging her ribcage, a breathless Constanze Herail sat up. "Those suitcases do not belong to him. Neither does that newspaper. He killed those two men for the suitcases. He shot Harrison to get—"

Song interrupted. "You lying little slut. You'll say anything if you think it'll help you get out of Saigon. The suitcases and the newspaper are mine. I want them."

Buf chuckled. "The man seems awfully interested in one measly old newspaper. Hey, you like the funny papers? Maybe you one of them people he don't read Batman he gets headaches and can't sleep at night. Me, I dig Wonder Woman. Man, she got those cute little blue panties and—"

"I want that newspaper."

Decker grinned. "Do I look like I give a shit?"

Decker thought, fuck Paul Jason Meeks where he breathes. The war was over. Time to stick it to Laughing Boy. Sneak in a little payback before the big iron bird took off for the world.

He said, "Newspaper stays here with the suitcases. You got a problem with that?" Decker didn't give a rat's ass about the newspaper. All he wanted to do was get under Laughing Boy's skin.

LaPorte, still crouched behind the desk, said to Song, "You got your health, man. Don't push."

Eyes almost closed, Song stared at Decker, who never blinked. Finally the Korean raised one hand, a signal to his men, and without a word walked towards the door. His men followed. Buf said, "Y'all keep in touch, you hear?"

When they'd left, LaPorte silently stared at the doorway. Finally he shook his head and looked at Decker. "Close, man. Too close. I got ice in my stomach."

Decker touched the Puerto Rican's shoulder. "Stay cool, bro'. We're going back to the world. Don't even think we're not. Right now, all we have to do is mess up a few machines then we're out of here. This time next week you're back in Brooklyn watching the Mets blow another game in the bottom of the ninth."

But the truth was they'd nearly had their tickets punched. Meanwhile the two Vietnamese came over to Decker to complain about Captain Song, about how he had shot their lieutenant and had been ready to shoot them. When Decker asked why, the Vietnamese went silent. Smoke and mirrors.

Suddenly he snapped his fingers. *The man on the floor.* Decker pushed past the Vietnamese and hurried to the man's side. The man literally looked like death warmed over. He was coated in plaster dust, was barely breathing and sat in a pool of his own blood. The woman, who said her name was Constanze Herail, was picking plaster bits from his hair. The man was Harrison Random, and Decker knew him.

Random was CIA and Decker had seen him at the embassy and around the CIA compound. He wasn't the brightest member of the intelligence community. Random might have done a better job if he hadn't spent so much time at the massage parlors along Nguyen Hue and Tu Do Street. At the moment, however, his mind wasn't on getting laid. Harrison Random was about to die.

In addition to an eerie brightness Random's eyes had a vacant stare suggesting he could already see the next world. His chest, thighs and hands were red with his own blood. His breathing was minimal. Decker felt for a neck pulse, finding one so weak he nearly missed it.

Constanze Herail told him that Song had shot Random in the back. Decker was about to ask why but decided it was more important to radio Jellicki for confirmation that Laughing Boy and his goons had actually left the building. Decker preferred not to have any surprises waiting for him in the hallway. He didn't trust Laughing Boy. The little gook was oilier than a can of sardines.

With the Vietnamese watching his every move Decker unhooked the hand radio from his belt then turned to face the front door. The Vietnamese also snuck in a couple of quick glances at the suitcases. Decker couldn't wait to find out what was in them.

He'd brought the radio to his mouth when he saw Schow barrel into the room, blowing past LaPorte and Buf like he'd been shoved from behind. The CIA agent stumbled before dropping to his knees, head flopping back on his shoulders. There was blood on his neck and flak jacket.

As Decker watched in amazement, Schow toppled onto his right side, head striking the floor. He lay motionless, with Buf chuckling and saying, my, oh my, and LaPorte shaking his head, and Decker thinking, the fuck's that all about. And then Decker saw Schow's hands. They'd been tied in the front with his belt. The CIA agent tried to speak, but only a harsh rasp came from his mouth. His throat had been cut.

LaPorte saw the blood and sprinted to Schow's side. At the same time Buf spun around to cover the door and that's when Schow literally exploded, the discharge turning most of the room into an inferno. The blast said grenade. One with a time fuse. Someone had pulled the pin, dropped the grenade in Schow's pocket, then pushed him in the room.

A screaming LaPorte was engulfed by flames. A few yards away Buf was hurled from the room and out into the hall. Decker drew the lucky card. He was in the rear of the room, with the Vietnamese between him and the blast. It was they who took the full impact of the explosion, shielding him unintentionally.

The reduced effects of the blast, however, were still strong enough to knock Decker off his feet and hurt him. He flew backwards, feeling the intense heat and the shock waves, before colliding violently with the disk control unit Random had been leaning against. Bouncing off the machine Decker landed on the floor beside the dying CIA agent and blacked out.

Seconds later he opened his eyes and felt a sharp pain in his back. There was a ringing in his ears and he was covered in plaster, punch cards and glass bits from computer monitors. He smelled smoke and could taste his own blood. He heard the crackle of flames along with

the hissing and sputtering of exposed computer wires. And he heard
the screaming of people in agony.

Dazed and breathless, Decker moved his arms a bit. Then his legs
and hips. Everything was still attached. He felt his balls rub against
the floor, meaning he hadn't lost his dick which was the first thing
you thought about in fire fights and explosions.

Somewhere to his left Constanze Herail screamed, "I'm blind, I'm
blind. Help me, help me."

Decker thought, I would if I could but I happen to be passing out
at the moment. He wondered how he'd managed to hold onto the
radio still gripped in his right hand. Didn't matter. He was looking
forward to being unconscious, to being out of it.

But instinct said don't give in. *Don't give in.* Decker forced his eyes
open. Again they started to close. This time he called on all his
willpower and forced them open again in time to see Song lead his
Koreans through thick black smoke and back into the room. Decker
willed himself to lie motionless. He was afraid, but out of that fear
came a hatred so strong he knew his eyes wouldn't close any time
soon.

He watched Song, a hand covering his nose against smoke, point
to the suitcases with his pistol. They were on Decker's side of the
room and far enough from the explosion to be relatively unscathed.
Slinging AK-47s onto their shoulders, two soldiers picked their way
through bodies and burning debris to retrieve the suitcases. And the
folded newspaper.

On their way out of the room one of the soldiers paused long
enough to hand the newspaper to Song. Quickly unfolding it, Song
looked inside and fingered something hidden inside the papers. Apparently satisfied, he refolded the paper.

The smoke was irritating Decker's nose and throat. To keep from
coughing he bit his lip until it bled. Through watery eyes he saw
Song speak briefly to Kim Shin and the remaining enlisted man. All
three Koreans now held pistols.

Then, as Decker watched, the three Koreans began shooting everybody in the room. Alive, dying or dead. The Koreans shot them
all.

Decker watched Kim Shin step into the hall, fire two shots into
Buf's prone body, then call down the hall in the direction of the

soldiers carrying the suitcases. Somehow they had angered him. Nobody angered him and got away with it.

Inside the demolished computer room, Song carefully stepped around a mangled printer to where a screaming LaPorte, legs blown off by the blast, lay near a metal desk. Aiming carefully, he shot LaPorte in the head three times. When his pistol clicked empty, he frowned, stopped firing and began to reload.

Several feet away from Decker a Korean enlisted man shot a Vietnamese who lay motionless behind a computer. Near an overturned stool the second Vietnamese, his face a blood mask, knelt in the middle of the burning debris and tried to push his exposed intestines back into his stomach. Skirting a burning printer the Korean soldier walked over to him and fired two shots into the back of his head. Then he stepped over the corpse and walked toward Decker.

Tightening his grip on the hand radio—shifting his arm to draw his .45 would be too dangerous—Decker willed himself not to move. The soldier drew closer and then he was looking down at Decker, pistol aimed at his head. Suddenly the soldier glanced to his right. Constanze Herail, glass embedded in her eyes, had gotten to her feet and, arms outstretched, was begging for help.

Decker used the distraction. Quickly pushing himself to his knees, he smashed the soldier in the balls with the hand radio, doubling him over. On his feet, Decker threw the radio at the soldier, then gripped his head in both hands and twisted, breaking his neck. As the soldier slumped to the floor Decker pulled his .45 and, screaming, shot him twice in the head.

At Decker's shout Song froze in the act of reloading and looked across the room. A second later Song, eyes wide in horror, threw his gun aside and sprinted from the room. A groggy Decker swayed, then dropped to his knees, the .45 falling from his hand. Crawling over to the dead Korean soldier he pulled at the AK-47 trapped beneath him. It would not budge. Decker pulled harder. The rifle came free. Aiming the Russian-made gun at the doorway, he pulled the trigger.

He had forgotten how loud and powerful it was. The noise tore at Decker's ears and eyeballs and he could feel the vibrations through his teeth. But the gun got the job done. No one was going to come near the door. There would be no more grenades tossed into the room. Not while bullets fed by the thick, plastic magazine tore off the door frame and gouged broad holes in the corridor wall.

On his feet, Decker continued firing, stumbling toward the door and swearing before God that he was going to kill Song. When he reached the hallway the AK-47 was empty. And so was the hallway. He looked around for another weapon, saw Buf's shotgun wet with his blood.

Gripping the shotgun, Decker, eyes blinded by tears, staggered down the corridor toward the staircase, bumping into walls, spinning around, losing all sense of direction. He called out for LaPorte and Buf, his voice echoing along the empty corridor and coming back. The black depths of grief drew closer.

He reached the stairs and made his way to the first floor, leaving a trail of blood. The shotgun became heavier. To keep upright Decker talked to himself, to LaPorte and Buf, and soon they were talking back, telling him to waste Song, to catch up to Laughing Boy and wax his ass.

Near the front door Decker dropped to his knees and began to crawl, following the white plaster dust footprints left on the carpet by Song. The shotgun, now forgotten, lay near one of the cubicles.

Inches away from the door he passed out.

FOUR

At 4:32 in the afternoon Det. Sgt. Manny Decker entered an almost vacant Mexican restaurant on Columbus Avenue and stood beside a woman who sat alone at the bar, her back to a picture window full of cactus plants. He watched her finish a Margarita, reddened eyes closed as she drained the glass.

After placing the empty glass on the bar beside an eelskin purse she picked up a half-smoked cigarette from an ashtray, took a quick drag, then stubbed it out. She looked at her watch and was taking a pack of Marlboros from her bag when she sighted Decker. Forcing a smile, she slid off the bar stool and into his arms.

As Decker held her close, a thousand sleeping memories came to life. Her name was Gail DaSilva and they'd once talked marriage. But that was before he'd returned from Vietnam a very different man from the one who'd left America as a young marine with clean hands and a pure heart.

He'd seen a lot and remembered too much. Shit, he'd come back feeling as though he were a thousand years old. A disappointed Gail had married someone else.

"Eight years," she said. "Eight long years. Can't believe it's been that long since we've seen each other."

"You're looking good."

"You're lying but that's okay. God, you're solid as a rock. Still doing your karate?"

"Still doing it. Karate, clean living and the power of prayer have made me what I am today, whatever that is. My old man thought exercise was a waste of time. Said if you're healthy you don't need it and if you're sick you shouldn't risk it."

"Wise fellow, your old man. I was so afraid you wouldn't show. Thanks for coming."

Burying her face against his chest, she wept silently. The detective closed his eyes. Being a cop for any length of time left you colder than a gravestone in winter. Decker wondered if he had anything to give. He couldn't weep for everybody, that's for sure.

Gail DaSilva, however, was a different matter.

Two days ago she'd telephoned him at the precinct. The day before, Tawny, her teenage daughter and only child, had gone off as usual to attend a private school on Manhattan's West 73rd Street. That evening she'd failed to return. A frantic Gail DaSilva wanted Decker to find her.

Manny Decker was in his mid-thirties now, slim and muscled, with dark brown hair, a mustache and a smile that made him seem congenial, which he wasn't. The first two knuckles on both hands were callused from years of hitting the *makiwara*, the karate punching board. A broken nose had much to do with his good looks. He'd acquired the cosmetic fracture while on a U.S. karate team competing in the Pan-American games when an opponent, a free-swinging Mexican postal clerk, had failed to pull a face punch.

Decker had earned his detective's gold shield in less than two years. In addition to precinct duty he was secretly attached to the Internal Affairs Division, which had recruited him as a field associate directly out of the police academy. Field associates reported police misconduct to department headquarters, making them the most detested people on the force. Discovery meant being ostracized, harassed and even physically attacked by fellow officers, who insisted that FA stood for "fucking asshole." The job was hazardous, at times dangerous. Decker liked it.

To reduce risks to themselves field associates maintained only one headquarters contact, a lieutenant or captain. Code names were used and meetings were held in out-of-the-way places. Decker had insisted that he and his contact, known simply as "Ron," never meet. Better to get a tin beak and peck shit with the chickens than be seen publicly with headhunters from Internal Affairs. Decker and Ron communicated by phone, Decker initiating all calls.

Decker was a loner, unable (unwilling, his ex-wife had said) to commit himself to anybody. He was an observer and lived a life free of commitment, a man on a stopover between womb and tomb, who fulfilled himself training alone in the *dojo* and who told himself he was blessed because his life now let him create his own laws. That was why he'd become a field associate, a fucking asshole. He'd wanted to make the laws himself.

In the restaurant Decker dropped his hat on the bar beside a Christmas wreath slated to be hung on the front door and unbuttoned his topcoat. He had to work at catching the eye of a young, hook-nosed bartender who was busy changing channels on a television set near the cash register. After electing to go with "Love Connection" the bartender turned his attention to the detective, who said, "Two coffees, black."

Gail took Decker's hands and pulled him onto the stool beside her. Petite and dark-haired, she was in her mid-thirties but looked older. She wore a smart black suit and white running shoes, which Decker had come to recognize as the uniform of professional women in Manhattan. He didn't much care for the look, finding it as ugly as homemade soup.

He'd last seen Gail on a chilly April afternoon at the Metropolitan Museum of Art when he'd bumped into her and her husband at a Van Gogh exhibit. She had married Max DaSilva, a chunky accountant who also owned a mail-order jazz record company. Decker remembered him as a man who seemed pleased with himself and displeased with everybody else.

In the telephone call about daughter Tawny's disappearance Gail had also clued Decker in on a life that was undergoing some changes. Shortly before their child's disappearance Max had asked Gail for a divorce. As he put it, he was nearly forty and it was time for a spiritual rebirth, a reawakening of interest in life. It was time to expand his soul, to increase his ability to give and to receive.

Gail said, you're talking shit, Max. Get to the point.

The point, as Gail told Decker, was that Max was banging a client, which was how he had developed a taste for psychobabble. His new love, a Swiss designer of costume jewelry, had pushed him into hypnotherapy as a means of bringing repressed feelings to the surface of his consciousness. As a result Max learned he'd wanted a divorce for years but lacked the balls to go for it.

Now that he was in touch with himself, he wanted to end his marriage to Gail and marry the woman with whom he said he wanted to live while he was alive.

Gail had a surprise for Max; she was as bored with him as he apparently was with her. Truth was, both of them had come to this state simultaneously. All they'd done the past few months was discover each other's faults, she told him. The magic was definitely gone.

Gail's response to Max had stunned him; he'd always underestimated her pluck. Then again, so had Decker and on more than one occasion.

Max had agreed to give Gail everything she wanted. Money, maintenance, a piece of the record company. Max wanted to remarry pronto. Gail could have custody of Tawny. Max preferred a clean break. Gail could even have their three-bedroom co-op located directly across from the Philippine consulate on East 66th Street. As divorces went, this one appeared to be hassle free.

Eliminating Max from her life would allow Gail to concentrate on her job with a children's book publisher where she had been a secretary for almost five years. She enjoyed the work, the money was good and she was about to be promoted to executive assistant. The future was looking so bright Gail was going to have to wear shades.

Another bonus. Life without Max would mean peace and tranquility at home because he and Tawny didn't get along. Max was easily agitated, supercritical and, before therapy, had believed in keeping his feelings to himself. Tawny was impulsive, restless and quick to speak her mind.

Decker hadn't met Tawny but he liked Gail's description of the kid's independence. If he hadn't been so unhinged after Nam, Tawny might have been his daughter. A photograph sent to him by Gail revealed a blonde girl-woman of extraordinary beauty who also seemed to have a touching combination of defiance and uncertainty. Decker saw her becoming the kind of woman who did nothing she didn't want to do.

As Gail told it, Tawny's reaction to the upcoming divorce was to say she preferred living with Gail and didn't care if she ever saw Max again. This brought on a doozy of an argument in which Max accused them of ganging up on him. It ended with Tawny running sobbing to her room and slamming the door. Max had barged in after her, provoking a nasty quarrel between the two of them. He'd lost his temper and slapped Tawny, causing Gail to freak out and slap him. It had been a very unpleasant scene, with tears, shouting and name-calling all around. The next morning Tawny had gone off to school and not been seen since.

"Have you received any ransom notes?" Decker asked Gail.

"No. I wish I had. At least then I'd have something to hold on to, something showing she was alive."

"I've been in touch with police runaway units, hospitals, morgues. No one fitting Tawny's description has turned up."

"What about the FBI? You mentioned something about contacting them."

"I did," Decker said. "But unless a missing-persons case is interstate they won't touch it. Right now we don't know where Tawny is. Let's hope she's still in New York. Gives us a better chance of finding her. An FBI guy promised me they'll post a missing-persons notice on her in their Washington headquarters. That's all he can do."

"I don't want excuses, I want my daughter back."

"Gail, listen. The FBI guy says we have a problem. There's no proof Tawny's been kidnapped. No ransom note, no telephone calls, no witnesses who saw her being abducted. He says all we can do is work with local cops and hope for the best."

Decker massaged the back of his neck. "Look, I work vice, drugs, dirty money and some things I'd rather not go into. I don't know that much about finding missing children and my informants don't either. But I'm willing to give it a shot. I'll make what contacts I can, fall back on some old ones and just get out on the street and try to make it happen. I'm saying we need all the help we can get and that includes the cops in your precinct."

Gail's chin dropped to her chest. "Max is out doing things on his own. He's been to her school, telephoned her friends, their parents. So far, nothing. He says he feels guilty for having hit her. I'm trying hard not to blame him for what happened but it's not easy. It is not easy."

Decker put an arm around her shoulders. "Ninety percent of missing kids return within twenty-four hours. I know it's been a couple of days, but Tawny could be on her way home right now."

He didn't tell her that most runaways who returned had been sexually molested. Or that thousands didn't return because they were murdered in a growing wave of ritual homicides or by serial killers who preyed on kids.

Gail placed her clenched fists on the bar. "I want my daughter back. *I just want her back.*"

She looked at Decker with red-rimmed eyes. "Max is Jewish and you know I'm Catholic, but we celebrate Christmas because Tawny likes it and we get a kick out of seeing her happy. I was planning to shop for her presents this week. She wants leather pants and a pair of shoes from Sacha. She always did have expensive tastes."

"Go shopping," Decker said. "Keep a normal routine if you can."

"I told the police about Tawny, like you said."

"I know. I checked in to let them know I was involved as a friend of the family. They said no problem, just keep them informed. They'll check her school to see if she's staying with friends and they'll ask around the neighborhood to see if she's been seen since her disappearance."

Which as Decker knew was just about all Gail would get from her precinct. Most police were at least approachable and often friendly, but the city's high rate of street crimes had created a police force that was overworked, burned out and, after years of seeing humanity at its black-hearted worst, very cynical. Fighting crime in this town was like trying to run a marathon with one foot.

Decker knew why cops didn't view Tawny's disappearance as urgent. Urgent was finding eight dead Dominicans in a Washington Heights apartment, the youngest six years old, the oldest eighty-three, all dead because one had burned the wrong people in a drug deal. Urgent was a twenty-two-year-old cop shot in the head while guarding the home of a Queens drug witness because druglords wanted to send a message to the community about the dangers of cooperating with police.

Urgent was not a spoiled brat who didn't come home from private school yesterday but who might very well come home when she was hungry enough.

Decker had suggested that Gail's cops dust Tawny's room for fingerprints to be sent by computer around the country and matched with those of unidentified dead girls her age. The answer he'd gotten was, "We're really busy right now, sergeant, but if anything develops we'll let you know." Fuck off, in other words.

Gail said, "It was Max's idea to run two classifieds on the front page of the *Times*, which we're doing starting tomorrow. One says Tawny, we love you and want you back. The other offers a twenty-five-thousand-dollar reward for her return, no questions asked."

Decker took a sip of black coffee, then pressed the cup between his palms to warm his hands. "The money will draw crazies, nutcases claiming they have information when they don't. But that can't be helped. Drink your coffee."

"I'd like another Margarita. Remember when I used to work here as a waitress, back when I thought I was a better singer than Judy Collins? A Margarita cost ninety cents. Now it's almost six dollars."

Placing a hand on Decker's arm, Gail turned to stare through the bar window at a young Hispanic couple outside on the sidewalk eyeing the restaurant menu. Decker followed her gaze. The man, small and tough looking, wore a green wool cap, matching down jacket, and gripped a newly purchased Christmas tree a foot taller than he was. The woman, lean with a big mouth, pulled a fake fur collar tighter around her throat and pointed to the menu. She said something to the small man, who ignored her.

"First week in December," Gail said, "and already they're selling trees on every other street corner. I started seeing Christmas ads in August."

She looked at Decker. "I've never been the victim of a violent crime in my life. Had my purse snatched once and my behind grabbed on the street a few times, but that's it. I don't know what it's like to have someone you love murdered. But it can't be any worse than having that person disappear and not knowing what happened to them. Jesus, I'm sitting here and I don't know if my daughter's gone forever or what."

Neither did Decker. Tawny could already be dead, an accident or murder victim. She could even be a suicide. Or she could be at home raiding the fridge while thinking of an alibi for her vanishing act. She could be at a girlfriend's house watching MTV. Or she could be chained in a cellar on Staten Island, where some geek was doing things to her that would shake the toughest cop.

The bottom line: the longer Tawny remained missing the less chance she would ever be found at all.

Recently the press had gone crazy with a story about a twelve-year-old Queens boy who had been missing three weeks. His corpse, minus head and hands, had been found in Long Island Sound by clam fishermen. Knowing that trapped gases caused a corpse to float, the killer or killers had slit the boy's stomach.

So far there had been no arrests. All the cops knew was that a middle-class white kid had gone alone to a tough black neighborhood in Queens to buy crack. Crazy, but when you're a druggie you've lost the power to think. Decker asked Gail if Tawny did drugs. If so, she wouldn't be the first kid her age to run into trouble making a buy. Gail said, "You're not talking about my daughter. Tawny would never touch drugs." Gail was willing to bet her life on that.

Decker caught the bartender's attention and pointed to Gail's empty glass. Nodding, the bartender picked up a clean glass, wet its rim with a section of lemon, then placed the glass upside down on a plate of salt. But not before changing the TV channels. Apparently "Love Connection" wasn't doing it for him.

Decker sipped black coffee, thinking it might be wise to grab something to eat while he had the chance. Maybe a beef-filled taco or a bowl of chili and some nachos. These days he ate on the run or not at all.

His precinct commander, monosyllabic Deputy Inspector Allan Huda, didn't mind him looking for Tawny DaSilva providing it was on Decker's own time. Words to live by, since Huda, Ayatollah Huda-Fuck to the troops, had a real nasty disposition when crossed.

So Decker put in a full day then hit the bricks to show Tawny's photograph to transit cops working Port Authority Bus Terminal; to shivering kids gathered in Central Park's Strawberry Fields to remember John Lennon; to scared runaways living in city garbage trucks amongst the trash on the West Side docks.

On the "Deuce," 42nd Street and Times Square, where runaways gravitated by the hundreds, he showed her photograph to black teenage pimps, three-card-monte dealers and managers of adult video stores. Downtown, it was bouncers in skinhead clubs, organizers of cockfights, a pair of Hell's Angels and owners of homosexual bookstores.

Back uptown, it was chickenhawks and a boss player on Eighth Avenue whose sniffling had less to do with an icy December than with Bolivian marching powder. Decker also showed Tawny's photograph to the owner of an all-night bowling alley on Broadway and to whores in an East Harlem after-hours joint who had so many wrinkles they had to screw their hats on. He hit places where a cop was as conspicuous as a bad toupee, where they were given careful thought and attention but precious little regard.

He came up empty.

No sightings, no rumors, no rumbles from any quarter. Apparently no one had seen or heard of Tawny Joanne DaSilva. On one level Decker could deal with it. After all, nobody won them all. On the other hand he was competitive; there was a side of him that never liked losing and rarely accepted defeat.

Karate had taught him to be unwavering, to persist and remain constant in his purpose. He was slick enough, though, to appear casual in his tenacity; he rarely made anyone feel arms were being twisted even when they were. His problem was an inability to let go after situations were no longer feasible.

In the restaurant Decker stood behind Gail, helping her on with a lambskin jacket as she reached for a pair of gloves lying near her purse. Both stared at the television screen, where the top story on the five P.M. newscast was the crash of a Pan Am jumbo jet in West Germany. Two hundred and thirty-three passengers and crew had died when the plane exploded in midair shortly after takeoff.

Gail said, "I know it's selfish, but I can't think of anything right now but Tawny. God forgive me, but I can't. *God.* How can anyone believe in God with all this insanity going on? Hundreds of people dying in a plane crash. My only child missing. Manny, please tell me she's alive."

"She's alive," Decker said, wondering if he'd done it again: lied to her as he lied to others in the course of being a cop. His ex-wife had refused to buy the argument that his job called for deceit, contending instead that lying of any sort was a corruption of his manhood. She was no longer in his life, leaving Decker free to lie under any and all circumstances.

A minute later he was looking through the bar window at Gail, who was now outside on the street, attempting to hail a cab. She'd invited him to her place for dinner the coming Friday. Max would be there. Maybe Decker could give him hope as he'd just done for her. Would he please come? He accepted the dinner invitation, hoping he wouldn't have to tell Gail and Max that some kids were on the street because home was hell.

Meanwhile, he was still hungry. Calling the bartender over, Decker ordered nachos, chimichangas, a small house salad with avocado dressing, and more black coffee. He was tired and would like nothing better than to eat, then stretch out on the bar. Sleep would have to wait. He'd committed himself to at least an hour on the Deuce tonight looking for Tawny.

Was he pushing his career to the breaking point? Maybe he'd bitten off more than he could chew with this Tawny thing. He had other cases. Jesus, did he have other cases. One in particular was a bitch. If Decker wasn't careful it could ruin his career or get him wasted.

For the last ten days he had been investigating the murders of two undercover cops who had been killed while working separate drug investigations in Manhattan. Like Decker, one officer, twenty-four-year-old Willie Valentin, had been recruited directly from the Academy. The other, twenty-five-year-old Frankie Dalto, had been deliberately kept out of the Academy.

They were outsiders, strangers to drug traffickers and virtually the entire New York police department. On the surface you couldn't find more ideal candidates for undercover work. Willie Valentin was assigned to infiltrate a Colombian cocaine ring; Frankie Dalto was to get close to a major black dealer working out of Harlem.

These weren't the usual buy-and-bust operations built around an undercover team: one cop making the drug buy, a second, "the ghost," watching nearby and, if possible, the field team, five backup officers, within view of both undercover cops. Valentin and Dalto had been assigned to bring down the fat cats, to work from deep cover where you couldn't have backup. There was no more dangerous way of making a drug bust.

The department had given Willie Valentin and Frankie Dalto the best training possible, but in the end it hadn't been enough. Both dead cops had been found in Decker's precinct, the area from West 59th to West 86th, and from Central Park West to Riverside Drive. Valentin's corpse, with two bullets in the left temple, had turned up in Riverside Park at West 79th Street. Frankie Dalto, shot three times in the face at close range, had been discovered in a trash dumpster on West 83rd Street and Broadway. Both had been taken out with a Hi-Standard .22, the handgun of choice for pro shooters.

Decker had been especially angered by the death of Willie Valentin, a stocky Puerto Rican with warm brown eyes and a passion for chess. A few years earlier, Willie had been one of his karate students, a seventeen-year-old teenager with a spinning back kick he threw at bullet speed. Decker had encouraged him to be a cop, not that Willie needed much persuasion.

Willie's father, also a cop, had been relaxing off-duty in a Bronx bar when a hired killer shotgunned him to death after mistaking him for someone else. At Willie's request, Decker had attended the funeral, sitting in St. Anthony's Catholic church in the Bronx with the elder Valentin's widow and eight children, each of them crushed by grief. Five years later Willie had been inducted into the police department, wearing his old man's badge. Three months later he was dead.

Decker had initially concluded that Willie and Frankie, both young and inexperienced, had gotten careless. They'd made a mistake somewhere along the line and paid the price. It was also possible they'd been executed by thugs who'd decided these two young "dealers" were worth ripping off for their drugs and money.

Word on the street, however, said the two had been given up. Given up by cops and killed by cops. *Killed by cops.* Which is why nobody was willing to come forward and say more. Police officers had power, which they carried around in a holster. Combine this power with a badge, and you had a man who could kill you without fear of punishment.

Rookie cops as well as older officers were now having second thoughts about going undercover. Had a police nightmare finally come true? Had drug traffickers penetrated the department's most secret operations?

Murder belonged to Homicide. Vice, Decker's territory, wouldn't catch this one. But because of Willie, Decker wanted in and was prepared to be a hard-ass on the subject. He foresaw two roadblocks.

First there was Homicide's paranoid pixie, the sad-faced Lt. Barry Pearl, who had more hair in his nose than on his head, and who would rather battle over turf than breathe. And of course there was the Ayatollah Huda-Fuck, who would rather stick his nose in a dog's ass for twenty minutes than tolerate an overachiever, especially one who lived life as recklessly as Decker had been known to on occasion.

Surprise, surprise. You're on board, said Pearl and Huda-Fuck when Decker asked to join the Valentin-Dalto investigation. Decker encountered no resistance to his request nor did the term overachiever come up.

Pearl and Huda-Fuck were not acting out of benevolence or good will. Decker's expertise was needed. His reputation was built on making drug cases, and these two murders were decidedly drug related. He'd gone after Colombian and black traffickers in the past, and while Willie's assignment had kept them apart, Decker knew more about him than anyone else at the precinct.

The top brass down at Police Plaza didn't like unsolved cop killings. Ayatollah Huda-Fuck and Barry Paranoid had careers to consider; at this point in their lives Decker was a gift from God. But if he didn't come through, his future was dark as a stack of black cats.

He began with a telephone call to Ron.

"So far we've managed to keep this thing out of the papers," Ron said. "Valentin and Dalto means we've lost three undercover guys. First time it's Fleming, a black kid who could have made the NBA he didn't hurt his knee. We said, it happens. I mean you win some, you lose some. We didn't like it, but we weren't looking over our shoulder, understand? Second, third time, well, I'm telling you there was a shitstorm around here. Internal Affairs is convinced there's a leak and until we plug it the entire undercover program's in big trouble."

Decker said, "Some people at the precinct aren't buying the leak theory. You know the drill. Protect the brotherhood at all costs. Bury your head in the sand. To hell with the smoking gun even if someone giftwraps it and drops it on your doorstep. Anyway, don't count on keeping this thing out of the press forever. Sooner or later somebody's gonna talk to reporters."

"We've got to plug the leak before that happens," Ron said. "Nail the bastard who's giving up our people before the press taps into what's going on. Let's face it, public confidence in the police isn't at an all-time high, especially when it comes to drugs."

"That's for sure."

"It has to be coming from inside. We catch the son of a bitch, then we put our own spin on this thing. Let everybody know we can clean house ourselves. Manny, if we can't put people in deep cover, we're fucked."

"I'm concentrating on Willie," Decker said. "Who he made buys from, who he partied with, who his enemies were."

"Start with his reports," Ron said.

"Good idea."

"You need anything on this, I mean anything, just sing out. One more thing."

"Yeah?"

"The person or persons you're looking for could be sitting at the next desk, hear what I'm saying?"

"I hear you."

"Don't trust a fucking soul."

Decker said, "I wouldn't trust my mother on this one, and she's been dead fifteen years."

FIVE

The morning following his reunion with Gail DaSilva, Decker entered DEA Headquarters on West 57th Street and Twelfth Avenue, a neighborhood made stagnant by abandoned passenger ship piers, outmoded automobile showrooms and timeworn taxi garages.

He had come to check out DECS, Drug Enforcement Cooperating System, a clearinghouse set up by federal drug agents to avoid duplication of effort in New York narcotics cases. All city, state and federal cases were logged in these files. DECS acted like a traffic cop, keeping the different investigations from covering the same ground.

Decker was interested in any profile sheets Willie Valentin had filed with DECS. Profile sheets contained a trafficker's physical description, family and criminal histories, aliases and list of known criminal associates. Some cops mailed the sheets to DEA, others personally brought them in. But all local or federal narcs, whether undercover or working openly, were required to turn them in.

Before getting down to business, Decker made his social calls, which meant schmoozing with agents, cops and secretaries to learn who'd been transferred, who was retiring to become security chief for a television evangelist, who was planning to breed Akitas in his spare time, who'd nearly lost a finger in a drug raid by reaching into a dealer's mouth to retrieve cocaine needed for evidence.

His biggest laugh was recalling the sentencing of a Pescia family underboss taken down two years ago by the DEA and Decker on drug charges. The judge had buried the mob guy. First count: thirty years. Second count: fifty years. Third count: thirty years, and so on for ten counts, the total coming to three hundred years, causing the underboss to say to the judge, "What do you think I am, a sequoia?"

It was forty minutes before Decker reached the DECS file room. He hugged and kissed Susan Scudder, the waiflike thirty-three-year-old who collected the profile sheets and recorded them. In the last five years she'd stockpiled quite a few from Decker.

There was a naive charm about Susan Scudder that he found appealing. A breathy little-girl voice made her foul mouth emerge more erotic than offensive. She was a hard worker, twice-divorced, and had a reputation for worrying too much. She fell in and out of love easily, usually with black agents or black cops.

Susan loved to travel. A bulletin board on the wall behind her desk was covered with photographs, postcards, and travel folders from Caribbean cruises, skiing trips to Aspen, package tours to Las Vegas. When things were lax at the office she wasn't above taking a daytrip to Miami or Bermuda. Decker found her to be a talker, a steady source of gossip and hearsay.

Decker was about to ask her for Willie Valentin's profile sheets when Alicea, Susan's young Hispanic assistant, said she had a phone call. The raised eyebrows on Alicea's thin face indicated that the call was personal. With a quick *excusez moi* Susan hurried to her desk, seized the receiver and pushed down a blinking button.

As she removed a clip-on earring and brought the receiver to her ear, Susan Scudder became another person. Her femininity and sensuality intensified. One small hand gently brushed both breasts and her face softened. Turning her back to Decker and Alicea, she whispered into the phone, then laughed, a lusty sound that made Decker want to drop his pants.

"She still going with Russell?" Decker said to Alicea.

"You know it. Too bad you can't get no more shoes from him."

Decker nodded. Too bad, indeed. Russell Fort was in his mid-thirties, a shaved-head, black ex-cop with a crooked smile and a sly, drawling voice. He had retired on partial disability eighteen months ago after getting chewed up by a Doberman pinscher when he'd tried to separate the dog and a woman who had been behaving in a very improper manner in Sheridan Square Park.

Fort had then gone into business, opening a running-shoe shop among the glistening boutiques and restaurants of yuppified Columbus Avenue. In addition to pricey footwear he offered headbands from L.A., sweatshirts from Milan, and striking-looking Navajo Indian jewelry. None of it was cheap. As Susan Scudder told Decker, the only people who could afford the shit Russell sold were what she called wine-and-cheese assholes.

Nevertheless she had steered Decker to the store, first arranging for him to get a twenty-percent discount. Decker liked Fort's shoes, but he found the ex-cop a bit hard to take. One minute Fort was hitting on female customers, the next he was cursing the teenagers he'd hired at minimum wages. He was also a guy who gave you answers before you finished asking the questions.

Recently Decker had gone to the store only to find it empty and a notice on the padlocked door saying that Fort's "Fast Track" had been closed for nonpayment of state and city taxes. This time Fort had gotten chewed up, not by a frustrated pooch but by life's all-time ballbuster, the tax man.

In the DECS room Susan Scudder continued her breathy and apparently indecent telephone conversation. Decker and Alicea were ignored. "I have a life to live," Decker said to Alicea. "How about running off copies of Willie Valentin's profile sheets?"

He and Alicea spoke briefly about Willie's death and how tragic it was, and when Alicea went into how cute Willie had been and how she'd wanted to go out with him, Decker politely cut her off, saying he was in a hurry.

Minutes later Alicea handed him a manila envelope with the copies he had requested just as Susan Scudder abruptly squealed, "Oh, wow. We're getting the *stretch* limousine this time? Far fucking out. I'm so excited I could wet my pants. I've got my things with me. What time should I be downstairs?"

What we have here is one very turned-on lady, Decker thought. Folding the envelope, he stuck it in a pocket of his topcoat. "What's that all about?" he asked Alicea.

Alicea's bulging eyes protruded even more as she prepared to channel a secret into the world. Whispering from behind her hand she said, "Russell Fort. He's taking Susan to Atlantic City for the weekend. They go there a lot. She's always telling me about it. I mean she wants people to envy her, you know? Russell loves the shows, the gambling, and I guess she does, too. She's always running off somewhere. That's Susan, right? They're leaving after she gets off work today. The hotel always sends a free limousine for Russell. He likes it when they make a fuss over him."

Decker's eyes went to Susan then back to Alicea. He tried to sound casual. "You wouldn't happen to know the name of their hotel."

Alicea frowned. "Hmmm, I think its Gold's Castle. Yeah, that's it. Wait here, I'll check with Susan to make sure."

Decker gently placed a hand on Alicea's wrist, keeping her in place. She shivered inwardly; Decker's touch made her think of Julio, the married Puerto Rican agent who was screwing her two afternoons a week in a motel four blocks away. Like Julio, Decker had eyes that removed a woman's clothes.

The detective grinned. "Don't bother. It's not important. I was curious, that's all. Tell Susan I couldn't wait. Thanks for the copies."

Decker had reached the door when Susan called his name. He turned in time to see her blow him a kiss, then laugh at something Fort said on the other end of the line. The detective smiled and touched the brim of his hat. A moment later she spun around to face her bulletin board. She never saw Decker's eyes harden.

One of the good things about being a cop was the power you had over people. You could tear their lives into little pieces and mail each piece to a different state in the Union. And you could do it legally.

Decker now set about trashing the lives of Susan Scudder and Russell Fort.

After leaving the DEA he gave Ron a buzz from a public telephone booth on the corner of 57th Street and Ninth Avenue, telling him about Russell Fort's failure in the shoe trade, Fort's relationship with Susan Scudder, and their upcoming trip to Atlantic City with a free limo provided by Gold's Castle.

Casinos gave free transportation only to high rollers, to people who could afford to gamble big. Russell Fort's store had just gone belly up. So where was he getting the bucks to while away the hours in Atlantic City? Inquiring minds wanted to know.

Decker also wanted to know the source of Fort's rent money. Commercial rents on Manhattan's West Side were steep. Fort's place had been small, but it was prime real estate and, as the monkey said when it pissed into the cash register, this could run into money. Figure the monthly rent at five figures minimum.

Decker saw Fort as having only one visible asset: a girlfriend with access to the kind of information drug traffickers would pay anything for. And speaking of girlfriends, was Fort faithful to Susan Scudder or was he, as Decker suspected, also dipping his wick elsewhere.

Thirty-six hours later Decker was told that Gold's Castle was furnishing Russell Fort with more than a free limo. He was getting meals, drinks, passes to all shows and a suite overlooking the boardwalk. He also had a fifty-thousand-dollar line of credit and the use of a car while in Atlantic City. The high-roller treatment was his for the asking. All this for a man who didn't appear all that solvent.

Fort was a compulsive gambler. Two months ago he'd spent fourteen hours at Gold's blackjack tables, walking away with one hundred and ninety thousand dollars. The next night he returned, only to lose every dollar plus an additional fifteen thousand. Gambling also made him a loser in the marital sweepstakes. A former wife complained in a divorce petition that Fort had forced her to have sex with two men as payment for a poker debt he owed them.

Fort had opened his shoe store with money from Li-Mac Associates Inc., a New Jersey realty company dealing in commercial property sales and mortgage financing. Li-Mac was a mob front; the Pescia family, operating out of New York and New Jersey, used it to launder proceeds from drug trafficking and illegal gambling.

"Business tax records show Li-Mac took over the store," Ron said.

Decker said, "Fort borrowed money from Paulie Pescia and couldn't pay it back. The bastard's lucky he had something Paulie wanted. Otherwise he gets his eyes shot out."

"Li-Mac put more cash into the place. I've got copies of bills for new paint jobs, new rugs, new cash register. Paulie probably thought the family had another laundry for its dirty money."

Fort, like most gamblers, didn't know when to quit. He'd skimmed store funds to feed his habit, his final act being to wager the store's tax money on the losing Mets in the National League playoffs. His life shouldn't have been worth dried spit.

Decker said, "So why's he still alive? Why isn't he buried under a Queens trash dump or crammed inside the cornerstone of a teamster union hall?"

"Because he's being protected by a man neither you nor anybody else wants to fuck with. Pescia's people, the other four families, no-body wants to take on this particular individual. I'm talking about Ben Dumas."

December suddenly felt more wintry. "I don't need this," Decker said. "I really and truly do not need this. Jesus. Ben Dumas."

Ben Dumas was a big, fortyish man who had been a smart tough cop until he'd left the force under a cloud. He spoke in a whispered monotone and was unfailingly polite. On the force he'd made big bucks by shaking down drug dealers, operators of after-hours clubs and the owners of gay bars, people in no position to complain. Complaints would have been risky, since Dumas was a vicious borderline psychotic who would kill without hesitation or pity.

His law-enforcement career ended when he was charged with attempting to sell an eight-year-old Puerto Rican boy for fifty thousand dollars to a Belgian businessman who belonged to an international pederasty ring. Dumas didn't fall all the way on this one. He avoided prison when the boy and his mother disappeared, presumably having fled to South America, and the Belgian jumped or was pushed from the twenty-eighth floor of a London hotel. No witnesses, no case. Dumas, however, was finished as a cop.

Currently he ran Ben Dumas Associates, a company calling itself personnel advisors. Decker knew it as a private detective agency with a suspect reputation. Dumas hired only rogue cops, men who, like himself, had been kicked out of law enforcement for breaking the rules. Decker hadn't been surprised to hear that Dumas and his goons were suspected of being contract hit men for the underworld.

Dumas was a mystery to most people, Decker included. He had racked up a handful of commendations for bravery, made his gold shield in a drug shoot-out that cost his partner's life, and supposedly had an above-average IQ. Yet how could you explain his motiveless viciousness? Was it insanity, sadism or just plain boredom? Whatever the reason, Ben Dumas was a man whose resentment apparently had no discernible source.

Decker rated Paulie Pescia as the toughest of New York's five Mafia bosses. Paulie had started out as an illegal immigrant and worked his way up to *capo di tutti capi,* boss of bosses. And he had done it in a field where life expectancy ranged between short and brief.

He was a man of respect, but let him touch Russell Fort and Du-

mas would show up at Paulie's house, ring the bell and shoot him
when he opened the door. To trespass against Ben Dumas was unsafe. He killed for a reason or he killed for no reason at all. Which
told Decker nothing about the man except that he was a hardcore
psycho, especially dangerous because he was uncontrollable.

"I don't have to tell you to be careful around this guy," Ron was
saying.

"Tell me anyway. I need to be reminded."

"I've got a man undercover with a hijacking crew, working Kennedy Airport. They're connected with Pescia's people. My man tells
me Fort's making payments on what he owes Paulie. Looks like Dumas bought Fort some time. If Dumas is Fort's rabbi, you can bet
there's a reason behind it. Dumas is the kind of guy who lowers your
heating bill by burning down your house."

Decker said, "Suppose, just suppose, that Fort is getting the identity of undercover cops from Susan Scudder. He then sells the information to Ben Dumas, who turns around and sells it to people who
could use time off for good behavior."

"It's possible. You think Dumas smoked Valentin and Dalto?"

"Maybe. Ben's a wacko, so who knows? He and his crew are
certainly capable of doing it. Or Dumas could have identified the
undercover officers and let the Colombians do their own dirty work.
One thing's for sure: show a dealer a way of identifying undercover
drug cops and you can name your price. You could end up with more
money than Michael Jackson. By the way is Fort a chaser?"

"Is a pig's ass pork? His lady friend should only know. Fort's made
a couple trips to Atlantic City without her and each time he's had
company. Last month he checked into Gold's with a black girl.
Maybe he wanted to change his luck."

Ron laughed, but Decker's thoughts were elsewhere. If Ben Dumas was a player, Decker could not afford a wrong move or a rash
act.

Ben fucking Dumas.

At five P.M., ninety minutes before his scheduled dinner at the
DaSilvas', Decker put himself through his first *dojo* workout in four
days. He was alone in the West 62nd Street karate club located
around the corner from his one-bedroom apartment. Formerly a

small hat factory, the club was now an airy hall with a shiny floor, high ceilings and windows looking down on the schmaltzy pastiche of Lincoln Center. Four days away from this place and Decker had missed it.

Only in the *dojo* could he find peace. Here he did not have to reason; he only had to do. For that reason he found karate not savage but serene.

He wore one of two *gis* he kept in the club. His right knee, twice seriously injured in karate matches, was protected by an elastic and steel brace. A sprained left elbow and right wrist were encircled by smaller elastic braces.

The intermediate class began at six, meaning the club was his for an hour instead of the usual two hours he would have preferred. For the past four days Decker's heavy caseload had forced him to abandon his daily morning practice. Late hours looking for Tawny meant sleeping late, which barely gave him time for a quick first-light run in Central Park, followed by a half hour's karate practice in the park's vacant bandshell. Then it was haul-ass down to the precinct before the Ayatollah began questioning his absence.

At six Decker planned to leave the *dojo* for that rarity in his life, a home-cooked meal. Gail had promised him the best scampi he'd ever tasted. Definitely an improvement over his own cooking, which leaned toward cold pizza and fudge ripple ice cream.

With today's *dojo* training limited to an hour he cut his warmup to fifteen minutes instead of the customary half hour. In that time he stretched his spine, hamstrings, trunk and arms. He rotated his neck, ankles, then pulled and twisted his fingers, wrists. He high-kicked twenty times with both legs front and back. Finished, he sat on the floor and massaged his feet to increase his energy.

After rising, he closed his eyes and took five deep breaths.

Ready to rock and roll.

Believing that battles were won during training, Decker went all out in practice. Even against an imaginary opponent he held nothing back. Punches, blocks, kicks were delivered with speed and power.

Today he chose to work on infighting, nullifying his opponent's attack by stepping into it. Stepping in also reduced the number of techniques an opponent could use. In close, the opponent's moves could be controlled. Infighting demanded the expert use of short punches, knee-strikes and low kicks. Above all, it demanded speed.

Decker attacked the head: bridge of the nose, eyes, chin, throat, temples, back of the head and neck. He used hook punches, uppercuts, elbow, forearms and knee-strikes. He went for his opponent's ribs, heart, abdomen, groin, again using elbow and knee. Finally he attacked the inner and outer thigh, knee, foot and ankle.

He attacked as he defended, defended as he attacked. He looked for flaws in his opponent, pulling or pushing him off balance to make his opponent's position poorer. Each time he attacked from the side, never facing his opponent head-on.

He perspired heavily despite an unheated *dojo* and an eighteen-degree temperature outside. The hour ended all too quickly.

He was showering when a student, a middle-aged bearded Hasid, came in to say there was a telephone call for him. Which was how Decker learned there would be no home-cooked meal with Gail and Max DaSilva tonight. Instead he was to go to a meeting in the U.S. Treasury office on Church Street in lower Manhattan. The feds had entered his life again. This was not good karma.

In a direct order from police headquarters, those very prominent folks down at One Police Plaza, Det. Sgt. Manfred Decker had been commanded to assist Treasury Agent Yale Singular until further notice. This association was to commence at once. Do not pass Go. Do not collect two hundred dollars.

Said additional duty was not to interfere with Decker's regular case load.

When he had called Gail to cancel he'd found himself speaking to a very worried lady. Max, she said, was being followed. Maybe it had something to do with Tawny's disappearance, maybe it didn't. Max had been relentless in searching for Tawny, bugging homeless people, thirteen-year-old drug dealers, homosexual prostitutes, anybody and everybody. Some hadn't appreciated having him question them for any reason. Max had frequently been told "outta my face or it's your ass."

Gail also had to wonder if Rashad Lateef Quai had anything to do with Max being followed. Mr. Quai, a black Muslim, was a postal worker who claimed to be a jazz-poet and who had submitted a tape featuring himself reading his own poetry while backed by himself on flügelhorn, sitar and bass. In returning the tape Max had called it the worst piece of crap he'd ever heard. Mr. Quai had not taken kindly to rejection. He had threatened Max with mail stoppage, personal and business, as well as with a serious "whupping."

Gail was on the verge of tears and Max was jittery. When could they see Decker? Tonight, he said. He'd show up after his meeting with the Treasury people. Tell Max to write down everything he could remember about whoever was following him. Age, race, clothing, any peculiarities. Have it ready for Decker when he arrived.

He heard Gail tell Max, heard Max in the background say he'd get right on it. Gail thanked Decker and reaffirmed her promise about delivering the best scampi. She'd been cooking for hours especially for Decker. It was the least she could do. Decker said he was looking forward to it and hung up. Time to meet Treasury agent Yale Singular, whoever he was.

Decker had worked with the feds before, rarely willingly, and each time he'd gotten screwed. They were experts at taking the credit for cooperative investigations that turned out successful, plus they had more money and power than local cops and never let you forget it. Because of that power Decker would now have to eat reheated scampi.

Yale Singular was in his early forties, a huge, heavy-jowled man with a thick neck and wide nose. He appeared to weigh at least seventy pounds more than Decker, who was one-seventy-five. Three-quarters of Singular's bulk looked to be muscle. By girth alone he dominated the room.

He wore a three-piece suit of tanned wool lined with black silk, a black bowtie, dark brown cowboy boots and a red silk pocket handkerchief. His eyes, under bushy brows, never blinked. He was said to have been the best linebacker in Texas A&M history, this in a state where football was a religious experience. Decker also found it interesting to note that Singular sported a Phi Beta Kappa key on his watch chain.

Singular did his talking perched on the edge of his desk, styrofoam cup of coffee in hand, often punctuating his soft Texas drawl with a chuckle. Decker thought it was one of the better acts he'd seen lately.

The Treasury agent was interested in Decker's investigation of Ben Dumas. Singular said, "I hear you're out to tie that boy's ass in a knot."

"We're working on it, yes." Decker had a bad feeling.

"I like the way you're going about it. Yes, sir, seems like you got a bunch of country-smart people kicking this thing around. Am I correct in sayin' that DEA don't know what you up to as yet?"

Decker shook his head. "No, they don't. Right now we're focusing on Ben Dumas and Russell Fort. Something tells me you know all this."

Yale Singular grinned. "Don't go frothing at the mouth, pilgrim. We know what we know and let's leave it at that. Which brings me to why you and me are having this little encounter. Now I'm not here to stop your investigation. I'd simply like to establish certain guidelines for you in connection with something we at Treasury got going. Let's say that we don't want you to overwind your watch."

"Two undercover cops have been killed," Decker said. "We think Dumas may have had something to do with it. Is Treasury trying to stop a homicide investigation?"

Singular held up a huge hand. "Rest your features, son. Just hush up for a mo'. Nobody's stoppin' you from exposing Mr. Dumas's wicked ways. No siree. You just proceed on course. We'd also like to see Big Ben get what's coming to him."

Singular said that Ben Dumas was suspected of supplying information to a certain counterfeiter wanted by the Treasury Department. This information was obtained in various ways, one of which involved tapping into police computers, something very hard to prove. The counterfeiter in question bragged of having a sixth sense about his customers and the police. But this so-called sixth sense was really information supplied by Ben Dumas.

Dumas was also suspected of coming up with the paper that made the counterfeiter's hundred-dollar bills the best on the market. Yale Singular wanted Decker to continue digging into Dumas but to share whatever information he dug up. Singular was big on eye contact. Decker got over the problem of holding his gaze by staring at the bridge of the Treasury agent's nose. All the while Decker listened quietly, waiting for the other shoe to drop. It did.

Decker was to stay away from the counterfeiter, who was expected in America very shortly.

Looking up at the ceiling, Singular rubbed the back of his meaty neck. "This oriental trader in funny money is an old acquaintance of yours. Two of you had a run-in over in Nam, where I believe he tried to punch your ticket. Name's Park Song, aka Laughing Boy."

To control his anger Decker began massaging his left forearm while taking deep breaths. He looked at his fingernails and chewed a corner of his mouth. Finally he left his chair, walked to the window and looked down at the traffic on Chambers Street. In Vietnam Decker had ended up fighting for his life when Park Song had ordered a Korean to kill him in what should have been a "friendly" karate match. Decker survived a savage bare-knuckle brawl only to have Song trick the U.S. military command into nearly trying Decker on murder charges. It had taken a high-powered stateside lawyer to keep Decker out of Leavenworth and get away with a verbal reaming. His hatred of Laughing Boy remained one of the most violent of his life.

Singular said, "We had an agent undercover who was starting to get close when Song took him out. Probably with information supplied by Ben Dumas. Before that happened we learned a few things. Ben Dumas is Song's eyes and ears in this country. He keeps Song posted on everything and I do mean everything. Customers, police, Dumas delivers information on 'em all."

Singular was now standing alongside Decker. "Hated to lose that agent. He was a good old boy. We got Song and Dumas down in our books for that one, and believe me when I tell you, we do intend to collect. Before he died our man gave us the names of a few of Song's customers. That's how come we know the gook's planning a humongous sale of the queer in our beloved country. His customers look to be buyin' big. For sure they're gettin' their money together and heading in our direction. Gonna happen here in the East, New York, New Jersey, we don't know for sure. But we do know it's goin' down in this general area."

Decker looked at Singular. "And you think I'm going to mess things up by going after Laughing Boy. I'll kill him or scare him off, right?"

Singular looked down at his pocket handkerchief. "Let's just say we've heard you're the sort who at times tries to exceed his capabilities. This and the fact that you have a long memory could present problems. Laughing Boy is mine."

The big man's smile disappeared. "I understand you are one of those martial *artistes*. You're s'pose to be able to put a man away with a touch of your finger, shit like that. My way's more direct—not that I'm sayin' I disbelieve in your skill or anything—but when I played football, what I did was, I rushed into the backfield, scooped up everybody in my two little arms, then tossed them all aside until only the quarterback was left. No finesse, you understand, but it got the job done. That's me. No finesse, but I get the job done."

He put a thick hand on Decker's shoulder. "Seems you ain't havin' much luck in findin' that little girl. What's her name? Tawny? Maybe you ought to forget about her, at least for the time being. Just concentrate on Ben Dumas and those two dead undercover officers and see if you can clear that up. 'Course, you will keep me posted. Christmas is comin' and you probably ain't done your shopping yet. You ought to get on that. Same old shit every year, ain't it? I mean you end up buyin' cheap soap for people you don't know, ain't that how it is?"

"Aren't you forgetting something?" Decker said.

"Such as?"

"When do I get sworn in?"

"Say what?"

Decker told him. He insisted on being sworn in as a deputy U.S. marshal. Experience had taught him it was the only way to survive working with the feds. As a deputy U.S. marshal Decker could serve federal warrants, subpoenas and pursue investigations across state lines. He could carry a gun interstate and onto a plane. And should complications arise, the feds wouldn't be able to screw him quite so easily. Working with the federal government was like being a fly on a toilet seat. Sooner or later you'd end up getting pissed on. The feds didn't like giving these powers to local cops. Yale Singular didn't appear to be an exception.

Not that Decker cared whether Singular was happy or not, because he was sure of one thing—Singular wasn't telling him everything. Decker knew that, just as sure as he knew Santa Claus was coming to town. He would have to stay alert around Man Mountain Yale, who was clearly nobody's fool.

"You ain't being asked to invade Grenada," Singular said. "Just stay in touch with me and mind your p's and q's when it comes to Laughing Boy."

"Either I get sworn in or you'll wait a long time for any of my reports. I mean a long time."

"A mite testy, aren't we? Showin' your ass a bit early in the game, it would appear." Singular's expression said he didn't like being pressured.

Decker pulled away from the big man's hand and began walking toward the door.

"Nine-thirty tomorrow morning," Singular said. "U.S. attorney's office. You been there before, I understand. And Sergeant Decker?"

The detective turned to look at him.

The grin was back. "I do not like being forced into a course of action. You just went down in my book as a bit of a strut fart. In the future I want you to remember that it was you who set the tone of our relationship. Stay well."

On East 66th Street Decker stepped from a yellow cab that had come to a stop behind two blue-and-whites parked in front of Gail's building. In a lobby dominated by a large Christmas tree decorated in blue lights he saw a uniformed policeman and policewoman talking to two Filipino women wearing nurse uniforms under winter coats. One of the nurses shook her head, saying, "I live on the same floor and it's so sad what happened, especially at this time of year."

Decker walked over to the uniformed doorman, a squat light-skinned black who had a boxer's thick ear and wore a torn cap with worn gold braid. The detective asked for the DaSilvas' apartment number and froze because the doorman's eyes said it all. Decker had been a cop too long not to recognize that look.

Shield in hand, he pushed his way between the nurses and identified himself to the two uniforms. His right eyelid twitched and he found it difficult to swallow.

Decker already knew what he was going to hear.

The female officer, young and black, her lips greased against the cold, said, "Yeah, it's the DaSilvas. They're both dead. Gun was in his hand. Looks like he shot her, then did himself. Fifth floor. I guess it's all right to let you go up."

SIX

For the past six months Ben Dumas had been a partner in the discotheque P.B., four floors of an old slaughterhouse on West 14th Street facing the West Side Highway and the abandoned piers bordering the Hudson River.

The desolate, rundown area housed New York's meat-packing industry while also offering the wares of various leather and S&M bars. Here a lease could still be had at bargain rates, a rarity in Manhattan, where landlords viewed rent gouging as a sacred trust.

Dumas had long held a bargain to be nothing more than an exchange in which each participant walked away thinking he'd cheated the other. The lease for his club, however, proved an exception to this rule. Commercial space in Manhattan could still run as high as four hundred dollars a square foot. P.B. was paying fifteen dollars a square foot on a ten-year lease. If anybody had got burned on the deal it had not been Ben Dumas.

P.B.'s main dance floor was a former gay bathhouse now decorated as a high-school gymnasium complete with basketball hoops, vintage jukeboxes and bartenders dressed like school-crossing guards. The second floor hosted live bands while the third floor offered upcoming experimental artists in live performances that included video, poetry, dance, film and conceptual art. The fourth floor, once site of the meat-freezing chamber, was the VIP lounge.

Whether Dumas would open the lounge tonight depended on how soon he concluded his business with Russell Fort. Dumas was waiting for him in the VIP area which was closed to the public in order to afford the two men privacy. Fort was twenty minutes late, not unusual for a man who was rarely on time.

Dumas was forty-three, a long-jawed, hulking man with receding sandy hair, and a wolfish smile which hinted at his compulsion to manipulate and connive. Forceful and intense, he preferred his own standards and habit of behavior to any authoritative direction. If provoked or offended, he went all-out for revenge no matter what it cost him. Having little interest in the welfare of others, he felt no inclination to curb a deep-rooted and coldblooded violence.

His disco, private detective agency and a gay bar he owned on Bank Street were all profitable. His game, however, wasn't money but total mind control over those associated with him. Club life allowed him to set a stage where he could watch the actors—employees and customers—perform under his direction.

In the spacious mahogany-paneled VIP room Dumas sat peacefully in a white wicker armchair listening to baroque lute music coming from a tape deck sitting on a pool table several feet away. Two empty wicker chairs were within reach. Resting on the nearest one was a hinged flat wooden box that when opened became a backgammon board.

Dumas sipped black coffee, smoked Lucky Strikes and watched his dog eat a large platter of raw hamburger mixed with chopped egg. The dog, named Oscar after Oscar Wilde, was a three-legged Great Dane and Black Labrador mix, a huge genial animal Dumas had acquired the day after resigning from the police force. Oscar, Dumas had decided, was a liberal because he wanted to please everybody.

Dumas and Fort were going to talk money. Despite his successful businesses, Dumas was in desperate need of cash. Almost everything he earned went toward the medical expenses of his lover, a slender forty-two-year-old Japanese psychiatrist named Ken Yokoi.

A year ago Yokoi had contracted AIDS, not through his homosexuality but because of acupuncture treatments he had received to ease severe bursitis. His insurance covered some costs, such as AZT and doctor visits, but it was Dumas who was paying sixteen hundred dollars a day to have private nurses serve Yokoi in eight-hour shifts.

The ex-cop's love for the dying Japanese was fanatical, which was why he had killed the acupuncturist, whose unsterilized needles had fatally infected Yokoi. Dumas had shoved an ice pick up the acupuncturist's nose and into his brain. Finding no evidence of violence, a coroner had concluded that the deceased had perished from natural causes, namely a cerebral hemorrhage.

Presently Dumas's bank account contained less than two thousand dollars, while a dwindling stock portfolio was worth only four thousand dollars. He drove an eight-year-old Honda Civic, owned two suits and lived frugally in the Village in a one-bedroom Hudson Street apartment facing the 170-year-old Church of St. Luke-in-the-Fields. He was comfortable with a spartan existence and could easily have lived this way for the rest of his life.

His love for Ken, however, demanded that Dumas make all the money he possibly could so that Ken could at least live a little longer. Dumas had always been a resourceful man, but when it came to Ken's illness there were things he couldn't do, things that could only be done with money.

P.B. was successful because Dumas had taken Ken Yokoi's advice and instituted a door policy favoring Asians. Japanese businessmen, tourists and local residents were the biggest spenders on New York's club scene, Ken had said. These days it was the East that begat money.

The idea of catering to Asians at his club appealed to Dumas, who had always found them charming and attractive. He took Ken's suggestion one step further by hiring Asians as half of P.B.'s work force. At times he found the delicacy and fragility of their beauty overpowering. Having them at P.B. was like owning a cage of beautiful birds.

In the VIP room Oscar looked up from his meal and eyed the tape deck, seemingly commending guitarist Jakob Lindberg for his work on Roncalli's Sonata in C Major. Dumas blew a smoke ring toward the ceiling, recalling how Ken had introduced him to Baroque music by saying it had been written in more cultured times and wasn't smeared with the shit of modern life.

Oscar returned to his dinner only to stop eating moments later and swing his oversized black head toward the entrance to the VIP room. As the dog stared at the door someone on the other side of it tried the knob on the locked door. "What it is, what it is. Ben, you there?"

Dumas left his chair, walked to the door and looked through a peephole, then unlocked a dead bolt, opened the door and with a slight movement of his head motioned Russell Fort inside. The two men shook hands as a smiling Dumas said, "Glad you could come." He pointed to the wicker chairs.

Tonight the chunky, round-faced Fort wore a purple velvet jumpsuit dotted with metal studs, a gold earring and gray lizard skin boots. A beige vicuña coat hung from his shoulders and he wore enough gold to cover the altar of a Mexican church. His eyes were hidden behind amber-lens Ray-Bans and his shaved head gleamed like the moon. There was a slight Caribbean lilt in his voice, a reminder that the first twelve years of his life had been spent in a Kingston slum.

Dumas noticed the drink in Fort's hand. Apparently our Mr. F. had stopped at the bar downstairs, probably charging his liquor to Dumas, who also wondered how many women Mr. F. had hit on downstairs before keeping tonight's appointment.

Dumas was not blind to the shortcomings of this particular African-American. Mr. F. was addicted to pleasure, making him unreliable in Dumas's book. He put good times, gambling and women in particular, before everything else. His life was instant gratification. He wouldn't wait an hour to be happy, something Dumas found true of black people in general.

In front of a wicker chair Fort drew the vicuña around him, sat down and put his feet up on a nearby butcher block that served as a coffee table. Dumas returned to his original seat, his right hand coming to rest on the backgammon board in the chair beside him.

Fort lifted his drink to Dumas in a mock toast. "Little toddy for the body, my man. Too much to drink isn't nearly enough, I say."

"Surprised you didn't fall in love downstairs on the dance floor," Dumas said. His whispered monotone was not unpleasant.

Fort sipped his Scotch. "Ain't looking for love, amigo. But, dig, I am always in the market for a little L.W.P. Lust With Potential, that is. Danced with a cute little Korean gal. Fine young thing around eighteen. I was planning on showing her my two inches."

"*Two* inches?"

Fort giggled. "Two inches from the floor, my man. Anyway, we're dancing when some Korean dude hustles over and drags her away. I was ready to throw down on the man, but I see he's got his crew with him so I chill out."

"You do complicate your life."

"Can't fuck all the ladies in the world, but at least you can try. Meanwhile, I'd like that dude who interrupted my dance to get it up the ass on national TV. So, let's talk about the money I'm going to make. I notice you got your raggedy-ass dog with you."

"Oscar's birthday is day after tomorrow. He'll be four."

Fort grinned. "Four years old with three legs. Be better the other way round, know what I'm saying?"

"I think I've got the gist of it." Dumas lit another Lucky and blew smoke at the ceiling. A vein throbbed in his left temple and he gnawed at his lower lip. Jesus, if Fort only had a brain. You had to wonder if his mother still bought his clothes. Dumas exhaled, put a smile on his face and stared at Fort for several seconds. Dumas's smile was icy. His unblinking eyes held a dangerous glint. On the backgammon board the fingers of his hand clenched into a fist, squeezed hard, then unclenched before slowly forming a fist again.

Had Fort observed Dumas more closely he might have been more alert to the danger. But behind his Ray-Bans his eyes were closed, so he missed any warning signal. He was wired, Jack, riding a fast train through a Peruvian snowstorm and feeling warm with joy and pleasure. Having soothed his soul with some dynamite flake, Fort was not afraid to deliver his black ass into the presence of Mr. Ben Dumas. Man had to be anxious around a dude who not only killed people but who'd once strangled a drug dealer's pit bull to death with his bare hands.

Fort had a gambling Jones to feed, else he wouldn't have been in the same city with this cold-blooded faggot, let alone the same room. It was a known fact that Dumas had an inadequate understanding of what it meant to be human. Dumas had a big head, people said, in order to get all the mean in. His street name was "Hitchcock" because he was considered a stone psycho.

Some said you couldn't even kill the dude because he was dead already.

Opening his eyes, Fort looked over his shoulder at the tape deck on the pool table. "Don't know what you call that shit, but it ain't music. You're in a disco, so you got to get on the good foot. Real music is all the way to the right of the dial, where they keep the black folks. Now that's gonna put some dip in your hips, some glide in your stride."

Snapping his fingers and humming Michael Jackson's "Smooth

Criminal," Fort rose unsteadily from his chair and stepped to the pool table. His vicūna coat slipped from his shoulders and fell to the floor.

Dumas also got to his feet. After stubbing out his cigarette in an ashtray on the butcher block he yawned and stretched his arms overhead, then picked up the backgammon board and followed Fort to the pool table. When Fort reached for the radio tuner Dumas lifted the backgammon board overhead and clubbed Fort on the right forearm.

Clutching his damaged arm, a screaming Fort dropped to his knees. Dumas swung the backgammon board again, striking Fort on the head, back and shoulders, tearing his jumpsuit with the sharp end of the board. Fort now sat on the floor clinging to the pool table by one hand and calling out to Jesus.

Hitchcock was really putting the hurt on him. Fort had never been worked over like this. The pain was everywhere—in his shattered arm, shoulders, even his brain. He felt as if his eyes had been ripped out. He was on fire.

No more. Jesus God, no more. He struggled to breathe as his brain asked a pertinent, and at this point, somewhat overdue question: *What the fuck had made him think Dumas wouldn't find out?*

By way of underscoring this timely query, a wide-eyed Dumas threw the backgammon board aside and kicked Fort in the stomach and ribs. After several seconds he stopped his attack, spat on the semiconscious black, then kicked him once in the spine before backing off. Fort released his precarious grasp on the pool table and slumped to the floor.

Inhaling deeply, Dumas sat in his chair and stared at Fort who was curled into a fetal position and coughing up ugly fluids. Oscar, his tail wagging furiously, looked at Fort as if to say, could I play too?

"That was to encourage your comprehension," Dumas said. "If I didn't need you, I'd have dropped the hammer on your ass here and now. Did you actually think you could get away with it? Yes, I suppose you did. You have an unlimited capacity for being stupid. Sit up. I don't like talking to a man's back."

Teeth gritted, Fort slowly rolled over to face him. It was seconds before he could speak. "Needed the money, man. Needed it bad."

His Ray-Bans hung from one ear; his chin was wet and there were dark stains on his jumpsuit. Under the pool table Oscar sniffed at a gold chain torn from Fort's neck during the attack.

"He needed the money," Dumas said. "Now that comes as a surprise. What we have here is a man who's in so deep he's traveling by submarine. I don't know why you gamble and I don't care. But I do care if your gambling costs me money. You tried a little hustle to finance that nasty habit of yours and as you may have guessed by now, I'm not in favor of it."

Dumas leaned forward, forearms on his knees. "Because of you I had to whack Tawny DaSilva's parents."

He saw Fort's jaw drop and his glazed eyes widen. "*You* killed them?" Eyes closed, Fort braced himself against a wave of pain. He took several deep breaths before speaking again. "Press said murder-suicide. Jesus, my arm."

"Suck on this," Dumas said. "Gail DaSilva told Manny Decker that her husband was being followed through the streets by some jungle bunny. Now an hour or so before the DaSilvas got iced this same jungle bunny phoned them and said he could get their daughter back. For a fee, of course. Three guesses as to the identity of this mysterious spear chucker. The first two don't count."

Fort remained silent.

Dumas said, "All the DaSilvas had to do is point you out and Decker would have taken it from there. My guess is he'd have pounded your balls into veal patties if you didn't do the right thing. How long would it have been before you told him I've got Tawny DaSilva? One second? Second and a half?"

"How'd you find out 'bout me and the DaSilvas, 'bout them mentioning me to Decker?"

"Dumb question."

"You bug their phones?"

Dumas rubbed the back of his neck. "I'm about to put you in the big picture. I went upside your head just now because this scam of yours to bamboozle the DaSilvas could have ruined a nice payday for me and Mr. Fox."

Mr. Fox was the pseudonym of Dumas's partner, an Englishwoman who had to be the classiest pimp in the history of flesh peddling. She lived in London, had more panache than Deborah Kerr and a great head for business. The lady's only fault was stinginess. If she were ever to commit suicide, she'd hang from the ceiling with one hand and choke herself with the other to save the cost of rope.

Dumas said, "I've already told you that Mr. Fox and I intend to sell Tawny DaSilva to Laughing Boy. What you didn't know is that we're getting one hundred twenty-five thousand apiece. You know why I need the cash."

Fort nodded.

Dumas lit a cigarette. "I had a choice. Either waste you for trying to screw me out of money Ken needs real bad, or waste the DaSilvas, thereby keeping Decker away from you, me and the girl."

Dumas tapped cigarette ashes into an ashtray on the butcher block. "Hear me and believe me. This thing's personal with Decker. He ain't about to let it go. You're still alive in this kinder, gentler America because Tawny DaSilva is worth a hundred twenty-five K and because that DEA tramp you're fucking can deliver information."

Fort painfully raised himself to a sitting position. "You don't have the facts of what was going on. I swear on my mother I wasn't going to tell the DaSilvas nothing. I was running a game on them, nothing more."

"I know what you were trying to do. You were going to take the DaSilvas' money and give them nothing. That's the sort of thing we've come to expect from lawyers and television evangelists."

"Dig, Susan told me about the girl, okay? Decker comes to see her and he tells everybody at DEA he's looking for Tawny. I mean it ain't no secret. Also, there was this ad in the paper offering a reward."

"Nail these words to your skull, Russell. I don't need another hand on the steering wheel. Tawny DaSilva is my business, me and Mr. Fox. I can just see the eyes pinwheeling in your head when you heard there was a reward for the kid's return. A couple of phone calls to the DaSilvas and suddenly you're among the affluent. And I'd never find out, right? Just grab the money and run. Russell, I think medical science will have to open up your ass to find your head. I really do."

Removing the Ray-Bans from his ear, Fort dropped them on the parquet floor. "I owe, can't you understand? Not Paulie Pescia but another crew. Had some bad luck on the NFL playoff games."

"There are times," Dumas said, "when I doubt if you can count past ten without taking off your shoes. I help you with Paulie Pescia and a minute later you're in hock to some other maggot. Russell Fort. A man who hits bottom then finds a hole in the bottom. Let's hear about your new creditors."

Fort wiped tears from his eyes with the back of his hand. "Guy's name is Spindler."

"Ruby Spindler. Loan-sharking, bookmaking and fencing. He's with the LoCasio crew in Brooklyn."

"Spindler's with LoCasio?" Fort said.

"Russell, you were a cop once, remember? We both know the greaseballs control all the gambling in New York. Spindler couldn't operate unless he had an arrangement with some dago. Don't look so uptight, it's just the whole world watching your life go down the tubes. Now here's what I'm going to do. You're into Spindler for how much?"

"A dime."

"Ten thousand? Russell, if I didn't know you I'd swear you were unintelligent. All right, listen up. I'm giving you ten K, which you're going to give to Spindler. You pay him off and that's all you do. Lose it gambling and I'll make you sorry you were ever born. I won't kill you, Russell, but you'll wish I had. Am I getting through?"

Fort nodded.

"Terrific. Since there's no free lunch in this life, you're going to pay me back. I have another job for you. Do this little chore and we'll call it even. You have a problem with that?"

"No problem, no problem."

"Good. First, you're going down to Washington and pick up some more paper for Laughing Boy. We sent him a pile, but he wants more waiting for him when he arrives. I understand he's turning out a ton of hundreds so he's hungry for all the paper we can lock up. You leave tomorrow evening. Follow the same routine you always do on a paper run. You stay overnight in Atlantic City, gamble a little and next morning go on to Washington where you visit your old diabetic Aunt Lorraine on H Street. Spend at least three hours with her. Everything's got to look righteous. Before you leave town you pick up Laughing Boy's paper. It's waiting for you at the usual place."

"My arm's killing me," Fort said. "Got to get to a doctor."

"I'm not finished. Take Slutty with you. As long as she feels loved she'll stand by her man. I'll front you two thousand for gambling and expenses. Don't piss it all away at the blackjack table."

Rising from his chair, Dumas walked to the pool table and squatted down beside Oscar. He scratched Oscar's neck and spoke to Fort without looking at him. "One more thing: I want Slutty to give you copies of all reports Decker files with DEA. Any requests for files, information, whatever. I want to know everything and I mean *everything*."

Fort said, "I'm telling you right now, man, Susan ain't going to do it. The woman's scared. She knows Decker got copies of Willy Valentin's profile sheets to find out who maybe gave him up. She didn't know those two cops were going to get smoked. Right now she don't want to give me nothing."

"Maybe she didn't know, Russell, but you did."

Fort closed his eyes.

"Can't put the toothpaste back in the tube, Russell," Dumas said. "Valentin and Dalto are history. Lie to her, Russell, tell her you didn't know they were going to die either."

"Susan won't give me shit, I'm telling you."

"Russell, Russell." Dumas's voice was soothing. He rose, smiled down at Oscar and patted the dog on the head. Then placing both hands on the pool table, he stared at a dart board on the wall across the room. Suddenly he grabbed up a pool cue, broke it on the edge of the table and shoved Fort to the floor. One knee came down hard on the man's chest while a hand pinned Fort's head to the ground. The sharp end of the broken cue was less than an inch from Fort's left eye.

"You like music, Russell, so I'll tell you what. How'd you like to be a singing eightball like Ray Charles or Stevie Wonder? Or how about we play the late Sammy Davis, Junior, and go for one eye. What do you say?"

Fort tried to wrench his head from under Dumas's hand and failed. "Don't, don't."

Dumas stood up and dropped the broken cue on the pool table. He was calm, as if nothing had happened. "Russell, can I count on you to convince Slutty to do the right thing?"

"I'll make her do it, I swear I will."

Dumas began rolling pool balls into corner pockets. "I sell information, Russell. I sell to drug dealers who want to know who their customers really are. I sell to CEOs who want to know who's stealing from the company. I sell to a husband who suspects the old lady's spending afternoons in a hot-sheet motel spreading her legs for her dance instructor."

He turned to look at Fort. "I sell to a woman who wants to know if her fiancé really has money or is just some loser with mental problems and a bad credit rating. But you see, Russell, before I can sell this information I must first collect it."

Folding his arms across his chest, Dumas sat on the edge of the pool table. "It's a fascinating field, Russell, this business of collecting information. As a cop I worked with police intelligence which really got me hooked. I also did a few things for the FBI and CIA. Lot of technology in this business, Russell. I use computers myself to find out a lot of things, but you know something? There's no substitute for what we call *humint.*"

He smiled down at a sniveling, beaten Fort. *"Humint,* Russell. It means human intelligence. Person to person. You find out something, then you tell me. Simple as that. No computers, no microchips, no satellites, no space stations. Just one human being to another. And that's where you and Slutty come in.

"Forewarned is forearmed, Russell. That's how I stay in business. I tell people like Laughing Boy everything they want to know about their customers and in turn they pay me. That's why I need your help from time to time. Otherwise there'd be little point to our relationship."

Dumas stood up and stretched. "Got to mind the store, Russell. Time to go downstairs before the bartenders steal me blind. You should have that arm looked after."

Fort leaned against a leg of the pool table. "I don't know if I can travel, man. I'm hurtin' bad."

A smiling Dumas said, "As soon as you have Laughing Boy's paper I want you to call me at the office. Use the prearranged code. I might want to set up a different meeting place. There's a chance Mrs. Da-Silva called Decker from outside her place and told him about the mysterious black man following her husband. Which means Decker could know more than we'd like him to know."

"You mean he could know about me and this counterfeiting thing?"

"If he's sniffing around Slutty he might already be on to something. I say might. We shall see, we shall see."

Fort shook his head. "Hey, man, prison ain't part of our deal. You get popped for counterfeiting and you're talking federal time. Real hard time. You're talking Atlanta and Leavenworth. Real shitholes, people die there. Cons are always killing each other over gambling and—''

Fort caught himself in time. He'd almost said faggots.

Dumas smiled. "I know all about federal prisons, Russell. You just leave Decker to me. You keep Slutty happy. And next time when you tie her to the bed, shove something in her mouth besides your joystick. The woman howls more than Lassie.''

"How'd you know about that?''

Dumas chuckled. "I love it when you whine. Don't ask any more questions, your mind can't stand the strain. I think you can use a drink. I'm buying.''

SEVEN

The cablegram annoyed Mrs. Rowena Dartigue because it forced her into a last-minute change of plans.

Park Song's wire arrived at her Georgian brick home on Chelsea's elegant Cheyne Walk at 6:10 P.M., not long before she was to attend the opening night of Mozart's *The Magic Flute* at Covent Garden. Having wrapped up his business in Rome and Paris the Korean was now in London. He'd arrived twenty-four hours ahead of schedule.

Mrs. Dartigue was to meet him at once. A telephone call, to be expected momentarily, would inform her of the time and place.

He'd signed the cable "Taps." Fred Astaire was most likely spinning in his grave.

She read the wire a second time before dropping it on a glowing pine log in the fireplace of her oak-paneled bedroom. Then she told Maureen Costello, her seventeen-year-old Irish maid, that she didn't wish to be disturbed. Mrs. Dartigue wanted to attend the Mozart gala—the Prince and Princess of Wales were honored guests—but disobeying Park Song was out of the question.

Wearing a delicately floral caftan, she stood in front of the fireplace and sipped jasmine tea as she weighed the possibility of ignoring the Korean's wire.

There were two points to consider.

Point one: In meeting him a day earlier she would collect her $125,000 from him that much sooner.

Point two: Defying Park Song was, to put it mildly, unsafe. Meeting him as requested was both smart and right.

She telephoned Lord Jasper Kinsman straightaway and broke the news to the paunchy seventy-year-old political has-been who was to have escorted her to the Mozart gala. "Sorry, darling," she said. "Can't make it. You'll have to go on without me."

His lordship made no protest, being as spineless as they come. He was, after all, the man who had inherited ten million pounds at age twenty-one and frittered it away by age twenty-three. For Mrs. Dartigue, Lord Kinsman's appeal lay in his lineage and willingness to accommodate her every whim and caprice.

Rowena Caroline Dartigue was in her late fifties, a slender, long-faced Englishwoman who looked years younger as a result of twice yearly sheep-cell injections in Switzerland, dyed blonde hair and alert gray eyes that rarely rested on one object for more than a few moments. Unusually intelligent, she could sense a person's most vulnerable spot. She was ruthless when she wanted something and viewed most people with distrust. Behind a charming facade she remained on guard, showing little of her true self.

She owned Rosebud, a fashion clothing-and-accessories shop in fashionable Beauchamp Place that had become a showcase for young design talent from Britain and the Continent. Many of the designers were fresh out of college, permitting Mrs. Dartigue to pay them a much smaller commission than she would have given established designers. Still, her prices to customers remained outrageously high.

"It's snob appeal, darling," she told her husband, Michael, a strapping American twenty-three years younger than she and for whom she had an intense if somewhat misguided love. "True snobs have this enormous appetite for overpaying and then boasting about it. Such people *should* be overcharged, don't you agree?"

Michael himself was overcharging Mrs. Dartigue, a practice that served as the foundation and justification for their relationship. The couple's marriage of six months was a trade-off—he'd married her for her money, she had married him for sex. Her most recent gift to him had been a new Mercedes 560 SL equipped with telephone, stereo, fridge and fax machine. In return he had promised to spend at least weekends with her for the next two months.

At thirty-five Michael Dartigue was still athletic, a large agile man with sleepy eyes, large nose and blond hair worn in a small ponytail. He was charming, amusing and fairly bursting with can-do, the sort of American whose energy instantly endeared him to English women tired of cold and unresponsive English men. Winsome traits aside, he had failed at everything since his glory days as a basketball star at the University of Miami. In his own words, he had left school and "hit the ground crawling."

He'd failed as a restaurateur, real-estate salesman, film producer, rock-concert promoter and drug dealer. Even Rowena Dartigue had to admit that her husband was shallow, unethical and had as much insight into the human condition as a walnut. He blamed his failures on a refusal to compromise, bad financial advice, betrayal by trusted associates and politics. "Not my fault I'm getting fucked over," he told Rowena. "You get knocked down once and the world won't let you up again. Wasn't for bad luck, I wouldn't have no luck at all."

In the area of his sexuality, however, Michael's confidence knew no bounds, an assessment happily shared by Rowena. She had never been with a man who had given her more enjoyable orgasms or done a better job of keeping up with her sexual demands. His erotic exuberance was dispensed as a reward for her financial generosity, and she was very satisfied. Michael made her feel young; he gave her back the days when life had wings, something for which she was willing to spend any amount of money.

As for Rosebud, it was not Mrs. Dartigue's primary source of income. The shop allowed her to show the tax man legitimate earnings and to travel abroad, presumably in search of new designers. It also permitted her the appearance of respectability while concealing her secret life and the true origin of her sizable income, which came from "white" slavery. Using the pseudonym "Mr. Fox," she sold teenagers and young adults to wealthy buyers from all over the world. Once a year she held an auction where her most attractive slaves were put on the block. The next such auction was scheduled in New York in less than three days.

She had also established the Lesley Foundation, a small charity designed to assist runaway and abused youngsters. Like her clothing shop, the charity served to launder her proceeds from the auctions.

Among others who used the charity to conceal large amounts of money was Park Song.

The Lesley Foundation also provided Mrs. Dartigue with slaves to sell. She had kept all this from Michael, who was not in her life because of his powers of thought. Only saints kept secrets, and Rowena's husband was no saint. As far as he knew she made her living from the shop. Her travels abroad were to find new design talent and to sell Rosebud's products to foreign buyers.

After the telephone call to Lord Kinsman she walked to a bedroom alcove whose curved shelves displayed a collection of antique bracket clocks. A nonbracket clock stood alone on the top shelf beside a small blue vase of yellow tea roses. This distinctive timepiece—a silver and translucent Fabergé clock—was worth more than all her bracket clocks combined.

Park Song had given it to her some months ago in exchange for an exquisite young girl from Austria. Mrs. Dartigue couldn't recall the girl's name, but given Song's enthusiasm for bloodshed one could be certain that the girl, whoever she was, had long since expired. The Fabergé, meanwhile, had doubled in value. Money did not buy happiness, but it did permit one to purchase the misery one preferred.

She'd asked Park Song to bring her a certain expensive item from Rome, to be applied toward the cost of a teenage American girl he planned to buy from Mrs. Dartigue and her American associate, Ben Dumas. The girl, called Tawny, was currently in New York and being guarded attentively by Dumas. Photographs revealed little Miss Tawny to be a cool, blue-eyed beauty with golden hair and a teasing appeal which certain men found absolutely irresistible.

Copies of those photographs, air-expressed to Song in South Korea, had excited such lust in him that in a telephone call to Mrs. Dartigue he'd been nearly speechless. On Mrs. D's part it required no abundance of intuition to realize she had Laughing Boy by the short and curlies on this one.

"A quarter of a million dollars," she'd said to him. "Seize the moment, darling, or Tawny goes to auction."

"I want her. Sell her to me this instant." The Korean was practically in heat, no surprise from one dedicated to the fulfillment of highly unsavory cravings.

"Gladly, dear boy. Two hundred and fifty thousand smackeroos and she's yours."

Song's voice shot up an octave. "Are you mad? I give you one hundred thousand, which is more than I've paid for any of your girls."

"Something close to physical pain hits me whenever an individual attempts to bargain because it means an effort's being made to cheat me."

"One hundred twenty-five thousand. I want this girl."

"Darling, you remember General Abuja, that dwarfish, pushy Nigerian who spent a fortune trying to introduce bull fighting into his country? You've done business with him, I believe. Well, he's been after me for months to uncover a tidbit like Tawny. As has an Italian prince. And do I have to tell you how many Arabs would love to devour this sweet child? Allow me to put it this way—should she go to auction I intend to *start* the bidding at two hundred thousand. Under these circumstances I'd say you're getting a bargain."

"And I say you're being damned ungenerous. You forget you've made a lot of money with me in the past."

"I wouldn't have made the money you speak of if I hadn't produced a worthwhile service. You're not being forced to deal with me, you know. No one's holding a gun to your head, dear boy. Feel free to choose alternatives."

The Korean was quiet, then: "You're a genius at getting people to believe you've got something they want. All right. Two hundred fifty thousand."

"Darling, nothing cheap is worth having. Half the money when we meet in London, the other half when Ben hands you the girl. Oh, when you're in Rome there's something I want you to pick up for me. Just apply it against the price of the girl."

"You know, I believe you'd sell shit out of your ass if you could."

Rowena Dartigue's face reddened. But she remembered who she was talking to. "Harsh words, darling," she said. "You seem to forget who introduced you to Ben Dumas, the same Ben Dumas who furnishes you with that notable paper that is so crucial in your counterfeiting endeavors."

"Forget? You won't let me forget."

"The same Ben Dumas who investigates the backgrounds of your potential customers, saving you hardship and suffering. Slander me if you must, but pay me you will."

"You're a bitch."

"Thank you for the compliment, darling. Now, here's what you're going to pick up for me in Rome."

Rowena Dartigue left her home and entered a waiting radio cab shortly before seven P.M.

Maureen had ordered the car, which turned out to be a shoddy Ford with torn seat covers, full ashtrays and a back door containing a mysterious rattle. Obsessed with cleanliness, Mrs. Dartigue's reaction to the vehicle's appearance was to flare her nostrils in disgust.

The driver was a pudgy fifty-year-old Sikh in an orange turban and full-length down coat, an illegal alien experiencing his first London winter and not pleased about it. Speaking Punjabi, he cursed into a hand radio, relaying Mrs. Dartigue's destination to the dispatcher, along with an obscene opinion of a freezing rain that had slowed traffic all over London.

She too hated rain; it reminded her of the awful moment when the most wonderful period of her life had come to a brutal end. For six years she and her beloved first husband Roger had enjoyed a happy and prosperous life in South Africa, until he had decided it was no longer possible to ignore that country's racist system of apartheid. On a rainy evening in Cape Town an assassin had shot him for publicly supporting black leader Nelson Mandela and his African National Congress. Roger had died in the arms of an hysterical Rowena without regaining consciousness.

She'd had no career of her own to fall back on. A strong interest in fashion included neither the talent nor the patience to persevere at it. She'd grown up alternating between being protected by affluent older men and being so penniless that she was sometimes on the borderline of starvation. Roger's death forced her to come to terms with a complex and unforgiving modern world. Come to terms with it in her own way.

She decided that if lasting love was unlikely in this universe then nothing mattered. The human race was a plaything in the hands of an unfeeling, uncaring God. And if God didn't care about anyone here on earth, why should Rowena? She'd always been good at getting whatever she wanted and not worrying about it. Just like God.

In the backseat of the Ford, Rowena, eyes hidden behind dark glasses, sat with a large envelope handbag on the seat beside her.

Designed by a seventeen-year-old Belgian girl, the bag was made of deep purple calfskin lined with purple silk. A big seller at Rosebud. It complemented Mrs. Dartigue's fur coat, a black ranch mink worn despite animal rights activists who weren't above hurling green paint on women bold or foolish enough to wear furs in public. Rowena Dartigue, who despised any restraint on her freedom, wore fur whenever she felt like it.

The Sikh's fussy driving infuriated her. He obeyed speed limits to the point of madness and stopped at every pedestrian crosswalk even when no one was there. Rain-slicked streets and backed-up traffic only added to her irritation. Mrs. Dartigue finally went to her bag for a Valium, washing it down with a sip of mineral water from a small silver flask.

It took the Sikh thirty minutes to drive from Chelsea to Parliament Square, the approach to the Houses of Parliament, and one of the busiest traffic roundabouts in London. Here weather and traffic forced the station wagon to creep along at a snail's pace past bronze statues of Disraeli, Winston Churchill and a tall rumpled Abraham Lincoln. Byron was right, Mrs. Dartigue thought. The English winter ended in July, to recommence in August.

From Parliament Square the Sikh turned onto the Victoria Embankment, following the River Thames and encountering only light traffic all the way to Waterloo Bridge. A right turn onto the bridge and Mrs. Dartigue, growing increasingly tense, was heading toward the South Bank. Not her favorite part of London, to be sure. Beggars living under bridges in makeshift cardboard shanty towns, London's uglier public buildings, deserted streets and sleazy pubs. It was absolutely Dickensian.

Just minutes off the bridge the Sikh pulled into Waterloo Station, stopping at the main entrance. He had been a wretched driver and since Mrs. Dartigue did not believe in rewarding incompetence, she tipped him twenty pence on a fifteen-pound ride. Tips were wages paid to other people's hired help, a practice she avoided.

She walked into the station, passing underneath the entrance arch, which served as a memorial to staff killed in the first World War. The station, Britain's largest, was nearly empty; it was hard to believe that nearly two hundred thousand people passed through it daily. Mrs. Dartigue walked briskly, eyes straight ahead, the envelope bag tight under one arm.

She shunned newsstands, bookstalls, fatigued baggage handlers and weary Jamaican ticket collectors on duty at the gate entrances to trains. Ticket windows were also ignored, most having closed for the day. Instead she continued walking until she reached the Waterloo Road entrance and stepped outside the building, stopping several yards away from a rank of black taxis.

The station overhang shielded her from the rain but failed to protect her from the damp chill. She trembled under her black mink; why in God's name hadn't she worn thermal underwear? It was cold as a well-digger's arse and getting worse.

She detested the rain. It had been raining that night in Cape Town when a man dressed as a priest had shot her first husband Roger to death. And it had been raining the morning she had left South Africa and returned to England carrying Roger's ashes. She had adored Roger so much that for months after his murder she'd slept in his bloodstained shirt. Damn the rain. She'd shed too many tears in the rain ever to find it wonderful.

Rowena walked to the rear of the taxi rank, then past it, stepping from the curb onto the rain-wet driveway. Ahead and to her left a pair of headlights flicked on and off once, twice, three times. Pulling the collar of the mink around her face, she walked faster.

A taxi turned from the street and into the driveway entrance, heading toward Mrs. Dartigue. To avoid it she hurriedly flattened herself against a damp wall until the taxi passed, then quickly walked toward a limousine parked with its engine idling, the privacy within protected by smoked-glass windows. Opening a rear door she entered the car and sat down beside Park Song.

The Korean lifted a flute of champagne to her in a toast. "Well, I suppose we can get started," he said. "David?"

David Mitla, in the front seat, mumbled to the chauffeur sitting beside him and the limousine rolled away from the wall. Seconds later the limousine stopped alongside the first cab and the chauffeur blew his horn. Three short bursts, a pause, then two more.

Switching on his engine the driver and his empty cab pulled away from the line. His "For Hire" sign was off.

The limousine followed him out of the station.

On his London trips Song followed rigid security precautions. For their mutual protection he refused to meet Mrs. Dartigue at her home or shop. Instead they met at night in a hired car and transacted their business while driving about the city. Because Song's chauffeur didn't know London a local cabbie was hired to precede the Korean's car.

"You look fantastic," Song said to Mrs. Dartigue. "I'd say marriage agrees with you. Yes, it most definitely agrees with you."

"A happy husband makes a happy wife," she said. Bit of a lie, this.

Yes, marriage had brought her immense sexual satisfaction but Michael didn't seem to be overelated with the legal union of man and woman as husband and wife. He continued to drink, use drugs and stay out long past curfew. All of this while pissing away her money with the enthusiasm of a drunken sailor on leave. God alone knew where Michael was tonight. He wasn't at home, that was for sure.

Song's limousine crossed Westminster Bridge, following the vacant taxi past the Houses of Parliament and St. James's Park, then on to Constitution Hill, which ran through the middle of Green Park. An excited Song pointed to Buckingham Palace on his left. "It's too dark for me to see," he said, "but would you know if the Royal Standard's flying over the palace? That's an indication the Queen's in residence, you know."

"Really? Yes, well now, come to think of it the Queen's flag has been waving over Buck House this week."

Mrs. Dartigue was lying again, having no idea where the Queen was and caring even less. Her fib, however, made Song happy. He seemed overjoyed that he and the Queen were in London at the same time.

Leaving Green Park, the limousine crossed Piccadilly and passed Wellington Museum before entering Hyde Park. On the park's South Carriage Drive, a solitary jogger, ominous in a gray hooded track suit, ran toward the car, then disappeared in the darkness behind the vehicle.

"Champagne?" Song asked.

"Please." Unzipping her bag, she reached in and handed him two sealed white envelopes. As he opened one she sipped her champagne, which was dry and chilled, an excellent vintage. Laughing Boy's hold on reality might have been fragile, but he certainly knew the difference between good wine and moose piss.

He removed three sheets of paper from the envelope and began reading. Rowena Dartigue gave him a few seconds, then said, "Per your instructions Ben faxed that to me this morning."

Song nodded and returned the refolded pages to their envelope. Coded information, as Rowena Dartigue knew, to be deciphered privately. This was a last-minute report on the people in London and New York to whom Song was planning to sell his counterfeit currency, bonds and securities.

He insisted that Ben Dumas run two investigations on the background of potential customers, to include personal, professional and financial history. The first was a preliminary examination when clients or business associates approached Song. The second occurred forty-eight hours before he met these same people to conclude a transaction.

Both reports were then matched, with special attention paid to changes and modifications. Should anything appear questionable Song would immediately cancel all dealings with the person in question. Should circumstances dictate, the person himself would be canceled. Ben Dumas produced reports that allowed Song to appear almost clairvoyant. Such knowledge had its price. Park Song was paying Dumas plenty for keeping him out of harm's way.

The second envelope. No coded information here. Just a one-page update on the health and well-being of Tawny DaSilva as requested by Laughing Boy. Rowena Dartigue allowed him to read in silence.

Finished, the Korean smiled and casually stroked the page with the back of his hand. "Time to pay the piper."

He opened a small refrigerator door, reached in and removed bundles of hundred-dollar bills, giving each one to Mrs. Dartigue.

"Cold cash." He liked his pun. "Fifty thousand, first installment on the down payment for Tawny."

"A thousand thank yous, darling."

His hand went back into the fridge. "And the rest."

He presented Rowena with a flat book-sized package covered in black velvet. She took a deep breath, pressed the package against her chest. As she unwrapped the parcel her hands shook ever so slightly.

"You dear boy. You dear, dear boy."

Quickly she removed the contents, an Egyptian-style necklace made of gold, rubies, diamonds, seed pearls and turquoise. The necklace came with a matching pair of earrings. Rowena had never seen anything so beautiful. The warmth she felt was nearly sexual.

Necklace and earrings, both over a hundred years old, were the work of the Giuliano family, Italian immigrants who had become nineteenth-century London's finest jewelers. Rowena especially craved this jewelry, which had been inspired by the Renaissance, specifically Hans Holbein's paintings. What pleased her most was the subtle chromatic sense, the use of stones for their color rather than their value.

The previous owner of the jewelry had been the wizened seventy-three-year-old Prince Stefano Cosenza of Rome, who had a passion for blonde adolescent girls, whom he half killed before passing them on to a brothel in Tunis. Needing money to cover stock-market losses, he had sold the jewelry, his wife's, to Rowena Dartigue for seventy-five thousand dollars.

She'd learned that Park Song had business in Rome and asked him to pick up Cosenza's treasures for her. And while Laughing Boy had acted with less than a whole heart, in the end he'd done as she asked.

To guard against thieves and opportunists such as her beloved Michael, she kept her Giuliano collection in a Shepherd Market Deposit Center. It was open 365 days a year, twenty-four hours a day, and offered excellent security. It also provided freedom from banking restrictions and the tax man. Only Rowena Dartigue could get near her safe-deposit box, which she did by matching her thumbprint and a photo ID with those on file at the depository.

Two keys were needed to access the box. She had one and the depository had the other, listing it not under her name but under a three-digit number changed every other month. Among items she also kept here were cash, personal papers and records on the money laundering conducted through her charity. She also kept listings of clients and their preferences in sexual slaves.

Rowena had furnished Ben Dumas and Ken Yokoi with a copy of these listings, permitting them to obtain suitable American youngsters for favored customers. Which was how Dumas came to know that Park Song would pay plenty for delectable little morsels like Tawny. Knowledge was freedom from destitution and indigence.

Rowena removed a pen flashlight and jeweler's loupe from her envelope bag, pushed her dark glasses on top of her head, fitted the eyepiece and switched on the flashlight, training its beam on the necklace. Necklace and flashlight were brought up to the loupe. Song giggled.

She smiled. "Orgasmic, darling. And decidedly genuine. You can just about make out the Giuliano mark on the back of the enamel. The necklace is signed *C. and A.G.*, which would be father Carlo and son Arthur. The mark's somewhat unclear, an indication that it's authentic. As are the stones. Positively orgasmic." She examined the earrings, pronouncing them authentic as well. Removing the loupe, she kissed Song on the cheek and again called him a dear, dear boy.

"Shall we conclude the rest of our business?" she said.

She watched the Korean pick up a small suitcase from the car floor and place it on the seat beside her. Opening the case he turned it around to allow her to view the contents—hundred-dollar bills.

"Eight million," he said. "Also genuine."

After plucking a bill from the suitcase, Rowena eyed it through the loupe. She did the same with four other bills taken at random from the bag.

"Right you are," she said.

She locked the suitcase, which contained Song's proceeds from his sale of counterfeit cash and securities on the continent. A sale aimed at saving his life.

He'd remained mum about his troubles with the Razor, but Ben Dumas had learned about them and passed the news on to Rowena Dartigue. Ben Dumas, who knew everything about everybody, whom she found rather likable in his primitive way, who enjoyed listening to her English accent and treated her with a certain deference merely because she was English.

Rowena would launder Song's eight million through her Lesley Foundation. Ostensibly a certain Hong Kong real estate company was advancing the eight million to her charity on a short-term loan. She would deposit the money with the Lesley Foundation's bank on the Channel island of Jersey. Later the bank would arrange for the Hong Kong company to receive bank drafts and guarantees against which it could borrow. Result: clean, untraceable cash for Laughing Boy.

Song's eight million dollars would yield at least eight hundred thousand in interest, to be divided equally between the Lesley Foundation and Rowena Dartigue. She would make the necessary payoffs to appropriate bank personnel.

"Drop me off at my depository," she said to Song. "I want to lock up my lovely gems for safekeeping. And secure your cash as well.

Tomorrow morning the money will be off to the Channel Islands. And do have the taxi driver wait for me at the depository."

"What about papers confirming my loan to your charity?"

"Should be in my hands late tomorrow afternoon. Ring me at the shop around three. You're leaving England when?"

"Assuming Dumas's information checks out and all goes well, I should be leaving day after tomorrow. I'll let you know if I'm taking my profits with me or leaving them here with you."

Silly little man, thought Rowena. Do you really think I don't know your secret? He had three ways of getting his money out of England and she knew them all, including the one he'd kept hidden from her. Route A: Song took the cash with him. Route B: he left it with Rowena to funnel through her accounts. Route C: the Asian special.

For Route C, Song had enlisted the aid of the South Korean government in moving his earnings hither, thither and yon. To be specific, he'd tapped into his country's diplomatic pouch. Rowena knew because Ben Dumas had told her. Clever little bugger that he was, Song also sent his counterfeit wares via this route, a means so safeguarded and dependable that it was unlikely police would ever catch on.

Ben Dumas wasn't supposed to know about Laughing Boy's mysterious smuggling route. However, Dumas never did business with anyone until he knew all about them, and that included Rowena. As he told her, Song would be a fool not to have a backup for getting his stuff into the country. And as they knew, Song was nobody's fool.

When Dumas learned that Song, while abroad, always visited a South Korean embassy or consulate, he knew what to do. He'd gotten in touch with a CIA contact and obtained the name of a code clerk at South Korea's consulate in New York City. The clerk was a CIA asset, a fact unknown to his Korean bosses. He also worked on a strictly cash basis.

It cost Ben Dumas five thousand dollars, but he (and Rowena) came to learn that Park Song was not keeping his eggs in one basket, that he had a backup smuggling route courtesy of the South Korean government. This information, Dumas told Rowena, was not to be passed around. She understood. If Park Song knew she was aware of his little scheme he'd skin her alive. What Ben had told her would remain a secret, words spoken in darkness and never to be revealed in light.

In the limousine Song said, "Still leaving for New York on schedule?"

Rowena Dartigue held up the Giuliano necklace. "Whenever you keep people waiting, darling, they tend to pass the time by speaking ill of you. I leave for New York the day after you do. My auction's scheduled the night I arrive. No chance to unpack, really. Feel free to attend. I expect the customary connoisseurs of fine young flesh to be on hand. Michael's been told the usual, that I'm going to New York to interview young American designers and to see about opening a New York branch of Rosebud."

Song lifted an eyebrow. "How is Michael these days?"

She returned the necklace to its box. "How is Michael? Working on another scheme to get rich, I would imagine. Ask me what it is and I couldn't begin to tell you. He's not seen fit to confide in me, you see. He's dropped hints of having an iron or two in the fire but nothing specific. Oh, before I forget, I have a little something for you."

Laying the jewelry box aside, she reached into her bag, removed a brown manila envelope and handed it to Song. The Korean removed a black-and-white photograph. For a few moments he was speechless. Then he whispered, "Impossible, I don't believe it."

He held an eight-by-ten glossy photograph of Dick Powell, Ruby Keeler, choreographer Busby Berkeley and director Mervyn LeRoy taken at the wrap party of the film *Gold Diggers of 1933*. Each of the four had autographed the photograph.

Song's voice was hoarse. "Priceless. Where did you get this?"

"From a young Frenchman who designs for me. He collects Hollywood memorabilia and came across this in some tacky Carnaby Street shop. He was quite pleased with himself."

"And you bought it from him?"

"Especially for you, darling." One more lie. She'd stolen the photograph from Georges, who had carelessly left it lying about the shop. Little Georges was heartbroken over the loss of his treasured relic, being a fan of movie queens and something of a queen himself. Anything that pleased Laughing Boy, however, could only advance Mrs. Dartigue's cause.

Song couldn't stop looking at the photograph. "I can't tell you how much this means to me. I worship these people."

"My pleasure, darling. My first husband, God love him, always said we are made kind by being kind."

The Korean tapped the photograph with a forefinger. "Their films will live forever. Like you and Michael, perhaps."

Rowena, her mind suddenly miles away, ignored his sarcasm. *Forever*. The sadness had hit her without warning. Turning from Song she stared through the tinted glass at the Serpentine, Hyde Park's artificial lake, where a strong wind sent dockside boats crashing into each other.

Michael. Forever.

She whispered into the darkness:

"Sigh no more, ladies, sigh no more,/ Men were deceivers ever;/ One foot in sea, and one on shore;/ To one thing constant never."

EIGHT

As Rowena Dartigue proceeded toward the Shepherd Market Deposit Center, her husband lay on a sagging bed in a two-room Soho flat sucking the toes of Nigella Barrow, a leggy twenty-six-year-old English croupier whose dark eyes were filled with dancing lights.

A cassette player on top of a nearby night table featured Smokey Robinson's sweet tenor caressing "Tracks of My Tears." From an adjacent closet a burly forty-six-year-old Scot with a bristling red mustache observed the couple through a cracked door. His name was Bernard Muir and he wore the uniform of a London policeman.

Pausing, Michael Dartigue removed a bottle of Advockaat from the night table and swallowed a mouthful of the thick yellow Dutch liqueur made from egg yolks and brandy. Then he poured the liqueur on the inside of Nigella's thighs and began licking it off. Whimpering, she pulled his head toward her with hands tipped with multicolored nails. As he sucked hard on her clitoris she pushed to meet his tongue, climaxing as she lifted her pelvis from the bed.

Eyes glazed, she collapsed back on the bed in a pleasurable stupor. "You're rough. That's what I want. Yes, that's what I want."

Michael wet a foot in the liqueur on the bed and rubbed it over her pubic area. "The saga continues," he said.

"I want to be on top," she whispered.

They traded places, she riding him in a frantic rhythm. "Twist my

113

nipples," she said. *"Harder."* He did as she ordered. "That's good," she whispered. "Ooh, that's good."

She climaxed first, screaming before biting his ear. When she clawed at his chest he quickly grabbed her hands. "Careful," he said. "My wife."

A winded Nigella hurriedly apologized. "Sorry, love. I keep forgetting. Forgive me."

Later they lay still, Nigella on top of Michael, her long auburn hair covering his chest as she listened to his heartbeat. "Just a few minutes more, love, and we'll be finished."

Two-minute warning. Except this wasn't basketball but a bigger game with a different kind of championship on the line. Two minutes to win or lose it all. Chump or champ in one hundred twenty seconds. Michael's heart was pounding. Too late to back out now.

Nigella said, "We're out of grass, but there's a bit of coke left. Like to do a few lines?"

Eyes covered by a muscular forearm, Michael turned toward the wall. "Let's just get it over with, okay?"

She slipped out of bed and turned down the cassette player. As if on cue the closet door opened and Bernard Muir, small truncheon in hand, entered the room.

At the bed he stared at Michael, tapped his palm with the truncheon. "Well now, young sir, what have we here? I'd say we've been more than a little indecent. Should detain you for this sort of thing, but I'm a fair man. Fact is, I'm in rather a forgiving mood. Let's do a deal, then. A bit of fun for myself and I'll forget about what I've witnessed in this room. Well?"

A silent Michael refused to look at the Scot.

Muir whacked his palm harder with the truncheon. "I said *well?"*

Michael whispered, "Please, officer, I'll do anything, but don't arrest me. Please don't arrest me."

Muir placed the truncheon on the bed, removed his dark blue trousers and a pair of white boxer shorts, dropping them on the floor. "So, you want me to do something to you, is that it?"

"Yes, I want you to do . . ." Michael's voice faded.

"Well, if that's what you really want."

Reaching into a breast pocket of his police jacket Muir removed a condom, tore off the wrapper and slipped the condom into his mouth. On the cassette Smokey Robinson held a high note on "Ooo Baby, Baby."

Wearing the police jacket and helmet a half-nude Bernard Muir crawled onto the bed and took Michael Dartigue's limp penis between his lips. Quickly his tongue expertly fitted the condom over the American. As Muir began to fellate, Michael, face to the wall, attempted to ignore what was being done to him. *Get it over with*, he thought. *Finish* this before I throw up. *I have no choice, remember, I have no choice.*

Shivering in revulsion, Michael slid from under the Scot and rushed to the bathroom, leaving Nigella Barrow to sit on the bed beside a nervous Bernard Muir.

Muir's square jaw cupped in one hand, she turned his head around to face her. Her dark eyes caught pinpricks of light from a red candle on the night table. "Did you enjoy yourself, Bernie?"

"Indeed. Absolute bliss."

Nigella smiled. "Getting him here tonight wasn't all that easy."

Taking his trousers from the floor, Muir pulled a small blue notebook from a back pocket. He smiled at Nigella, teasing her by gently waving the notebook in front of her face. Heart pounding, she watched him hungrily, resisting the temptation to snatch the notebook from him. It was only after he had torn out the first three pages and handed them to her that she realized she'd been holding her breath.

Three pages from a cheap notepad. Muir's payment for his just-concluded fling with Michael. Three little pages containing information worth millions.

She kissed Muir on the cheek and offered him a cup of tea, knowing it would be refused.

The Scot looked at his wristwatch. "Wish I could, but I'm due at work in forty minutes. Going to have trouble getting there as is. Not easy traipsing about in this weather."

"I understand. And we'll send your share to Liechtenstein as you asked."

"Wouldn't look right if I suddenly came into a large amount of cash here in Britain. The money will be quite safe in Liechtenstein. The bankers there are even more closemouthed than the bloody Swiss."

Suddenly Muir seemed less amiable. He spoke to the ceiling, his voice hardened. "Eddie Walkerdine's giving me a chance to get my own back, and I intend to make the most of it. My employer, stinking wog bastard that he is, says I'm too old. Says he has to sack me because these days guarding money has become a young person's game. The man's a swine, an unsurpassed Indian swine."

He looked at Nigella. "I'm still fit, you know. Work as hard as anyone he's got. It's been years since I've reported in sick. But that isn't stopping Mr. Ravi Sunny from getting rid of me. First of the year and I'm out on my arse. No pension. Haven't been there long enough to qualify for one, he says. Know what that bastard's giving me after twelve years of faithful service? A check for one hundred pounds. And a plaque, of course. A bloody *plaque*."

He got up from the bed. "Well, let him discharge me, but I'll be leaving with a damned sight more than a bloody plaque. Bet on it."

Nigella watched Muir walk to the closet, remove an empty suitcase and carry it to the bed. Into the case went the policeman's jacket, helmet, trousers and truncheon that had been rented. Back at the closet, Muir reached in among her clothing and removed a gray suit, matching topcoat, dark brown cap.

Dressed, he picked up his umbrella and suitcase, then looked around the room. "I believe I've got everything," he said to Nigella. "No time for a wash, I'm afraid. My regards to Mr. Walkerdine. Those notes I've just given you should solve his problem. If he needs anything else he knows where to reach me. When I check my Liechtenstein bank in two weeks I expect to find my share on deposit."

Nigella said, "Thank you again, Bernie. Your money will be there as promised. Eddie's a man of his word."

Touching the umbrella handle to his cap in farewell, Muir turned to leave, then stopped. "Goodnight, Michael," he said in a loud voice. "I had a lovely evening."

From the bathroom came the sound of breaking glass. "Fuck you, you sperm-brain dickhead!"

Muir said to Nigella, "It's his musical use of the language I'll miss the most."

Eddie Walkerdine was a small, forty-two-year-old Englishman with receding dark wavy hair and a gap-toothed demonic smile. He wore a tuxedo with a white carnation in the lapel, black Gucci loafers and a gold pinky ring containing a star-shaped sapphire. Clenched in his front teeth was a small black cigar.

He and Nigella Barrow were seated on her bed when Michael Dartigue, freshly showered, emerged from the bathroom in gray slacks and white turtleneck. Michael sat down beside Nigella, who took his hand and kissed it. Both watched as Walkerdine silently inspected the information received minutes before from Muir. Humming tunelessly, the little Englishman studied the pages.

Two months earlier he had begun work on a plan to acquire money for his permanent move to Marbella, the most glamorous and chic of Spain's Costa del Sol resorts. His plan, if successful, would yield ample funds to meet fixed expenses—alimony and child support to two ex-wives, a yearly allowance to another woman whose eight-year-old son he'd fathered; the expense of private nursing care for an ailing mother.

There would also be enough to buy a restaurant on Marbella's marina, a small hotel near the casino complex of Puerto Bancus and a block of new flats just outside the resort. Here was the prize he'd been chasing from birth, and now it was within reach.

From the moment he had learned the properties were for sale he'd burned with a need to own them. At present they still belonged to Ned Clegg, the forty-year-old Australian newspaper proprietor who needed cash to expand a four-hundred-horse stable. Two months ago he'd offered to sell his Spanish holdings to Walkerdine for twenty million dollars, slightly under market value. The catch: Walkerdine had to pay the full price in cash and no later than the end of December.

Done. Walkerdine would have the money, every penny, and on time. He avoided financial particulars, which was just as well, since to acquire the money he intended to rob the Shepherd Market depository of some fifty million pounds, give or take a few million.

He saw no reason why he shouldn't pull it off. Energetic and shrewd, he planned his moves carefully, showed strength when challenged and prided himself on knowing when to walk away from a lost cause. A one-time bus driver who had never known his father, he had clawed his way out of London's oppressive East End by expertly playing up to the weaknesses of those who could advance his ambitions. Despite a simianlike appearance, women found him clever, forceful and erotic.

Walkerdine managed the Riviera, a Leicester Square discotheque which he'd turned into one of London's most successful clubs by catering to prosperous blacks. Unwelcome at up-market clubs where nonwhite faces were greeted with "Members only," affluent blacks also avoided clubs patronized by lower-class blacks, places that were often rowdy if not menacing.

Whites were welcome, but the Riviera's primary patrons remained moneyed black people, some of whom were African and Caribbean millionaires. Visits by blacks celebrated in American entertainment and sports had given the club cachet. Walkerdine and Michael Dartigue had met when the American had dropped in with black friends who were professional basketball players in the States and Europe.

Walkerdine earned eighty thousand pounds a year, plus what he skimmed, which provided him with an annual income of over a hundred thousand pounds. The skimming was a response to the club's owner, a skinny Lebanese with ties to the Amal militia, who had broken his promise to make Walkerdine a partner.

In September Walkerdine had married for a third time. His bride —who hated England, where she suffered endless colds—was Gina Branchero, a twenty-five-year-old Spanish model born in Marbella and who longed to return there because it supplied more sun in a day than London did in a month.

Walkerdine had met the voluptuous Gina while on holiday in Marbella, where she'd been the mistress of a resident Arab sheik who was a major arms dealer and owner of the largest yacht in the marina. Irked by Gina's demands that he dump his harem of twelve wives and marry her, the sheik was glad to rid himself of "Miss Sangria 1986."

Gina wasn't alone in wanting to chuck England's filthy weather for life in the sun the year round. Walkerdine's asthma was getting worse, aggravated by England's cold, damp climate. The previous spring a Harley Street lung specialist had warned him that inhalers, pills and injections were no longer enough for his respiratory problems. Unless Walkerdine moved to a warm dry climate he would eventually suffer a possibly fatal asthma attack.

And there were the effects of Walkerdine's working in discos, bars, private clubs and restaurants for twenty-five years. He was tired of the eighteen-hour days, the conniving club owners, the protection money, the bent coppers out for payoffs, the witless food suppliers, the predawn knife fights among drunken patrons. Not to mention dealing with drug overdoses in the ladies' room, arrogant rock stars and their thuggish bodyguards, employees who took off for Majorca without a by-your-leave, bartenders who molested waitresses and stole liquor by the case. Most of all he was tired of working for other people.

For years he had vacationed in Marbella, where his wit and arrogance had made him a popular figure among expatriate Brits, wealthy Arabs and film stars living in tax exile. He enjoyed sipping champagne and charming the pants off the truly rich while tanning himself on their huge yachts moored in the port marina. What he most wanted was to live there with Gina for the rest of his life. He owned a small villa behind Marbella's Puerto Bancus casino, and a marina flat, both of which he rented out for most of the year. Income from these properties, alas, would not cover Walkerdine's fixed expenses and also allow him to live the good life among the resort's fat cats. Income from Ned Clegg's properties, however, would.

Two months ago, on a Tuesday night, Walkerdine's future, in the form of an inebriated Bernie Muir, had staggered into the club. Tuesday at the Riviera was "Gay Night." Nothing too wild. A bit of dancing, silly contests of one sort or another and a chance for gay people to relax among themselves without incurring the wrath of intolerant straights. The idea had been Walkerdine's, his way of boosting business on what had been the slowest night of the week.

Bernie Muir had been a Gay Night organizer. Walkerdine didn't particularly care for him, finding the Scot a moody loser who always picked the wrong man and couldn't wait to tell the world about it. Muir also drank too much; he'd had a skinful when he'd bitched to Walkerdine about being chucked out. Muir spoke of getting his revenge for being unfairly sacked, and Walkerdine dismissed it as whisky talk.

He had even made a joke out of it. Rob the place, he said. Let's team up and rip off every single safe-deposit box at the center. Both of them could use the money. Good idea, Muir said, then proceeded to tell him how to go about it.

After spending a sleepless night reflecting on Muir's words, Walkerdine sought him out the next day. Both men took that night off from work and talked for six straight hours. This time there were no jokes.

Walkerdine figured his life was more than half over. He was sick of waiting for circumstances to make him rich. It was time he created those circumstances himself.

Walkerdine, seated on Nigella Barrow's bed, crushed his small cigar in an ashtray resting on a crumpled pillow, then stood up. Scratching his chin with Muir's notes, he smiled at Michael. "You look none the worse for wear, sunshine," he said.

Michael rubbed the back of his neck. "I weirded out when Muir finished, but I'm okay now. Fucking guy's dippy. Dressing up like a cop. Jesus. If you ask me, the man's going through life with his headlights on dim."

Walkerdine grinned. "That was the deal, sunshine. We get information on the security at the Shepherd Market Deposit Center and he has his way with you. That was Bernie's price. Your manly body, plus two hundred thousand pounds. Sex and money. Makes the world go round."

Walkerdine tapped Michael on the shoulder with Muir's notes. "Say what you will, the wanker kept his word. It's all here in black and white. Location of closed-circuit television cameras, perimeter alarms, cipher locks. Number of guards on duty after midnight. Important thing is we now know that the telephone lines are connected to perimeter alarms. Cut one, you cut both. No calls in or out. No distractions."

Nigella fingered Michael's ponytail as he said to Walkerdine, "You say when the telephone lines are cut no calls go in or out. Fine. Now suppose we're in there punching all those boxes when somebody phones the guards and can't get through. Seems to me that's when the shit hits the fan."

Walkerdine shook his head. "You're not in America now, cowboy. We Brits are a bit more relaxed in certain areas, and security, fortunately or unfortunately, is one of them. We lack your crime and therefore your paranoia. Over here your American security is as out of place as testicles in a convent. Muir says security's lax. Things are pretty dead around the depository at night. Clients rarely drop in after ten, and there's never more than one or two after-midnight calls a week."

"How about the guards?" Michael said. "I don't dig being used as a firing range."

"Let me repeat—you're not in America now. Don't dwell too much on receiving a bullet in your irreplaceable backside. The guards don't have guns. Theoretically an alarm has to go off, *then* the security company sends over armed guards. But when we cut the wires there isn't going to be any alarm. The security company's located on the other side of London, meaning that under the best of circumstances it takes a while before they arrive at the depository. The center relies on strong locks, strong doors, alarms of course, and on the fact that it's never had a robbery in its history. It's a juicy apple ready to be plucked and I say we do the plucking."

A click from the cassette player signaled the end of the Smokey Robinson tape. As Nigella rose to change tapes, Walkerdine lit another small cigar and blew smoke at the ceiling, then stared at Michael before speaking. The American struggled to hold his gaze.

"No backing down, sunshine," Walkerdine said softly.

Michael rose from the bed. His face was red and his temples were throbbing. "I don't take shit, I don't give shit. Where the fuck do you get off saying I'm going to wimp out?"

Up went Walkerdine's hands in an apologetic gesture. "Sorry, guv. Sorry. Didn't mean to offend. It's just that I'm in too deep, as the bishop said to the actress. You haven't met the two men who'll be working with us, but trust me when I say they don't take kindly to broken promises. Should we cancel our little adventure between now and Thursday, well, I'll have to explain things to this pair of villains, who in turn may demand a further explanation from you. Hard men, we call them over here. From the East End of London, where crime isn't just one way of life, it's the only way of life. They're the type who'd stick a glass rod up your granny's arse then tie her to the back of a lorry and drive off into the country making sure to hit every bump in the road."

A grinning Michael said, "You want to try and do this thing without me? Want to fence what's in those safe-deposit boxes all by yourself? Speak up, I can't hear you."

"You know bloody well I daren't get rid of the stuff in this country. That's why I had to bring you in."

"No more phone calls, we have a winner. Fast Eddie ain't as dumb as he looks. You're the one who tells me we're apt to find everything from gold bars to false teeth when we hit the depository. But you fence so much as a paper clip and Scotland Yard or whoever the fuck it is will tie your asshole in a knot. You might as well wear a T-shirt saying you pulled the job. And that's where Big Mike comes in. I know how to get rid of the stuff. You don't. I got contacts in New York who can fence what we heist. You don't. I know how to make things disappear. You don't. Am I getting through to you?''

Walkerdine forced a smile. "No disrespect intended, Mike. Only two days until we do this thing. Got a slight case of nerves, I guess. We shouldn't, either of us, get our bowels in an uproar. If I've offended you, I apologize."

As Marvin Gaye sang "Give It Up" Nigella walked from the night table and stood beside Michael. Taking his hand in both of hers, she said to Walkerdine, "You can count on Michael. He'll do his part, believe me."

Her intervention gave Walkerdine a moment to calm down. Getting into a shouting match with Michael Dartigue was a waste of breath. Why tell this cretin that robbing the safety-deposit box belonging to his own wife would probably be the only way he'd ever get enough of her money. Walkerdine was not one for saying the wrong thing at the wrong time.

Not a bad girl, Nigella. Had a few brains, which she rarely bothered to use, unfortunately. Half the men in London, Walkerdine included, had screwed the ass off her. Had she really fallen for Michael Dartigue? A spoiled overgrown child who had the attention span of a two-year-old? As usual, she'd let some chap sell her a bill of goods. This time it was Dartigue, who'd laid it on thick by promising he'd chuck his wife after the robbery and take Nigella to the States with him. He'd also gone on about his intention to set up Nigella with a hair salon in Miami.

Walkerdine didn't believe Dartigue gave a hoot about Nigella. The bugger was only using her to snatch his wife's money. Walkerdine was willing to bet that after the job Dartigue would hit the gas getting away from Nigella. She'd been better off when she was selling it to rich Arabs at a hundred quid a time. At least she knew where her next meal was coming from.

Taking his topcoat and hat from a chair, Walkerdine said, "Duty calls. You lovebirds coming to the club tonight?"

Michael shook his head. "We have a few things to go over. Maybe tomorrow."

Walkerdine slipped into his topcoat. "Tomorrow, then. Oh, when you drop by the club you must try our new drink. We call it the Afrodisiac. Don't laugh, Nigella. Rum, grenadine, vodka, bitters, bit of mango, fresh limes, fresh cream. Absolutely sensational. Guaranteed to put lead in your pencil, believe me."

After Walkerdine left, Nigella spoke first. "Eddie's too clever by half," she said. "He's what you call a bit tricky. Sneaks up on you, he does. Chips away at you. Bit here, bit there and before you know it he's got you. Eddie's only out for Eddie, remember that."

Michael nodded. "I hear you."

He looked at her face, seeing the love which had nurtured him the past two months, a love that sometimes turned him into a fool who didn't know what he was saying, and which made everything about her precious. It was a love he'd tried to resist, which had finally overwhelmed him and was now his master. It was a love which had made him stronger than he'd been in years while leaving him vulnerable and afraid of losing it.

An uncertain Michael said, "I've got a lot riding on this and you know it. You also know Fast Eddie better than I do, so you make the call. Do I pull out or do I go through with it?"

Nigella dropped her eyes. "He's a first-class manipulator, Eddie is. We just have to be on our guard, that's all. You're the only thing that matters to me in this whole thing. I can do without the money if I have to. I can also do without Eddie and his little schemes."

She stared up at him. "You really can't just walk away, you know. I don't think you could live with yourself if you did. And we both know it has nothing to do with Eddie. I think you should do what's important to you."

Michael shook his head. "I'm Florida white trash and that's about all I'll ever be in this life. The one thing I had going for me was basketball, which I learned from blacks, which pissed off my parents since they hated blacks with a passion. My father, especially, got all bent out of shape over my choice of friends. He was a Baptist minister, the Ayatollah of his day. Gave me some fundamentalist bullshit about how I'd violated divine law because blacks were cursed by God and could never enter heaven. Nigger only gets to heaven, he said, if God makes him white."

Michael sat down on the edge of the bed and stared at the floor. "One day I'd had enough of his bullshit, so we just went at it. I swung at him and he went upside my head with his cane. I really freaked out then and knocked his ass into the goldfish bowl. Funny as hell, him lying there and goldfish flopping all over the rug. Would have killed him if my mother hadn't pulled me off. Don't forget, I was a big kid, tall for my age. Ended up with them kicking me out of the house. Told me to move in with my nigger friends. I did. I was sixteen."

"Andres's family, they took me in. Talk about poor. They didn't even have a bathroom. Had an outhouse out back. You bathed in a washtub set up out in the backyard. Cold weather, you put the tub in the front room. What little they had they shared with me. Good people, especially his mom. The best, bar none."

Michael smiled. "Me living in a rundown house in Liberty City with eight spooks. Had to sleep on the living-room floor but I didn't mind. When our sneakers wore out, me and Andres would tape them together because we didn't have ten bucks to buy new ones. Wintertime, we wore pajamas under our pants to keep warm. Great times. We got recruited for the University of Miami the same day. Same day. His mom came to every home game. Should have seen the looks when she pointed me out on the court and said, 'That's my son.' Whatever I know about the game, Andres taught me. His family was my family and he was my brother. Andres is the best. Period. End of discussion. I fucking love that man. Can't walk away from him now. I just can't."

Nigella sat down on the bed beside Michael and took his hand. "Do the job," she said. "Do it for your friend, not for Eddie Walkerdine. Do it for Andres."

For Andres.

Eight days ago, on a mild November morning, Michael and Andres Valentino had met at Florida State Prison where Andres was doing ten to twenty for manslaughter. It had been three years since Andres had used a screwdriver and hammer to jam a couple of cash machines on Collins Avenue in North Miami Beach. When two bank guards showed up to service the machines Andres pulled a sawed-off shotgun from a shopping bag, took twenty-two thousand dollars from the guards, then shot them. One guard had died, the other had lost an arm.

Prison was a long way from the University of Miami, where Michael and Andres had both made second team all-American. Only Andres had got a shot at the NBA. Drafted by the Detroit Pistons on the eighteenth round he'd been cut in training camp. Too slow. Michael hadn't even been drafted. Not big enough, read the scouting reports. Not fast enough, not tough enough.

As a pro he'd played a year in Italy, averaging twenty-six points a game for Milan and being a party animal until word had gotten around about him and Marisa Algeri, wife of the team's owner. Michael was alive today only because friends had bundled him into a car bound for Switzerland minutes before three men with guns had kicked down the front door of his Via Pontaccio flat.

In the prison visitors' room he sat and stared at his reflection in the glass barrier separating guests from inmates. Getting lines in his face. Getting gray, too. And there was *that sound*—steel gates slamming over and over, a sound echoing in his head since he'd set foot in this place. For days after each visit Michael heard that sound in his dreams. Sometimes it was so scary he'd wake up with colitis.

Michael wanted a cigarette, but there were No Smoking signs around the room. He was searching his pockets for gum when he saw Andres Valentino enter the visitors' room accompanied by a balding, paunchy corrections officer. A tall, flat-nosed thirtyish black with a large, friendly face, Andres allowed the CO to guide him by the elbow to an empty chair between a Haitian and a Cuban inmate.

Andres wore an orange jumpsuit, gray Reeboks and a green knitted skull cap over a shaven head. A black patch covered his left eye, and fresh stitches ran down the left side of his face and neck. He sat only after the CO signaled him to. *Andres Valentino, the most daring point guard in the history of Florida collegiate basketball, waiting to be told he could sit down. Jesus.*

Ignoring Andres's cut face, Michael picked up the phone. "Hey, dude, good to see you."

"I thank you for coming."

Andres spoke with an inmate's awareness of the importance of words. Words determined one's very survival in a situation as unsafe as prison. His speech, therefore, was guarded, the words carefully chosen.

Michael said, "How you living?"

"Twenty-four seven, my man. Twenty-four hours a day, seven

days a week in the place where you don't pay no rent and there ain't no rules. You looking good. Your lady treating you fine, I see. I dig that jacket."

Michael touched it. "Suede. She's got connections in the fashion business. Gets a discount on everything."

Andres chuckled. "She treating you well, which means you still gettin' the most out of your dick. Dick take you where your brain never could. Then, you always was a man who made himself available toward people of the female persuasion."

Both chuckled.

Michael said, "Your face, man. What happened?"

Andres touched the patch with long brown fingers whose nails had been bitten down to the quick. "Least I be able to see out of my eye. Ain't gonna be like it was, but I still got it. Gonna have them scars, too. Ran into some trouble with one of the Jamaican posses in this place. Dudes carry razor blades in their mouths. Spit them out then cut you faster than a cat can lick its ass. Had a discord with a Jamaican who said I paid his boyfriend to suck my dick. Didn't have to pay that fool at all."

Andres sighed and began biting his nails. "Anyway, this boy's lover, he jealous and he tries to shank me. Had a metal piece he broke off from under his bed. Had a real cutting edge on it. I stomped his butt good. Wasn't the end of it. Last week his Jamaican friends come at me in the yard. Muslims stopped them from killing me, but not before I get my face cut up."

Michael shook his head. "Man, I am sorry."

"What goes round, comes round. People be waiting to see what I do about it. Got to do something. Can't let a dude put his mark on you without no payback. Next thing you know, the idea get around you weak. If I want respect I'll have to make a move on the brother who threw them niggers on me."

Michael thought, I could be sitting on the other side of the glass, some of the shit I've pulled. Selling steroids, sinking boats for insurance, passing bad checks, promoting rock concerts that never happened, selling fake timeshares, raising money for films that were never going to be made. Only thing he'd been lucky at was keeping out of jail.

Michael leaned toward the glass partition, anxious now to tell Andres why he'd taken time away from his business in New York to fly down here. "That lawyer you told me about last time I was here. Cuban who used to be on the parole board. He still around?"

Andres studied Michael. "You mean DeLaquilla. Yeah, he still around. Still in business, but the man is very expensive. Charge you for breathing the air in his office. Heavy dude. No sense going to him unless you got a great big piggy bank."

"You said he's connected, that he can get you an early parole or put you in a work-release program."

"Seen it done. Guys with money, had eight, ten years to go, they hired DeLaquilla. Before you know it they get paroled or ended up on the outside living in some halfway house and working a nice civilian job. But it costs. Fifty K, maybe more."

"I can get the money. Is DeLaquilla righteous?"

"Your old lady, she give you the bread?"

Michael snorted. "No way will that woman help me get some spook out of jail. She loves herself more than she could ever love anybody else. Buys me what I want, but getting cash out of her is like pulling teeth. Got to come to her every time I want something. Pisses me off, which is why I'm dumping her."

Andres laughed. "You just got married and you quittin' the bitch? You a man of angles, Jack. Definitely a man of angles."

Michael told Andres about Eddie Walkerdine's plan to rob the Shepherd Market Deposit Center. When he'd finished, Andres scratched his head and nodded. "Sounds cool. One thing, though. Why he bring you in? Like, why didn't he do it with his own people. He got his inside man, so why he need you?"

"He has this little problem fencing the stuff. Doesn't want to do that in England and he's right. Enter Big Mike. Remember when I had that restaurant down here in West Palm Beach?"

"Seafood place. You was fronting it for some people from New York." Using a forefinger Andres pushed the tip of his nose to one side.

Michael nodded. "Yeah, I know. You don't fuck with these greaseballs, not twice anyway. Long as you kept your word, though, they weren't too bad. At the time they were expanding out of New York. They were the first mob people to make contact with certain Cubans down here and have them reach out for Castro. Had this crazy idea about getting him to let them reopen the casinos in Havana."

Michael grinned. "Fucking Castro almost went for it, but the Russians made him turn it down. Didn't want the Americans getting back into the country. Anyway, these clowns, these olive-oil salesmen, they wanted to expand in Florida and one thing they needed was a local name to front a restaurant. Seeing as how I'd been a hoops star in my college days, I got the gig. These guys also paid me to be a mule. Carried cash and pharmaceuticals to New York, Atlantic City, Montreal, London. That's how I met Rowena, my wife."

Andres said, "Pharmaceuticals is what got me in here. Crack makes you paranoid, man. I smoked some rock before I hit the bank, made me think them two guards was going to kill me. They weren't, but I didn't know that. Anyway, I'm listening."

Michael said, "After we hit the depository the greaseballs will fence the stuff. But not for free. Whatever cash we rip off, they're only giving us fifty cents on the dollar. Everything else they take forty percent off the top. When I get my share I'm buying you out of this place."

"Man, I can't let myself even dream about something like that happenin'. If you can pull that off . . ."

He took a moment to get control of himself. "Momma ain't doing so well, ain't been out of bed since the stroke. You did good sending her the bread—"

"Hey, nigger, don't give me that shit. Momma V's the only mother I got. Besides, it wasn't all that much. When I get a few bucks, mom always gets a taste. You know that."

"I know, man. I know."

"Left something in your prison account. Money, cigarettes. Anyway, listen up, because I don't have much time. I flew to New York to wrap up things with the Italians. Got to check in with them before I go back to London. They don't do business over the phone. Told them I had to fly down here to see my family, which is the truth."

Andres said, "Man, you 'bout the only one who ain't forgot I'm here. My own blood don't want to know from me anymore. All I got is you and thinking about what it was like back when we was in school, back when all we did was play hoops and chase pussy. After we leave school everything turn to shit."

"I hear you," Michael said.

"Hoops keep me alive in here, but it ain't like playing when you free. I go up for a rebound and for a few seconds prison ain't under my feet, know what I'm saying? For a few seconds I got no contact with this place 'cause I'm flying. Then I come down and I'm still here, man. Still here. Don't get no easier. Hoops ain't no good unless you free, and I ain't free."

Michael said, "On our mother, man. I swear on our mother I'll get you out. I swear it."

He watched Andres reach inside his jumpsuit, which had no pockets, and remove something that he held up to the glass for Michael to see. For Michael the sight of it brought on a sadness he couldn't hide. What he saw was a newspaper clip, a photograph of the University of Miami basketball team shot during a game in his and Andres's senior year.

The photograph, taken the night the team had won the NCAA semifinals by a point, showed the five starters huddled together during a time-out. Every Florida newspaper had carried it on the front page. The shot had also run in sports pages across the country.

Uniforms dark with sweat, their faces animated with joy, pride and fatigue, they clung to each other, five against the world, Michael in the middle with his arms around the necks of Glenn, Ahmad, Jon and Andres, Michael the only white in the photograph. Two days later they would play for the national championship and lose by ten points. But the photograph from the semifinals had been taken on the greatest night in their lives. This had been the best game they would ever play as a team.

As Andres watched from behind the glass, Michael tried to stop the tears from coming, but couldn't. Right hand on the glass, he covered the photograph, but tears soon made it impossible to see.

NINE

Park Song had checked into a fifteen-story French chateaulike hotel in London's Piccadilly. He was registered under the name Henry Yue Lan, with a passport describing him as a Chinese stockbroker born in Taiwan and now living in Macao. It was one of several aliases he used on his business trips to the West.

Song had chosen this particular alias as a private joke. The festival of *Yue Lan*, the hungry ghosts, was celebrated in Hong Kong every July. On this day hungry ghosts wandered the earth and could only be appeased by paper money, fruits, food and other gifts. Song's mind was always on money, so why not travel the world as Mr. Hungry Ghost?

The hotel in Piccadilly had an exterior of Portland stone, a marbled entrance hall with gilded ceilings, an arcade of exclusive shops and a life-sized bronze sculpture of a half-nude woman in its Art Deco lobby. The woman was a nineteenth-century Irish courtesan who had built the hotel with the three hundred thousand pounds she'd charged an East Indian diplomat for the privilege of spending one night with her. Song was amused to learn that she had died when a young actor had asked her to marry him and she laughed, provoking the actor to strangle her on the spot.

The hotel's French restaurant overlooked a private garden, boasted thirty-one champagnes on its wine list and served the finest smoked salmon soufflé Park Song had ever tasted. His enthusiasm for good food was no pretense. To do anything well, one first had to eat well.

At 6:43 on the morning after his meeting with Rowena Dartigue he entered the sitting room of his hotel suite and switched on an overhead chandelier, then a pair of Art Deco bronze lamps. He wore a black track suit edged in white, a yellow headband and rice straw slippers. He carried a pair of tap shoes and a small cassette recorder. A towel hung from his neck.

He planned an hour's *Taekwon do* practice and a bit of tap, followed by breakfast with bodyguard David Mitla and the judo-adept chauffeur Han Choi. Then he would get on with the business of selling counterfeit money and securities. By tonight he should be out of this country, where it never stopped raining. Then it was off to New York, the final stop on his excursion to stay alive. New York, where he would collect the big money and the American girl he had bought from Rowena Dartigue.

At a damask-draped window Song placed tap shoes, cassette recorder and towel on the sill, then looked down over the Buckingham Palace garden wall twelve stories below. Nothing to see. His vision was eclipsed by darkness and rain. Nor did it help to know that the Queen had landscaped the garden to ensure privacy. Since the garden was as close as Song had ever come to seeing the Royal Family in person, he stared at it for several minutes.

Breathing deeply, he peered through the window and vigorously massaged the base of his skull with both thumbs. Then with the bottom of his fists he lightly pummeled his arms, torso and legs. His skin tingled and he felt a bit warmer. The English weather chilled the blood. He needed to get his blood stirring again.

Song crossed the room to an Italian marble fireplace, where he placed his towel, tap shoes and cassette recorder on the mantelpiece. Kicking off his sandals he began jogging in place, knees high, arms moving rhythmically. Five minutes later he stopped, circled his neck, swung his arms. Warming up wasn't enough. *Taekwon do* was basically a kicking art. A practitioner had to be limber enough to kick head high.

Gripping the edge of the mantelpiece with both hands Song began stretching. He lifted his right leg, easily placing his heel on the mantelpiece, which was level with his chin. When he'd stretched the leg, thigh and hip on one side of his body, he turned to the other. In *Taekwon do* it was leg flexibility above all. Flexibility equaled speed and speed equaled power.

He stretched carefully, allowing his muscles to extend of their own accord, doing everything smoothly, without force or unwarranted pressure on joints and ligaments. In Seoul his private gymnasium included the latest body-building equipment plus simple pulleys and ropes. By looping one end of a rope around his foot and pulling on the other end Song could raise his kicking leg to any height. For power he had a pair of large training bags that allowed him to practice full-impact as well as flying kicks.

Stretching completed he began foot sparring, a form of training in which hand techniques were forbidden. Using front, side and back kicks, he attacked an imaginary opponent, first the head then the body. Next he switched to roundhouse and hook kicks, striking with speed, accuracy and power.

Finished, Song collapsed into a tapestry-upholstered chair, his jacket soaked with perspiration. The strict mental and physical discipline of *Taekwon do* was demanding. But the reward for practicing this martial art, whose roots went back fifteen hundred years, was increased bravery and an unyielding spirit.

After drying his perspiring face and neck he laced on his tap shoes. Then he stepped to the fireplace and turned on the cassette recorder. As Fred Astaire began to sing "Too Marvelous For Words," Song started a slow time step on the slate hearth. Dancing relaxed him. It was also when he did his best thinking. Closing his eyes, he let Astaire's voice warm him. He wasn't tired anymore. His weariness had evaporated. He began to hum along with Astaire.

As he tap-danced he made a mental rundown of the day's schedule. *Pick up the counterfeit money and securities before his customers arrive. Decide whether to leave the money from these sales in England with Rowena or send it back to Seoul. Get the loan papers from Rowena covering the eight million dollars he gave her last night. Get David Mitla to confirm their flight arrangements from London to Montreal.*

From Montreal they would make their way to New York by rented car, crossing the U.S. border away from any customs agents or border patrol. Song clicked his heels together. All roads led to the beautiful little girl named Tawny. She might be bitter at first, but in his hands she'd eventually become as sweet as honey.

Today he expected to make four million dollars from just two customers. One was a seven-foot Nigerian who ran a travel agency on Thurloe Street when he wasn't occupying himself with insurance and credit-card fraud. The other was an Indian couple who arranged marriages for a living while indulging in gold, diamond and drug smuggling on the side.

Rowena had endorsed the Indians, who had occasionally found an Asian child for her. As for the Nigerian, Song knew him slightly, having met him two years ago at a party in Rome hosted by one of Song's customers. Ben Dumas had checked out the Nigerian and the Indians, finding nothing to make Song reject either buyer of his counterfeits. Song was now free to engage himself in commercial pursuit, to haggle in the marketplace.

With each hour, however, his schedule became tighter. He had only four days to raise the rest of Youngsam's thirty million dollars. Song would make the deadline but only by a day.

In New York, his last stop, he had arranged sales that should yield him eleven million dollars. This, plus sales made in Hong Kong and Europe, plus what he expected to make today, should put him over the top. He'd have Youngsam's thirty million and a three-million-dollar profit. But for the next ninety-six hours fortune had to be on his side or he was finished.

The sweetest part of this deal was the three-million-dollar profit. This would allow him to stop counterfeiting for a few months, work on his tap dancing and devote himself to shaping his little American girl into a perfect woman. Only through money, his heartbeat, could Song live and be happy. Anyone who believed money wasn't crucial should try raising thirty million dollars in three weeks while under a death sentence.

Daylight was creeping through the hotel window when David Mitla, barefoot in a short terrycloth robe, entered the sitting room. Ignoring Song, he flopped down on a tufted sofa, reached for a telephone on a fruitwood coffee table and ordered breakfast for three. Self-confident and outspoken, the former paratrooper didn't hesitate to mock Song's breakfast of a coddled egg and soda crackers. After hanging up the phone Mitla said, "Your Joan Crawford special is on the way."

At the hearth Song did a three-hundred-and-sixty-degree turn, clicked his heels together three times and spun around again. On the sofa Mitla lit his first cigarette of the day, blew smoke at the chandelier, then asked what time he and Choi should pick up the goodies, Mitla's name for Song's counterfeit currency and securities.

"Nine-thirty," Song said. He was now dancing to James Stewart's unique vocalizing on "Easy To Love." "Gives you and Choi an hour and a half. I've telephoned and you're expected. Everything's ready and waiting. Is Choi up?"

"He's up. And he's got both windows wide open. Ice was starting to hang from my nose."

Song had a private room while Mitla and Han Choi had to share, annoying the Israeli, whose calm never revealed his true feelings. Even those who thought they knew the slender, bearded Mitla found him as elusive as quicksilver. He'd led a dangerous life, one he'd never spoken of to anyone, including a wife in Israel who ran their small software business from a cliffside home overlooking Haifa Bay. She also managed his other investments, which included a movie theater on Haifa's Hanassi Street and citrus orchards on the Sharon Plain.

He told her nothing of his role as a mercenary. She knew that he possessed a lust for warfare, that he'd fought all over the world since he was fourteen. She also knew there was a chance he'd return to her in a coffin, or vanish, never to be seen again.

Mitla made more money as a bodyguard to Park Song than when training bodyguards and assassins for Colombia's *los magicos*—the Medellín drug barons. Which was why—putting a bent for privacy aside —he'd accepted rooming with the brawny, twenty-six-year-old Choi, who could bench-press over five hundred pounds and had once broken a man's back for stepping on his foot in a discotheque.

Each morning Choi, who carried his judo silver medal in its original case with him, did two thousand push-ups followed by several minutes of duck walking to strengthen his legs. Then he meditated in front of an open window for ten minutes. If the window was sealed, Choi would turn the air conditioning to high.

Mitla, who considered Choi a bit deranged, rated his own martial arts skills as good but nowhere near good enough to take on the Korean in a fight. Should that day ever come Mitla intended to shoot Choi. Since Choi preferred settling arguments using his judo skills, taking him on bare-handed was the equivalent of rushing to your death.

Song said, "After the pickup, you and Choi return here, no stops, no detours. While you're gone I'll set up appointments with my buyers."

Song's counterfeit dollars and securities were waiting at the Korean embassy on Palace Gate, a street of grand houses located a stone's throw from Kensington Palace. The goodies traveled by diplomatic pouch, courtesy of Colonel Youngsam, who was well compensated for his assistance. Thanks to Youngsam and his intelligence agents at embassies around the world, Song's property was safer than it would be in a bank vault. So long as Song satisfied the Razor's greed he had a friend at court.

"I have to wire money to my wife," Mitla said.

"Do it before you go to the embassy. I don't like you and Choi stopping anywhere while carrying the product. I want to leave England tonight, which means everything must run on schedule."

Mitla stubbed out his cigarette. "Whenever we come here it's always pissing down outside. I hate this gray country, hate the cold weather, hate the cold people. If I had to live here I'd go crazy."

Song stopped dancing and toweled his face. "I hear New York's very cold, so make sure you have your woollies."

Mitla jammed both hands in the pockets of his robe. "Speaking of New York, how's our friend Dr. Ken Yokoi doing these days?"

Song tossed his towel onto the mantelpiece, then resumed tapping. "You should hear Rowena. She's terrified of catching the disease from Ken. Doesn't want him anywhere near her. Don't worry, we won't be dealing with Ken, who in any case refuses to see anyone except his precious Ben. We'll be dealing with Mr. Dumas. And Rowena, of course."

Mitla knew what Song did with little girls like Tawny DaSilva and he dealt with it by simply ignoring the matter. Other than being a bit too competitive at times the Korean was not a bad guy to work for. In any case, how long would Mitla stay a mercenary if he turned down a job just because the offer came from a man who had a few loony ideas about women? He'd been around long enough to know that powerful and influential men in Africa, South America, Europe and the Middle East committed sex crimes and ritual killings daily. A mercenary's very livelihood depended on disregarding the inadequacies of such people. It had yet to occur to Mitla that a love of war had contaminated him.

Experience had taught him, however, that people were little more than wolves gnawing on each other. Even Machiavelli, Mitla's favorite writer, had called the people a wild beast. Big Mac was right. In any case, morality was a luxury mercenaries couldn't afford. A soldier of fortune wasn't hired because he loved Christ.

Mitla accepted the fact that his job had him doing things no rabbi would say a *brocha*, a blessing, over. What mattered most was the rush of adrenalin whenever he went into battle. What mattered was the intense edge of excitement. Except for his wife Messalina, everything else in the world was nothing. At thirty-eight she was three years older than Mitla, the widow of a fellow paratrooper. She was a Sabra, a native-born Israeli, energetic and, like him, inclined to do as she pleased. He had been attracted to her because she was the strongest, most outspoken woman he'd ever met.

The tap-dancing Song broke into the Israeli's reverie: "Wake up, Mr. Mitla, time is money."

Mitla walked toward the room he shared with Choi. Behind him a cheerful Park Song added his adenoidal whine to Gene Kelly's husky tenor in "Singin' In The Rain."

Shortly before one in the afternoon Park Song, in red silk robe and matching slippers worn by Nelson Eddy in *Naughty Marietta,* concluded his first sale of the day in a hotel suite darkened by the December downpour.

The customers were Mr. and Mrs. Prokash, a jovial Indian couple who exchanged two and a quarter million dollars for eight million dollars in fake hundreds and Hong Kong securities. A gray-haired, meaty woman in her early fifties, Mrs. Prokash wore a pink and yellow sari under a ragged cloth coat and did most of the talking. Her husband, a slender, fiftyish Bengali with a durable smile, deferred to her, occasionally removing the pipe from his mouth long enough to say, "Veddy good, veddy good."

The couple had been accompanied by their two eldest sons, one in a three-piece suit, the other in jeans and a Chicago Bears sweatshirt. Both quietly sat down in front of the counterfeit money stacked on the fruitwood coffee table which they eyed in awe and wonder. Song thought, no woman will ever bring you two lads a greater joy than that which you now see before you.

It was mother who prodded her anxious sons into reaching into their jackets for the pocket calculators, notepads and ballpoint pens needed to tally the counterfeit. As they counted, the sons packed the fake money and securities into five suitcases carted along by the family. At no time did Mrs. Prokash's small dark eyes leave the money passing through the hands of her two offspring.

If there's trust among thieves, Park Song thought, it doesn't extend to this crew. Mother didn't trust her children nor did she appear to have much respect for hubby who was left to stand around with his hands in his pockets while turning the air blue with pipe smoke. Mr. Prokash, poor bastard, had married a tsar, not a wife.

At mother's request Song had allowed her sons to be present at the buy. They were needed, she said, to carry home the counterfeit notes and securities. Rather than lose a badly needed sale, Song agreed. Nothing in the Prokashes' background had indicated the use of violence in their dealings. Still, Song insisted that both sons be unarmed, a fact confirmed by Mitla's thorough body search.

Firearms, Mrs. Prokash said, frightened them all no end. Minus bodyguards or weapons of any kind they'd taxied to the hotel and planned to taxi back to their flat on Lady Margaret Road in Southall, London's largest Asian quarter. Song's reaction was to whisper to Mitla, I hope I never become that adventurous.

Song and the Prokash family made their respective counts in silence. To speed his tallying Song used a counting machine borrowed from the embassy, a device which amazed the Indians but not enough to switch from counting by hand. The old ways had always worked well for her, Mrs. Prokash said, so why change at this point?

Mitla, meanwhile, moved restlessly about the room with a silenced 9-mm fifteen-round Taurus in his right hand, an Uzi dangling from one shoulder and a .357 Magnum tucked in his waistband. An air of menace clung to the Israeli, discouraging the Indians from speaking or even looking at him. His eyes flicked from them to the front door, from there to the house phone then back to the Prokashes. Like a snake Mitla, even when calm, hinted at a swift, unpredictable violence.

Choi, somber in dark suit and white socks, stood with his back to the front door, arms folded across his massive chest as he too eyed the Prokash family. In contrast to Mitla he never moved. His breathing was imperceptible. The only sound in the room was that of rain and wind against the windows.

The tallying concluded, Park Song shook hands with the Prokash family, then escorted them to the door. They were as eager to depart as he was to be rid of them. The Nigerian was due shortly, and after doing a deal with him it was off to America.

The Prokash family gone, Song felt like dancing. He was richer than he had been one short hour ago, certainly cause for rejoicing. He looked at his Mickey Mouse wristwatch, a souvenir of his trip to Florida's Disney World three years ago. Twenty minutes until two. Twenty minutes before Katsina Jonathan, the gargantuan forty-two-year-old Nigerian, appeared with $1.8 million. Events were on schedule. Song's destiny would be decided by him, not by Colonel Youngsam.

Mitla and Choi had finished carting the Prokash money to Song's bedroom and were seating themselves in the living room when there was a sharp knock at the door. *"Police. Open up."*

Song came off the sofa. He felt chest pain, shortness of breath. In an attempt to stop a sudden headache he pressed the heels of both hands to his temples. *No,* he whispered.

On the other side of the door a voice spoke in a cockney accent. "Mr. Henry Yue Lan, we know you're in there. Kindly open the door. We would like you to help us with our inquiries, if you please."

Song paced back and forth. Stopping abruptly, he pulled a red silk handkerchief from a robe pocket and tore at it with his teeth. He didn't see Mitla step to the house phone, pick up the receiver and listen. Near the Israeli a silent Choi rose from the sofa, face impassive as always. Eyeing Song, he waited for instructions.

Slamming down the receiver, Mitla said, "Line's dead." He nodded toward the front door. "They're not police. This is a holdup."

Song stopped chewing the handkerchief. A small piece of cloth clung to his wet chin. "How can you be sure? *How?*"

Mitla slipped his Magnum into a pocket of Song's robe. "How can I be sure? Because I'm suspicious that the house phone's been cut off just when you come into two million dollars. Because with your record the police put a gun to your head *then* they announce themselves."

Song looked at the front door. "What if you're wrong? What if those guys are real police?"

"We'll find out soon enough."

Mitla whispered into Song's ear. As the Korean listened he beckoned Choi to his side. Seconds later Mitla raced across the room and into Song's bedroom, leaving Song to hurriedly relay instructions to Choi.

"Mr. Yue Lan, sir. Don't make it hard on yourself. We simply want to ask you a few questions."

Song said, "I'm coming now, officer. Yes, I am."

His deferential voice was misleading. Gone were all signs of fear and dread. A calm, cold-eyed Song watched Mitla close the bedroom door then shifted his gaze to the front door. His hatred of anyone attempting to rob him knew no limits. If the "policemen" calling on him were thieves Song proposed to crush them completely.

Choi, meanwhile, was excited at the prospect of a fight. He felt the icy hatred emanating from Song and knew how explosive the counterfeiter could be. Song was a generous man to work for, but he was also a proud man who didn't like being insulted, tricked or cheated.

Followed closely by Choi, Song walked to the front door. When he opened it his smile was straightforward and heartfelt.

"Good afternoon, officers. I'm Henry Yue Lan. What can I do for you?"

"You can begin by standing aside and allowing us to enter your premises. How's that for starters?"

The speaker was a stocky, thirtyish cockney with small features set in a large red face. He was flanked by two younger men, faces half-hidden by police helmets. All three wore dark ponchos over navy blue uniforms.

Hands in the pockets of his robe, Song backed into the room, followed by the three policemen. The red-faced leader and a tubby bucktoothed man strolled casually past him, taking in the posh surroundings. The third constable, a worried-looking thin man with a drooping mustache, stayed just behind Song and Choi.

Keeping his back to Song the red-faced cockney said, "I'm Constable Fowler. Like to discuss a bit of passport difficulty with you, if I may." Eyes on the chandelier, he turned around to face the two Koreans.

Song's smile never faded. "Is there something wrong? I thought my passport was in order."

Fowler took another slow look about the room. "Before we go

into that, I believe there's a third gentleman traveling with you. Would you, by any chance, know where he can be found?"

Song nodded towards his own bedroom. "At the moment he's taking a hot bath. I think he's coming down with a cold. He's not used to this sort of weather."

Fowler blew into his cupped hands. "Know what you mean. Filthy weather, this. Bucketing down out there and the cold's enough to freeze the balls off a brass monkey. Pleasure and pain, we calls it. That's cockney for rain."

"Really?" Song said. "I never knew that."

Fowler sighed. "You say your friend's having a bath. Well, they tell me cleanliness is next to godliness, though you couldn't prove that by me mother-in-law. What a foul creature that one is. Allow me to compliment you on your choice of slippers. Red with gold braid. Matches that robe nicely, it does. Very nicely. Don't see much of that where I come from. I suppose the more sensitive little birdies appreciate proper dress more than the rest of us."

As the mustachioed constable near Song and Choi snickered, the tubby, bucktoothed man stepped behind Fowler and whispered in his ear. Fowler nodded. Then jerking his head toward the bedroom the cockney said, "Constable Quillan here will go look in on your friend just to make sure he's washing behind his ears, after which we'll get down to business. Constable Quillan, do your duty."

Quillan swung his hands from under his poncho and produced a sawed-off shotgun. Song showed no reaction; his smile remained in place.

As Quillan walked off toward the bedroom Fowler said, "I'm sure you gentlemen won't mind remaining here with me and Constable Dawson until Constable Quillan returns with a report on your mate. Dawson?"

Backing toward the fireplace, the mustachioed Dawson brought his own sawed-off shotgun from under his poncho, training it on Song and Choi.

"I thought British policemen didn't carry guns," Song said.

Fowler folded his hands, the backs of which, were tattooed with eagles and roses. "Oh, but we do, sir. In special cases we most definitely do."

"And this is a special case?"

"Oh, indeed, sir. Which reminds me. If you don't mind, I'd like to

scrutinize the pair of you for weapons. Just a formality, you understand."

He took the Magnum from Song and a fifteen-round Czech CZ-75
pistol from Choi. "For shame, going about England armed to the
teeth like bloody pirates. Have you no faith in our policemen?" He
placed both pistols on the mantelpiece, then resumed his position by
the sofa.

"Never liked guns meself," he said. "More likely to shoot yourself
than the other fella."

Removing his helmet, the balding redheaded Fowler wiped his
forehead with the palm of one hand, then returned the helmet to his
head. A bloody joke, him dressing up like a copper. Him who'd
spent three of the last four years inside for assault, theft and fraud.
The same Reginald Emmett Fowler who'd been a boxer and a book-
maker and not very good at either, who was about to heist more cash
than Ronnie Biggs and his thirty villains had in the Great Train Robbery of 1962. Reginald Emmett Fowler, who was pretending to be a
formidable copper but, truth to tell, had to hide both hands under his
poncho because he had the bloody shakes.

At the bedroom Patric Quillan used the barrel of his shotgun to
push open the door. Millions of dollars and we're in for a fat share,
Fowler had said. Us, and the individual what sent us. They'd be
going after a slitty-eyed little bastard who was sitting on a pile of real
lolly and a good amount of the fake stuff besides. No worries about
genuine coppers either. In Fowler's words, Mr. Henry Yue Lan was
not exactly God's most noble work.

Quillan took three steps into an empty twin-bedded room lit by a
single lamp on a night table. Three steps before he stopped dead and
stared unbelievingly at the money. "Gor blimey," he whispered. He
heard water running in a small bath across the room, but his mind
was closed to everything except the money. Spread across one of the
beds was a beautiful big pile of American money. Quillan thought,
I've died and gone to heaven, I have.

Patric Ian Quillan had finally gotten lucky. No more drug dealing
with the Yardies, the Jamaican gangsters who'd as soon shoot a man
as look at him. No more teaming with Dawson to go debt collecting
for loan sharks who were forever demanding you break some poor
bugger's kneecaps as a Please Remit notice. This rainy day in Picca-

dilly was the best day of Quillan's stinking life. Glory be to God, it was.

Such thoughts consumed only seconds. But they were seconds in which he forgot why he'd come to the bedroom, in which he'd become distracted from the task at hand. Reluctantly moving away from the money, he looked at the bathroom, where the door was slightly ajar. The sound of running water indicated that the bloke inside preferred a full tub. On a stuffed chair near the bathroom entrance someone had left what Quillan thought were ballet shoes with steel taps. Probably belonged to that wog in the red slippers who had to be taking it up the arse from the other two. Tightening his grip on the shotgun, a confident Quillan walked toward the bathroom. Nothing to fear from this crowd of Nancy boys.

His mind, however, was still on the money. Should he tuck a few handfuls under his poncho before reporting to Fowler? Why not? Every man for himself in this world. At the bathroom entrance he stood beside the stuffed chair and gently pushed the shotgun against the door, the money very much on his mind.

Preoccupied, he never saw Mitla rise from behind the stuffed chair and with one hand grip the shotgun by the barrel, simultaneously pressing the silenced Taurus against the helmet strap under Quillan's jaw. Mitla fired twice, holding onto the shotgun as Quillan went limp and crashed into the bathroom door. The door swung open and Quillan landed on the tiled floor, knocking the bloodied helmet from his round head.

In the living room Fowler raised his voice. "Constable Quillan, would you kindly tell us what's going on in there?"

Mitla stepped into the doorway of Song's bedroom and aimed his Taurus at Fowler's head. "Quillan can't come to the phone right now."

Fowler froze momentarily, staring at Mitla, then yelled, "Get him, Dawson."

Dawson stepped away from the fireplace, thinking, I can't hit the bugger from this range. Shotgun's for close work. A bit nearer's what I need, then I'll have him. In his excitement he forgot Song and Choi. He took two steps toward Mitla and in doing so placed his back to the Koreans.

Choi seized Dawson from behind, pinned his arms to his sides and lifted him from the floor. As Dawson yelled, Choi tightened his already ironclad grip and broke the slender Englishman's arms. The shotgun fell to the rug. Choi dropped Dawson to the carpet and sat on his chest. Then crossing his hands at the wrist, Choi seized the lapels of Dawson's jacket, tightened the collar around Dawson's neck and choked him to death.

Mitla, his gun still pointing at Fowler's head, entered the sitting room.

Song raised his hand. "Don't shoot. I want him alive."

Fowler looked at the entrance, seeing only Song between himself and the door. Get by the wog, he thought, and I'm as free as a bloody bird. Tough on you, Henry Fuck Yue Lan. You and your red slippers.

Fowler didn't need a gun; they'd said they weren't going to shoot him, hadn't they? Therefore his fists ought be enough to hang this scrawny little queer out to dry. A tiny punch-up, then Fowler would quick-step down the hall and put this disaster behind him. Let Dawson and Quillan fend for themselves.

He tore off his helmet and hurled it at Song, who ducked, the helmet passing harmlessly over his shoulder. As Song kicked off his slippers Fowler, fists held shoulder high, rushed him. Song waited two seconds then quickly spun around, and back to Fowler, kicked him in the face, firmly driving a callused heel into the cockney's nose.

Arms flailing, Fowler staggered backwards, a throbbing pain spreading throughout his head. Blood gushed from a crushed nose. His vision was blurred. Worse, he was seized by confusion and had lost all sense of direction.

Feet apart, he shook his head to clear it. Damn this bastard who'd got in a lucky shot. One lucky shot. Fowler could take him. He bloody well could.

He stumbled forward, forearms in front of his damaged face for protection. He saw Song take two steps to the right, wait, then take one to the left. Maybe Fowler was a bit more cautious but he wasn't all that impressed. He was going to reveal some fancy footwork of his own and in the process he'd push Mr. Yue Lan's yellow face through the back of his yellow neck.

But the hurt in his head wouldn't go away. Again he shook his head to clear it, and that's when Song kicked him again, driving the edge of his right foot into Fowler's rib cage. The kick knocked the wind out of Fowler, who felt as though he'd been hit by a car. Breathless, he panicked. Turning his back to Song he looked for an escape and found none.

Stepping closer, Song kicked him in the spine, dropping the stricken Fowler to his knees. The instant the cockney touched the carpet Song, showing no mercy, moved in to finish him. Leaping forward, he punched Fowler behind the left ear, knocking him unconscious and into the fruitwood coffee table.

"Nice, but I thought you wanted him alive," Mitla said. "His friends are history."

He walked over to Fowler and felt his neck pulse. "Well, he's still with us. Does this mean a certain tap dancer's losing his touch?"

Song, who'd been calm during the fight, now raised his voice. "How did they know we were here?"

"Your presence in London isn't exactly a secret. Rowena, the Prokash family, Katsina Jonathan. Colonel Youngsam. Dumas. They all know you're here."

"I don't care what it takes, I'm going to find out who betrayed me and I'm going to deal with them. I won't have the bastard walking around knowing my plans. I will not have it."

Mitla said, "My money's on the Nigerian. Rowena and the Indians aren't cowboys. Rowena doesn't have to lift a finger to get your money. You handed it to her, remember?"

"If I'm dead she doesn't have to return it."

"Good point, but if Jonathan doesn't keep his appointment I'm betting he's our man."

"If he is, I'm not leaving England until he's dead. At the moment I intend to devote my attention to Constable Fowler or whoever this bastard is."

"Can't you put off having your fun just once? You want to get back at him. I understand that but I don't think we have the time. Give me two minutes and I can have Fowler singing in Hebrew. He'll talk, believe me. Then we terminate him, we get out of here and let your embassy clean up this mess. Whoever sent these guys knows where we are. I don't like that. I say we find another hole to crawl in and do it fast."

Song spoke in a whisper. "Everything happens in threes, it's a law of nature. This business with these *policemen* was the first setback. I will suffer two more, mark my words."

He held up three fingers. "Three men they sent after me. Three. It's a sign."

Mitla said, "You're forgetting something. You survived this blow. I say it means you'll survive the others as well."

Song looked at him. "You really think so? You really think I can survive the other blows?"

If you don't, Mitla thought, there goes my money. Flattery was called for. "I see no reason why you can't achieve what you set out to do."

Smiling, Song placed a hand on the Israeli's shoulder. "Thank you, my friend. I need to be in control again. Do you understand?"

Mitla nodded. Of course he fucking understood. Song wouldn't feel right until he'd *controlled* this Fowler character. Putting it another way, Song intended to cheer himself up by torturing the poor bastard.

"Fifty-thousand-dollar bonus if you see me through everything. *Everything*. You understand?" Song said quietly.

Mitla sighed. "Just speed it up, all right?"

Song smiled like a child told he could go out and play. "One hour," he said. "You and Choi start packing. I'll call the embassy and tell them we've had a bit of trouble. Youngsam has thirty million reasons for coming to my assistance."

Fowler was having a nightmare. He lay naked in a lush green jungle on cold hard ground. A freezing rain beat down on him unmercifully. He had the worst headache of his life. His body ached, especially one arm that felt as though it were on fire. Worst of all was the snake. The huge yellow snake that gnawed at Fowler's hand and sent stabbing pains throughout his body. He opened his eyes and screamed, a cry heard by no one because his mouth was taped.

He wasn't dreaming.

He lay naked in a bathtub, right wrist handcuffed to a faucet. Both ankles were lashed tightly together with a belt. Cold water gushed down on him from a gold-plated tap. The snake was the nude Henry Yue Lan, who knelt outside the tub and with a straight razor was slicing the tattoo from the back of Fowler's left hand.

Though weakened by the beating he'd received just minutes ago, Fowler still struggled to pull his bloodied hand away from the Kore-

an's grip. Song dug a thumb into a nerve inside Fowler's wrist, sending pain up the man's arm. Resistance dealt with, Song resumed the
task at hand.

But when the agony in the left hand again became too much
Fowler again tried to pull the hand away. This time Song pressed the
wrist nerve harder, keeping his thumb in place. Fowler writhed,
splashing Song with blood-tinted water. From the cassette came the
rich voice of Judy Garland singing, "I'm Old-Fashioned."

Song said to Fowler, "When I remove the tape you will tell me
who sent you. I will ask you just once, but I'm sure you will tell me
the truth."

He stared at the cockney through half-closed eyes. "Did you know
that everything happens in threes?"

Lips pursed, he dug the straight razor into the back of Fowler's
hand, making an incision around the feet of a blue eagle clutching a
pink rose in its talons.

TEN

Because Manny Decker believed people phoned only when they wanted something he wasn't keen on receiving telephone calls.

But on the morning following the alleged murder-suicide of Max and Gail DaSilva a call came into the precinct which demanded some degree of attention if not courtesy on his part. A woman named Karen Drumman telephoned to say that she, like Decker, believed the DaSilvas had been murdered.

Decker had never heard of Miss Drumman so he said, that's interesting, thinking, please, lady, keep it short and to the point. He wasn't in the best of moods, having had only four hours' sleep. He also hadn't eaten breakfast, and was looking at a twelve-hour work day. And he'd just come from the U.S. Attorney's office where a sullen Yale Singular had reluctantly witnessed his swearing in as a U.S. Deputy Marshal.

Last, but by no means least, Decker felt responsible for Gail's murder because if he'd shown up for dinner on time last night she might still be alive. Sooner or later his guilt was going to push him towards some kind of self-inflicted punishment. Some people had one of those days. Decker had one of those lives.

His gut instinct said Gail's killer had known that Decker was going

147

to be late in getting to her place, therefore giving the killer time. Had Gail's phone been bugged? If so, why? In seeking an answer to this question Decker would be poking his nose into someone else's boiling pot. Someone who'd gambled he could ice two people before Decker arrived. Someone who was slicker than wax on a marble floor.

Miss Drumman had a pleasant voice, slightly husky but precise, as though she'd taken speech lessons at some point. Decker wondered what she looked like. She sounded foxy. Then again she could be coyote ugly.

Karen Drumman said she was Gail's best friend and also Tawny's godmother. According to her she'd known Gail since they'd shared a Second Avenue walk-up back in the seventies when both had tried for a show-business career, Gail as a singer, she as an actress. They hadn't made it. We only lacked three things, Miss Drumman said, talent, luck and the abnormality it takes to go on stage and bare your soul in front of strangers. Decker thought she didn't sound too bitter about failing, leading him to wonder if she'd ever seriously wanted to be an actress in the first place.

These days she was a headhunter, she told him, a recruiter who located qualified candidates for high-paying executive jobs in advertising. She worked for Ralph Sharon Associates on East 42nd Street across from the Daily News building. However, Gail's death had upset her so much that she'd taken the day off.

She was at home, in her apartment only three blocks from Gail, and down to her last three Valiums. Decker, fresh out of pity, stayed silent on Miss Drumman's short supply of pharmaceuticals. He had no inclination to give his soul to a stranger, even one with a dynamite voice.

Miss Drumman had got his name from Gail, and while she had him on the phone she wanted to thank him for trying to find Tawny. Decker wondered if Miss Drumman was who she claimed to be and decided he'd find out in the course of investigating Gail's murder. He knew this much: on the phone Miss Drumman sounded angry, sad and she cried a lot. Decker thought she had a naive charm.

He was aware that any investigation of Gail's death would be handled by her local precinct, which had official jurisdiction. Department rules said that only investigating officers were allowed on a crime scene, meaning Decker shouldn't have been permitted to enter the apartment the previous night.

However, he'd known one of the victims and was a cop himself, so he'd been given permission to come inside the DaSilva condo, providing he didn't get in the way. But should he decide to dig deeper, he didn't need to be a college graduate to know he'd better not get caught. Everybody had a scheme that wouldn't work. This could well be Decker's.

His own precinct wanted him on the Valentin-Dalton homicides, while the Treasury Department craved his assistance in nailing Ben Dumas and Laughing Boy for passing funny money. Decker knew he should play it safe, that he should take care of business and stay focused on the task at hand, a time-honored way of keeping one's career on an upward trajectory. On the other hand he loved cutting corners. He enjoyed jumping over the fence with the alarm going off. So what if he occasionally did something that went beyond dumb and reached all the way to stupid?

As the foxy-sounding Karen Drumman told him that the DaSilvas would never embrace murder-suicide, Decker remained hunched over his desk reading the green sheet, a list each station house received every morning of all crimes committed in the city during the previous twenty-four hours. Max and Gail were on the list.

They had ended their lives as crime statistics, along with a dead three-year-old Hispanic girl found in a burning suitcase on a South Bronx back lot, a pair of human hands found in a paper bag left in an East Harlem apartment lobby, a Brooklyn man struck over the head with a ketchup bottle after an argument over a two-dollar debt, and the usual dead goats, chickens and cats found by Central Park foot patrols each morning, the leftovers from Santería and voodoo rites performed in the park the previous night. Decker wondered if even planned parenthood could stop crime. He doubted it.

Meanwhile, something Miss Drumman said stopped him from reading the green sheet.

"I have a photograph of you and Gail taken down in South Carolina when you were in the Marines," she told him. "I think it was just before you went off to some special military school. I thought maybe you might want it. Gail never forgot you. She spoke of you quite often."

Eyes closed, Decker massaged the bridge of his nose with a thumb

and forefinger. "Could you describe the photograph to me, please?"
He took a deep breath, exhaled, then cleared his throat. His heartbeat quickened. He wanted to hear what Miss Drumman had to say
about the photograph. On the other hand he wished she'd never
called.

She said, "You're both outdoors on a parade field it looks like.
You're wearing a formal Marine uniform. She's wearing your Marine
hat. It's a white hat. Your hair's cut very short and you both look so
young, so happy."

We *were* young and happy, Decker thought. We had it all ahead of
us. The dark days had yet to come and nobody had poisoned the
wells. He smiled, remembering how short his hair had been. High
and tight like the Corps demanded. Sides clipped short so that no
hair showed when a cap was worn, the hair on top approximately a
half-inch long.

Karen Drumman said, "I let Gail look at some of my wedding
pictures and when she returned them, the one of you and her somehow ended up with mine. I never got around to returning it. I'm
pretty sure she'd want you to have it."

"Thanks," said Decker, whose instinct told him to ignore the photograph, something he couldn't bring himself to say to Miss Drumman. The most painful memories were those involving something
you didn't do. This photograph would only remind him of what he
hadn't done about Gail.

Karen Drumman said, "Any news about Tawny? I can't sleep for
worrying about her."

"I'm sorry, but there's nothing to report. I'm not giving up on her.
Especially not after what happened to Gail." Guilt would devour him
if he even thought of giving up.

"I understand," Karen Drumman said, sounding touched by his
determination. "You know, it's strange," she said, "first Tawny dis-
appears, then a few days later Gail and Max are murdered. If that
isn't bad karma, I don't know what is. You can't call it an accident
and you can't call it coincidence, so what do you call it? Doesn't it
seem to you as though someone was out to get Gail and her family?"

Decker reached for the dregs of his black coffee. Miss Drumman
had a point. There was bad luck and worse luck and there was what
had happened to the DaSilvas. Cops and press were floating a sce-
nario that had Gail walking out on Max who didn't want to live

without her so he shot her twice in the heart before turning the gun on himself. Decker thought that anyone who believed this shit had the kind of head you can see through.

Max may have been a schmuck but he wasn't a psycho, at least not according to Gail. Meanwhile, the press was calling him a disillusioned yuppie whose pursuit of money had left him mentally unbalanced. As one happy-talk newscaster put it, Max had felt unhappy and unloved and so he had chosen a quick bullet in the head over the slow death of crushed ideals and old age. Decker thought, right, and you're so dumb you couldn't hit the ground if you fell.

As for Gail, she wasn't someone who'd lost control of her life. She was getting divorced, not having a nuclear meltdown. She wasn't dumping Max, they were dumping each other. They'd both been ready to start new lives. People with something to look forward to don't usually kill themselves. Nor do they whip up an elaborate dinner for three, with expensive crystal and silver service laid out on the table and four bottles of Montrachet chilling in ice buckets.

"You wouldn't happen to know if Max owned a gun?" Decker asked Karen Drumman.

"You got to be kidding," she said. "Max was a lover, not a fighter. He'd sooner stick pins in his eyes than go near a gun. Some black kids robbed him at gunpoint in the subway three years ago. Scared him so much he never rode the subway again. Went everywhere by cab or limousine after that. That's also why he owned a car and a jeep. Cost him a thousand a month in garage fees but he didn't care. Gail hated guns more than Max did. She said with Tawny at home she'd never have one in the house."

Decker ignored his ringing phone. The switchboard could take messages. Let's say Miss Drumman was correct and Max hadn't owned a gun. Then who did own the brand new Beretta 84, .380 caliber, 9-mm short barrel used to put two bullets in Gail's heart and one in Max's right temple?

In a call to Gail's precinct that morning Decker had learned that no permit had ever been issued for the Beretta. The serial number had also been filed off. The gun was virtually untraceable, a shrewd move on Max's part. Except why go to all that trouble if you're going to kill yourself. And whose fingerprints were on the gun? Max's, of course. Whoever concocted this scam was one smooth snotball. He'd thought of everything. The man had imagination, not to mention a natural and exuberant sense of style.

There'd been no signs of forced entry, meaning Max and Gail had let their killer into the apartment. They'd trusted him. Why?

Responding to complaints about loud music, Ivo Popovich, the building's assistant manager, had used a spare key to enter the Da-Silva apartment after Gail and Max hadn't answered the house phone. Mr. Popovich claimed to have found husband and wife dead on the living-room floor. He then left without touching anything and made a telephone call to police from his office. *Why had Gail and Max let the killer into their apartment?*

"Gail told me Max was planning to raise the reward for Tawny," Karen Drumman said. "Maybe somebody came there to rob them. Could be they thought Max kept big money around the house."

Decker placed the receiver between his shoulder and chin, then opened his notebook. "Robbery's out. The place hadn't been tossed."

He checked his notes. He'd been right. The apartment hadn't been touched. There'd been loot on the premises that no self-respecting thief would have passed up unless he'd been born without hands and eyes. Such as twenty-one hundred dollars in cash. And nine credit cards, jewelry, checkbooks, cameras, two fur coats, three VCRs, two home computers, and a Proton stereo. Also the keys to Max's two-year-old Mercury and new four-wheel-drive Jeep, both of which were downstairs in the building garage. The shooter had come there to do two people, not fill a pillowcase with stolen property and rush off to the nearest fence.

Karen Drumman said, "Detective Decker, two days ago Gail told me Max was being followed by a black man. He thought it might be someone he'd previously had trouble with. Could this person be a factor?"

Decker rubbed the back of his neck in an attempt to wake up. Earlier he'd gone to the precinct bathroom for a quick shave and looked in the mirror. What he saw looking back at him was like something out of *Night of The Living Dead.*

"I can't say more about it at the present time, but the man you're talking about doesn't figure in this at all."

Bulldog Drumman, girl detective. Give the lady credit for bringing up a good point. Interesting that Max had gotten whacked just before he furnished a description of a spook who'd been following him around for a couple of days.

So Miss Drumman knew about Max's troubles with Rashad Lateef Quai, the black postal worker who wanted to stop selling stamps and switch to making music. Did knowing this make her righteous? No way. She could be anybody; until Decker knew otherwise he was going to be cautious and speak slowly. Cops who talked too much were cops dumb enough to drown on dry land.

After checking out the Beretta, Decker had checked out Mr. Quai. Forget about him tailing anybody. For the past seventy-two hours he'd been in jail, charged with stealing forty-two thousand dollars from the post office to pay his phone bill. Addicted to telephone sex, he'd spent hours each day in some very expensive phone conversations. Max's black man was not the lecherous and hot-to-trot Mr. Quai.

Time to end this conversation with Miss Drumman, who talked too much about the past to suit Decker. There were things he didn't want to recall. Recalling them made him feel very lonely. Miss Drumman could put the photograph in the mail if she wanted to. End of story.

As though reading his mind she said to Decker, "I don't think I should put the picture in the mail. It might get lost, and I'm sure it means a lot to you. It meant a lot to Gail. I could meet you somewhere and give it to you if you'd like."

Decker shook his head. Jesus. What was he going to say—mail the thing and get out of my life? She'd see that as an insult to Gail and she'd probably be right. Besides, she was almost out of Valium so why give her a hard time.

"That would be very kind of you," he said to her.

"I'm having dinner with a client this evening," she said. "Something I can't get out of. If it's not too inconvenient, maybe you could drop by the restaurant and pick up the photograph."

"Address?"

"Corner of 64th and Madison. It's called Bougival. It's across the street from my apartment. Gail and Tawny and I used to have Sunday brunch there when Max was spending weekends with his little friend from Switzerland."

She had a warm, throaty voice that made Decker wonder again what she looked like. "Don't worry," she said. "I won't keep you. I

know you're busy. Just ask for Brenda. She's the maître d'. She'll
show you to my table. By the way, I have other photographs of Gail.
I'll bring along a few and you can take your pick."

"Thanks," Decker said. This time he meant it.

She said, "Right now I'm listening to Mozart's Requiem, which
seems appropriate if a bit depressing. Music reminds me of Max and
his gadgets, his stereos, computers, tape recorders. I hope they have
them where he's going. He was gadget-happy. He even dictated
memos to Tawny on a microcassette recorder. Imagine dictating a
memo to your own daughter. But he dictated everything. Memos,
letters, telexes, everything. He kept a dozen recorders in the apartment. Used to drive Gail crazy finding them everywhere she
turned."

Decker stopped rubbing his neck. Shit, was it possible? He quickly
turned the pages in his notebook until he found what he was looking
for. There it was in black and white. Or rather, there it wasn't. He
was looking at the list of personal effects found in the apartment, stuff
the killer had ignored.

No microcassette tape recorders. Stereo equipment, computers,
but no microcassette tape recorders. There hadn't been any in the
apartment. Not one.

"Miss Drumman, are you sure Max kept microcassette recorders in
the apartment?"

"Is there some kind of problem?"

"Just answer the question. Are you sure about the microcassette
recorders?"

"I'm sure. Gail had me over a lot lately to talk about her troubles
with Max, so I saw the recorders myself. The latest one was a present
from a Japanese record distributor Max had just signed with. Gail
showed me how it works. It's no bigger than a book of matches and
has a fantastic sound. Wouldn't mind owning one myself, except
they're not sold over here."

Closing his eyes, Decker nodded his head. "That's what he did.
Son of a bitch."

"Excuse me?"

"Nothing. Just thinking out loud."

The killer had taken something from the apartment after all. He'd
taken the microcassette recorders. Every goddamn one. When the
killer entered the apartment Max had probably been dictating a de-

scription of the black man he'd planned to turn over to Decker. To protect this spook the shooter had taken out Max and Gail.

Slick Rick, you just made your first mistake. If you'd walked off with only one recorder, I'd never have known. But you're a smartass. You don't trust anybody, so you had to take them all. Ran Dobson was right. Being too clever is dumb.

Turning to a blank page, Decker made notes. The killer had been watching Max and Gail. Maybe tapping their phone. Otherwise why hit the DaSilvas just before they were to tell Decker about the black dude? The timing and the missing tape recorders said it all. Someone had wanted to protect this dude in the worst way. Karen Drumman's phone call had been a gold mine and not a waste of time. Cops lived by information, and Miss Drumman had produced more than her share.

Decker said to her, "All right if I show around eight-thirty?"

"Eight-thirty's fine."

"Good. See you then."

He hung up, leaned back in his chair, absentmindedly clicking his ballpoint pen. Karen Drumman was right. We're talking superior bad karma. But it did seem odd that the DaSilvas should have so much bad karma all at once. An unseen hand was pushing the pieces around the board.

He reached for his notebook and wrote Tawny DaSilva's name and the date she had disappeared. Below it he wrote the names Gail and Max DaSilva along with the date of their deaths. He underlined this date twice.

ELEVEN

It was almost 8:45 that evening when Decker and his partner Det. Ellen Spiceland entered Bougival, the East 64th Street restaurant named for a French village often seen in Renoir and Monet paintings.

The restaurant was a long narrow room with a small side room near the far end. Both rooms had low white-tiled ceilings, candles on every small table and walls of exposed brick hung with Renoir and Monet prints. Decker automatically disliked the place because it was on the East Side, not his favorite part of town.

He distrusted the area's phony gentility and the inflated aura of self-esteem on the part of people living there. As for Bougival, it struck Decker as being no different than a thousand other East Side joints. Look for the raw spinach salad, front doors made of frosted glass and drinks with cutesy names like Fuzzy Navel and Harvey Wallbanger. Bougival tended to cater to a yuppie crowd—young, white and prosperous, an assembly of wrinkle-free thirtysomethings in the morning of their lives, minds untainted by experience. The men wore preppy clothes that were neither in nor out of style; the women wore suits or dresses that stressed uniform affluence over individuality. The one black face in the room belonged to Decker's partner, Ellen Spiceland. If this bothered her, she didn't show it.

She was a thirty-three-year-old beige-tinted woman with high cheekbones, reddish hair and a flattened nose that had been crushed at thirteen when she'd resisted a rape attempt by a Harlem minister. The precinct called her "Bags" because she entered sinister bars and after-hours joints with a hand in her purse gripping a .38 Smith & Wesson. As she told Decker, coming out on top didn't mean anything. Coming out alive did.

She was heading home, but at Decker's request had agreed to keep him company. She lived on the East Side but far from the "Silk Stocking" district where Gail and Karen lived. For Ellen Spiceland, home was the edge of Spanish Harlem, in a large apartment on a block that was considered relatively safe because it rarely had more than two murders a year. These days she was handling alone much of the caseload assigned to her and Decker. Buying her a drink tonight was his way of saying thanks.

For now she was stuck working a dozen ongoing cases by herself, but she wasn't bitching. Decker needed help; Gail, Tawny and Willie Valentin were not burdens he could easily shift to God or a shrink. Which didn't stop Bags from realizing that she was earning markers. Ultimately Decker would have to pay up.

In Bougival she eyed the Renoir and Monet prints, most of which she recognized. She was married to a Haitian artist, her third husband, and a self-obsessed bore to whom she was devoted. They stayed together because her strength reminded him of his mother and because it didn't bother her to give generously to him while getting nothing back. Decker, who stayed out of her personal life, wondered if she was a masochist or just liked a challenge.

When necessary Bags could get down. Two years ago she and Decker, "Black and Decker" to coworkers, had shown up at a West 83rd Street apartment to arrest a Cuban male suspected of having raped an eighteen-month-old baby girl. The Cuban, one Raul Gallaraga, opened the door, a thirteen-round Browning automatic in his left hand, and aimed at Decker's throat. Three shots were fired. Decker, ready to die, only heard the first.

It was Ellen who shot Gallaraga three times in the gut, firing through the beaded bag she'd received from Henri on their third anniversary. Decker replaced the ruined bag with a two-hundred-fifty-dollar Courrèges purse, the best he'd been able to find at Saks Fifth Avenue. And when she told him she'd wanted to kill a maggot like the Cuban for twenty years, Decker told her thanks for waiting.

Brenda, the maître d' who led Decker and Ellen to Karen Drumman's table, was in her late twenties, a lean, deadpan blonde in a tuxedo, with lengthy blood-red fingernails and eyebrows which had been tweezed and redrawn. Ellen whispered to Decker, "Bet she doesn't read on the toilet or pick her nose. You ever see a more icy-looking woman in your life?"

Decker said, "I think she'd tie you up on the first date."

Ellen looked around. "I didn't know Manhattan still had this many white people. I feel as though I'm in a sanctuary for endangered species. Next time I'm bringing my camera."

Decker took her arm. "Behave yourself, Bags. They don't understand you like I do."

"You know, I look at these guys and I think it must be hard going through life not being able to get it up."

Decker was still smiling when Deadpan Brenda left them at a table near an apparently empty back room and occupied by two people. One was Karen Drumman, a slender red-haired woman in her early thirties, tanned and dressed in an olive green jumpsuit, matching suede high heels and a studded black leather belt with an oversize gold-plated buckle.

Decker liked the two ivory chopsticks in her hair and the high heels. He liked her eyes, which were a clear blue and focused on him without blinking. He liked it that when they shook hands she smiled and held his a little longer than necessary. Truth was, they liked each other on sight.

The other person at the table was Jean-Louis Nicolay, a small gray-haired, baby-faced Frenchman in his forties who wore a well-cut, double-breasted dark suit, pale lavender shirt and yellow silk tie. There was a pink cloth flower in his buttonhole. Decker figured the suit at around fifteen hundred, not including alterations. The cost of Nicolay's shoes probably equaled the weekly take-home of a first-grade detective. Monsieur Jean-Louis didn't need company. Anyone loving himself enough to spend that much money on clothes was never alone. Decker disliked him immediately.

From the looks of things Nicolay had been hitting on Karen Drumman and getting nowhere. He had a hand on her knee and his little mouth near her ear. Karen Drumman wasn't buying. Her indifference to the well-tailored Jean-Louis impressed Decker, who was suspicious of people in expensive clothes. People like that usually wanted to be seen as more than they were.

Ignoring the Frenchman, Karen Drumman had been slowly tapping a water glass with a sesame-seed breadstick. Every so often she'd stop tapping to pick up seeds from the table and drop them in an ashtray. Jean-Louis was making every guy in the room look good.

At the sight of Decker, the Frenchman abandoned his quest to get lucky. Smiling, he sprang from his chair, gripped Decker's hand with both of his and in heavily accented English introduced himself as Bougival's owner. Decker introduced himself, but said nothing about being a cop. You had to be careful with citizens these days. They tended to view cops as the custodians of ethical conduct, so telling them you carried a badge usually put a damper on the party. Decker merely gave his name, then introduced Ellen as Mrs. Spiceland, a business associate.

Jean-Louis addressed Ellen as *madame*, kissed her hand and said the pleasure was all his. Head bowed, the Frenchman didn't see her wink at Decker and gently nudge him with her hip. She was being flattered by a pro, leaving her wary but no less charmed. Decker thought, monsieur's got all the right moves. Monsieur probably didn't make any noise while eating his soup, either.

Decker watched Ellen thank Nicolay for his kind words, doing it in French, which she'd learned from her Haitian hubby and which now shocked Nicolay into raising one eyebrow. Having experienced French snobbery firsthand in Saigon, Decker knew monsieur was surprised to find that an American, a black woman no less, spoke *française* fairly well. Give Jean-Louis credit. In seconds he'd recovered and moved on to the business of being a flirtatious host.

He and Ellen began speaking in French, the language bringing back memories of Saigon for Decker, memories of a letter from Gail that had included the Emily Dickinson lines—*Unable are the loved to die/ For love is immortal.* He'd carried the letter around with him until the writing had faded and the paper had fallen apart and he'd gotten out of Vietnam alive.

Decker enjoyed the fact that Ellen had caught Jean-Louis being a tad condescending. Bags was quick, capable of going from zero to ninety in a second like a cheetah. She could not be easily deceived or imposed upon.

Earlier today she'd stopped Decker from screwing up his investigation of Gail's murder. He'd begun with the Beretta, realizing that like many guns it could have been acquired from a gunrunner who purchased weapons in Florida, then legally sold them in New York to any deviate who could pay. As a cop, Decker didn't view gun ownership as a right. He saw it as a disease.

For now he decided to ignore the Florida–New York firearms connection and play an educated hunch, namely Kennedy Airport. The Beretta was Italian-made, a foreign gun. Gail had been killed by a new one, a piece in mint condition. Decker was looking for a recent import. Kennedy Airport was as likely a place as any to go digging.

OCs, organized crime members, regarded Kennedy Airport as their very own shopping mall, except they never paid for anything. Maybe some wiseguys had grabbed a gun shipment from the airport not too long ago. When these slimeballs weren't extorting money by threatening airlines with labor trouble they were stealing any piece of cargo that wasn't nailed down.

Hijacking from Kennedy, the world's richest port, remained one of the mob's most profitable enterprises. Aiding and abetting OCs in this lucrative undertaking were those shipping clerks and loading-dock foremen who were habitual gamblers, born losers who paid off debts to mob bookmakers and loan sharks with cargo information on valuable consignments, trucking timetables, airport security. Gamblers ended up betraying everything and everybody. Decker found them to be dimwits who ultimately turned into shitheads.

He'd said to Bags, "I'm reaching out for the Bureau of Alcohol, Tobacco and Firearms," which was the branch of the Treasury Department dealing with guns. "The T-boys should know about gun heists at Kennedy." Since Decker was now a deputy U.S. marshal, why not use his new clout? Yale Singular was using him; why shouldn't Decker return the favor?

"Because it's stupid, that's why," Bags said. "Gail's important to you, but be cool. Yes, he's using you. Take down Ben Dumas, he told you, then get off the set. Stay away from Laughing Boy no matter how much you despise the man. You may not like that part of the deal, but does this mean you should be simpleminded? You want hijacking intelligence, you know where to go. And I don't mean fat boy."

"Safe, Loft and Truck," said Decker, knowing he'd just been reprimanded and knowing he'd had it coming. The police department's

Safe, Loft and Truck squad dealt with burglaries, safecrackers and truck hijackings, keeping updated intelligence on perps, organizations, informants, fences, arrest records.

"You got that right," Bags said.

Decker had almost made a mistake and all because pride demanded that he do to Yale Singular what Singular was doing to him, namely, pull strings and make the other guy jump. Bags was square on target. Yes, Singular was using him, but why should Decker compound the problem by passing on his theories about Gail's death to the fat man?

Cops disliked feds and with good reason. Feds usually took whatever you offered and gave you zilch in return. Tell Singular that Decker was looking into Gail's murder and the T-man would use that bit of news on his own behalf. Singular had already made it clear that he didn't think Decker should be out looking for Tawny. In the race to be loved the fat man was bringing up the rear.

Anybody could slip up, but only a schmuck persisted in his mistake. Luckily this was one mistake Decker could recall before it cost him anything. That's why he liked Bags. She knew when to rein him in, doing it in a way that didn't make him feel like a halfwit.

Decker knew several of the sixty or so detectives assigned to the Safe, Loft and Truck squad, which dated back to the turn of the century. He reached out for Det. Lowell Chattaway, a red-faced forty-year-old mick with breath like a drain and a propensity when drunk to crawl under dinner tables and bite diners of either sex on the thigh.

According to Chattaway two cases of Beretta 84, .380 caliber, 9 mm short barrels from Milan had been stolen from a Kennedy cargo terminal over Thanksgiving weekend. An informant claimed the heist had been the work of a crew connected to the LoCasio family. To make matters worse, some four hours after leaving the airport the Berettas had disappeared again.

Credit this to the LoCasio sales force, which had gone about its job in a pragmatic and businesslike manner. Before snatching the guns, Joe LoCasio, the family *padrone*, had customers lined up and ready to buy. The stolen Berettas had been sold quickly. Unfortunately, the snitch didn't have the buyers' names. When and if the snitch got lucky Chattaway would buzz Decker.

Progress. And with only one phone call. Decker owed Bags, no getting around it. Part-payment. So tonight he invited her to join him and Karen Drumman for a drink.

At Bougival, Jean-Louis Nicolay ordered complimentary drinks for Karen's table. A gaunt young waiter with dark wavy hair and a weasellike face was assigned to handle their every need. Nicolay himself passed out large handwritten, one-page menus and described the day's specials, which included Tunisian couscous, rabbit stew and basboussa, a semolina pastry with almonds. He seemed to enjoy playing host so much that Decker didn't mention he'd only dropped by for a drink and to pick up some old photographs. Take away monsieur's illusions about being important and you took away his happiness.

As Nicolay and maître d' Brenda disappeared into a small passageway leading to the restaurant's back room, a relieved Karen Drumman said to Decker, "My client canceled at the last minute. Came down with the flu. His whole family's had it, now it's his turn. You two arrived just in time."

She looked over her shoulder, then back at Decker and Ellen. "Jean-Louis was inviting me to one of his *special* parties." She shivered in revulsion.

"And he smells so nice, too." said Ellen.

"I'm no prude," Karen said. "I've been married and divorced and I've dated some, though not all that much, I'm afraid. But Jean-Louis's a bit kinky for my taste. We went out a few times after I broke up with my husband. That was two years ago. I suppose I wanted reassurance that I was still attractive. Anyway, the relationship went nowhere. Jean-Louis is into life in the fast lane and that's not for me."

She said to Ellen, "You're a cop, too, right?"

"Manny's partner."

"I thought so. I sensed Manny didn't want Jean-Louis to know he was a cop so I kept quiet. Was it you who was checking up on me today? My office called me at home to say some policewoman had dropped by to ask whether or not I worked there. Are you two always this cautious?"

"Doesn't mean we're not nice people," Decker said, wriggling his eyebrows à la Groucho.

She said, "I guess," and smiled at him, making Decker feel he'd said something funny. Bulldog Drumman was definitely worth a trip across town in subfreezing weather. In the cab Bags had teased him, saying that Karen was probably ugly enough to scare a dog off a meat truck, that when she came into the room the mice jumped on chairs. Not this time, Bags. Karen Drumman had looks and smarts. Dig the way she'd kept quiet about Decker being a cop.

She had something else, Decker decided. She was sweet, and sweet was rare in New York, where if a man breathed he could make a woman angry. As a woman once said to Decker, if they can put one man on the moon, why can't they put them all there? Karen Drumman definitely wasn't of that school.

Decker, with an assist from Bags, had learned that Karen was from Denver, had been in New York fourteen years and lived alone with two cats. She was divorced, earned good money and did volunteer work at a Gramercy Park foundling hospital one night a week. She had a sad smile and lines around her eyes that Decker found attractive. She appeared warm and feminine, the sort of woman who aroused a man's protective instinct. Experience, however, had taught Decker that such women could usually take care of themselves.

Ellen said, "Let's hear about this party. We're not going to arrest anybody. I just like to know about those things." Bags loved gossip and would tell you so in a minute.

Karen looked down at the table. "Lord help us. Jean-Louis insists the party's very high-class. Only the best people from here and overseas, he says. A select clientele, is how he put it. I'm under no obligation to, you know, do anything. If I go, that is. I can watch or join in, my choice. This is a very unusual party, according to him. Look, what it is, is some kind of orgy."

The table went silent as the weasel-faced waiter brought drinks. When he'd left, Karen stared into a white wine spritzer sitting in front of her. "Jean-Louis has some weird ideas about women and sex, which is why I stopped going out with him. There is such a thing as too much."

"You wouldn't want to define too much," Ellen said.

Karen abruptly turned to Decker. "Anything new on Tawny? Stupid question. If there were I'm sure you'd have told me."

Decker said, "Before leaving the station house I checked with the National Hotline for Missing Children and the National Runaway Switchboard. Nothing. Tonight I'll phone a couple more people and see if they've got anything. But to be honest it doesn't look good."

He didn't tell her what a hotline caseworker had said, that because

of the growing number of adult males craving sex with children it
was more dangerous to be a kid now than it was ten years ago.
Pedophiles took pictures of children they'd kidnapped and traded
the photos among themselves as you would baseball cards. It was
frightening to think about, the caseworker said, but Tawny's photograph might already be in somebody's collection.

Karen said, "Tawny, Gail and I were supposed to see the Christmas show at Radio City Music Hall. We go every year. After the
show we usually have dinner at one of the Rockefeller Center cafés.
It's a nice little party. All girls, no men, lots of fun."

Karen lowered her voice. "Speaking of parties, it reminds me why
Jean-Louis and I agreed to disagree. He's into wild parties, can't get
enough of them. I despise that kind of stuff. He even invited me to
something called a sex-slave auction, can you believe it? He said it
would all be just in fun. Just a bunch of party-goers having a laugh."

"The man appears to be in perpetual heat," Decker said.

"I couldn't believe he actually used the words 'sex-slave auction.'" Karen said. "According to him, some people actually let
themselves be bought and sold at these things for sexual purposes.
He says it's not a crime because they do it voluntarily. He says it
happens once a year, sometimes once every two years. I guess he
could be pulling my leg, except Jean-Louis is no choirboy."

Bags touched Decker's arm. "Mr. Nicolay asked me what kind of
business we're in."

Decker waited.

"I told him we were systems analysts," she said.

Decker grinned. "You always say that. What happens when somebody asks you what a systems analyst does?"

"I refer them to you."

He nodded, reached for a large brown envelope near Karen's
purse, pulling it toward him, not really in a hurry to examine the
contents. *Afraid of your own memories, my man? Afraid to behold
what life has taken away from you? What you let slip away.* He
reached inside the envelope and pulled out the photographs.

The Parris Island graduation-day shot. *Gaze upon a grinning Manfred Freiherr Decker, named for Baron Manfred von Richthofen, the
legendary Red Baron and First World War flying ace. A skinny,
shaved-head Decker in dress blues and sharpshooter's medal and
looking pleased with himself. Hell, why not.*

And there was Gail with her arms around him, looking lovely in his white service cap, hoop earrings and a black leather mini that showed off her great legs. Well, we were masters of the future on that day, for damned sure. After a while it became too hard to look at the photograph. But there was no escaping his memories of her.

The other photographs. Decker and Gail at Coney Island, where they'd gone on his final leave before he was sent to Nam; Gail and Tawny backstage at a school play, Tawny in ballerina tights and minus her front teeth; Gail, Tawny and Karen in overcoats, earmuffs and boots on line at Radio City Music Hall; Gail and Decker in formal dress, on the dance floor with Ivan and Lucette LaPorte, the four of them mugging for the camera at Ivan and Lucette's wedding.

Lucette had been three months pregnant when she and Ivan married. To make her eligible for any military benefits Ivan had decided to marry her before going overseas rather than wait until he returned from Saigon. As he told Decker, I don't trust the future. With Lucette I know what I got, but if I wait too long I could lose it. Decker would remember those words long after LaPorte was dead and Decker had broken up with Gail.

He returned the photographs to the envelope, then dropped it on the pile of menus. Ellen was showing off her knowledge of art, pointing to a Monet landscape and telling Karen the history. Decker reached for his black coffee, not sure if he should go home and get some rest or stay here with Karen Drumman. They were definitely interested in each other. Why not go for it?

The waiter reappeared with his order pad. Ellen said she and Decker weren't eating. Karen said neither was she and quickly looked at Decker. The waiter, annoyed that he'd be getting a lousy tip from this table, practically snatched the menus from the table and stepped into the passageway leading to the back room.

Touching Decker's shoulder Karen pointed toward the back room. "Better catch our waiter. When he took the menus I think he also took the photographs," she said.

"Can't have that," Decker said. He stood up, thinking, this should be fun. Weasel Face had an attitude problem. Then again most queens had an attitude problem.

He left the table for the back room, feeling Karen Drumman's eyes on him. He'd make his move when he returned. With Bags watching it ought to be some show. Be that as it may, Decker would be dumb if he didn't try to get to know Karen Drumman.

The back room was a smaller replica of the larger one down to the checkered tablecloths, small blackboard listing today's specials, and the Charles Aznavour songs flowing from unseen speakers. Only one table was occupied. Across the room three men sat eating and talking quietly near a small wood-burning fireplace. Otherwise the back room was empty except for Weasel Face who stood just inside the doorway to Decker's right washing down pills with Diet Coke. Decker didn't know the number of calories in Diet Coke, but he knew it didn't contain booze, which is what he smelled coming from the can.

He was about to ask for the photographs when his attention was drawn to the three men. Two were Koreans, burly and flat-faced in dark suits, skinny black ties and crew cuts. The larger one was in his late twenties, with a bad complexion, and the sizeable neck and chest of a dedicated weightlifter. Hired muscle, Decker figured. Earns his pay by protecting his employer in a stern and frightful world.

The second Korean, who also looked inclined to take the hard line, was in his mid-thirties, with thick lips, a wide nose and horn-rimmed glasses. Decker thought, both these dudes look meaner than a bear with a sore ass.

Jean-Louis was the third man and the only one not eating. He was doing most of the talking, which Decker decided resembled pleading more than it did an exchange of ideas. Nervously fluttering his hands the Frenchman spoke rapidly, apparently anxious to get his point across. Decker thought, he's sucking up to the boys from the Far East who couldn't care less. Jean-Louis's campaign to win hearts and minds didn't seem to be panning out.

Suddenly Decker's heartbeat quickened and his mouth went dry. His legs felt weak. Dazed, he walked towards the Koreans. He knew the older dude, fucking knew him. And if the guy was who Decker thought he was, it raised a big problem, namely did Decker kill the son of a bitch now or later. A horrible memory, long asleep, stirred within the detective.

First to spot Decker was Jean-Louis who leaned forward and whispered to the Koreans, bringing a quick reaction from the one Decker had recognized. Fork in hand this Korean looked over his shoulder, spotted the detective, and recoiled as if he'd just spotted Freddy

Kruger. Leaping from his chair he stared wide-eyed at Decker, head moving side to side with short, jerky movements. Decker thought, you prick, it is you.

The younger Korean, *Muscles,* rose from the table more deliberately, moving with the arrogance of someone who was used to being feared and respected because he could break your face. Fingers clenched into sizable fists, he eyed the detective as though he were the most useless pus head on the planet. Red alert, Decker thought. Big Boy wants to earn his pay.

But the detective's primary interest, only interest, remained the Korean wearing hornrims, a man who was supposed to have died in Vietnam fourteen years ago. Decker hated him enough to kill him on the spot. The Korean in hornrims was Kim Shin, formerly a captain in South Korea's Tiger Division.

Fourteen years ago. National Police compound. LaPorte and Buf. Laughing Boy. And Shin. In the back of Decker's mind the grenade exploded again and he heard the screams.

An investigation into the National Police compound killings had been a joke. The CIA and the Defense Department didn't want another American media story about greedy allies and atrocities; they wanted a cover-up. They wanted to kill any news about Laughing Boy's sale of U.S. intelligence files to the NVA since it would only point to America's failure to protect its own people. To survive this shit storm the CIA needed a scapegoat.

Nor was the South Korean government anxious to see a valued intelligence agent like Park Song punished by a foreign power. The dead marines were America's affair and the missing files only meant Vietnamese would continue killing each other, a matter of no importance to the Koreans. The Koreans also noted that to gain support for the war on Communism, America had turned a blind eye to South Vietnamese drug-dealing. For the same reason let the U.S. now apply that same blind eye to Park Song and the plates. It was in the U.S. interest to forget about the plates since Congress and the media would be furious to learn about their existence.

Under such circumstances a mere marine corporal was expendable.

Manny Decker, fall guy. Somebody to take the weight for the missing plates and murdered Americans. He was in the computer room when everybody—Marines and Vietnamese—had died. The blind Miss Herail didn't count. Paul Jason Meeks got into the act, contending that Decker's injuries could have been the result of a double-cross by unknown associates. Park Song claimed Decker had lied about him in revenge for Song's having beaten him in a karate match. Decker was looking at twenty to life in Leavenworth.

Deliverance arrived in the form of Gerald Twentyman, a heavy-set, big-nosed Georgia country lawyer who'd help put a peanut farmer named Jimmy Carter in the state governor's mansion. Twentyman was Buf's father, a former Second World War Marine who'd been wounded on Saipan and whose slow-walking, slow-talking ways hid a steel-trap mind. He wanted to know the truth about his son's death and had been in politics long enough to know when the government was modifying facts to suit its convenience. This whole business, he told Decker, had all the smell of a dead skunk lying in the hot sun.

Twentyman would get to the bottom of this mess, starting with taking on Decker's legal defense. Over CIA objections Twentyman entered testimony from Private Jellicki, who swore he'd seen Song and some Korean soldiers rush out of the National Police compound carrying four suitcases. Next Twentyman had Georgia's senior U.S. senator promise that if the CIA wasn't more forthcoming there'd be a congressional investigation into the matter of the stolen files that had ended up in NVA hands.

Finally Twentyman tracked down Constanze Herail, locating her in a Hong Kong home for the blind. She'd lost her sight when the exploding grenade had propelled flying glass into her eyes. Her deposition linked Laughing Boy Park Song to the plates, the murders of the CIA agents and the Marines. Decker was exonerated, receiving an official apology and a belated letter of commendation from the Corps. As Twentyman said, "We cut them Washingtonians high, wide and deep. I think Maxey can rest a little easy now."

Decker walked away from the proceedings convinced that nothing was more dangerous than a government out to cover its ass. As for Kim Shin, he'd been reported killed by a Cong sniper on the last day of the war. Decker hadn't wept. His hatred for Shin and Song was going to last a lifetime.

Now, in the Bougival's back room, he stopped a few feet from the two Koreans, feeling his chest tighten. Fourteen years or no fourteen years, there was too much bad blood between him and Kim Shin for something not to happen. Happen right then and there. He sensed he'd just witnessed a little episode not meant for public viewing. Meaning he'd caught Kim Shin and Jean-Louis with their hands in the cookie jar.

Slowly, carefully Decker removed his shield from inside his jacket and held it up. He had a duty to try and lessen the tension, to keep the peace. How would Kim Shin react? "I'm a cop," he said. "Detective Sergeant Decker, Twentieth Precinct. Everybody stay calm. Let's not get excited."

Kim Shin glared at Jean-Louis. "A *policeman?*" he said. "You allowed a *policeman* here? You stupid fool. When I tell him what you've done he'll kill you."

A shaken Jean-Louis sprang from his chair. For a few seconds he stood and silently pleaded with Kim Shin, then he was hurrying toward Decker. Forget about savoir-faire and kissing ladies' hands, Decker thought, the man's scared shitless. Whether it was Kim Shin or a party of the second part, monsieur was scared of somebody. Then again, one had to wonder why Jean-Louis was hanging out with a dirtbag like Kim Shin in the first place.

Arms outstretched with the intention of pushing Decker backward, the little Frenchman said, "Leave at once. Go, go. You don't belong here. Return to the other room with your friends, I order you to leave."

Decker stiff-armed Jean-Louis in the chest, stopping him. The two made eye contact and held it until Jean-Louis nervously looked away. "Getting physical with cops isn't just wrong, *monsieur,*" Decker said, "it's loud wrong. If you don't want to be arrested for assaulting an officer I suggest you get the hell out of my face and sit your little ass down somewhere. Anywhere. Meanwhile, I'd like to talk to Mr. Shin, whom I haven't seen in a long time. I'm interested in how he managed to return from the dead. Maybe he's on some kind of diet I should know about."

Jean-Louis's response was to take two steps backward, circle right and run from the room. Kim Shin, eyes on Decker, whispered to the young Korean, who nodded but said nothing. After a few silent seconds Kim Shin shouted, "Why do you come here? Why do you follow me?"

Decker said, "Follow you? I didn't know you were alive until now."

"A lie," Shin said. "You follow me. You disobey orders."

Decker thought, am I really hearing this? What the hell was this pudgy little shit talking about? "Orders?" he said. "What *orders?*"

Cross-examination would have to wait. Kim Shin issued a command in Korean and Muscles moved confidently toward Decker. Up-close and personal, Muscles was truly ugly, with pig eyes and a face like a car bomb. He was some ten years younger than Decker, two inches taller and at least fifty pounds heavier, little of it fat. And as Decker knew, he would be good at his trade. A ready for prime time player.

Decker's skin began to tingle. He felt lightheaded.

Muscles elected to dispense with subtlety. He started with a side-kick, right knee to his chest as he loaded up for the most powerful kick in karate. Decker, alert and focused, had looked at Muscles's face and read his moves. The Korean had stared at his target, revealing his game plan. Warning Decker.

Muscles kicked sideways, driving his foot at Decker's rib cage. Had it landed the kick would have broken ribs and the fight would have been over. Decker sidestepped and evaded the attack. At the same time he grabbed a chair by the back, lifted it shoulder high and swung. He connected, clobbering Muscles on the left arm and hip, banging him hard enough to crack the chair. Muscles did not go down.

Decker didn't like that. Didn't like that at all.

The Korean stopped long enough to rub his elbow, then he punched the palm of one hand, a loud, ominous sound. His small eyes got smaller, a trickle of spittle emerged from the corner of his mouth. Then he shuffled toward Decker.

Still gripping the wreckage of the broken chair, Decker quickly backed up. When he had five feet of space between himself and Muscles he dropped the shattered chair on the floor, jammed a foot down on it and pulled at a chair leg. He'd barely freed it when Muscles, arms outstretched, threw himself on Decker.

Swinging the chair leg, Decker banged the Korean across both knees, this time getting more of a response. Muscles stopped, rocked back on both heels and looked down at his knees. Then standing on one leg, like a doggie at a hydrant, he lifted the other leg off the ground and shook it. A smile. He felt just fine. Hands up to protect his face, he shuffled forward.

Fighting panic, Decker swung at the Korean's wrists, putting his back and hips behind the blow, expecting to drop the dude this time. Wrong. With a quickness unexpected in a big man the Korean grabbed the chair leg in mid-air, yanked it from Decker's grasp, broke it over his knee and tossed the pieces aside. Decker thought, Christ. Jesus Christ.

The detective backed into a table, fought against losing his balance, and that's when Muscles hurled himself on Decker, sending them both crashing onto a wooden floor smelling of lemon-tinged wax. They landed hard, in a tangle of empty chairs and tables, unlit candles and salt-and-pepper shakers.

For Decker it was instant pain. He banged his left shoulder and hip. His head bumped into something hard. And he was on his back, a bad position to be in with Muscles on top: the man weighed a ton and was determined to put Decker away.

Refusing to panic, Decker jammed a thumb in Muscles's left eye and kicked at the Korean's shins. The Korean's head snapped back. He reached for Decker's hand, but before he could grab it Decker yanked the hand back, then drove the heel of his hand into the Korean's nose. Without hesitating, Decker gripped Muscles's left ear, twisted and yanked downward, nearly tearing it from the Korean's head.

Blood spurted over both men. Muscles did not cry out but he was hurt. Rolling clear of Decker, he flopped back on the floor beside the detective. Decker sat up first, in time to see Muscles reach inside his jacket for a gun. The Korean's hand was on his shoulder holster when Decker threw himself on top of him and twice punched him in the balls, short chopping blows so quick that Decker himself wasn't aware of what he'd done. Muscles's jaw dropped. Cupping himself, he writhed from side to side, bloodying cloth napkins on the floor around his head.

Decker stood, and when the Korean made one more, although weak, attempt to pull his gun, Decker kicked him in the head. Muscles fell back and lay still.

The hairs went up on the back of Decker's neck. It wasn't over. *Behind him.* He looked over his shoulder in time to see Kim Shin swing an unopened bottle of red wine at his head. Stepping into Shin, Decker blocked his arm inside on the elbow and pushed it down. Then he smashed a forearm into Shin's face.

As Shin staggered backward, Decker, feeling a hot red mist of anger, swung his right leg in a short circle and smashed his shin into Kim Shin's right thigh. Screaming, the Korean sat down on the floor, leg crippled by an attack so damaging that many fighters rated it as more devastating than a kick to the balls.

Face bloodied, a weeping Shin clutched his damaged leg and slumped to his side. Decker stepped closer, lifted his right leg and drove his heel into the Korean's stomach. He'd just kicked Kim Shin in the stomach a second time when three uniformed policemen, followed by Bags and Jean-Louis, rushed into the room.

It was Jean-Louis who shouted, "Arrest him! He's attacking a Korean diplomat! Arrest him!"

TWELVE

It was almost noon when Ben Dumas used his keys to enter Ken Yokoi's Greenwich Village townhouse. Behind him stood Oscar, who sniffed at Dumas's worn attaché case while wagging a short, nearly hairless tail. Among other items the case contained a box of mint-flavored dog biscuits, Oscar's preferred nosh.

Also in the attaché case were 300 milligrams of an experimental aerosol drug called pentamidine, a powder that when mixed with sterile water was used to prevent a life-threatening pneumonia that attacked AIDS patients. Dr. Paulo da Sé, the baggy-eyed seventy-year-old Brazilian who dispensed Ken Yokoi's unauthorized treatments, had recommended at least three doses a month, saying that without these treatments Yokoi would die immediately. Dumas purchased Yokoi's pentamidine on the black market, paying twice the list price of one hundred dollars per dose. Outpatient pentamidine therapy, which also included doctor and inhaler machine costs, ran into thousands of dollars. Money was Dumas's defense against being alone.

Before being stricken, Yokoi, a small, fortyish Japanese with a large, square head and sleepy eyes, had been a charismatic man whose vitality had swept away anything in his path. As a psychiatrist he'd conducted a private practice from his townhouse, where he'd grown prizewinning roses. He'd also found time to mold a slim,

173

muscular physique through body building, jogging and *kendo*, the traditional Japanese fencing.

They had been attracted to one another on sight, Dumas by Yokoi's intellect, Yokoi by Dumas's primitive strength. Both were gay, had a keen sense of order and needed constant excitement which they somehow always managed to find. When their anger was aroused, both could destroy someone and never feel a moment's guilt. What impressed Dumas most about the Japanese psychiatrist was his ability to control and direct others, something Dumas prided himself on doing well.

Yokoi's red brick townhouse was located on Washington Square South, only doors away from where Eugene O'Neill had lived. It faced Washington Square Park which guidebook writers continued to call the symbolic heart of the Village long after it had ceased to be true.

Nowadays the park was a hangout for drug dealers, college students from nearby NYU, the homeless, folk singers, break dancers, street magicians and EDPs, emotionally disturbed persons.

In the mahogany-paneled lobby of the townhouse Dumas removed his hat and topcoat, hanging them in a walk-in closet. Then for a few seconds he studied a splendid floral arrangement on a nearby rattan table. It was a seasonal arrangement, one popular throughout Asia. Known as Winter Promise it consisted of stark Manzanita branches, azaleas, carnations and leaves of thistle, the mixture representing a promise of spring. The arrangement was one of the best Dumas had ever done.

Traditional oriental flower arranging was his hobby. Ken Yokoi had suggested it as a means of relieving the stress involved with police work. Before meeting the psychiatrist Dumas had never thought of himself as having a talent for anything aesthetic. But with Yokoi's encouragement he'd demonstrated a gift for arranging fresh and silk flowers.

Still carrying the attaché case, Dumas walked through the living and dining areas that were linked by symmetrical arrangements of rattan and Regency chinoiserie furniture, oriental rugs and Thai tables. Each room also had floor-to-ceiling bookcases, a fireplace, bleached wooden floors and Japanese folding screens decorated with hand-painted scenes of the four seasons. Chinese Chippendale gilt-wood pier mirrors enhanced the beauty of both rooms.

In a large kitchen with overhead racks of brightly colored utensils, Dumas filled a saucepan with water, then opened a door leading to the backyard. Tongue against the back of his front teeth he whistled sharply. Oscar bounded past him, leaping through the doorway and into a small backyard whose space was almost entirely filled by a thriving greenhouse.

Outside, a chilly December wind stirred Dumas's thinning hair as he looked around for Oscar's feeding bowl, finding it on top of a coiled garden hose lying in front of the greenhouse entrance. After pouring the mint-flavored dog biscuits into the bowl he placed it and the saucepan of water beside the garden hose. Eat up, Big O., he said to Oscar.

While the three-legged dog devoured his lunch Dumas squatted beside him and stared at the greenhouse. Early in their relationship Yokoi had said to Dumas, "You are more than most men—more intelligent, more truthful, more destructive. By extension you must also be more creative. You're unhappy enough to be creative."

Unhappy? Definitely, Dumas thought. Years of dealing with mutts, skells and maggots made all cops unhappy. But he wasn't creative. He was a cop, thorough and efficient, coldly self-reliant and stubborn. Sure he had a few smarts; he read the New York *Times*, occasionally attended the opera and was a member of the Metropolitan Museum of Art. He also collected travel books, a hobby he'd developed during four years in the navy, which he'd joined at fifteen after lying about his age. But as he told Yokoi, this didn't mean he was Leonardo da Vinci.

On the other hand he enjoyed puttering around Yokoi's small greenhouse. The fragrance and beauty of the plants was a new and gratifying world, far removed from the shabby Bronx apartment he'd shared with a widowed father and an uncle, both of whom had sexually abused him until he'd run away from home at the age of fourteen.

The greenhouse, Yokoi decided, touched something too deep in Dumas for him to talk about, something buried beneath the wall Dumas had erected as a defense against society's contempt for cops and gays.

"You've accepted your tactile side," Yokoi said. "Now accept the other Dumas, the one who has something beautiful within him."

"Assuming there is another me," Dumas said, "I'd weaken myself if I gave in to it. I'd lose the edge I need to survive on the streets."

Yokoi took his hand. "From the moment we admit to being gay we live with an emptiness inside. We're not wretched people and we're not ugly. But society does its best to make us feel worthless if not entirely unessential in the overall scheme of things. We pretend we don't feel this disapproval. The truth is, we do. That's why it's so important for you to accept your total self. Don't go through life like a bird with only one wing. Total self-approval, Ben. That's what you need. That's what we all need."

Encouraged by him, Dumas revealed an interest in classical music, Asian culture, and of course flower arranging. He'd even begun dressing better. His quick mind allowed him to understand these new ideas and concepts at once. But it was the love shared by him and Yokoi which made this learning process both exciting and pleasurable. Dumas came to rely on the Japanese psychiatrist as he did no one else.

As for Yokoi, he was captivated by the big cop's sensuality and unpredictability. No lover had ever given him as much excitement and pleasure as the man he called "my noble savage."

Because of an enormous sexual appetite Dumas had rarely remained faithful to one lover for any length of time. The three-year affair with the intriguing and cultured Ken Yokoi represented a milestone in the big cop's life. It had produced a spiritual as well as physical sharing. Not only was Dumas faithful to Yokoi but he never lost his temper with the Japanese psychiatrist. After a lifetime of searching he'd found someone in whom he had complete trust.

They'd met the night Dumas killed India Sabogal, the bigchested thirty-two-year-old Puerto Rican wife of his partner Det. Luis Sabogal. India had been hard-talking, giving Luis, a gloomy-looking, thirty-seven-year-old Rican, some sleepless nights. She'd had enough of his fooling around with other women and wanted a divorce.

To make matters worse she'd threatened to go to Internal Affairs and tell all unless he came up with big bucks as part of the final settlement. This declaration was not to be taken lightly. India Sabogal knew enough to send Luis and Dumas upstate until they were old men and the liver spots were showing through their gloves.

She knew they'd robbed drug dealers of drugs and cash, shaken down Manhattan after-hours clubs, provided information on search warrants and supplied guns, walkie-talkies and police shields to Dominican and black drug gangs. She knew that gay prostitutes had provided Dumas with sexual services in exchange for drugs and money taken from the police evidence locker; that Dumas and Luis Sabogal had drowned a drug dealer in his bathtub then walked off with a suitcase containing fifty-five thousand dollars and two kilos of cocaine.

Luis Sabogal said to Dumas, "The bitch wants two hundred fifty thousand cash, tax free, or she gives me up."

"*Us.* She gives *us* up," Dumas said.

"I haven't got that kind of bread and if I did I wouldn't give it to her. Woman's got to go. Soon as possible she has got to go. But I can't do her. She's my wife. Anybody else, I got the balls. But I can't do India."

Dumas said, "And I guess that means me, amigo. I'm just thrilled to be a part of it all. Yes sir, I am really thrilled."

"Look, it ain't all my fault," Sabogal said. "I swear on my mother's grave, I didn't tell her everything. Okay, some things I told her. I mean she's my wife. The rest she picked up herself. India's no retard."

"Let's talk about when and where it goes down. I want to know if India jogs, if she goes to church, if she ever visits her relatives. I want to know if she does drugs. I want it all, *partner.*"

Halfway through Sabogal's rundown on his wife, which included the fact that she was a cokehead, Dumas held up one hand in a stop signal. "The ball," he said. "That's where it happens. That's where you get your instant divorce, sport."

"You shitting me? You're saying you plan to walk up to my wife and smoke her when she's surrounded by thirty, forty citizens. And when she knows what you look like. Christ, get real. I been to a couple of these balls and I know for a fact they draw hundreds of people."

"Doing her like that sort of adds to the excitement, doesn't it?"

Sabogal rolled his eyes up into his head, thinking, sure as shit he's gonna do it. Five years partners with this wacko and I should know him by now. He's gonna do it. Thank God I won't be there when this one goes down.

In three days India Sabogal and her brother Danny would attend the House of Grandeur Ball, part of New York's drag scene, which held little appeal for the butch Dumas. These balls were combination fashion show/beauty pageants put on by black drag queens who'd been organizing them in their communities since the 1920s.

Using a dance style called *voguing,* after the magazine, competitors showed off fashions designed and made by themselves. Harlem dancers had invented *voguing* as a parody of the white fashion world that had barred them for years. The House of Grandeur Ball would be held on Halloween. Perfect, Dumas thought. Perfect.

Drag queens competed in these balls as a *house,* a unit. In this subculture, with its own rules, language and culture, India's brother Danny was a superstar drag queen who performed under the name Miss Fleurette. He was a popular singer-dancer at gay clubs, and while they'd never met, Dumas knew him by reputation. India Sabogal was devoted to her brother, serving as his manager, chauffeur and protector. She also designed clothes for him and the "House of Grandeur."

"From now on India's my problem," Dumas said. "You just make sure that on Halloween you're surrounded by a lot of people, say from ten that evening until one next morning. Now tell me about the ball, especially about backstage or wherever the queens get dressed."

"You might need an invitation. India keeps some around the apartment for family and friends. Whenever her precious Danny's performing she likes a full house. Dude's a highstrung little prick who's always hitting us up for money."

Dumas shook his head. "No invitation. When I show up it won't be at the front door."

Halloween. At 11:22 on a mild fall night Ben Dumas entered the First Avenue Projects on the Lower East Side, site of the House of Grandeur Ball.

Populated by Latins, Chinese and blacks, the First Avenue Projects was a public-housing development located in a rundown neighborhood of abandoned tenements, vacant lots, shattered windows and graffiti-covered walls. Residents also included a few elderly Jews, survivors of pogroms in Russia and eastern Europe, who were now too poor to leave the area. Vandalism and the ravages of time had given the surrounding streets a desolate, menacing feeling.

Dumas wore a black wig, sunglasses and a scruffy army overcoat purchased at an Eighth Avenue pawnshop. He had pasted Band-Aids across the bridge of his nose and stuffed cotton in his mouth between the gum and top lip. Draped over his right forearm was an evening dress made of hand-dyed silk. In his waistband was a .22 Magnum with the serial number filed off and a silencer attached to the barrel. To prevent the gun from slipping down into his pants Dumas had wrapped three oversized rubber bands around the grip.

Clipping India Sabogal with people around would be tricky, but Dumas wouldn't have it any other way. The more pressure, the more pleasure. Putting himself at risk was a process of self-renewal.

On the project grounds Dumas followed a group of people in brightly colored Mohawk haircuts, leather facemasks, chains, spikes, rubber dresses and Velcro hightop sneakers. In front of him a chubby Oriental man in a sarong and pearls smoked a joint. To Dumas's left a bearded white male in a hoopskirt held hands with a gaunt black male in miniskirt and bustier. Dumas thought, either I'm heading toward the ball or I'm marching in some freak-and-geek parade.

He looked up at the sky. A full moon. Still the project grounds remained poorly lit. Vandals and junkies had destroyed or stolen most of the outside lighting, including street lights, bulbs and a few hundred feet of electrical wiring. Down here they'd saw a cat in half and sell both parts. Dumas welcomed the semidarkness. It made him that much harder to recognize.

He didn't need lights to know that his size thirteens were crushing empty crack vials by the dozen. Nor did he need to see the faces of local residents and drug addicts who lounged on broken benches and hurled insults. However, he could see black and Latin youths yelling obscenities from surrounding apartment windows. One of them threw a D-battery, a lemon-sized chunk of metal that barely missed two bony women dressed in matching white tuxedos and studded dog collars.

Holding hands, the women quickened their pace. The rest of the group, Dumas included, hastily followed. He wasn't scared. But a sure way of calling attention to himself was to show more balls than his fellow fun-seekers.

On reaching the west wing of the projects the crowd stopped at the entrance to a basement auditorium. Guarding the door was a thirtyish Latin butch queen in camouflage fatigues, backed by a Rottweiler chained to the doorknob. Pinned to the dog's studded collar was a button that said, *AIDS is like a balloon—one prick and you're gone.*

Leaving the crowd, Dumas walked to the rear of the auditorium, past addicts and homeless men crouched at the building's barred, broken windows. The ball didn't start until midnight, so what were these dirtbags staring at? Then from the auditorium came sounds of *salsa*, cheers and applause. The junkies and their pals were enriching their lives by watching a dance contest, a warm-up prior to the main event.

The queens take this stuff seriously, Luis had said to Dumas. The House of Grandeur, composed entirely of Latins, was to compete against other Latin and black houses for cash prizes and trophies. Danny de la Vega, India's brother, was expected to cop first prize in the top categories of best face and best female impersonator, the drag equivalent of two Oscars. Celebrity judges included a famed Italian fashion designer, a celebrated Japanese fashion photographer and two transvestites who sang with a downtown rock group called the Booty Sisters.

Behind the auditorium Dumas watched three Latin drag queens walk down a small staircase and disappear into the building. Smoking joints, the trio hummed "Tara's Theme." He looked around. Nobody close by, nobody looking at him. Removing the .22 from under his overcoat he concealed it under the silk dress he'd draped over his right forearm. Let's do it, he whispered. He felt unruffled, untroubled. His smile was natural and unprompted.

He walked down the short iron staircase leading into the auditorium. Guarding the doorway was a black bodybuilder in a flat top and wearing a Trump Plaza sweatshirt, green stretch shorts and white cowboy boots. With him was a skinny Dominican butch queen with dyed orange hair and a nose ring. A folded straight razor hung from her neck on a thin gold chain.

Past them, Dumas could see a low-ceilinged passageway with people rushing back and forth. Tonight the *voguing* contestants were using the area and its offices, supply, laundry and boiler rooms as changing rooms. It would be total chaos back there, Luis had told Dumas. Confusion up the ass. But that's where you'll find India.

Dumas, extending the dress toward the bodybuilder, said, "For Danny de la Vega." Under the dress the .22 was aimed at the man's navel. A reflex action, nothing more. If Dumas couldn't get in he had no intention of icing the man. He'd simply leave and take out India some other time.

As the Dominican lustfully viewed the dress, the bodybuilder, displaying his cool by wearing mirrored sunglasses, jerked his head toward the uproar inside, a signal for Dumas to enter. The big cop stepped into the passageway.

Confusion up the ass was right. Dumas found the passageway like the subway at rush hour. The tunnellike area was crammed with people. Some leaned against graffiti-splattered walls and drank cheap wine from styrofoam cups. Others pampered themselves with unregistered chemicals. Dumas could have made enough drug busts in this hallway to fill the police property room twice over.

He saw friends calming down nervous drag queens who were suffering from precontest jitters. Men and women carrying gowns and women's shoes squeezed past drag queens who were posing for photographers. Dumas stepped on something that appeared to be a small dog but which turned out to be a long black wig. Two queens, makeup and mascara running, held each other and cried. Against his inclination Dumas found the commotion around him exciting.

What he didn't like were the smells—the urine odor found in projects all over the city, compounded by the body odor of contestants and spectators. He also didn't like the heat, the result of too many people jammed in a small space. The sooner he dropped the hammer on India Sabogal, the sooner he could quit this loony bin and take off the overcoat. The wig, which had started to itch, was also a problem. As for the ghetto blasters, forget it. Anyone who liked that noise should have his ears nailed to the floor.

According to a makeshift directory taped to the door, the changing area for House of Grandeur was to the right, in the laundry room. Dumas began walking in that direction, free arm on the dress to keep anyone from grabbing it and heading south. Down here they'd steal the teeth out of your mouth, then come back for the gums.

As expected, the laundry room was crowded, people spilling through the doorway and out into the passageway. Inside, drag queens were having clothes fitted to the beat of the *salsa* coming from two ghetto blasters. It took Dumas a couple of minutes to get from the hallway and inside, where he stood near the entrance and looked around for India Sabogal.

She was twenty feet away, in front of a broom closet she was using as a clothes locker. Tonight India wore a hot pink jumpsuit, black satin pumps and a false chignon. Dumas watched her finger a sleeveless blue silk dress being fitted on the prettiest drag queen he had ever seen. Had to be Danny boy, and what a luscious little morsel he was.

At least two people in the laundry room could identify Dumas, one being India Sabogal, the other a hunk who worked as a bartender at a Jane Street gay bar. He had been one of Dumas's lovers, an association that had ended six months ago when a jealous Dumas had broken both of the kid's arms.

India Sabogal's back was to Dumas now as he pushed through the crowd toward her. He had almost reached India when she threw up both hands in frustration and walked away. One of her two Latin assistants pointed to Danny's hemline, apparently a problem. Danny, meanwhile, was in his own world. Stretching one arm overhead he examined an imitation diamond bracelet worn over a long blue evening glove. He was still admiring his junk jewelry when India stepped into the nearby broom closet in search of something. Time to punch big sister's ticket.

Dumas pressed forward. Four more steps brought him to the broom closet, where India Sabogal now knelt with her back to the room. He watched as she impatiently rummaged through a suitcase filled with scraps of dress material. From cursing in Spanish she suddenly switched to cursing in English.

Dumas looked around. Nobody watching. Time to get down.

Keeping the silenced .22 under the dress, he pressed it against the back of India's false chignon and fired twice. She fell forward, landing on the suitcase, her chunky body half in, half out of the closet. One bejeweled hand knocked over a pair of green leather high-heeled shoes.

Dropping the dress on India's corpse, Dumas shoved the gun under his overcoat and suit jacket and into his waistband. Just one more drug-related killing in Fun City. India had been a cokehead, remember?

He made his way through the crowd, not hurrying and feeling more relaxed than he had all day. *A clean hit with a roomful of people looking on and he was going to get away with it.* Outside on the project grounds he ducked into the first empty apartment lobby he saw and took off the overcoat. After making sure the pockets were empty, he removed the wig, cotton balls and dark glasses, putting them in a jacket pocket. He unscrewed the silencer from the .22, placing it and the gun in another jacket pocket. Later he would break the gun down, then dump pieces and silencer into a sewer.

Whistling "Tara's Theme," he left the projects. A block away on Second Avenue he placed the overcoat on top of an overflowing trash basket. In five minutes the coat would be the property of some junkie or booze hound. Call it a slight atonement for having blown away India Sabogal.

Meanwhile, Dumas was hungry. He began walking downtown toward East Houston Street and a Chinese place that had some of the best *moo goo gai pan* in Manhattan. It wasn't smart to wander around here at night, but Dumas was in a mood to walk. Did he fear getting mugged? Anyone who wanted to try was free to step up and take his best shot. Other than an occasional panhandler or junkies out looking for victims, the area was deserted.

Tonight, as Dumas headed toward East Houston, he wondered if he ought to charge Luis for having clipped India. Hadn't been for Luis and his big mouth they wouldn't have had any trouble with the woman. Why shouldn't Luis compensate his partner for services rendered? Dumas was still kicking around the idea when he saw it.

Trouble. Which was the last thing Dumas needed while trying to leave the site of a homicide in which he figured rather prominently.

The big cop stepped to his left and stood still, merging with shadows cast by empty store fronts. Eyes narrowed, he stared straight ahead. At the end of the block four males, young Latins, stepped from a battered blue Ford parked half on the sidewalk, half on the street. Standing shoulder to shoulder they waited for two men and a woman crossing the street and heading in their direction.

Dumas thought, what the hell do I do now? The Latins were going to fiend these three citizens, no doubt about it. One spic gripped a length of chain; another had a knife or a screwdriver, Dumas wasn't sure which. A third bore a machete on his shoulder as though it were a rifle.

Oblivious to any danger, the well-dressed citizens remained deep in conversation, strolling along with no more concern than backpackers had on a nature hike. One was a short Caucasian male with a full head of gray hair and a matching gray suit which Dumas guessed cost a small fortune. Beside him was a tall, blonde woman in a tweed skirt, blue blazer and boots. The third potential vic, who was doing most of the talking, was a small Asian male with expressive hands and horn-rimmed glasses. Dumas thought, three chumps begging to be ripped off.

The trio proceeded along a trash-ladened sidewalk, past shops which lay filthy and uninhabited behind rusted steel gates; past a filthy, half-naked black man lying at the base of a corner street light. Uptown folks out slumming, Dumas thought. Maybe down here to catch an experimental play or attend a gallery opening or dine at some "in" restaurant located off the beaten path.

Like Dumas maybe they'd read *Bonfire of the Vanities* and now wanted to see for themselves how New York's underclass lived. He could only shake his head at the arrogance which had brought these turkeys down here this time of night.

His first reaction was to back off, to let the robbery go down. If these respectable, upstanding folks got hurt, so what.

Let Dumas start playing cop and he'd have to explain to his superiors exactly why he'd been in this area at this particular point in time. *Detective, would you mind telling us how you just happened to be on the Lower East Side the night your partner's wife was having her brains blown out at a drag ball?*

Let these schmucks get taken off. Next time they'd think twice before strolling around a shithole like this after dark. If they lived, that is.

But even as he debated his next move Dumas found himself tiptoeing down the block, closing in on the taco benders who'd backed the vics to the corner street light. Situations like this brought back bad memories, all tied in with abuse he'd suffered as a kid. Each time he trashed some asshole he was really getting even with his father and uncle. That's why he'd become a cop. That's why he'd never stopped hating those two old men in the Bronx who'd made his life hell.

Dumas kept to his left, staying near the buildings and in the shadows, stepping over empty whisky bottles and beer cans and trying not to tread on syringes discarded by junkies. When he was almost on the Latins he pulled his Smith & Wesson from its belt holster and shifted it to his left hand.

Then reaching into a back pocket he took out a blackjack, a carrot-shaped piece of black leather and black masking tape with a lead center. A guaranteed bruisemaker, bone-breaker and life-taker. Slipping his hand through an end strap, he tightened the strap around his wrist. The *red buzz,* that wild anger forever in his heart, had made him almost feverish.

Killing India Sabogal had been fun. He hadn't felt the slightest animosity towards the woman. She'd had to go, he'd done it, and that was that. But this little exercise with the four Latins, now that was different. Call it personal. Watching the taco benders swoop down on citizens was a reminder that Dumas had once been a victim. That's why backing off was unthinkable. If Dumas could be said to fear anything it was his memories.

Hands behind his back, he stepped into the light of the street lamp. Spit trickled from a corner of his mouth. His cold eyes never blinked. The *red buzz* had pushed him into a brief madness. The rage in him knew only the will to destroy.

Like any wolf pack, the one Dumas now prepared to confront didn't just want money; it also wanted to exercise power. The tall, blonde woman was the target of a chunky, dark-skinned Dominican who used the tip of his machete to toy with a string of pearls hanging from her neck. Rigid with fear she attempted to maintain her composure. Speaking in an English accent, she forced herself to display a calm she didn't feel. "Take what you want," she said, "but please don't harm us."

The chunky Dominican brushed her breasts with the back of his hand. As she flinched he said, "Maybe I want something else. Maybe I take you up on the roof. We get some wine, some dope. We party all night long. I be good to you. Real good."

Eyes closed, the terrified woman shook her head.

As two Dominicans began a search of the male vics a fourth mugger, a tall pockmarked teenager with one end of a bicycle chain wrapped around his fist, sensed someone behind him. He turned and Dumas clubbed him in the collarbone with the blackjack, dropping the teenager screaming to the pavement.

A slender, dark-skinned teen who'd been examining the contents of a victim's wallet never got the chance to turn around. Striking from the rear, Dumas whacked him in the right elbow. The kid shrieked, threw the wallet up in the air and clutched his shattered arm. Seconds later he staggered forward, tripped on the curb and fell to his knees in the gutter.

The kid with the machete was caught by surprise. After a quick look at his prostrate associates he eyed Dumas for a second or two before saying, "You fucking crazy or what. I kill your ass, man. I kill your ass." Blade resting on his shoulder, he took two steps towards the big cop.

But he stopped dead in his tracks when Dumas's left arm came up and pointed the Smith & Wesson at his face. The Latin turned into a chubby, breathing statue. But his nostrils flared and he tightened his grip on the machete.

"Want to drop that?" Dumas said softly.

Eyes hot with hate, the Dominican hesitated. Dumas waited, gun hand steady. Finally, the Dominican opened his hand and the machete dropped to the sidewalk. Dumas quickly swung the Smith & Wesson around to cover the fourth mugger, a bug-eyed little crackhead with rotten teeth. Nothing to worry about here, because this one had no *cajones*. Positioned between the two male victims, he hadn't moved to join the combat. Either he'd been scared or he'd had a great deal of faith in machete man's know-how.

As the *red buzz* subsided, Dumas spoke quietly. "Turn around and assume the position," he said to the doper, who complied, facing the streetlight, legs spread, hands touching the gray metal post.

The machete man, however, was still hanging tough. "I smell shit," he said, "must be a cop round here some place." He spat, narrowly missing Dumas's left shoe. "Had my heat with me, you'd have gone down. For sure, your cop ass would have gone down."

A smiling Dumas said, "There's a time and place for attitude, chico." He kicked the machete man in the balls, returned the Smith & Wesson to its holster, then almost as an afterthought slugged the man in the forehead with the blackjack, knocking him to the ground, unconscious.

Dumas looked at the victims, thinking, All right, let's hear it. Police brutality, violation of civil rights, racism toward ethnic minorities. Surprise. Not a word from the trio. Not a single expression of indignation at such unkind treatment of "our Latin brothers."

The blonde woman, in fact, nodded her head in approval. The Asian, a Japanese, eyed Dumas with intense interest. There was something sexual about it. Talk about a far-out bunch.

He patted down the doper, who had a sharpened screwdriver tucked in his belt. Dumas also found a plastic wallet containing a one-dollar bill, two subway tokens, change and a single condom. And he turned up three vials of crack, which he crushed under his heel, making the perp a bit misty-eyed.

Now the hard part. How to keep this little skirmish from tying him to the killing of India Sabogal.

The small Japanese, who had a big head and sleepy eyes, stepped forward to assume the role of spokesman. Taking Dumas's right hand in both of his, he said, "You saved our lives. I can't tell you how grateful we are." His hands were extremely soft and he never took his gaze from Dumas's face.

The Englishwoman, not as young as she had appeared from a distance, said, "If you hadn't come along I dread to think what might have happened. I'm Rowena Weymouth. Dear God, I'm still trembling. You were magnificent. Absolutely magnificent."

Dumas lit a cigarette, anything to hide his annoyance with this crew whose stupidity now threatened his survival. However, he did enjoy listening to Rowena what's-her-name speak. She had a beautiful English accent, very upper class, something he heard only on television or in the movies. If she'd said I'm third cousin to the queen of England, Dumas would have believed her.

Of the three, the little man with gray hair and suit to match remained the most frightened. Mopping sweat from his brow with a red silk handkerchief, he whispered to himself in French as though not convinced it was over. Dumas didn't like the man's smile. It was too wide. Wide smiles belonged to frightened people and frightened people were weak people and not to be trusted.

Hand extended, the man said, "Jean-Louis Nicolay. Thank you, thank you, thank you. So grateful, *monsieur*, so very grateful."

"You people don't belong down here," Dumas said. "You were only asking to be ripped off."

The Frenchman's wide nervous smile grew even broader. "Ah, *monsieur*, we were to go to the First Avenue Projects for a costume show. *Oui*, a costume show. We had dinner at a restaurant a few blocks away. I am thinking of buying it. I am in the restaurant business, you see. Afterwards I thought we could walk to the show, it's not so far away. I thought it would be safe to walk such a short distance."

Dumas said, "You thought wrong." Why couldn't these three clowns just go away and let him get on with his life?

He was pondering his next move when he noticed something odd.

They were eyeing each other like people with something to hide. He'd been a cop long enough to know when he was being stonewalled. These three had suddenly developed chronic speech impediments. What were they covering up?

The sleepy-eyed Japanese stared at Dumas, who'd finally figured him out. The dude was gay and watching Dumas kick ass had definitely turned him on. "Am I correct in assuming you're a policeman?" he said.

Dumas thought, time to play Let's-Make-A-Deal. He'd smelled it coming when the trio stared at each other and had that short wordless conversation. For some reason these citizens didn't want cops prowling around their lives.

Dumas smiled. "I'm a police officer, yes. You people want to press charges against this group?" Yeah, right.

Again the trio eyed each other. Silent signals flew back and forth. It was all Dumas could do to keep from laughing out loud. Eventually the Japanese said, "There's no need to carry this any further. None of us was injured, thanks to you, officer. Speaking for everyone, we'd rather not press charges."

Dumas dropped his cigarette to the pavement and stepped on it. "Whatever you say."

The Japanese pointed to the Dominicans. "What about them?"

Dumas smiled. "Looks to me as if they're lost in thought. I think we ought to leave them alone."

Throwing back her head, the Englishwoman let loose with a rousing laugh. "Marvelous. Bloody marvelous. I like this man."

Eyeing the machete lying near her feet she said, "Could we get out of here? At the moment I haven't the slightest interest in some bloody drag show. The last thing I want to see is some man swishing about in granny's undies. What I could use is a stiff gin and tonic."

Smiling, she took Dumas's arm. "And you, sir knight or Clint Eastwood or *whoever* you are, you shall join me."

The Frenchman looked at the Japanese, ready to follow his lead.

"Perhaps we should forego the show," the Japanese said. Reaching out he touched Dumas's bicep. "Please forgive me for not introducing myself," he said. "I'm Ken Yokoi. Dr. Ken Yokoi."

*　*　*

DECEMBER/WASHINGTON SQUARE. Dumas entered the master bedroom of Ken Yokoi's townhouse in time to see a plump forty-year-old Jamaican nurse with two gold front teeth hook Yokoi up to an intravenous solution. A highly concentrated food formula, the solution nourished AIDS patients who were unable to eat.

Bedridden and bald from chemotherapy, a scrawny Ken Yokoi lived connected to oxygen and assorted life-giving tubes. Because he was now powerless and weak he permitted only Dumas to see him. As a psychiatrist he'd controlled everything in his life and that of his patients. AIDS, however, was something he couldn't control.

When the nurse had left them alone Dumas kissed Yokoi's forehead then stroked his cheek. "Can I get you anything, babe?" he said.

Slowly shaking his head, Yokoi spoke in a hoarse whisper. "Where's Oscar?"

"In the backyard with his mint-flavored dog biscuits. I think he's the world's first three-legged gourmet."

"Rowena?"

Dumas took Yokoi's hand. "She arrives from London tomorrow evening. I'm picking her up at Kennedy then we're driving straight to Astoria, right to the house. Auction starts the minute she gets there. Checked out the slaves last night. They're as ready as they'll ever be. As usual I've got extra security on the house until this thing is over."

"And our friend Park Song?"

"Laughing Boy comes in tomorrow. Or the day after. You know him. He thinks he's tricky. Gives you an arrival time then switches at the last minute to keep you off-balance. He'll show up, though. He's hot for that little blonde kid we're holding for him. And he has to sell enough funny money to come up with Colonel Youngsam's thirty million dollars. Rowena has my final report on the buyers Song's planning to meet here. He should have it by now. Not having heard anything, I assume all's well and he's on his way."

Yokoi took a deep breath then said, "He is one very strange man. Doesn't want women around for any longer than it takes to screw them and kill them."

"You sound like a feminist."

"And you're hung like an amoeba."

Holding hands, they laughed. After a few seconds of silence Yokoi asked about the customers who were planning to attend Rowena Dartigue's sex auction the following night.

Dumas shook his head. "It's amazing how worked up they are for this thing. Spoke to two of them last night. They can't wait. One's Osteros, the Colombian banker who's got this thing about teenage redheads with small tits. Also spoke to that Swedish airline pilot, the one you think looks like Kirk Douglas in *The Vikings*. He's still into twelve-year-old black boys."

Dumas chuckled. "Takes all kinds, I suppose. Speaking of which, Rowena tells me our friend Laughing Boy can't wait to get his grubby paws on Tawny DaSilva."

Yokoi concentrated. Finally he said, "Tawny. Tawny. Is she one of my patients? So hard to remember. So hard."

A depressed Dumas kissed Yokoi's hand, thinking, nothing prepared you for watching someone you love die of AIDS. Not religion, not years of being a cop, not any philosophy you thought you believed in. Nothing prepared you for this. The suffering dragged you down, made you think, and in the end there was no limit on the pain. Yours and his. It had been years since Dumas felt this inept, this inadequate.

Ken had days when his mind was as sharp as it ever was. Other days it was painfully obvious that AIDS was getting to his brain. Actually it wasn't strange that Ken thought he'd treated Tawny Da-Silva. It was Ken who, from among his more unstable and attractive patients, selected many of the sexual slaves marketed by Rowena Dartigue, apart from those Rowena chose herself from the Lesley Foundation.

Occasionally Jean-Louis Nicolay found a prospect from among individuals encountered through his East Side restaurant or the Manhattan swing clubs and orgies he attended. But it was Ken who worked on the prospects' minds, convincing them to admit they were inherent submissives, sexual animals born to obey their masters.

Rowena Dartigue paid for the therapy, the upkeep and the house in Astoria, Queens, where they were confined until auctioned. Other than that rare London sale to a trusted customer, the auctions were held outside of England. As Rowena said to Dumas, "I believe you Americans have a saying: one doesn't shit where one eats."

She also provided customers from around the world via the money-laundering she conducted through the Lesley Foundation. As

Ken told Dumas, Rowena Dartigue's talent was to exploit your needs whatever they happened to be.

Through his detective agency Dumas ran a check on the candidates to insure they didn't have relatives or friends who might make trouble. His agency also provided security for the Queens house. But in Dumas's opinion neither he nor Rowena was as important to the operation as Ken.

Every so often the tightfisted Rowena bitched about having to pay Ken big bucks. But she was forced to admit that without the esteemed Dr. Yokoi they would each be eating cheaper cuts of meat.

Until a month ago, when his respiratory problems had suddenly worsened, Ken had treated submissives from his bed, hiding his deteriorating appearance behind a black satin robe, gloves and a black leather face mask.

In the bedroom Dumas leaned close to Ken and said, "Tawny's not a patient, babe. She's the kid Nicolay put me on to, the one who used to come into the restaurant with her mother."

Yokoi closed his eyes. "I remember now. You brought her to see me. Lovely child. She should make Park Song happy even if he isn't into long relationships."

Dumas agreed. Tawny DaSilva was going to die, and die ugly, and all because Nicolay had bought the downtown restaurant he'd been scouting the night Dumas had saved his tush from the beaners. To buy the property Nicolay had borrowed a hundred and fifty thousand dollars from Yokoi at a straight ten-percent interest, a good deal as interest rates went. But because the Frenchman couldn't hold onto his chef the restaurant had folded within three months of opening. Nicolay then proceeded to ignore his debt to Yokoi, no surprise to Dumas. At Yokoi's request, unfortunately coming after the loan had been made, Dumas ran the frog through the computer.

The cop learned that Nicolay, something of a sex freak, had operated restaurants in Nice, Tangiers and Saigon. He'd also occupied himself with such sidelines as gun running, pimping and counterfeiting. Luck, political connections and the timely disappearance of witnesses had so far kept Nicolay out of the joint.

He'd been the one who'd brought Rowena and Ken together. Nicolay and Ken had met at a Manhattan sex club. The Frenchman had met Rowena Dartigue by washing money through her Lesley

Foundation. To such a man, welshing on a debt was no worse than picking your nose.

After contracting AIDS Ken's need for money became critical. Dumas did all he could financially, then demanded that Nicolay pay what he owed. The Frenchman responded by handing over fifty thousand dollars, then pleading poverty. He was rebuilding the kitchen in his East 64th Street restaurant, he said. He also had tax troubles and the unions were making his life miserable. All he needed was a little time and he'd produce the rest.

Dumas suspected Nicolay was deliberately stalling, anticipating that Ken's death would cancel the debt. The Frenchman was a calculating little prick who'd lost his shirt more than once because he tried to do too much and never knew when to quit. He also had few qualms about taking advantage of others' bad luck. It was Dumas who freed him from the misconception that he wouldn't have to reimburse Ken Yokoi.

The week before Thanksgiving the big cop made an unannounced appearance at the Frenchman's apartment on Central Park South and delivered what he termed *the final notice.* At the close of their dialogue a sobbing Nicolay, looking down at the blade of the Swiss Army knife pressed against his balls, vowed to repay the balance of his loan within the week.

Which was why the next day, a Sunday, he invited Dumas to Bougival restaurant, seating him three tables away from a lovely adolescent girl having brunch with her mother and a slim, red-haired woman. Pointing to the girl, Nicolay said, "Her name's Tawny DaSilva. I think she can make us both rich. Ring Rowena and see what she says." The Frenchman's hands shook so badly he had trouble lighting a cigarette. Dumas looked at her for several seconds, then returned to his quiche lorraine.

Twenty minutes later, in a trans-Atlantic telephone call from the restaurant office, Dumas described Tawny to Rowena Dartigue. "Well *done,*" she said. The AIDS scare had increased the demand among certain prudent adults for youthful sex partners, minors considered less likely to have the dreaded illness.

Dumas then said to Rowena, I want a bigger payoff this time. His fee for checking out the girl's background and a bonus at the end of the upcoming auction wouldn't be enough. Not with Ken's treatments costing as much as they did. It was possible that Miss Tawny could bring as much as a quarter of a million dollars.

Dumas demanded half, nonnegotiable. Since Rowena had little choice, she agreed. She hated parting with money, but as a sensible businesswoman she knew with whom she was dealing. In Dumas she was dealing with a man whose love was mad and knew no limits. Better a fiscal adjustment on little Miss Tawny than arouse Ben Dumas's enmity for refusing to help Ken Yokoi.

In his bedroom Ken Yokoi looked from his intravenous food solution to Dumas. "This auction's the first I'll miss since getting together with Rowena. I'm counting on you to bring me up to date on the gossip. What's wrong? You're looking ultra butch, which means you're brooding. What about?"

"Decker," Dumas said. "The man's getting closer and I don't like it. He's following Tawny's trail and she's leading him to my doorstep. I thought icing her parents would keep him away from me and Russell Fort. Then last night he goes to Jean-Louis's restaurant to meet this lady friend of Tawny's mother and he spots Kim Shin and Jean-Louis having a heart-to-heart in the back room. Decker and Shin's bodyguard go at it. Decker not only kicks the guy's ass, he gives Shin a tune-up as well. Since Shin's got a diplomatic passport, this brings the matter to the attention of the police department, the Korean mission and the U.S. government."

"Then what's the problem?"

"The problem is Russell Fort gets Park Song's paper, which he passes to me and Jean-Louis. We pass it to Kim Shin at the Republic of Korea mission here and he gets it to Song. Now suppose Decker starts wondering why Jean-Louis and Shin are so buddy-buddy. Suppose he somehow links Jean-Louis to me. That shit at the restaurant last night wouldn't have happened if Decker hadn't been tracking little Miss Tawny, as Rowena calls her."

"Fort still in Washington?" Yokoi said.

"Should be on his way back with the extra paper Song asked for. Kim Shin was bitching that we weren't coming up with the paper fast enough. I figure Colonel Youngsam's holding Park Song's feet to the fire and Song's passing it on. Jean-Louis was trying to calm down Kim Shin when Decker showed up. I might have been there if I hadn't had to go to Astoria and get things ready for Rowena."

Dumas held up two fingers. "My second problem with Decker.

Couple days ago he visits DEA and picks up the profile sheets turned in by those two undercover cops who got whacked by drug dealers. I got fifty thousand per for fingering them. No regrets, babe. We needed the money and that's that. Anyway, I'm wondering how close Decker is to learning that Fort's lady, Susan Scudder, gave up those two undercover guys."

Yokoi smiled. "This Decker, he's a summer cold. You just can't get rid of him."

"I know all about Decker. He'll keep coming at you and he'll be so smooth about it that if he told you to go to hell, you'd actually look forward to the trip. What happens when he learns that Jean-Louis knew Kim Shin and Laughing Boy in Saigon? What happens if he leans on Jean-Louis and the frog gives me up? By the way, Saigon's also where Decker had a run-in with Shin and Park Song."

Ken Yokoi slowly lifted a forefinger. "Did you or any of those psychopaths who work for you run Decker through your trusty computer?"

Dumas nodded. "Better believe it. The man's squeaky clean. Or maybe I should say he's yet to be caught dirty. Very into the martial arts. Supposed to be good at it. One thing: a few years back he quit the cops and went to work for a private security firm. Then after a couple guys at the company got themselves smoked in mysterious fashion Decker resigns and he's back on the cops."

Closing his eyes in thought Yokoi said, "And what does this tell you?"

"There was some talk about revenge, about how Decker had gone to work for the company just so he could get those two guys. He was never accused of anything. To this day nobody knows who did those suckers."

"You think Decker murdered them?"

"He has his moods."

A smiling Yokoi opened his eyes. "Don't make me laugh. It shakes the tubing loose." He put a finger to his lips in a request for silence. He was thinking. Dumas waited.

Finally, Yokoi said, "Don't kill Decker. Not yet. Not until I tell you to."

"Whatever you say."

Yokoi held up a forefinger. "Everyone has a hostage to fate. Children, wife, loved ones of some kind. That's where we hit Decker. In his support system. Find out who he's attached to and you've found his weakness. That's how we take him out of the game without risking a direct confrontation."

"Might piss him off. Make him harder to deal with."

"And it could take the legs right out from under him. Look how paralyzed America gets over its citizens being held hostage by a bunch of ragheads. Think of a mother's fear when her child is late coming home from school. This thing could go either way. I think it's worth the risk."

"I understand."

"Force him to defend himself on different fronts," Yokoi said. "If you become too reckless and go after him directly, you risk getting destroyed. I know you don't mind getting destroyed, but, for my sake, please consider this only as a last resort. Position yourself so that you can surprise him. Your helping Colombians to kill cops is one thing. Killing Decker is another, unless, of course, it becomes a matter of life and death. Then do what you must. Meanwhile, I want you to outthink Decker, not just react to his agenda."

"You're calling the shots, babe."

"Decker's got trouble. He beat up a Korean diplomat, remember? That's bound to bring a negative reaction from two governments, ours and theirs. For Sergeant Decker, I'd say this means new problems. Problems involving finesse, tact, subtlety."

Yokoi coughed twice and went silent. Dumas looked toward the door and the nurse. Yokoi said, "No, it's okay, okay. Playing these little games keeps me alive. About Decker, his most glaring weakness appears to be his sense of guilt. Based on your phone taps of the DaSilvas, I'd say he feels guilty for not marrying Tawny's mother. That's why he wants to find Tawny and whoever killed her parents."

Dumas said, "Had to do it, babe. I had a man on the taps and when I relieved him I listened in and heard them tell Decker about some black guy who'd been following the husband. They'd have identified Fort and that son of a bitch would have identified me."

"I'm not blaming you, hon. You did the right thing. Don't doubt it for a moment. Right now, let's talk about Decker. Guilt. That's what's driving him. Let him live, at least for now. But remember what I said about his support system. Be prepared to use it against him. Maybe give him a chance to feel some more guilt. Play with the man's head."

Dumas nodded. "You told me when to quit the force. When to open my own agency with rogue cops. Great idea. I've got eight pros working for me who'll climb all over anybody's peace of mind if I tell them to. You made the discotheque happen, you got me together with the people who sold me the Bank Street bar and you brought me into Rowena's setup. Wasn't for you I wouldn't have a pot to piss in."

Dumas looked at Yokoi. "I have to know, babe. Russell Fort, Jean-Louis. Which one can hurt me the most?"

"Fort. Like you say, there's a chance Decker's already onto his girlfriend. If so, that's where you could start hemorrhaging."

"And Jean-Louis?"

"How do you put it? He knows the drill. Jean-Louis's been arrested before, so he should be able to handle that end pretty well. All he has to do is keep quiet, let a lawyer do the talking, then post bail and skip the country. He also knows what you and Song can do to him. If that doesn't keep him quiet, nothing will. Still, you never know about these things."

He paused to catch his breath, then, "Fort and Susan Scudder. My suggestion is you plug these leaks before it's too late. By now Miss Scudder knows you used her to kill two undercover cops. And she knows that Decker is hot on the trail of whoever did the killings. I know you've put the fear of God into Mr. Fort, but should Miss Scudder turn out to have scruples or fear for her own safety, you can assume she will refuse to betray any more policemen."

Yokoi paused again for breath. "Mr. Fort's gambling will always be a major weakness. No gambler knows when to quit. As you've already noted, Mr. Fort's pathetic attempt to extort funds from the DaSilvas has brought Decker within smelling distance of you and Tawny. You can threaten Fort until the rivers run dry, but because of his gambling habit you will never be able to trust him. Or his little friend. Fort and Miss Scudder can bring you down."

Dumas sighed. "If I didn't need Fort to supply me with Laughing Boy's paper I'd seriously consider sending his ass to that big watermelon patch in the sky."

"What's wrong with making your own arrangements with his source? Eliminate the middle man, as they say."

"Now why didn't I think of that." Dumas was about to say more when he saw Ken's sunken eyes go to the door. Dumas didn't bother turning around. The Jamaican nurse was efficient. She had given Dumas twenty minutes. After that she would return to resume her work and he had better not get in her way.

"Back in a little while. Going to look in on Tawny," Dumas said quietly.

"You know how to handle her?"

"I've had the best teacher."

Five minutes later Dumas, carrying his worn attaché case, stepped from a small private elevator and into the warm basement of Ken Yokoi's townhouse. After switching on the light he checked the door to a small wine cellar, turning the handle and examining the lock that he had installed himself.

The wine cellar had not been tampered with. A final pull on the door handle, then Dumas checked the boiler thermostat. Which reminded him: he'd have to make arrangements for the December oil delivery to the townhouse. Ken was dying of AIDS. No need for him to freeze to death as well.

Dumas resumed walking, heading toward the far end of the basement and a light over a green metal door. He had just passed a washing machine and several metal file cabinets containing the records of Yokoi's past patients when the metal door slowly opened.

A stocky, baby-faced Korean cradling a Uzi stepped through the doorway. He wore a Mickey Mouse sweatshirt, shoulder-length black hair and gray trousers held up with a belt and suspenders.

As Dumas reached the doorway the Korean silently stepped aside and Dumas entered a small concrete room lit by a fluorescent lamp, containing a cot, metal folding chair and a card table. He frowned at the aroma of garlic and cigarette smoke. On the floor were copies of Korean newspapers, girlie magazines, empty pizza cartons and empty McDonald's bags. A small black-and-white television set was tuned to John Wayne's *Sands of Iwo Jima*.

Stepping to the rear of the room, Dumas rested one hand on a second metal door and peered through a glass panel. Then he looked at the Korean. "Everything okay?"

Smiling, the Korean nodded. "Everything okay."

"You touch her, you're dead. If Park Song doesn't kill you, I will."

"Everything okay."

"You'd better hope so, amigo."

Removing a key from a hook to the right of the door, Dumas unlocked the door and entered a second concrete room, closing the door behind him. Slightly bigger than the first room, this one also had the same overhead fluorescent light, cot, blankets, card table, folding chairs. Unlike the other room it had a private toilet. A closed-circuit camera looked down from one corner of the ceiling. Under the camera Tawny DaSilva lay on the cot facing the wall.

Hearing the door open she looked over her shoulder, face almost hidden by her long blonde hair. She was dressed in the same long-sleeved, cream-colored blouse, blue pin-striped skirt and white boots she was wearing when Dumas kidnapped her five days earlier. After a few seconds she sat up, combed the hair from her face with her fingers and looked at him with red-rimmed eyes. He was impressed by her eye contact. The kid had to be scared, but she still managed to hold his gaze. Give her points for guts.

"I want to go home," she said. Which was what she had said the last time Dumas had looked in on her. She spoke quietly but firmly. She was making a huge effort to stay calm, to avoid coming apart. Dumas had to admire that. A lot of men would have come apart under such circumstances. The kid was special.

Dumas sat on a folding chair and opened his attaché case, keeping its cover between him and the girl. He switched on a microcassette recorder he had taken from the DaSilva apartment the night he'd killed Tawny's parents. He lit a cigarette, inhaled deeply, then blew smoke at the closed-circuit camera. After a few seconds of silence he pointed to the food on the card table. "You don't like cheeseburgers and French fries? I thought every kid went for that. You have to eat something, you really do."

Later Dumas would play this tape for Ken, who would also look at the closed-circuit films and make his recommendations to Park Song. These recommendations would be the first steps used by the Korean in forming the girl into his perfect lover. In the next few minutes anything she said or did, her slightest reaction or response, would speak volumes to Ken. Park Song considered Ken's opinion on the training of his girls to be invaluable.

Tawny said to Dumas, "Why are you keeping me here? Why can't I see my mother? You're not a policeman. You say you are but you're not."

The kid had smarts too. He'd flashed his old police shield to stop her in the street. He'd also used it to get inside her parents' apartment the night he'd smoked them.

Using her sleeve, Tawny wiped tears from her eyes. "I don't want to stay here anymore, I want to go *home*."

Sensing someone behind him, Dumas looked over his shoulder. Well, well. Baby Face had got tired of watching John Wayne win the war in the Pacific and had quietly opened the door to see what was happening. Munching a Devil Dog, he stood in the doorway, taking in the show. Dumas stared at him until the Korean stepped back into the small room and closed the door. If Baby Face was bored with the Duke, let him change channels.

The Korean was one of Shin's people, either someone from the Republic of Korea mission or a local muscle with whom Shin had a working relationship. Dumas didn't know and didn't care. His own men were tied up working agency cases or guarding the auction house. Song had reached out for his old pal Kim Shin, ostensibly a deputy consul with the Korean mission but actually a member of the KCIA. As Dumas had told Ken, this proved you could get good service in New York, providing you were willing to spend thirty million dollars.

Ken's basement, used to put up submissives temporarily, was a good place to hide Tawny. Hiding her made more sense then confining her in the Astoria house, where steady customers might be upset to learn they couldn't bid on her.

Ken had also allowed Laughing Boy the use of the townhouse for any deals involving his funny money. If he so chose, the Korean could now conclude his counterfeiting and slave activities in one spot. He'd earned the privilege of convenience by agreeing to pay a quarter of a million for Tawny.

Dumas said, "Tell you what, Tawny. Why don't we call your mother and see what she has to say about all this. You're here because of her, you know."

Tawny wiped her eyes again. "I don't understand."

"She's given us legal custody of you. Total legal custody."

Fist clenched at her side Tawny got up from the bed. "You're a liar. I know you're lying."

Dumas thought, five days in this rathole and she's still fighting back. Kid, you're something. "Tawny, it's true, she just doesn't want you anymore. I'm sorry, but that's the way it is."

"She'd *never* do that. Mom would never do that. You're a dirty liar." Defiant. And attached to her mother. Laughing Boy's going to have his hands full with this one. Turning her out isn't gonna be easy.

Reaching into his attaché case Dumas removed a cellular phone, extended the antenna and punched several numbers. Then he brought the phone to his ear and listened. As a recorded female voice began to recite the tri-state weather report for the rest of the day he said, "Yes, Mrs. DaSilva? Ben Dumas. I'm fine and you? Good. Mrs. DaSilva, I have Tawny here with me and I just wanted to confirm our deal. Yes, I told her but she doesn't believe me."

As he spoke into the phone Dumas watched the girl. Her eyes never left his face. Messy hair, puffy eyes and still beautiful. And strong, too. She was an inch from breaking down but she held on. Held herself together and refused to look away from him. It was Dumas who almost blinked.

"Yes, that was our deal," he said into the phone. "You've been paid and we now have legal custody of Tawny. Like you told me, this is something you had to do and—"

"*Mom*. I want to speak to her. Let me speak to my mother." Not afraid to stand up to adults. Watch this one, Laughing Boy.

Tawny ran at Dumas, who quickly said, "Thank you, Mrs. DaSilva. We'll talk later." He switched off the phone and pushed in the antenna.

Screaming and weeping, Tawny clawed at him and attempted to grab the phone from his hand. "I don't believe you, I don't believe you."

A smiling Dumas easily fended her off, thinking, everything went down just the way Ken said it would. Then again, was Ken ever wrong? *How would they manage without him when he was gone?*

Stepping back from Dumas, Tawny returned to the cot and sat weeping. Head bowed, she cried aloud. As her body shook with her sobs Dumas closed his attaché case and stood up. He felt no sympathy for the kid. Didn't hate her, didn't love her. Ken mattered, she didn't. Ken was more important than a thousand Tawneys.

Dumas started towards the door. When he turned for a final look at Tawny, he found she'd stopped sobbing and sat with a shocking calm. This time Dumas blinked. Was this kid a freak or what? She sat up straight, maybe the way her mother had taught her to do, and used her fingertips to wipe tears from her eyes. Then she placed her folded hands in her lap and quietly said, "You didn't talk to her. I know you didn't."

THIRTEEN

It was 1:58 A.M. when Michael Dartigue, Eddie Walkerdine and two hired thugs began robbing the Shepherd Market Deposit Center.

The center was a plain, windowless room, thirty by thirty feet, with a low ceiling, closed-circuit TV monitors and metal walls lined with safe-deposit boxes. Protecting the boxes was a steel vault door two feet thick and seven feet in diameter, equipped with a primary combination lock, time lock and locking bolts. A local alarm connected the door to Fedor SecuriCom which protected the depository.

From a tiny foyer a lone night guard manned a panel of buttons controlling alarms for the front door, vault, floor and ceiling. The center's owner was Ravi Sunny, a roly-poly thirty-six-year-old Indian born in Calcutta, where he had worked as a butcher before immigrating to England with a thirteen-year-old wife at age twenty-five. In 1980 he had sent his wife back to her family in Delhi and begun buying slum property in London, which he quickly resold at a profit. Fond of London nightlife he regularly made the rounds of trendy clubs, restaurants and casinos, most recently in the company of a black stripper named Helen Bedd. The deposit center was his sole piece of real estate in a secure area.

Located in fashionable Mayfair, Shepherd Market was a small, exclusive square of little white houses, antique shops, pubs and boutiques. The deposit center occupied the ground floor of an eighteenth-century house whose remaining floors had been rented out to an advertising agency, a silver/goldsmith and a folk-art gallery. Flanking the home were a Rolls-Royce showroom and a real estate agency.

An edgy Michael had entered the deposit center first, nose burning from cocaine he'd snorted to give him the balls to go through with the robbery. Front door and vault alarms weren't used during the day when the center had its heaviest traffic. Nighttime was a different story. That was when guards checked all photo ID's before admitting anyone inside.

A lone customer, Walkerdine said, wouldn't arouse the night guard's suspicion. On the other hand four wicked-looking faces at the front door was another story. It was Michael's job to make sure *everyone* got inside.

He had disguised himself in a dark blue raincoat, brown leather cap and false red beard. He wore sunglasses, deerskin gloves and carried a small suitcase. His hair had been cut short and dyed red. And he had shown a phony ID to Joseph Lexy, a horse-faced forty-year-old Irishman who was the night guard.

The ID featured Michael's doctored appearance, left thumb print and the three-digit number of a fictitious account. Bernard Muir had supplied the ID card, improved upon by Walkerdine who had added such details as the alias William Henry Pratt, the real name of Walkerdine's favorite actor, Boris Karloff.

Michael had shoved the ID through a slot in the depository's eight-inch-thick oak front door and into Lexy's nicotine-stained fingers. Seconds later Lexy switched off the front alarm and Michael was inside. To spare Lexy the trouble of searching depository files and finding no matching ID, Michael pulled a .38 Smith & Wesson from a raincoat pocket and pressed it against the Irishman's spine.

This time it was Michael who cut off the alarm, admitting Walkerdine and the two others into the foyer. All three wore ski masks, dark trousers, black turtleneck sweaters and surgical gloves. One, a short barrel-chested man with turned-in toes, carried a small suitcase in each hand. The other, a big thick-necked man, carried one large suitcase.

The barrel-chested man was Patrick Markey, a thirty-two-year-old West Indian and ex-con whose crimes included arson, computer fraud and horse theft, the last at a Paris racetrack where he'd been a stable boy. Under his ski mask Markey's face was missing most of a left ear, courtesy of a razor-wielding sweetheart who'd caught him in bed with her sixty-two-year-old mother.

As Markey set his suitcases down, the other man, an oversized twenty-eight-year-old cockney named Harry Zwillman, joined Michael in wrestling the terrified Joseph Lexy to the floor. Zwillman, a convicted car thief, burglar and strong-arm debt collector, then placed a knee on Lexy's neck, pinning the guard face down. With a jerk of his head Zwillman motioned Michael away.

Michael backed up three feet to stand in front of a battered green file cabinet. Here he removed his topcoat to reveal a security guard's uniform. As he laid the topcoat on top of the file cabinet he found himself wishing he had more blow. The coke had speeded up his heartbeat and given him a dry throat. On the upside he was psyched, ready to go hog wild and hit the ceiling. He'd felt this way before. Same high energy level he'd experienced during the last quarter of a game, team down by one, seconds to go and him bringing the ball up the floor, knowing nobody could stop him from going to the hole for two and the game.

Michael had expected to be afraid tonight and he was, just enough to keep him on his toes. His main feeling was excitement at being in on the robbery. It was easy to see how people got hooked on stealing. You didn't do it just for the money. You also did it for the kicks.

Heart pounding, Michael watched Walkerdine go to work on the guard. Taking a cigarette lighter from his back pocket, the little Englishman thumbed it into flame. Markey, meanwhile, opened a suitcase and removed a quart-sized orange juice carton. He poured half of the contents on the neck, back and thighs of a weeping, squirming Lexy. The smell of gasoline filled the tiny foyer.

Walkerdine said, "You're dead if you don't answer my questions. First, where's the junction box?"

The junction box was the point at which telephone lines and perimeter lines were connected. Walkerdine knew the answer; he'd already gotten it from Bernard Muir. But to protect Muir, that information had to be forced from the night guard, thereby removing suspicion from the Grand Duchess, Walkerdine's name for Muir.

A terrified Lexy struggled to get out the words, his speech blocked by this latest reminder of the way his life had taken one nasty turn after another. No problems with the night shift, the Fedor people had said. Bloody liars. Twenty-four-hour access to the boxes was necessary, but there were nights when no one showed up for hours. Most guards favored day hours, preferring to spend evenings with their families.

That's why the night shift paid a bit more.

Lexy had no family, not these days, so he became a bat. The night hid his sorrows—two broken marriages, stillborn children, automobile accidents, failed alcohol rehabilitation. At night he could dream of what might have been had heroin not gotten in the way of his architectural studies at Dublin's Trinity College.

Now from the floor of the foyer he looked up at fire in the hand of a madman crouched over him. Staring into the flame, Lexy found his voice. "Downstairs," he said. "The junction box is downstairs. But you first have to get into the vault."

Walkerdine said, "Right. Now, I need three more things from you. I want you to cut off the vault alarm and open the door to the deposit boxes. Then I want you to cut off the floor and ceiling alarms. Finally I want you to tell me tonight's code."

"Code?"

Walkerdine grabbed Lexy's collar and held the cigarette lighter to the guard's nose. "You fuckfaced twerp. Go feebleminded with me and I'll roast you. Every security company telephones its night guards two or three times to see if anything's wrong. When the call comes in you either say everything's fine or you give a prearranged answer that says you've got trouble. For the last time, what is your bloody code?"

"When they ring me someone will ask, 'Is the new wage to your liking?' If there's difficulty I'm to reply, 'Time and a half won't do. I want more.' The fellow at the other end then says, 'Why don't we let the union decide.' That's it, there's no more, I swear."

Walkerdine stood up. "On your feet, sunshine. You'd better be right about the code."

A shaken Lexy rose and turned off the alarms, allowing Walkerdine, Markey and Zwillman to enter the vault. Michael, posing as the night guard, remained in the foyer. Should depositors appear, he was to show them into the vault. There they would have their hands cuffed, eyes and mouths covered with duct tape. Now cuffed and taped was the gasoline-soaked Joseph Lexy, who lay on the floor just inside the vault's entrance. His hands had been cuffed in front to allow him to use the telephone when his nightly call came in.

With Lexy unable to see their faces, Walkerdine, Markey and Zwillman took off their ski masks. Walkerdine and Markey reached into their suitcases, removed hammers, chisels and small crowbars. From the large suitcase Zwillman pulled out three empty duffel bags. Walkerdine said, "Merry Christmas, lads. Let's carve the turkey, shall we?"

Michael had demanded to be allowed to break into his wife's safe-deposit box. In his steady pursuit of ready cash, he had gone through Rowena's handbags, jewelry boxes and private papers more than once. He had come across her deposit center ID hidden in the closet and filed the information away for a rainy day. In mental matters she'd always sold him short. Well, he was about to outsmart the bitch.

Rowena's account number was 212. Walkerdine trailing him, Michael found the box. Top row, far wall, among the larger boxes. Nothing small for Rowena.

Michael could open Rowena's safe-deposit box, Walkerdine said, but he couldn't take anything. Just dump the contents into the duffel bag held by Walkerdine, who with Markey and Zwillman looked on as Michael went to work on the box with a crowbar. It was nearly five minutes before Michael pried the box open.

Holy shit. *Money.* American hundreds and fifties. An awed Walkerdine whispered, bloody Christ almighty. Markey and Zwillman slapped each other on the back in congratulations. Michael was speechless. What the hell was going on here? *Where did Rowena get this much money?* She'd never mentioned it to him, that's for sure. Well, she could kiss it all goodbye. Turning to Walkerdine, Michael shoved a clenched fist in the air. "All *right!*"

Walkerdine took his arm, glanced at the prone Joseph Lexy, then whispered to Michael, "Good work, sunshine, but let's keep our voices down, shall we? Now, while I hold the bag do you think you could transfer all that lovely cash from the lady's account to ours?"

Using both hands Michael proceeded to scoop Rowena's money from the safe-deposit box and drop it into Walkerdine's bag. How much cash was there? Had to be *millions.* She'd also salted away some fantastic-looking jewelry that had to be worth a bundle. Michael chuckled. How could stealing be wrong when you could walk away with this much?

Halfway through removing the money Michael came across two black looseleaf notebooks. Walkerdine said, "No, no, sunshine. No reading material for us. You keep them as a souvenir. Just concentrate on the cash. Wonderful woman you married. By the look on your face you knew nothing about this."

"Man, if I had known this much money was in here I'd have paid this place a visit long ago."

"Gotten us off to a fine start, she has. How can you not love a woman like that?"

Markey and Zwillman, meanwhile, went to work tearing at the boxes in hopes of uncovering a similar bonanza. Feeling generous, a beaming Walkerdine allowed Michael to take a pair of Rowena's fancy earrings for Nigella. One pair shouldn't hurt anyone. Earrings and notebooks to start with. The real payoff would come later, when the haul had been laundered and made untraceable.

Back in the foyer a turned-on Michael took up his position as night guard, still wondering how Rowena came to have so *much* bread. Was she dealing drugs or what? Some of the money, but not all, had probably come from Rosebud. According to Walkerdine, who was good at figures, Rowena's stash amounted to between ten and twelve million. Maybe more. You didn't make that kind of money selling handbags and leather belts out of one small store. And how about all the expensive jewelry? Rowena hadn't picked that up at Woolworth's. Michael snapped his fingers. He knew where she'd got the money. She was stealing from that charity of hers. She was ripping off underprivileged kids. In that case, fuck her.

From the foyer Michael looked into the vault, where Walkerdine and the others were prying safe-deposit boxes from the walls before dumping the contents into the duffel bags. The three worked quickly and quietly. Cash, jewelry, coin collections, bonds, securities went into the bags. Everything else was tossed aside, including pornographic photos, wigs, personal papers, keys, false teeth, baby shoes, urns containing ashes of loved ones, lacy underwear. Drugs were also left behind. "A small kindness on our part," Walkerdine said. "When the owners see what's happened here they'll need something to soothe their nerves."

In a plan worked out between Michael and Joe LoCasio, the

Brooklyn-based Mafia capo was to fence the goods. Sometime this morning all three duffel bags would be sent to New York via air freight for a late-night arrival at Kennedy Airport. They would be addressed to a Queens motel, care of a LoCasio underboss registered there under a false name. By arriving late, the bags would be left in the air-freight terminal overnight to await morning inspection by customs agents, who usually ignored night cargo until the next day. During the night, members of the LoCasio family would walk into the warehouse and walk out with the bags. Simultaneously the cargo manifest would be changed to show that no such duffel bags had ever arrived.

Immediately after the robbery Michael would leave for New York, where Nigella was waiting for him in a Manhattan hotel. Walkerdine was to follow on a later plane, meet Michael and together they'd settle up with the LoCasios. After Michael received his share of the clean money he and Nigella were heading for Miami, where the first thing he intended to do was file for divorce. The best part of his marriage to Rowena was the thought of leaving her.

He had thirty thousand dollars from the sale of the Mercedes given him by Rowena which he'd sold to a Kenyan architect he'd met at Walkerdine's club. Otherwise Michael was leaving England with only one suitcase and the knowledge that for the first time since Miami U. he was a winner.

Coincidentally enough, Rowena was leaving for New York tomorrow on business. Good luck to her. Michael didn't expect to run into his wife in New York, but if he did, fuck it. Far as he was concerned their marriage was history.

In the foyer Michael kicked around the idea of running off with the duffel bag containing Rowena's millions, the one now lying at Walkerdine's feet. Nice idea but don't dwell on it. For sure, Walkerdine and his boys would come looking for him. Then there was the LoCasio family. With dagos, a deal was a deal. Break your word to them and you'd be lucky if all they did was shove a wrecking ball up your ass.

Michael also had to think about Andres and Nigella, the two people he loved most in this world. For their sakes he couldn't mess up this deal. He'd promised Andres his freedom and Nigella a new life, one that included her own beauty shop in Miami. Money was the only way he could have them with him in the future. Money would set them all free. Above all it would free him from Rowena.

Meeting Nigella at the Belgravia Casino, where she worked, had pushed him into dumping Rowena. Nigella was a magnetic force, drawing Michael to her with a warmth and calm completely absent in Rowena. Theirs had been an instantaneous hunger for each other, one filled with sex, genuine affection and a real interest in each other's problems.

In addition to everything else, Nigella, Michael felt, had been protective without suffocating him. There was a bond between them that had been missing with other women in his life. Like him, she'd put her faith in the wrong people and suffered for it. She had been too sexually obliging, making for complications she herself didn't always understand.

During the three hours they spent clearing out the boxes no customers showed up. Credit an icy rain with helping to keep people away. Only one security call came in; remembering Walkerdine's cigarette lighter, Lexy said the right things.

In the foyer Michael passed the time chain-smoking and fantasizing about how he intended to spend his share. Rowena's notebooks were forgotten. At the moment Michael was too psyched to read anything. He'd check out Rowena's notebooks on the plane.

He stared through a bullet-proof glass panel in the front door at rain-soaked Shepherd Market. The rain should stop soon. At least he hoped so. Otherwise there could be trouble taking off from Heathrow. He walked over to the vault. Walkerdine, Zwillman and Markey were stuffing the bags until Michael thought they were going to burst.

He watched a perspiring Walkerdine stop, light up a thin cigar and blow smoke toward the ceiling. Then the Englishman walked over to Michael. "We're packing it in. Be dawn soon. Might as well use the rain and darkness to hide our pretty faces. Come inside and change your clothes. You're leaving for the airport."

Clenched fists held overhead, Michael exhaled for a long time. "We did it. Goddamn, we did it."

Walkerdine touched Michael's arm. "I'd say so. We're bloody tired, the lot of us. Leaving a dozen or so boxes untouched, but such is life. I prefer we leave while God still seems to be on our side."

"That's right, that's right. So, I guess I'll see you in about twelve hours or so."

"My regards to Nigella." Walkerdine handed him a hundred-dollar bill. "You two have some champagne on me. Don't worry, my boy. This particular bill happens to be me own hard-earned money. You lovebirds deserve a bit of bubbly. Michael, I thank you for everything. This whole thing wouldn't have been possible without you."

Michael frowned. "Without me and Bernie Muir, you mean."

Taking Michael's hands in his, Walkerdine said softly, "You were fantastic. Held up your end. Did all I asked of you. Didn't fall apart. You're a bit of all right, Michael Dartigue. Now it's off with you. Mustn't keep our New York friends waiting. Have a safe trip and do give Nigella a kiss for me, would you?"

NEW YORK/6:10 P.M.

Michael leaned against the door of Nigella's Central Park West hotel room, shivering, and held her tightly. He had just arrived from Kennedy and still wore his raincoat and leather cap. They'd kissed, but not passionately. His mind had been miles away.

His bloodshot eyes now had a vacant, near-haunted look that went right through her. He'd whispered her name, saying, "Hold me, hold me." She did, put her head against his chest and waited for him to tell her what was wrong.

In a tired voice he said, "The robbery went okay. The bags are on the way here like we planned. It's just that something, something happened." He raised his arms so that she could see what he was holding in his hands.

"Rowena's notebooks," he said. "From her safe-deposit box. I read these things on the flight coming over here, and I have to tell you, I'm scared. I mean I am really scared. Rowena is into some very heavy shit."

A concerned Nigella looked at him. "Tell me."

"She's involved with people I don't ever want to deal with. People way out of my league. People who'd kill me if they knew I had these notebooks."

"My God."

"Rowena's laundering money for them. *Big* money. She's washing it through that kiddie foundation she's got. Her customers come from Europe, America, Asia. Something else. She's *selling* kids to some of these people. Fucking selling children for sex slaves to anyone who'll buy."

"You must be joking."

He clutched the notebooks. "It's all in here. Names, prices, the kind of kids these sick bastards prefer. The charity's a scam. Rowena uses it to launder money and dig up kids for sale. This woman doesn't deserve to live. See for yourself. Here, take a look at this shit."

Minutes later an upset Nigella handed the notebooks back to him. "What do we do now?"

"Don't know. I just know I have to get as far away from that woman as I can. I don't ever want to see her face again. Know why she's coming to New York today? She's coming to hold a fucking *auction*, to sell kids. Some Jap shrink and a private eye named Ben Dumas run the thing with her. Jesus, it's all here in black and white."

Nigella took his hand and led him to one of two twin beds near a window overlooking Central Park twenty floors below. "Get some rest, love. Sleep, then we'll talk about what to do next."

"LoCasio's people are supposed to call and let me know the bags are in the warehouse. I have to set up a meeting with them. Walkerdine's gonna call, too. I'm not even hungry. Reading those notebooks killed my appetite."

Nigella took off his cap. "Fine. Forget food but get some rest. I'll wake you when LoCasio's man calls."

"Wake me when Walkerdine calls, too."

"Does he know about the notebooks?"

Michael shook his head. "No. If he did I don't think he'd have let me take them. The guy's a hustler, he'd have tried to use them to his own advantage, I'm sure of it. Thing is, you don't mess with these people. Man, I'm telling you, you don't."

Nigella said, "Out of those clothes and lie down. I'll wake you when the phone rings."

Three hours later Michael woke up to find Nigella sitting across the room, watching television with the sound turned low. Still groggy with jet lag, he yawned and blinked several times before he could focus enough to see what she was watching. It was CNN, the cable news network.

"No calls?"

She shook her head. "No calls. The robbery made the telly, though."

"What did they say?"

"You're a rich man. According to Scotland Yard you gentlemen got away with more than forty million dollars."

Michael pressed the heels of his hands to his temples. "Jesus Christ. You're kidding. *Forty million?* Is that great or what."

He was reaching for his cigarettes on the night table when the telephone rang. One second into the first ring and he seized the receiver, jamming it against his ear, squeezing it with both hands. His heart started flip-flopping.

"You Michael Dartigue?" Male voice. A hardass Brooklyn greaseball who's probably been told he looked like Al Pacino and sounded like Robert de Niro.

"I'm Michael Dartigue. Who's this?"

"Fuck's wrong with you, you crazy or what? You know who you dealing with?"

"Zip it, asshole. I don't have time for this. Get off my line."

"You got time for me, cocksucker. I'm with LoCasio. Want to tell me what kinda game you running?"

"I don't understand."

"Well, understand *this*, assface. No bags. They didn't come in. We checked the flight, we checked the air-freight office, we checked the cargo manifest. We even got in touch with somebody at Heathrow Airport. Them bags were never on the fucking plane. They never left England."

Closing his eyes Michael said, "No, no. Can't be. It can't be."

"I tell you what can't be. You can't dick us around and get away with it, that's what can't be. We had a deal, hotshot, and you didn't hold up your end. Instead of getting a piece of forty million we got shit. I think maybe we should all get together and have a chat."

FOURTEEN

At 10:35 on the morning following the fight with Kim Shin and his bodyguard, Decker was sitting on a dark green leather sofa in Yale Singular's downtown Manhattan office. He sat with a cup of black coffee in one hand, a folded copy of the New York *Times* in the other, and watched as the Treasury agent was chewed out by someone at the other end of the phone. Singular was catching hell because Manfred F. Decker, a newly appointed U.S. deputy marshal assigned to him, had trashed a diplomat attached to the South Korean embassy.

At one point a red-faced Singular glared across his desk at Decker, who smiled and lifted his cup in a toast before sipping from it. Decker assumed Singular didn't appreciate the gesture since the big man narrowed his eyes and began wrapping the telephone cord around a sizable fist. Finally Singular hung up and buzzed his secretary to hold all calls. Then he placed both palms down on his desk and stared at fingers gnarled by a collegiate football career that had seen him set a collegiate record for tackles by a middle linebacker in the Cotton Bowl.

At Texas A&M he'd combined sports and scholarship, leading him to believe there wasn't much beyond his ability. In addition to football honors, which included two years first-team All-American, he'd graduated Phi Beta Kappa, thanks mostly to a near-photographic memory. But three operations on his right shoulder had kept Singular out of the NFL, which hadn't upset him too much since the working life of a pro player rarely exceeded five years.

He decided against following his father and two brothers into banking, and as a football celebrity with some brains got a position on the Washington staff of a Texas senator, through whom he got a close-up look at the Secret Service. An arm of the Department of the Treasury, the service did more than protect the president and vice-president. It investigated federal crimes such as counterfeiting, forgery of government bonds, theft of treasury checks and threats against foreign diplomats, all of which were more interesting than banking. Singular also liked the camaraderie among the agents, which he found reminiscent of that among football players. And there was the advantage of having the government behind you, which gave a man power without having to run for political office.

It was the senator, a lanky, beetle-browed man with tiny eyes and lips, who sounded a warning about government service. "You're working for politicians now," he said to Singular, "and with all the power they got goin' for them, its dumb to expect they ain't gonna use it against you one day. Like LBJ once told me, ain't no good ever come of being around people who'll do anything to get elected."

In Singular's office neither he nor Decker said a word until Singular leaned back in his swivel chair and spoke to the ceiling. "The Justice Department, State Department and U.S. Attorney's office are chewing my balls off because of what you did to that Korean diplomat. Now I get to come down funky on you."

He glanced at Decker. "Guys like you really grind my gears. You think you know it all and the rest of us don't know diddly. I told you to walk easy, but it seems the only thing you need to make you go off half-cocked is a warning. Well, city boy, if you're a jackass don't be surprised if people ride your behind into the ground. You been gettin' by on bad attitude for too goddamn long."

Decker said, "I guess I should be worried."

"Listen, hotshot, even your own people think you stepped in it this time. Your precinct commander, the brass down at Police Plaza, they can't wait to put the strap to you and the day ain't even half gone."

Decker held up the copy of the *Times*. "By the way, in case you're interested, I wasn't drinking and I didn't start the fight. Those stories are bullshit."

"Your problem has turned into my problem. Allow me to explain. I don't give a shit who started the fight, you or some passing Eskimo. You look bad, which makes me look bad. A deputy U.S. marshal whipping up on a foreign diplomat. Jesus, if that don't take the cake. Goddamn it, didn't you hear anything I said? I *specifically* told you to concentrate on Dumas and those dead undercover cops. Forget Tawny what's her name, I said."

Decker said, "You also said keep away from Park Song. By the way, her last name's DaSilva. And what's she got to do with Kim Shin?"

"Know something, boy? I think it's all getting away from you. There's an advantage to understanding essentials, so before we get to talking 'bout how many inches you gonna lose off your pecker, permit me to expound on life as we know it. This country's forking over three billion dollars a year for South Korea's defense. Despite all the friends them Koreans have in Congress, and they got a lot, some folks say this is too much protection for a country that's enjoying a trade surplus with us. Might be they have a point."

He unwrapped three sticks of Juicy Fruit, rolled them into a ball and popped it in his mouth. "At the same time you could say we're caught between a rock and a hard place. North Korea's building a nuclear reprocessing plant. Meaning our troops ain't going nowhere, 'cause under those circumstances we can't afford to pull 'em out. We also hear there's secret talks going on between North and South Korea about the possibility of reunification. So where does this leave us God-fearing white Christians?"

Singular shifted the wad of gum from one jaw to another. "It leaves us still wanting to be a player and to do that, we need friends. Like it or not, we have got to keep in good with the South Koreans. We can start by not stomping a mudhole in their diplomats. Unbeknownst to you, we've got some very delicate negotiations going on with the Koreans. They pay just one percent of their defense costs. Uncle Sam pays the rest. We're picking up the tab to protect the very people who're putting our workers out of business. Ain't that a hoot?"

"These delicate negotiations have to do with us trying to talk them into forking over more money for their own defense. But when American policemen start beatin' up on Korean envoys, well, just imagine what this does to the diplomatic process. You see my point?"

Decker placed his coffee cup on an end table and crossed his ankles. "What I see is a man who's playing fast and loose with the truth,
who's jerked me around from the beginning. I see a man who
brought me on board to keep me from making waves."

For a few moments Singular attempted to blow bubbles with his
gum, then finally gave up. "Detective, your history shows that you're
an unhappy man. Unhappy people either think too much or too little."

Decker grinned. "The way I look at it, it's a sick world and I'm a
happy man."

Singular smiled in spite of himself. "For a man who's sitting on the
anxious seat, you don't look all that forlorn to me. You're going
around acting like Dirty Harry, which only confirms the liberals'
theory of cops being assholes. You've also made the federal government's shit list and that is not in your best interest, I can assure you.
So why are you sittin' there looking happier than a pig in shit? You
know something the rest of us don't? Or could it be you're just not in
your right mind?"

Decker said, "Well, let's see how wacko I am. I know the South
Korean government's involved with Laughing Boy's counterfeiting."

Singular stopped chewing.

Decker said, "I think our government knows it, too. That's why
they're pissed at me for clobbering Kim Shin. I think you've been
told it's okay to take down Laughing Boy, providing you don't make
waves. Sounds a bit like the war on drugs to me, the one we really
don't want to win. Because if we did we'd never have sucked up to
shitheads like Noriega. We'd also stop dealing with ninety percent of
the politicians in Latin America."

"You're pursuing a dicey line of inquiry, detective."

"Now why would I do that?"

Singular resumed chewing. "You were saying something about the
government telling us to go easy on Song?"

"In Saigon, Shin and Song were best friends. They stole the plates
together. You know the ones I mean. The ones the CIA tried to send
me to Leavenworth for, which they claimed didn't exist and which
they don't want anybody to know about."

"Cut to the chase, Decker."

"In Saigon, Shin worked intelligence. I think he still does. Like
they say, once a spook, always a spook. These days he calls himself a

diplomat but that's SOP for the spy business, isn't it? I think we both know he's using his position to help his old friend Laughing Boy. The look on your face says I'm right. I guess this means *you've* got a problem. You want to get Song, but you have to do it without provoking his friends in high places. Life's a bitch, ain't it."

Singular lifted a forefinger. "They say you're a regular Wile E. Coyote. One slick son of a bitch. You fight like a Jap, you think like one, and you always come up with a way to outwit the fine print. I think it's time you learned you can't win 'em all. Time to kick your butt."

"Before or after I tell you where Song's getting his paper?"

Singular stopped chewing his gum. "You're tricky or good. Which is it?"

Decker leaned back, hands behind his head. "Last night at the restaurant the cops kept me in Nicolay's office until they could check my ID. My partner came in and handed me my overcoat. I'm sitting on Nicolay's desk at the time so I dropped the coat on his Rolodex. Eventually I got the OK to leave, so I did."

"With your overcoat *and* the Rolodex," Singular said. "Makes one wonder who molded your character."

"I get home and the first thing I do is check out the names on the cards. Nicolay's got Kim Shin's number at the Korean embassy and his home number. He's also got several numbers for telephones in Seoul, no names, but I'm checking that out to see if any of the numbers belong to Song. Nicolay's also got some numbers for Ben Dumas and Russell Fort. He's got numbers for people all over the world. France, England—"

"Who's Russell Fort?"

"An ex-cop who knows Dumas and who's also into the wiseguys on account of a gambling habit. Fort and I know each other, so I can say there's a better than even chance he's dirty. Under Fort's name I found a listing for his aunt, a Mrs. Lorraine Buckey who lives in Washington and who used to work for the Bureau of Engraving and Printing. You know, where the money's printed?"

"I can do without the civics lesson. Just tell me about the paper."

"Mrs. Buckey's a diabetic and not in the best of health. That's Fort's excuse for dropping in to see her whenever he's in Atlantic City. Another name on Fort's card is that of Mrs. Buckey's son Arnold. He works at the Bureau of Engraving and Printing. In the department that has access to the paper on which our currency's printed.''

Closing his eyes Singular flopped back in his chair. "Jesus H. Christ. Goddamn paper drove us crazy. We know he's using the real thing, 'cause his bills have those red-and-blue threads running through them. That's the one thing a counterfeiter can't duplicate, them little threads.''

He opened his eyes and looked at Decker. "Drove us up the wall wondering how he managed to get all the paper he needed. The little bastard's doing two things. He's bleaching one-dollar bills, removing the color without wrinkling the bill. And he's using real paper, clean paper, in larger amounts than any counterfeiter's ever done before. We knew he had to be getting it from somewhere, we just couldn't figure where. How'd you learn about Fort's family so fast?''

"I had DEA fax its Washington office this morning. The minute I read the words Bureau of Engraving and Printing it started making sense. We know Dumas does a security check on Song's customers. And it's common knowledge that Dumas is Fort's rabbi. I'd say Fort pays for that protection by getting paper from the Bureau of Engraving and Printing, then passing it on to Big Ben. Song had the plates. All he needed was the paper. Nicolay's a player, too. Otherwise he wouldn't be hanging around that dirtbag Shin.''

Singular rolled his eyes. "Jesus. We give that little gook the plates, then we give him the paper. And you wonder why the world thinks this country's losing its mind. How do you figure Nicolay?''

"He's second-string. He's on the team, but he doesn't have too much clout. Kim Shin was dumping on him and he just sat there and took it. If Fort and Dumas are supplying the paper I doubt if they're leaving it on the Korean embassy's doorstep. Nicolay could be the drop. There's one way to find out.''

Singular toyed with a thick gold wedding band on his ring finger. "The record says you know how to use people. Who you gonna turn your magic on?''

"Fort. He's a gambling man. I think he's feeding his habit two ways: with the currency paper and by betraying undercover cops. His girlfriend's also a player. She works at DEA here in New York and has access to information that would appeal to Dumas. Main thing is, she's a lady who'll do anything for love. My gut says she gave up

Frankie Dalto and Willie Valentin. Turn Fort and we plug the leak on undercover cops. And you're a step closer to popping Laughing Boy."

Singular was quiet. When he spoke his voice was slightly more relaxed. His eyes, however, were icy. "We're gonna want to get together with Mr. Fort and discuss the matter of that very authentic paper used by Mr. Song."

"No problem. You can talk to him all you want. After I nail his ass for complicity in the killing of two undercover policemen."

"I can see we might have a jurisdictional problem, but we'll let that slide for now. You tell this to any of your people? Might win you a few friends."

Decker shook his head. "When I caught the undercover homicides I was warned not to trust anybody. We knew the leak had to be coming from inside, so I thought it wise to retain a suspicious mind. Dumas still has friends on the force. When I move on him I've got to be sure. I won't get a second chance. Not with a guy that smart, that tough and that crazy."

Singular picked up a letter opener and gently jabbed his palm. "Might be a good idea to throw a rope over Mr. Fort and drag him into the barn for safekeeping. Maybe convince him confession's good for the soul. Listen up. I wasn't supposed to tell you this, but I don't want you walking outta here thinking I've got used to the smell of politics. Never have, never will."

He sighed. "Even a cowboy like you has to play by the rules once in a while. Can't always do what you want, so you close your eyes, hold your nose and press on. There are times, believe me, when going along with the program sticks in my craw. I just want to piss on my desk, go through that door and keep walking 'till I hit Amarillo. About this little girl you're after, this Tawny what's her name. Before Song killed that agent of ours a year ago the agent came up with some information about a Mr. Fox—"

The telephone rang. Singular picked it up. "Goddam it, Nina, I told you to hold all calls. I—"

Frowning, he looked at Decker. "I see. Yes, he's right here."

He held out the receiver to Decker, who knew the signs. Something was wrong, and on a scale of one to ten it had to be at least a six. Singular looked as if he wished he were anywhere but in the room with Decker. If the news was this bad far away, Decker could only guess how bad it would be close up.

At Singular's desk Decker picked up the receiver and braced himself. "Detective Sergeant Decker."

For a few seconds he listened, then he closed his eyes. The news could not have been worse. And it rated more than a six. All he said was, "Jesus. I'm on my way," then he handed the receiver back to Singular.

"Squad car's waiting downstairs for me. My partner's been shot. They're not sure if she's going to make it."

FIFTEEN

Thirty-three hours after the robbery of her safe-deposit box a frantic Rowena Dartigue sat in the nearly empty departure lounge at Heathrow Airport and sipped cognac from a small silver flask. Her 11 A.M. flight to New York would be boarding in twenty minutes.

Twenty minutes closer to meeting Park Song, who was either in New York or due to arrive there shortly. Twenty minutes closer to being confronted by him on the subject of his missing eight million dollars. The same eight million she had accepted for safekeeping and which had now disappeared along with her cash, jewelry *and* notebooks describing her activities in detail.

Of all her money-laundering customers, only Song had money in the box. Only Song.

Frightened and confused, Rowena had contacted Scotland Yard in hopes the thieves had missed something, only to learn that her safe-deposit box had been cleaned out. The bastards hadn't left so much as a paper clip. She specifically inquired about her notebooks and jewelry, which she described in all their elegant particulars.

Some of the other victims had refused to discuss their losses with the police, preferring to keep certain information out of official channels. Later Rowena wondered if she should have asked about her missing property, but this was hindsight. So desperate was she to

221

retrieve the notebooks and the jewelry that she would have talked to the devil himself had she thought he could help.

She'd thought of canceling her New York trip. But that would be admitting she had no intention of repaying Song, or worse, that she'd been in on the robbery. Avoiding him was an admission that one was never too old to learn new ways of being stupid. Either Rowena contacted him straightaway or she wouldn't live out the week.

Her hand shook as she brought the flask to her lips. At the moment all she could think of was Song's well-deserved reputation for being cruel and without pity, particularly when he suspected he'd been cheated. Of course he would blame her for his loss. Hadn't the Korean spymaster Youngsam blamed Song when the Frenchman plundered their bank? The thought of Song's rage brought on agonizing spasms in Rowena's back, followed by a weakness in her hands and feet. Fear had drained her energy.

She swallowed more cognac, desperately trying to convince herself that Song wouldn't kill her when they met in New York, that he'd give her a chance to repay the money and keep them both alive. Too late Rowena remembered just how easily she had dismissed Park Song's homicidal whims merely because they had not affected her directly. She had closed her eyes to certain unpleasant truths and now had to pay the piper.

Stunned and frightened by the robbery, Rowena's initial reaction had been to rush to her bedroom, refuse all phone calls, and devour a bottle of cognac with the intention of rendering herself insensible. Park Song wasn't the only person she had to fear. She also feared what could happen to her should he and the others mentioned in her notebooks learn of their existence. Rowena's fear was such that she considered killing herself before deciding she was much too cowardly to go through with it.

Michael. God alone knew where he was at this moment. Not that he would be of much use in a crisis. He was an eternal adolescent, glib and empty-headed, steadfast in his pursuit of the new and different. Supposedly he was working on a deal which could mean a trip to the States to meet with the people involved. Had he been with Rowena right now perhaps his presence might have provided her with some comfort.

Weeping uncontrollably, she placed another small log in her bed-room fireplace then crawled under a pair of down comforters. How in hell could she go on with her life after this? *How?* She'd always seen herself as unique and unequaled, far above the common herd. This calamity was a brutal reminder that, in the end, she was just like other people.

In bed she stared at the fire. Its blaze threw a crimson glow on the parquet floor. It was comforting, a friendly companion inducing her to become solemn and reflective.

As a pretty and outwardly normal adolescent living in the London suburb of Clapham, she'd been introduced to sexual abnormality by William Cobden, a moon-faced, fifty-four-year-old vicar and con-firmed pedophile. Although Cobden had originated the depravity, the oversexed Rowena revealed herself to be an eager student. It wasn't long before she became the leader in their sex play which included posing in front of Cobden's automatic camera for porno-graphic photographs.

Nor was Cobden the only grownup with whom she cheerfully fornicated. An uncle, a police constable and a local rent collection agent were just some of the older men who enjoyed her precocious favors.

What made Rowena different from other youngsters who were sexually active with adults was a refusal to view herself as a victim of child molestation. From the beginning she endorsed the Reverend Cobden's belief that sex between grownups and children was both acceptable and correct. As a youngster she found it exhilarating to exercise power over men who were respected pillars of the commu-nity and, in some cases, old enough to be her grandfather.

Eventually her sexual misconduct became too embarrassing for Rowena's pub-owner father who threw her out of the house one day before her fifteenth birthday. Within the week she became the mis-tress of a fifty-five-year-old West End mobster.

Her disregard for convention was suspended at the age of twenty-two when she became the wife of Roger Weymouth, the husky, forty-year-old manager of a sports car business on Park Lane. Warm and affectionate, the successful Weymouth was Rowena's first husband and the only man she would ever truly love.

Two years after their marriage they moved to Cape Town, where he took over as manager of a large American automobile business.

The move was traumatic for Roger's sister Finola, a short, skinny, tight-lipped woman with, and the director of, a London children's charity called the Lesley Foundation. Deeply attached to her brother she'd opposed his marriage to Rowena whom she saw as oversexed, headstrong, mercenary and frivolous.

In turn Rowena suspected that at the bottom of the prudish and unwed Finola's drinking problem was a lust for her own brother. For Roger's sake the two women remained civil to one another, though Rowena knew the truce would last only so long as the other wanted it to.

In Cape Town, Rowena was the virtuous and loving wife. Her past, which Roger knew of and accepted, was behind them. He provided her with the personal attention her self-centered approach to life demanded, while in bed he was forceful and innovative, delivering all the pleasure she could wish for. In turn, a besotted Rowena gave him a loyalty she'd given no other man. With Roger she no longer felt the need to prove she was still the seductress.

While Rowena may have been leading a restrained existence, the same could not be said of all of their Cape Town friends. Jean-Louis Nicolay, a French restaurateur whom Roger had backed in a beach-front café, periodically invited them to wife-swapping parties, invitations refused by the couple. Nor did they share Nicolay's interest in sex with black and white runaways whom he'd use, then casually dispose of. A child, he said, was the magic elixir which kept a man young. If this testimony triggered any response in Rowena she refused to show it.

Neither she nor Roger wanted offspring of their own. Rowena was too possessive of her husband to see a child as anything but a threat, while he preferred having a beautiful young wife to himself. For six years they enjoyed a happy and prosperous life until the day he decided it was no longer possible to ignore South Africa's racist system of apartheid.

Against the advice of white friends and business associates, Roger openly supported strikes by black workers and the radical African National Congress led by Nelson Mandela. He also participated in a demonstration in the town of Sharpeville to protest against passbook laws, which restricted the movement of blacks in all-white areas. Police brutally suppressed the demonstration, killing seventy people. Roger himself was grazed by a bullet, suffering a minor leg wound.

Immediately after this incident the ANC, the Communist Party and other black groups were officially outlawed. The government also increased its violence against anyone opposing apartheid. Although afraid of what might happen to Roger, Rowena admired her husband's determination to speak out for what he believed in.

"South Africa's a beautiful country," he told her, "but the future has little value here. There's too much hatred and out of that will come destruction. You mark my words."

A month later the destruction he predicted showed up at their door. On a rainy evening a tall dark-haired white man dressed as a priest came to their home, rang the bell, and when Roger appeared shot him in the chest three times. He died in the arms of a hysterical Rowena without regaining consciousness. An anonymous caller threatened that unless she left South Africa within forty-eight hours, she would share her husband's fate.

Taking the warning seriously, Rowena called on the assistance of Jean-Louis Nicolay, who stuck by her during this terrible time. He arranged Roger's immediate cremation and Rowena's flight to London with his ashes. Roger's financial affairs, however, were not so easily disposed of. Rowena and he had lived well, but his death revealed that he owed back taxes. There was also an outstanding bank loan, other creditors and, of course, death duties. When the estate was finally settled Rowena received barely enough money to live on for six months. She was not only alone, she was penniless once again.

In London, Roger's sister Finola proved surprisingly sympathetic to her sister-in-law. She gave Rowena a job with the children's charity and found her a cheap flat in Bayswater. Grief drew them closer, and they forgave each other. Eighteen months later Finola died and Rowena grieved not merely for Finola but for the loss of the last link to her Roger.

She was now in charge of the charity which had become a losing financial proposition, paying her only a minimal salary. No longer inclined to be a dirty old man's darling, she struggled to keep the charity afloat. Public support, however, was hard to come by. People were willing to give away their old clothes and junk they no longer needed, but parting with cash was another matter.

Two months after Finola's funeral she heard from Nicolay, who supposedly had come to London on holiday. He had a favor to ask of Rowena. Would she launder some money, twenty thousand dollars to be exact, through her charity's bank account? It was a simple task and no one need ever know. She could keep the interest and use it for good works.

Rowena was shocked, not by his request but by the notion of acquiring so much money for so little effort. A bank slip or two, and it was done. The question of legality never arose in her mind. She was three weeks behind in her rent, and her landlord, a lecherous Cypriot, had given her twenty-four hours to pay up or start granting him her sexual favors. Rowena found Nicolay's proposition infinitely more attractive.

The jubilant Frenchman said this was just the beginning. With future racial conflicts in South Africa a foregone conclusion, smart money was starting to flee the country. During the next few weeks alone Nicolay was prepared to launder several hundred thousand dollars through Rowena's charity. After that he would be moving to Saigon, where he had friends and where the war between North and South Vietnam had created numerous opportunities for profit. If Rowena handled the South African money correctly, Nicolay would also send her money from Asia to wash.

Rowena, bored with the charity, had been thinking of walking away from it. There was just no money to be made and the children were getting on her nerves. In the light of her new arrangement with Nicolay she could reconsider her distaste for philanthropic labor. That is when the Frenchman told her there was another way of making money from her little charity.

He had a friend in New York, a Japanese psychiatrist he had met there some months ago. Recently the psychiatrist, Dr. Ken Yokoi, had been obliged to resign from the staff of a small New Hampshire college after a sexual scandal involving a teenage male freshman. Yokoi had just opened a Manhattan practice and specialized in therapy for disturbed people who had trouble accepting their own sexuality. Part of the treatment involved putting these patients together with men who were stronger, authoritative and often affluent.

Nicolay told her these men were sometimes more comfortable with young people than with adults. They were willing to pay money to find the right young person. Would she be interested in playing a part in such an arrangement, one which could prove *extremely* profitable?

Rowena invited Nicolay to the Ritz for tea and for a further discussion of the ways in which the philanthropic Lesley Foundation could be made more lucrative.

In Heathrow's international passenger terminal now, Rowena paused with the flask in front of her lips. Behind dark glasses her eyes were hawklike, narrowed. A frosty smile found its way to her lips. The idea that had just come to her was a daring one, but worth trying if she wanted to go on living.

She stood up, capped the flask and looked around for a telephone. She could feel blood rushing to her head. The excitement taking her over now was almost sexual. At the same time a sense of relief left her much calmer.

A bearded Arab in *kaffiyeh* headdress and business suit stepped out of her way with exaggerated politeness. Sweeping past him, Rowena headed for the duty-free shop. If it had no telephones, someone would certainly tell her where to find one. She began to walk faster, her mind spinning with the details of the plan she had devised to save herself.

She would telephone Ben Dumas straightaway and offer him whatever he wanted to kill Park Song. Get Song before he got her. She was going on the offensive. She would bloody well put out the fire herself. It was as simple as that.

Ben was killing people for everyone else. Why not for her? He could terminate Song when the Korean came to collect little Miss Tawny and at the same time collect one hundred and twenty-five thousand dollars. There would also be a bonus, namely half of little Miss Tawny's new sale price. Rowena would sell her to the highest bidder at the auction which should bring one of the fattest fees of the night.

Half the purchase price would go to Ben. Yes, it was a good deal of money to hand over to hired help, but with her life on the line no price was too great to pay for survival.

As she neared the duty-free shop Rowena allowed herself to feel triumphant. She had just solved what had appeared to be an insurmountable problem. Her life was about to return to some sort of order. *And* she would not have to liquidate her holdings, which was what she had intended to do if Song had accepted her offer of repayment.

Liquidate everything in sight then beg, borrow or steal the rest. The sale of her home and the shop, plus all of her bank accounts, might yield three to four million dollars. Sending Song on to a better world not only guaranteed her survival but was infinitely more practical. The thought of Song applying cold steel to her breasts inspired Rowena to think positively.

At the duty-free shop a young Sikh directed her to the telephone. Without thanking him, Rowena dashed off in the direction indicated, praying she'd be able to reach Ben. He was due to meet her at Kennedy Airport, but she wanted to speak to him this instant.

SIXTEEN

Dumas, cellular phone to his ear, sat on a windowsill in Ken Yokoi's bedroom, staring across the street into Washington Square Park at a light afternoon rain which had cut the number of freaks outdoors to a minimum. On a park bench a homeless old Hispanic man eyed a dead, bloodied rooster lying at his feet, the memento of a downtown cockfight. In the center of a dry fountain a cadaverous blonde woman in a quilted jacket practiced Tai Chi with a somber grace.

Turning, Dumas waved to Yokoi who lay in bed hooked to an IV for his twice-daily feeding. The Japanese weakly lifted a hand in reply. A second later Dumas, a wolfish grin on his face, spoke into the phone. "We've got a deal. See you when you get here."

Pushing down the antenna, he laid the phone aside. Then he faced the window again, shook his head, and chuckled softly. For a few seconds he watched a tall black drag queen in a white wedding dress, bombardier jacket, and pink parasol skate into the park from Bleecker Street. Then he looked at the cellular phone. Rowena, Song, and God knows who else, he thought. Talk about excitement. What we have here is a bunch of seedy characters with so many irons in the fire you can't see the fire.

Leaving the window he sat on the edge of Yokoi's bed, took the dying man's hand and repeated the telephone conversation.

229

Yokoi managed a brief smile. " *'O, what a tangled web we weave when first we practice to deceive.'* Or as grandmother used to say, trust everybody but cut the cards. You did fine, just fine."

"Did what you told me to. No more, no less."

"The successful outcome of a conflict sometimes demands you end a relationship. That's why you must be emotionally detached during any confrontation. Otherwise, you can't evaluate it properly. You won't know the strengths and weaknesses of any position, your own included. Keep a cool head and you should be able to make people do exactly what you want them to do."

Dumas nodded. "I went after Decker's support system instead of Decker, like you said. Shooting his partner has slowed him down. The last few hours he's been out of our hair. Looks like we'll finish the auction and dispose of Tawny without any interference from him."

Again Dumas flashed his wolfish grin. "Park Song and Rowena are supposed to be a couple of deep thinkers but they couldn't carry your jock. They're out in the world thinking they're movers and shakers while you lie here and run circles around them. I love it."

Yokoi said, "Always take the long view, big guy. And once you decide what you want, act quickly. He who hesitates gets fucked. Where's Park Song now?"

Dumas hooked a thumb towards the cellular phone. "He told me he's a hundred miles past Albany which should put him in the city sometime this afternoon. It's raining, but if the roads aren't too bad he should be here before Rowena's plane lands at Kennedy."

Yokoi said, "Dear Rowena. The lady who sees homicide as the solution to her problem. Death is her way of saying we no longer have a deal. Looks like big doings in the Big Apple tonight, by golly. We have our annual auction of firm, young flesh, and we're being honored by a visit from Park Song and Rowena Dartigue, our very own king and queen of depravity. What was that business about Song having trouble in London?"

"Besides losing eight million dollars in the deposit center robbery, he tells me three phony English cops tried to rip him off at his hotel. Song wasted all three then went after the guy who sent them. Seems the mastermind was the Nigerian, Katsina Jonathan. I'd already checked him out and he was okay. But apparently at the last moment he got greedy."

"Katsina Jonathan," Yokoi said. "Lovely name."

"He probably wasn't so lovely when Song and his friends got through with him. Song says they worked him over then burned down his travel agency with him in it. But not before they'd broken Jonathan's back and cut out his tongue, leaving him nothing to do but lie on the floor and bake. Our African friend was probably hotter than a goat with two dicks."

Yokoi chuckled. "Goat with two dicks. You're getting worse in your old age. As for Laughing Boy, talk about your morose behavior. Doesn't pay to catch him on a bad day, does it? You said he hasn't heard from Rowena. So how'd he learn about the robbery?"

"It made the front page of the International *Herald Tribune.* After reading the story and shitting in his pants, Song contacted the London embassy. It was they who learned that Rowena had asked Scotland Yard if any of her property had been left behind. The answer was no. The lady had a clean box, so to speak. She seemed particularly interested in her missing jewelry and notebooks."

Yokoi smiled. "Clean box. What are you, a gynecologist?"

"Song told me he wants me to ask her about those notebooks which were important enough to have been kept in a vault. My guess is, were he to hear something he didn't like, Rowena would wish she'd never been born."

"I'd say whoever robbed the safe-deposit boxes has those notebooks. I also think those notebooks have something to do with why she's willing to pay you to send Park Song on to his next life. Didn't think she had it in her. Shows you how much I know about women. Does she know about the Nigerian?"

Dumas shook his head. "She didn't mention it when she called from Heathrow. The safe-deposit heist is enough for her at the moment, especially with Song out there looking for her. You heard me try to calm him down a few minutes ago. Losing eight million clams at this stage of his life has him climbing the walls. Which doesn't mean he's forgotten Tawny. He's still hot for the kid."

Earlier that morning Dumas had visited Tawny in the cellar, finding the kid increasingly depressed but still a tad rambunctious. Deciding to play with her mind he said, "Your mother just telephoned to say she's sending over some of your clothes."

"I don't want to talk to you," Tawny said. "You make up stories." She sat on the edge of her cot, schoolbooks at her feet.

"Your mother said she's sending your favorite dress."

"Oh? Which one?"

Taken by surprise, a grinning Dumas said the first thing that came to mind. "You know the one. The one your girlfriends say looks so cute on you."

Tawny nodded. "Oh, you mean the yellow one with the blue trim."

"That's the one."

The trap was sprung. But it wasn't Tawny who'd fallen into it.

She eyed him with contempt before lying down on the cot and turning her face to the wall. "Yellow looks like puke. I hate it. I don't own any yellow dresses."

Dumas cocked an eyebrow. Not bad, kid. Not bad at all.

Later Yokoi said, if you're wondering what's keeping her together, it's her hatred for you. Song should know this little woman is going to be a trouble and a worry, as the Arabs say.

Now Yokoi said, "The Kisaeng Obsession. Where will it strike next, I wonder. And Song definitely blames Rowena for the safe-deposit robbery?"

"For that, and for the problem with the Nigerian. Considering how bent out of shape Song is over this thing, I'd say Rowena made the right decision to whack him. In her position I'd have done the same thing."

"The end of an era. The bonds that unite are about to be torn asunder. What time are you leaving?"

Dumas looked at his watch. "In a few minutes. I'll return before I go to the auction. I want to be here when the paper and the counterfeit money is dropped off."

"Speaking of paper, you haven't forgotten Russell Fort?"

"Funny you should mention it. Today's his last day on earth, as a matter of a fact. As soon as he delivers the latest batch of paper he's gone. I've got to make this double hit for LoCasio, so I'm having somebody else take out Fort. After he's gone I should be able to convince Aunt Lorraine and Cousin Arnold to deal with me direct. If they refuse there's going to be a family reunion in nigger heaven or wherever Russell's soul happens to be."

"You really have to do these LoCasio hits yourself?"

Dumas nodded. "Joe personally asked me as a favor. He wants it done right which is why he went out and got the best, namely yours truly. This one's a double-dip, two for one, so it has to be done right. It's got to do with his pride, so there can't be any slipups. After it's over Joe will owe me. I'll be in a position to come to him for a favor. Take the long view, remember?"

They held hands in silence then Yokoi said, "Try not to get yourself killed. If anything happens to you, I'm pulling the plug. You're all I have in this world. No family, really. A few friends, but no one like you. When you go I'm gone anyway, so why prolong the inevitable? Besides, this house wouldn't be much fun without you. Who else is going to make me such great flower arrangements?"

"Stop acting like an old queen."

"I am an old queen."

Dumas kissed him on the forehead. "I'm coming back, I promise."

"There are three ways it could go wrong," Yokoi said. "The Rowena–Park Song business. The auction. And this double hit for Joe. Any one of them could be trouble."

He closed his eyes. "Good, bad, everything happens in threes. Anyone ever tell you that?"

SEVENTEEN

As Ben Dumas left his lover's townhouse to commit two murders, Decker got up from a chair alongside the hospital bed of a sleeping Ellen Spiceland and inspected the thermostat. Sixty-five degrees. Too cool. He turned it up to seventy.

The afternoon rain had caused outside temperatures to drop, chilling the room. Decker preferred warm weather because it eased the stiffness in bones and joints he had damaged in over twenty years of karate. Warm weather kept him loose, which increased the speed and power of his techniques. Cold weather tightened the body, forcing him to increase the prepractice stretching that was necessary to avoid pulled muscles.

Professionally Decker saw the advantage of cold weather. It kept people indoors, shielding them from each other and cutting down on street crime. Freezing temperatures, snowstorms and heavy rain sometimes did as much for a cop's peace of mind as a bullet-proof vest.

When Bags had been shot yesterday morning she hadn't been wearing a vest. There'd been no need for one, not when she'd been planning to spend eight hours behind a desk at the precinct. As she told Decker after surgery, she'd left her apartment and was about to lock the front door when someone shot her in the back three times with what turned out to be a High Standard .22.

234

One bullet grazed a shoulder, resulting in a flesh wound. The other two had done more damage, injuring a kidney, piercing a lung and forcing doctors to remove her spleen. In time, she would recover and be able to return to duty, provided she felt like it. Decker had known cops to recuperate from a shooting, then become too scared ever to set foot inside a precinct house again.

He'd hate for that to happen to Bags, for her sake and his. Their friendship was one of the few things he trusted in life. Her value hadn't really been known to him until he'd heard she was near death. Then he'd almost come apart. The thought of losing Bags had been a sharp reminder of just how much he depended on her. Who else knew everything about Decker and liked him anyway?

She hadn't seen the gunman's face, but while she lay on the hallway floor after the shooting she had seen his baggy gray pants and tacky brown shoes as he raced upstairs toward the roof. Her husband, Henri, who had responded to her calls, also reported hearing someone run upstairs. Once on the roof the shooter had apparently crossed over to another building, walked down to the street and made his escape. Whoever the bastard was, he'd known his way around.

On their own time a dozen officers from Bags's precinct had joined local cops combing the neighborhood for clues. They had talked to everyone—news vendors, beat cops, whores, winos, storekeepers and street derelicts. At the same time they'd rummaged through garbage cans, dumpsters and vacant lots, hoping to find the gun used in the shooting. They had come up with nothing. No clues, no witnesses, no motive. All they had learned was that Bags was a popular lady who had even earned the respect of local drug dealers.

No, the dealers hadn't tried to smoke her. Killing a cop was bad for business, brought down too much heat and kept customers away. They pledged their support in solving the crime so that things could get back to normal quickly as possible.

In the hospital room Decker eyed the flowers and baskets of fruit from Bags's well-wishers. Calls and telegrams had poured in, from relatives, friends and cops who didn't know her, all pulling for the policewoman whose near murder had become New York's latest media event. The mayor, police commissioner, borough president and television cameras had come and gone. The switchboard was now holding all calls until further notice, and there was a twenty-four-hour police guard outside her room.

Decker, meanwhile, was losing sleep over why someone had tried to whack his partner. Had it been a case of mistaken identity? Maybe a perp from an old bust had tried to even the score. Somehow he didn't think so. If that had been true the shooter should have come after both of them, not just Bags. Unless Decker was next. If someone had planned a crisis to divert him from his current cases they couldn't have done a better job.

He had been among the first to donate blood for Bags. Before the day was over more than three hundred policemen and women had come forward to do the same. Most hadn't heard of her until the shooting. All they knew was that a cop had been shot in the back. It wasn't necessary to know anything else.

Decker turned from the thermostat and looked at the sleeping Bags, who had tubes in her nose and both arms. She looked so *small*. Who the hell hated her enough to shoot her in the back? Henri was also in the room, sleeping in his clothes on a cot near the window. He had dropped his veneer of a world-weary sophisticated artist and fallen back on his roots, which meant turning to voodoo to save his wife's life.

He had come to the hospital wearing what he called a magic shawl. Hanging from his neck were three gris-gris, small idols, and he had also put three peppers under his tongue. Cops working with New York's large Hispanic and Caribbean population knew that witchcraft and cults were more common than the average citizen would believe. So Decker wasn't surprised when Henri excused himself, saying he was going off to hide the peppers somewhere in the hospital. Henri wasn't trying to burn down the place. All he wanted to do was keep his wife alive. Henri spoon-fed Bags homemade gumbo, making sure the hospital staff never saw him do it. Did any of this make a difference? All Decker knew was that the doctors were staggered by her rapid progress. As was he.

In the hospital room he walked to the closet, found his overcoat and removed cards taken from Nicolay's Rolodex. He returned to his chair and bit into the remains of a tunafish sandwich before sitting down. Karen Drumman, who had visited the hospital, had brought him sandwiches and coffee. At her invitation he had spent the previous night at her apartment, located within walking distance of the hospital.

He had slept on the couch, hardly speaking to her, too incensed about the shooting to do more than grunt when she said goodnight and went to her bedroom. If it took him forever, he was going to find out who'd shot Bags and why. This morning he'd been up, showered and gone before Karen had gotten out of bed. But not before making a few telephone calls and leaving a note to bill him for the charges.

As rain lashed the hospital window he sipped cold coffee and examined the Rolodex cards he'd put in a certain order. There were Dumas's cards, his personal and business numbers and addresses. Then a card for Russell Fort and one for Nicolay, listing lawyers, accountants, apartment and summer home. Then a card for Kim Shin and other Koreans, most but not all of them at the Korean embassy here in New York. Decker suspected that some of these names were aliases for Park Song.

And then there was Mr. Fox, whose card contained several London telephone numbers. Decker had heard that name in Singular's office. The problem was, he couldn't remember when and how he'd heard it. Since he didn't know how Mr. Fox fit into the picture, he placed his card last in the pack.

This morning Decker had telephoned Mr. Fox's numbers from Karen Drumman's apartment and learned they were for a clothing shop called Rosebud, a house in Chelsea and a children's charity. All of the numbers had a common link—a woman named Rowena Dartigue, who either owned the properties or ran the businesses. Make that two things in common. In each case, whoever answered the phone had never heard of a Mr. Fox.

Singular. What the hell was it the fat man had said? Decker closed his eyes in concentration, breathed deeply and made his mind blank. He relaxed. Waited. Then, *About this little girl you're after, this Tawny what's her name. Before Song killed that agent of ours a year ago the agent came up with some information about a Mr. Fox.*

Singular had said something else, too. *I specifically told you to concentrate on Dumas and them undercover cops. Forget Tawny what's her name.* And Decker had said, *What the hell's Tawny got to do with Kim Shin?* As usual Singular had ducked the question.

Opening his eyes, Decker stared at Mr. Fox's card. Song and Mr.

Fox had been tied together by a dead Secret Service agent. Meaning they'd been in business together. Why had Singular mentioned them in the same breath as Tawny? Decker walked over to the window to stare down at a rain-soaked Fifth Avenue and Central Park. Dumas and Song. Song and Mr. Fox. Decker began shuffling the cards again.

Dumas supplied Song with intelligence and currency paper. What was "Mr. Fox" supplying the Korean with? Singular didn't want Decker digging too deep, that was for sure. Texas Fats wanted a go-slow on Dumas and Song. What the hell for? To avoid an international incident, obviously, but what kind of incident?

Back to the cards. Dumas and Fort. An impatient Decker placed them side by side on the windowsill. Max and Gail had been killed right after telling Decker about Max's being followed by a black man. Decker stared out at the rain, not daring to breathe. Fort and Dumas.

A ringing telephone brought him out of his dark vision. He hurried to pick up the receiver before Bags was disturbed. He was ready to ream the caller. No one was to call here unless it was an emergency. Grabbing the receiver he turned his back to Bags and whispered, "Detective Sergeant Decker. Who the hell put you through?"

"Lowell Chattaway. I thought it was important, so I touched base with your precinct and they said go ahead and call. Sorry to hear about Bags. You want help on this, you got it."

"Thanks, Lowell. What's up?"

"You asked me about those Beretta 84's ripped off from Kennedy by the LoCasio crew. You made it sound important. I just hope it has nothing to do with anything you and Bags are working on, but you never know."

"Appreciate whatever you have."

"Our snitch just reported in. Says LoCasio's people sold three Berettas to the CIA. Not those dickheads down in D.C. but the Ben Dumas detective agency. The *convicted, indicted, arrested* agency. Guys who can't keep their hands off other people's property, who'd steal the pennies from a dead man's eyes."

Decker closed his eyes. He had just found the last piece of the puzzle. The smoking gun had now been placed in Ben Dumas's hand. Crazy Ben had whacked Gail and Max DaSilva. As for a motive, Decker was ready to bet his pension that it had everything to do with whatever Russell Fort had going with Gail and Max DaSilva.

"I owe you one, Lowell," Decker said, then hung up without waiting for a reply. When he turned around, Bags was staring at him.

"How we doing?" she whispered.

Decker remembered that it had been Bags who had put him on to Safe and Loft in the first place. Remembered she had helped him trace the gun now being linked to Gail and Max DaSilva's killer.

He took her hand in his. "I know who wasted them, Bags."

EIGHTEEN

Russell Fort sat on an unsteady chrome barstool in the cramped office of Jean-Louis Nicolay's restaurant and watched silently as the Frenchman examined the paper—eight packages of blank notes wrapped in heavy paper and bound with steel strips. Just hours ago it had been the property of the Bureau of Engraving and Printing. The frog had it now. After him it would belong to a Korean whom Fort had never met and didn't want to meet.

He sat with his back to a heavily barred ground-floor window which was virtually opaque with soot and grime. He had been forced to tuck matchbooks under the stool to keep it balanced on the slightly uneven floor. At the moment Fort was more concerned with cash than with equilibrium. He was not getting paid for this load which had left him in a bad mood.

He had owed the LoCasio people, a debt that had been paid by Dumas. As a result Fort was getting zilch for this last batch of paper, which meant he'd have to come up with five thousand dollars for Aunt Lorraine and Cousin Arnold. The deal was ten thousand a load —half to Fort, half to his Washington relatives. Unless he produced five K pretty soon Aunt Lorraine and Arnold would turn off the tap, something Fort would have to explain to Dumas. And if all Dumas did about it was slap him bald-headed, as Aunt Lorraine might say, Fort would be lucky.

He lit a cigarette, moving gingerly because he still hurt from the beating given him two days ago by Dumas. His forearm was in a cast and he had two cracked ribs, which made it hard to lift his arms or lean to either side.

Fort and Susan Scudder had returned from Washington in a rented Olds, Susan doing most of the driving, Fort nodding out on Percodan in the back seat. He had taken the wheel in New York, where a light rain had slowed traffic to a crawl. Because of the bad weather they had arrived at the restaurant more than an hour late, which caused a jumpy Nicolay to curse out Fort for not being on time. Fort shut him up by threatening to go upside the little frog's head with his cast. Taking shit from a turkey like Nicolay wasn't part of the deal.

The trip to Atlantic City, Fort's cover for the Washington trip, had been a drag. Not only had the blackjack tables gobbled up most of the two thousand expense money fronted by Dumas, but Susan had turned out to be a problem. He'd had to explain how he had come to get beaten up, so he'd fallen back on the truth. Told the bitch everything—how Dumas had grabbed Tawny DaSilva, how he had tried to rip off the parents' reward money, how Decker had become a player. He had also told her that Dumas had iced mommy and daddy.

Susan had freaked out. What the hell had Fort got her into? Wasn't it enough that he'd involved her in the death of two undercover cops? And now *this* shit. Fort said, that's life, little mama. Fool with the bull and you get the horn. They'd tied themselves to Ben Dumas and now had to live with it.

Susan said, "Live with *this*, asshole." She then proceeded to curse Fort for bringing a creep like Dumas into her life. This trip to Washington was the last thing she'd do for these animals, Fort included. He was never to ask her for another thing or she'd go straight to Decker, or even the DEA, and turn them all in. If she had to go down, so be it. But she'd had it with these crappo, zero minus excuses for men.

Fort surprised himself by not reacting. He played Mr. Cool which was how to handle yourself around the ladies if you didn't want to end up looking like chump change. The painkillers helped. They left him so laid back that he couldn't have come on strong if he'd wanted to.

So he didn't slap Susan around for getting in his face. Didn't curse the bitch or make her cry. Why crack the whip when he needed her to keep Dumas off his ass? All he'd said was, we'll talk about it later, then closed his eyes and pretended to be asleep, leaving her to drive and think she'd won this round.

Later, when he felt stronger, he'd sit the lady down and clue her in. Recite the facts of life to her, beginning with the news that you did not say no to Ben Dumas. The best way to get around Susan was to take her to bed and work on that body until she was tearing at the sheets. Fort was her Sweet Daddy—get between her legs and he'd bring her around. For sure.

In Nicolay's office Fort slid off the stool, a set of western saddlebags slung over his cast. No payoff to shove into the bags this time. All he had in there was a ballpoint pen filled with cocaine, a Tom Clancy paperback, a cheap notebook and a fifteen-shot Browning 9-mm. Normally he'd sling the saddlebags from his shoulder, but not now. Not with his ribs giving him so much grief.

A smiling Nicolay extended his hand. "Forgive my earlier outburst, my friend. You understand I am under much pressure to have things ready when our Korean friend arrives tonight."

"Well, we all have our problems. See you around."

"Are you absolutely certain you and Susan cannot stay for dinner? Please be my guests. Tonight we are featuring a sea bass guaranteed to melt in your mouth. And for dessert a lemon ribbon cake with homemade lemon ice cream."

Fort shook his head. "Some other time. We're beat from all that traveling. I just want to crash and rest this cast. We'll drop off the car, then head straight to her place. You just make sure Ben knows the paper's here."

"You leave that to me. I shall call him immediately and say how magnificent you have been. Well, goodbye, my friend. Forgive me if I do not go to the car and say goodbye to Susan. I must set up for dinner."

Despising Nicolay for his role in Tawny DaSilva's kidnapping, Susan had refused to set foot in his restaurant. Fort had handled the situation by lying, saying she was having her period and feeling sick and preferred to stay in the car. It was a lie that verged on truth. Susan was sick. Sick of Nicolay.

The Frenchman walked Fort through the empty restaurant and to the door, where they shook hands. He watched Fort cross the street, get into a blue Oldsmobile and chat briefly with Susan, who seemed upset. At that time of the month, all women were upset, were they not? When the car pulled away Nicolay returned to his office, where he made a phone call.

His end of the conversation was brief: "They have just left. No, they are going to drop off the car, then go straight to her place. Yes, I'm sure. Quite sure."

When Russell Fort and Susan Scudder left the pizzeria at Broadway and 79th, they walked toward a brownstone one block away where she had a one-bedroom apartment over a Cuban-Chinese restaurant run by a Chinese family who had immigrated to Cuba, then fled when Castro had taken over.

Susan carried a large pizza, Fort a plastic bag containing a bottle of red wine and a box of Mrs. Field's pecan brownies. At four-thirty in the afternoon it was already dark outside. The rain, now a light drizzle, had tied up traffic and reduced the number of pedestrians to a handful. It hadn't kept the panhandlers off the street, however. In the space of a few yards Fort and Susan were approached by three street people holding paper cups and asking for spare change. He gave nothing, insisted Susan give nothing and told them all the same thing—get a job, man, and stop bothering people.

Susan, who loved her food almost as much as she loved sex, was now more relaxed. She spoke of the many Christmas catalogs she'd received this past week, of her intention to take up tap dancing next year, of her rent having doubled during the eight years she'd lived in the neighborhood.

By the time they neared her building Fort had an arm around her, remembering how he'd liked her from the moment she'd come into his store for a pair of running shoes and begun flirting with him. Bottom line was, he had himself a sweet lady in Susan. A bit garbage-mouthed at times, but sweet.

At the moment she looked like a kid in that green raincoat and floppy purple hat. A very sexy kid. He was anticipating a mellow evening with just the two of them. At the same time he wondered if he could get a bet down on the Knicks, who were two-point favorites over Houston at the Garden tonight. Whoever took his action would have to extend credit, because Fort didn't have a bean.

At the corner of Broadway and 80th they crossed the street and turned left, heading toward Susan's brownstone several yards away. A young Hispanic couple who had been on the other side fell in behind them. The man, small and tough-looking, wore a green wool cap, matching down jacket and carried a Christmas tree taller than he was. The woman wore a coat with a fake fur collar that she held tight around her throat with one hand. Neither had an umbrella.

At her building, Susan and Fort started up the single flight of stone steps leading to the entrance. The Hispanic couple continued walking, then stopped suddenly and drew pistols from their coat pockets. Turning, they fired at Fort and Susan.

On the top step Fort had stopped and drawn Susan to him for a kiss in the rain, seeing her eyes light up, and that's when he saw the shooters from the corner of his eye. He thought, protect Susan, and he shoved her away, sending her screaming down the stairs. Then dropping the plastic bag with the wine and brownies, he reached for the saddlebags.

He heard *pop-pop-pop*, felt a sharp pain in his thigh and collapsed on the steps, landing on his right hip. A bullet tore the heel from one eelskin boot. To his left two holes appeared in a ground floor window. His adrenalin was flowing as it had that night on Eighth Avenue when a crazed homeless man had tried to take away his gun and Fort had shot that sucker six times.

Fort shoved his hand into the saddlebags, his senses picking up images—the smell of red wine, the feel of the rain-wet steps hard against his spine, the bright orange of flames from the shooters' guns. He was out of control, crazy to save his own life and Susan's.

He took a second bullet through the shoulder; a third whizzed by his ear, gouging away a piece of the stone steps. By now Fort had found the Browning. Thumbing off the safety he fired through the leather, fired four times, hitting the man in the chest and driving him back into a fire hydrant. Another bullet, this one from the woman's gun, struck the stairs between Fort's legs, missing his balls by inches. He returned fire, knocking the hat from her head. With that the woman turned and ran toward West End Avenue, disappearing into the darkness.

Hand still in the saddlebag, Fort limped down the stairs and crouched over Susan, who lay on the sidewalk, the rain washing away her blood almost as fast as it flowed from the hole in her neck. Her eyes were open, bright and unseeing in the street light. Fort shook his head. "Goddamn," he whispered. "Goddamn."

"Decker. Who's this?"

"Russell Fort. Precinct said I could talk to you at the hospital in an emergency. I didn't tell them who I was."

"I bet you didn't."

"I told them it had to do with those dead undercover cops. They said call here, that you were with your partner. Look, two of Dumas's people tried to smoke me, but they got Susan instead. She's dead."

Decker closed his eyes. "I'm sorry. You said Dumas's people did it?"

"Before we go into that, I want your word you'll get me into the Witness Protection Program."

"Yesterday we might have had something to talk about. Right now I don't think you can buy into the game. I know you used Susan to get profile sheets from DEA to learn the identity of undercover cops. And I know you're supplying currency paper to Dumas, who's passing it on to Park Song. When the feds pick up your Aunt Lorraine and Cousin Arnold, you can turn out the lights, the party's over. You'll have to give me something else, Russell. Like who killed Gail and Max DaSilva."

Fort was silent. Then, "I think you know, man. If you know this much about my business, then you know the rest. Susan said you were smart."

"I need more. I need you to go into court and testify against Ben Dumas. Otherwise, you and I have nothing to talk about."

"I want a deal, then we'll talk. I'm an ex-cop, man. I wouldn't last a week in the joint. Look, I'm not just doing this for myself, I'm doing it for Susan. It's finished for me. The one thing I can do now is see Dumas's ass in the joint for what he did to her. I have an ID from the guy I shot, a Spic named Espinosa. He worked for Dumas's detective agency. Look, I don't have all day. I took two bullets and I need a doctor. The cops are probably after my ass for smoking Espinosa. I need protection."

"Give me a reason."

"Dumas got his information on Valentin and Dalto through me and Susan. I'll say that in court."

"Where are you?"

"Something else. That kid Tawny you been looking for? Dumas, he's got her. He killed her folks to get her."

Decker felt his mouth go dry. He cleared his throat twice before speaking. "How do you know that?"

"He goddamn *told* me, that's how I know."

"Fort, listen, where are you?"

"Oh shit, man, I got to go. Couple guys across the street staring at me. If they're Dumas's I'm dead."

Decker was on his feet, heart racing. Don't blow it, whatever you do, don't blow it. You're so close. Fort could tie Dumas to four murders—the DaSilvas, Valentin and Dalto. And Fort knew Decker was looking for Tawny. *Did he know where Tawny was?*

Decker had to talk Fort into coming in. Whatever witness deal Fort wanted, he had. The spade was worth his weight in gold. Promise him anything, but get him to come in. "Russell, let's deal. I'm a federal marshal. You want it, I can get you into the Federal Witness Program. Money, new ID, you name it. Just tell me about the Da-Silva killings. You said Dumas killed Tawny's parents to get her. What the hell does that mean? Where are you?"

"In a phone booth on Broadway and—oh, man, those two guys are coming over here."

Decker squeezed the telephone receiver. "Tell me where you are. I'll come get you myself. Russell? *Russell?*"

The line went dead.

NINETEEN

The knock on Michael Dartigue's hotel room door came shortly before 4:45 in the afternoon. Whoever it was tapped twice, not too loud, not too soft. Michael, who had been chewing his nails while watching a rerun of "Hawaii Five-O," suddenly looked toward the bed, where Nigella Barrow, in a blue silk robe, froze in the act of painting her toenails. They eyed each other fearfully. Finally Michael dried his palms on his jean-clad thighs and went to the door.

Hand on the knob, he closed his eyes, opened them and cleared his throat. "Yes?"

"I'm from LoCasio." A soft-spoken voice, polite. Not like the greaseball who'd telephoned yesterday with the news that the forty million dollars from the London robbery had not been sent to New York as promised. The one who sounded like he gargled with razor blades.

Michael opened the door and was greeted by a smile from Ben Dumas, who said, "May I come in?"

"I'm sorry. Sure, come on in. I'm Michael." He extended his hand.

"Fred Hannah," Dumas said. They shook hands as he entered the room. "I won't stay long," he said.

At the sight of Nigella Barrow he took off his hat and smiled. Michael introduced them and Dumas took her hand. "My pleasure."

247

Then Dumas reached into his topcoat and took out a two-inch vial of white powder, holding it between thumb and forefinger. His eyes went to Michael, who, chewing his lower lip and frowning, stared at the vial.

"First things first," Dumas said. "Before you dive into the party favors let's clear up a few points. Like Joe's guy said over the phone this morning, Joe did some thinking about that little talk you and he had yesterday. He wants you to know he's sorry for coming down on you so hard."

A relieved Michael breathed deeply. "Hey, these things happen. I understand. He did what he had to do." He nodded at Nigella as if to say, I told you everything would work out okay.

Dumas said, "Joe understands everybody got jerked around by Eddie Walkerdine so why hold anything against you? I mean, the way Walkerdine saw it, cutting you out was a lot cheaper than giving you a third or whatever it was you were supposed to get."

"Fred, I told Joe the truth. I swear. No way would I fuck with a heavy hitter like Joe. I mean, no way. I'd have to be out of my mind to even think of doing a thing like that."

"I know. But you have to see it from his position. You promised him something, you didn't deliver, and this made Joe look bad. Not just with his own people, you understand, but with the competition. Actually, it made him look confused, mixed up, fuzzy-headed, you might say."

Michael shook his head. "Fred, you don't know how bad I feel about that."

Dumas held up a hand. "Like I said, Joe understands. By the way, Walkerdine's turned up in Israel."

"Son of a bitch. You sure?"

"We're sure. Joe's got friends all over. With a load as big as this there's just so many places you can go to fence it, especially with all that jewelry. You can't resell stolen jewelry unless you break up the original settings and that takes skilled people. Men who can do this kind of work are few and far between. Everybody knows who they are."

Michael roared. "I love it. Fucking Walkerdine's going to get his ticket punched. I love it. You guys going to take the stuff away from him, I hope?"

Dumas sighed. "It's not that easy. Depends on how much of it he's got rid of and who he's selling it to. Looks as though he's got some kind of deal going with an Israeli he met in Spain. Anyway, back to you. You realize you owe Joe and—"

Michael put up his hands. "Hey, man, anytime I can do a favor for Joe . . . You want me to be a mule, whatever, you just say the word."

Dumas's smile was wolfish. "Great to be young and alive, isn't it?"

A grinning Michael, one arm around Nigella's waist, nodded. "Fucking A."

Dumas handed him the vial. "Party favors. Joe thought you seemed a little high-strung so that's why he promised to help you out. You two are free to leave New York any time you want. Your problems are over."

Michael swooped up a smiling Nigella in a bear hug and gave her a big kiss. "All right! You hear that? It's over. Man, it's over and we can relax. Is that great or what?"

He released Nigella and took Dumas's hand in both of his. "Man, am I glad you dropped by."

A smiling Dumas said, "If you don't mind, I'd like to stay and join the party." He took another vial from his pocket. "Brought my own."

Michael whooped. "Let's do it."

He ran into the tiny bathroom, then returned with Nigella's cosmetic mirror and a single-edge razor blade. By then Dumas and Nigella had placed two straight-back wooden chairs at a small table near the front alcove.

These being the only chairs in the room, a gracious Dumas insisted that Michael and Nigella sit. He would stand. He smiled at the haste with which Michael dumped his white powder onto the mirror and used the razor blade to divide it into eight thin lines. At the same time Nigella rolled three hundred-dollar bills into thin tubes. Dumas poured his powder on a small white saucer, using a small penknife to separate it into four thin lines. When Nigella gave him a rolled hundred he thanked her. Both Michael and Nigella seemed to warm to him, to relax in his presence.

Anxious to celebrate his reprieve from Joe LoCasio's retribution, Michael snorted first. Placing one end of a rolled hundred in the cocaine and the other in his right nostril he inhaled one line, then tucked the bill in his left nostril and inhaled a second. He did two more lines before flopping back in his chair, glassy eyed and grinning, traces of the white powder visible in his nose hairs. Giggling, he urged Nigella to dig in. This was some dynamite shit.

Dumas watched them for a few moments, then snorted two lines of his own powder, nodded approval and waited for the drug to take effect. Not on him but on Mickey and Judy, who didn't know they were about to put on a show. Neither seemed to notice that Dumas had put his gloves back on.

Suddenly Michael turned red-faced, clutched his heart and inhaled loudly through his open mouth. Eyes bulging, he went rigid in his chair. Nigella, meanwhile, sat with her hands on her throat, gasping for air. She looked at Michael in time to see him fall to the floor, where he lay twitching and vomiting.

She started to turn toward Dumas but fell, her head hitting the table. Then she lay still. Michael's body stiffened, then relaxed, his legs quivering briefly before he lay motionless near his overturned chair.

Dumas had given them one-hundred-percent cocaine, pure and uncut Bolivian marching powder with nothing added. They'd indulged themselves on nose candy strong enough to lift an elephant two stories off the ground and spin him around in the air three times. Stuff strong enough to bend steel and raise the dead. Well, it hadn't been entirely uncut. Dumas had added strychnine. Pure cocaine and rat poison. When you care enough to send the very best.

Didn't pay to make a fool out of Joe LoCasio. No, sir.

Dumas thought, Rowena, Rowena. You sure can pick 'em. This was the first time he had met Michael face to face. At Rowena's request he had investigated Michael Dartigue before their wedding and passed on his findings, which showed the guy to be a stone loser. Rowena, however, had chosen to ignore the facts. She'd got all excited about nothing, then gone ahead and married him.

Dumas picked up his saucer and went to the bathroom, where he washed off the white powder—milk sugar—in the basin. After drying the saucer with a bath towel he left it on top of the toilet, then looked in the mirror and sighed at the continuing loss of his thinning hair before returning to the room.

He found Rowena's notebooks right away, remembering how Ken had said that a man who would rob his own wife would do anything, including read her most private thoughts. There was always a chance that Michael's accomplices might have the notebooks, Michael not being the greatest brain on the planet. Dumas was to stay alert, and if he got lucky he was to bring the notebooks back to Ken for an up-close and personal inspection.

Dumas flipped through the notebooks, which were written in Rowena's ornate, elegant handwriting. He wasn't really surprised she'd kept such records. She was a meticulous, even fussy woman in many ways. The books might simply have been a way of keeping track of sexual preferences, customers and prices. Or they might have been a way of keeping certain financial records away from the taxman, banking authorities and law enforcement.

She could have been planning blackmail at some future date, though Dumas doubted this. Rowena, by now, knew her limitations. Her only mistake had been falling for the wrong man, a guy who would never live long enough to know better.

When Dumas saw his own and Ken's names, an eyebrow went up. Can't have people seeing this. Ken would decide how best to use the notebooks, after removing their names, of course.

LoCasio knew nothing about these notebooks. Michael, for his own reasons, hadn't mentioned them. He'd told Joe about the earrings, Rowena's no less, probably in an attempt to win sympathy for having gotten the shorts from Walkerdine. He'd wasted his breath. Joe had just one thing on his mind and that was to get even with Michael for jerking him around.

Which was where Dumas came in. He doubted if anybody was going to get excited about two cokeheads who'd ODed on high-class flake. Things like that happened in Fun City every day.

Dumas looked around for the earrings and found them without any difficulty. Very nice. Typical of Rowena's good taste. He dropped them in a pocket of his overcoat along with his "drug" vial. Rowena would have her earrings back within hours.

Moments later Dumas exited the hotel room, leaving a Do Not Disturb sign hanging from the door. He really was going to have to do something about his hair.

TWENTY

It was 7:12 P.M. when Rowena Dartigue, carrying a bottle of duty-free cognac in a blue plastic bag, stepped from the international arrivals building at Kennedy Airport and followed the dumpy Puerto Rican pushing her luggage cart.

She walked under the overhang, remaining near the building and away from the curb where a December rain pelted a taxi rank. Usually the downpour did little for her peace of mind; she'd always found rain synonymous with calamity. Today, however, she could not be happier. Ben Dumas was meeting her. Since he had agreed to kill Park Song, Rowena was ready to tolerate any amount of precipitation.

Along the curb a line of newly arrived passengers queued for taxis. Rowena's mind was on a limousine waiting to take her and Ben Dumas to the auction in Queens, the New York borough she found so depressing. The cognac she carried might remove the chill from her bones, but nothing could eliminate her distaste for lackluster Queens. If God ever decided on a second flood, Queens would be the proper place to send it.

As she walked Rowena reminded herself of the risk in asking Ben Dumas to kill Park Song. Ben was unpredictable; his motives were often obscure, his behavior erratic. Of all Rowena's friends and acquaintances he was most likely to do the unexpected. Like an acrobat he kept his balance by saying one thing and doing another. The inner madman in him could explode at any moment.

There was always the possibility he might betray her, that he might tell Song of her impassioned wish to see him dead. Rowena pushed that appalling thought from her mind. She was upset enough; to dwell on further unpleasantries would be self-defeating. But let Song learn she wanted him done in and he'd come after Rowena with mind-boggling ferocity. For her to continue living Ben Dumas must be willing to unleash his own brand of ferocity on Park Song.

But people were unreliable and the future uncertain. Complications could very well muddy the waters. Rowena, however, was counting on love to save the day. Ben's passion for the doomed Ken Yokoi was costing him a small fortune in AIDS cures. This fact, to Rowena's way of thinking, made Mr. Dumas susceptible to manipulation. She was in a position to exploit his need for money and would be foolish not to. By taking advantage of his difficulty, she would solve her own.

Song's murder carried a high price tag. Rowena had had no choice but to make Ben an offer he couldn't bloody well refuse. But as she followed her luggage cart past the taxi rank, a thought suddenly occurred to her. Perhaps it might be wise to up the ante. Ben's loyalty was, after all, for sale. So why not make certain he stayed bought? Lock up his fidelity, so to speak. Rowena, old girl, give yourself a pat on the back. This new offer to Ben would assure Song's demise as well as her own peace of mind. Three cheers for Mrs. Weymouth-Dartigue, if you please.

Her new offer: Ben would receive all monies from Tawny's sale at tonight's auction. A quarter of a million dollars in cold cash. Twice the value of her original proposition. And that was just for starters. She also intended to make him a full partner in the slave business. Share and share alike from the first dollar. What could be more generous than that? This new arrangement would lessen her future earning power, but now wasn't the time to quibble. Park Song's death was worth whatever it cost.

From the beginning of her relationship with Ben Dumas, she felt she had handled him with ease. He so admired her English accent, her aristocratic bearing, which he called *class*, a word which Americans apparently saw as the ultimate praise. His admiration was her margin. Rowena gave him points for being shrewd and street smart, but she herself was rational and cerebral, more strategic attributes in any battle of wits. In their relationship she had been the pilot, the one who'd taken the wheel. Her decision to amply reward him for killing Song should keep Dumas dancing to her tune.

She looked up at a gray December sky. America offered her the same filthy weather she had in England. Ben had picked bloody Queens for the auction house because of its proximity to his detective agency. The house, a private two-story home, was owned by a Panama-registered corporation which in turn was owned by Rowena. A middle-aged Hungarian couple, discreet and trustworthy, lived on the premises and were the owners of record.

Yokoi and Nicolay had worked out a procedure for adult customers at the house. These were Yokoi's patients, attractive young men and women desiring sexual domination and who had entered the auction at Yokoi's suggestion. Their stay was brief, no more than forty-eight hours before a sale. Those not sold or paired were asked to leave the house immediately but not before videotaping an admission that they were there of their own free will. This admission was insurance against attempted blackmail or any filing of criminal charges. As for rejected youngsters, they were put back on the Manhattan streets, returned to Rowena in England or sometimes passed along to U.S. pimps for a price.

Rowena sent over youngsters from her London charity in the company of two old queens who had been with her for years, the group arriving a day or two before the auction. House security was maintained by Dumas's men, as ghastly a bunch of villains as Rowena had ever encountered. Sales were cash only, no refunds. Rowena's takings never went below two million dollars per sale.

Tonight at the airport baggage-retrieval she had been met by a fleshy Puerto Rican bearing a sign with her name. Mr. Dumas, he said, was waiting for her in a car. The well-mannered Ben, who usually helped her with the baggage, had obviously decided to maintain a low profile. Perhaps he couldn't stand the cold rain, for which Rowena didn't blame him. She couldn't wait to get into the car herself.

A three minute walk then Rowena saw the Puerto Rican point to a silver stretch limo parked behind a small green bus that commuted between the airport's various terminals. Suddenly she felt excited, relieved and safe. Above all, *safe*. Ben would be thrilled with her new offer. She knew it, she bloody well knew it.

Rowena tapped the Puerto Rican on the shoulder, nodded at the limo's open trunk, then quickened her step, leaving him behind. The limousine's open back door beckoned to her, a beacon in a shadowy world.

An anxious Rowena, oblivious to "Silent Night" coming from the radio of a parked taxi, weaved her way through a cluster of newly arrived Japanese tourists. Then she dodged a nurse pushing a mummified old man in a wheelchair and stepped from under the overhang, ignoring the rain and its effect on her black mink. She couldn't wait to see the look on Ben's face when she told him that he was her new partner, effective immediately. By making him happy she would insure her own happiness.

Limp with relief, she slid into the back seat of the limousine. Elation seized her; she was now protected from the terror that was Park Song. Gloved hand patting her chest, she took a deep breath. Everything was going according to plan. Her plan. She would pull through this mess in grand style. "Ben, darling, you don't know how glad I am—"

Rowena's jaw dropped. Seized by fear, she turned cold, hot, then back to cold again. She leaned backward, a hand fumbling for the door behind her. But any escape was cut off: the door slammed shut, its lock clicking immediately. Rowena, heart beating wildly, held her breath. She tried to swallow but couldn't.

In the back seat with her, humming "White Christmas" and filing his nails, was Park Song.

Neither he nor Rowena spoke as outside the limousine the chauffeur Choi paid off the porter, then resumed his position behind the wheel. David Mitla, a Toronto Blue Jays baseball cap pulled low over his eyes, turned around in the front seat to stare at Rowena. As the limousine pulled away from the terminal she covered her mouth with both hands to keep from crying out.

Song buffed the nails of his left hand on the velvet lapel of his gray topcoat. "And may all your Christmases be white," he said to no one in particular. Then to Rowena, "Change of plans, Rowena. I decided to pick up your Tawny myself instead of having her brought to me. I am quite anxious to see her. Did you have a nice flight? British Air is one of my favorite airlines. No other one serves such excellent cheddar cheese. And those afternoon teas. Wonderful.''

Rowena placed her handbag and the cognac on a copy of the *Wall Street Journal* on the seat between her and Song. She had to compose herself. Present a calm front and act as if nothing was out of the ordinary. *Where in God's name was Ben?*

She had been caught off guard. Truth was, she had hoped never to see this psychotic little bastard again. Now she would have to answer his unnerving questions about his missing eight million dollars. She'd have to weigh her every word. Her life depended on it. Could she maintain her composure until Ben arrived? If she didn't, God help her.

She removed her gloves, opened her fur coat and forced herself to pat Song's thigh in greeting. A deep breath, then, "Park, darling, what a lovely surprise. Afraid I don't share your admiration for B.A. cuisine. Bloody tea they serve tastes like moose piss, if you ask me. Ran into a bit of turbulence over Newfoundland. Pilot had to fly above a storm for nearly an hour.''

She cleared her throat. "By the bye, where's Ben? I believe he was supposed to meet me." Her voice was too high, she'd have to control it. *Concentrate.*

Park Song looked at David Mitla. "Ben. Yes, he did say something about getting together with you. He decided it might be best if you and I had a little tête-à-tête first.''

Song touched her arm gently. "There is the matter of my eight million dollars which has gone missing.''

Rowena looked down at her clasped hands. "Believe me, Park, I feel as bad about that as you do. I wanted to explain things but had no way of contacting you. You're always on the move and—''

"I understand. Explain things, you said.''

"Park, I accept full responsibility for what happened to your money. I want you to know that straightaway. You handed over the cash in good faith, so it's up to me to make good. You'll get back every penny, I promise.''

Song aimed a forefinger at David Mitla. "See, I told you she was resourceful. Never underestimate Rowena, I said.''

Mitla shook his head then turned front.

Song dug at the cuticle on his right pinky. "Eight million dollars. I can counterfeit that much in hours except I'm in a situation where counterfeiting isn't practical. I need that money."

"I promise you'll have it."

"Is that what you told Ben?"

"I don't understand . . ."

Song stared through a tinted limousine window at the expressway. "Did you tell Ben you would return my money?"

"May I please have some air?"

Song pressed a button in his armrest. To Rowena's right a window slid halfway down and an icy gust chilled her face and teared her eyes. Eyes closed, she continued facing the window. *Had Song learned about her plan and eliminated Ben? Dear God, no.* She must not look frightened, she must take control.

Desperation gave her strength. She turned to Song. "Where is Ben?"

Song returned to filing his nails. "Home administering unto Ken. They have a crisis of their own, if you remember. He'll meet us here at the house before the auction's over."

"Are you sure?"

"I just finished speaking to him. Give him a call on the car phone, if you like."

Rowena forced a smile. "I'll see him soon enough at the house. He *is* coming to the house."

"Of course. That's what you pay him for, isn't it, to jump when you say so?"

"Park, you know that isn't true. Ben's very much his own man. We both know that."

To calm herself Rowena massaged her forearm, a trick she'd learned in yoga class. If Song felt she had power over Ben, then it must be true. She was elated. Scared but elated. The stout and sturdy Ben Dumas, the one man who could hold his own with Park Song, was very much alive. And he was Rowena's man.

She decided that Song's surprise appearance at the airport was due to his being a lustful pervert who couldn't wait to get his hands on a thirteen-year-old girl. *Ben was still alive.*

Rowena considered telephoning him from the car then decided against it. She had the shakes and there was always the chance she'd say the wrong thing which could be fatal. Park Song was nobody's fool. He would pick up on a word, a tone in her voice. Who knows what he'd do after that. As badly as she wanted to talk to Ben, now was not the time. Her deliverance would have to wait until she met him at the house.

Suddenly, she got a fantastic idea. A bit dangerous, perhaps, but worth the risk. She would take the offensive with Park Song. Keep the bugger off-balance until she met up with Ben. At which point she would insist he kill Song immediately. As for Choi and the Israeli, Ben had enough men to dispose of these two if need be.

Rowena had bought Ben's allegiance. Now she had to buy some time with Song. Lead him in circles until Ben could take over. She felt a bit of confidence creeping back. The wily Oriental gentleman sitting beside her was about to get hoodwinked.

She said, "Park, I didn't want to tell you this until it was a *fait accompli.* That is, until I actually had the cash in hand. But I've shipped a dozen more children over from London and I intend to demand top dollar for each and every one. That should produce a tidy down payment on what I owe you."

Song smiled.

Rowena said, "Remember I once mentioned that some estate agent had a filthy rich Arab ready to pay a bloody fortune for my home? Well, I got in touch with the agent before leaving and his Arab friend's still interested. All this trouble in the Gulf has the ragheads anxious to return to London so they're buying property in England like crazy. I'm sure I can get at least two million pounds for the house. That's nearly half your eight million dollars right there."

A nervous Rowena was lying through her teeth. Indulging in a bit of terminological inexactitude, as Churchill might say. There would be no extra children at tonight's auction. And her beloved house was not for sale at any price. But for the moment deception would have to become a condition of life.

Song eyed the nail file. "I expected no less of you."

Rowena beamed.

"You didn't disappoint me," he said. "You acted according to your nature. You truly did."

A smiling Rowena said, "Well, I owe you, don't I?"

"And I owe you as well," Song said, and stabbed her in the thigh with the nail file.

Rowena screamed and kicked him in the leg. Ignoring the pain Song said, you fucking bitch, and reached for her throat. Rowena scratched his face with both hands, drawing blood. An enraged Song, however, had her throat in an iron grip. Rowena pulled at his wrists. Song's grip, however, was immovable. She started to black out. Her head ached and blood ran from a corner of her mouth. She heard Song's voice, cursing in English and Korean, coming from far away.

Suddenly, he released Rowena and shoved something in her mouth. A small, hard object with sharp edges. As Rowena began choking, Song pushed her to the car floor and kicked her in the stomach. Rowena spat out the object. Gasping for air, she lay huddled at Song's feet and massaged her throat.

Song watched in silence as she picked the object up from the car floor.

"Taken from your husband," he said. "I believe you know how he came by it."

Rowena was holding a Giuliano earring stolen from the depository.

Her throat was raw. Forced to whisper, she said, "Where did you get this? Someone stole it from my safe-deposit box—"

"Someone? Is that what you're calling your husband these days? I got this from Dumas, by the way."

"I don't understand . . ."

"Your husband and some of his associates robbed the depository. Dumas and I are certain you helped them get inside. Your precious husband is no great brain. I can't see him tying his shoes without assistance. You played me for a fool, waited until I'd given you enough money to make it worth your while, then you struck."

"You're mad. I never took a penny from you. Why should I after all these years?"

"Your husband is a very expensive toy. Always in need of money for one foolish scheme or another. It all fits. The robbery, followed by your intense desire to see me dead. As you must realize by now, Dumas filled me in on everything."

Rowena shook her head. "I never asked Ben to—"

"Never asked Ben to—what? Go on, finish what you were saying."

Rowena closed her eyes.

Song said, "He's nobody's fool, your Ben. Killing me might solve your problems but it wouldn't do much for him. My murder would be a millstone around his neck. Important people in South Korea and

America would come down on him quite harshly for such an action. He thought it through and decided, wisely I think, to reject your proposition and instead seek a deal with me. Let me point out he's being well paid for switching sides."

Rowena said, "Park, believe me there's been a misunderstanding. I'm not the type to kill anyone. You know that."

"Ben taped your conversation and played it back for me."

Rowena closed her eyes.

"You tend to underestimate people," Song said. "At the same time you have too high an opinion of yourself. Ben's priority is Ken. Doing your dirty work would only shorten Ken's life. Did you think of that? Obviously not."

As the limousine turned onto the rain-slicked expressway Song leaned toward Rowena. A second later she cried out as his fingers dug painfully into the soft area around her right kneecap. When he took away his hand Rowena took a deep breath. There was no feeling in the leg.

Song said, "You're going to tell me everything. About the Nigerian you sent to rob me in London, about your foolish husband and his friends who cleaned out my account."

Still on the floor, Rowena sat up, back against the front seat. "Michael—"

Song removed Rowena's bottle of brandy from its plastic bag and held it up to the backseat light. "Michael's dead. Dumas saw to that. He says no charge for ridding you of that fucking idiot."

Rowena wept.

The limousine hit a pothole, splashing water on the windshield. There was no traffic in front and very little behind.

Rowena covered her face with both hands.

Song chewed a thumbnail. "Michael's death was business. He disappointed some people who weren't nearly as tolerant of his shortcoming as you were. For what he did to me, I'd have killed him myself. Torn out his fucking heart and pissed on it. Don't waste my time by telling me Michael is innocent. Thanks to Dumas I know who he did the job with. I also know the name of his fence and the name of the little cunt your darling Michael was running away with. That's right. Your husband was leaving you for a younger woman."

As a weeping Rowena covered her ears Song said, "Dumas drives a hard bargain. As if topping your offer wasn't enough, I also had to throw in a hundred thousand dollars worth of counterfeit."

In the front seat David Mitla snickered.

Rowena said, "I don't want to die. Please, don't kill me."

Song eyed the brandy label. "If you bought this at the duty-free shop, you were ripped off. They actually charge you more than do regular shops. Did you know that?"

Suddenly he screamed, "Where's my money?" and clubbed her on the head with the bottle.

Shrieking, Rowena curled up into a ball. An enraged Song repeatedly struck her until she remained still. "Bitch," he shouted. "I want my fucking money."

In the front seat David Mitla signaled Choi to stop. As the limousine pulled off the expressway, the Israeli turned and took the bottle from Song's hand. "She can't get you your money if you crush her skull."

He climbed into the back, knelt over Rowena and felt her neck pulse. Then he looked at Song who sat with his head against the window, eyes closed and breathing heavily. Mitla said, "She's dead."

Song opened his eyes. "Not so. I only hit her a couple of times."

Mitla flopped onto the back seat. "More than a couple, I would say. You got carried away, which is nothing new."

A frowning Song said, "What do I do now?"

"Let's start by ridding ourselves of the corpse. Remove all identification then push her out on the highway. Let a truck or a bus run her over. Should make her death look like an accident and keep an investigation to a minimum."

Song nodded. "And my money?"

"First things first." Mitla handed Rowena's purse to Song. "Have Choi get out and come around to this side. Traffic's not too heavy. But let's wait until it's clear before putting her body out."

It was ten minutes before the expressway was empty. Working quickly in the cold rain, Mitla and Choi dropped Rowena's corpse into a large puddle of water then raced back to the limousine. The limousine had just rolled back onto the expressway when they saw the headlights of an oncoming vehicle coming behind them. As Song and Mitla looked over their shoulders, the vehicle, a school bus, ran over Rowena's body.

TWENTY-ONE

At approximately the same time Rowena Dartigue's body was being crushed by a bus from the Safian Private School for Children, a yellow taxi was carrying Manny Decker past Ken Yokoi's Washington Square townhouse in rainy darkness.

He had time for a quick look at the residence before the cabbie, an aristocratic-looking Russian Jew, turned left at the corner of Yokoi's block and stopped in front of a store selling occult books, incense, New Age music and aphrodisiacs. After paying the fare, Decker stepped onto a deserted, wet sidewalk, pulled down his hat and opened a cheap umbrella purchased minutes earlier from a Senegalese street peddler near Bags's hospital. When he was certain he was unobserved he pulled his .38 Smith & Wesson from its belt holster and slipped it into an overcoat pocket. Face behind the umbrella, he walked toward the townhouse.

Two men had been moving about on the townhouse steps: Kim Shin and his bodyguard Muscles, Shin with adhesive tape across the fractured nose Decker had given him in their recent battle. Shin stood at the top of the stairs, back to the open door of the townhouse. From under a huge umbrella he watched his bodyguard carry suitcases to a Volkswagen van parked curbside. Decker had surprise on his side. But that wouldn't help if more Koreans suddenly came through the door.

He had no backup, no search warrant. Only Spiceland knew he was coming here, and she'd given her word to tell no one. Decker was playing a lone hand, not too smart when it involved withholding information from a hardass like Singular. Mr. Manfred Decker was shoveling shit against the tide.

He had to neutralize Dumas or Fort would never come in from the cold and nail Dumas for Tawny's kidnapping, the DaSilva murders and the undercover-cop killings. As long as Dumas was free, Fort would stay missing. To get his cooperation, Decker had to take Dumas off the streets.

Calling for backup was out of the question. Any contact with police would only have alerted Dumas, who had friends everywhere. He'd make a countermove and somebody, maybe Tawny, would suffer for it. If Decker wanted to rescue Tawny he had to go it alone.

At the base of the stairs he kept the umbrella over his face and stopped to let Shin's bodyguard pass in front of him, a suitcase in each hand. Decker felt a rush and the fear that always came before trouble now left his insides cold. He was pumped.

He dropped the umbrella, jammed a shoulder into the big Korean's spine and ran him into the van. The bodyguard hit the van headfirst, a jolt to the skull and brain that would have knocked most men senseless. Not this one. He was hurt but still conscious.

Decker watched him drop to his knees, hands gripping his head, then collapse on his side, glassy-eyed stare fixed on Decker, who let him see the .38, let him get a good look, before covering Kim Shin.

A slightly built man in an anorak who had been walking a schnauzer in Decker's direction came within several feet of the townhouse, saw the trouble and stopped dead. Without hesitating he picked up the schnauzer, and ran in the opposite direction, the dog's leash trailing behind him. Another public-spirited citizen who couldn't wait to get involved.

When Kim Shin raised his own umbrella for a better view of what was going on, Decker said to him, "Do something stupid and I'll paint the stairs with your brains. Come on down, hands behind your neck."

He considered wasting Shin, of dispensing wild justice here and now. There wasn't a cop who didn't feel that way about one perp or another. Some acted on it and were lucky enough never to get caught. Decker's nature ran to revenge, and Shin definitely had it coming. The gook had attacked first—fifteen years ago in Saigon. Ice him now and there'd be one less worry.

The downside: Decker would also have to kill Muscles, the only witness. Not smart. Whacking two men with diplomatic immunity? Forget payback.

He watched Shin drop his umbrella. The Korean was half-hidden in the darkness, but the nighttime did not hide the hatred in his voice. "You must be insane," he said to Decker. "I will see to it that you pay for this. I will demand that you be sacked immediately."

"Move it, and put your hands behind your neck before I put another hole in your ass." Decker motioned Shin to the van, where the diplomat looked down at the dazed bodyguard now struggling to his feet. Shin started to speak, but Decker silenced him; he pushed the diplomat against the van and kicked his legs apart. Eyes on the bodyguard, Decker quickly patted down Shin. The diplomat was clean.

The bodyguard, however, was packing. Decker ordered him to remove his yellow slicker and suit jacket, half expecting him to make a move. But he appeared weak. Or maybe he remembered the beating Decker had given him. In any case he followed orders. Free of his slicker and jacket, his .45 in a cut-down shoulder holster could easily be seen.

"Face down," Decker said. Eyeing Decker, the big man lay down but not in a hurry. The guy was looking for a chance to attack. Decker jammed his .38 into the back of the bodyguard's neck, letting him feel the pressure, letting him know how easy it was to get smoked on the Big Apple's streets. The touch of the .38 on his skin seemed to chill out Muscles. Decker easily relieved him of the .45.

He ordered both Koreans into the front seat of the van, Shin behind the wheel. "Cuff yourself and the bear to the steering wheel," he told Shin. When the Koreans were shackled, Decker removed the ignition keys and threw them into Washington Square Park. His heartbeat was slower. The fear was under control.

Decker walked to the rear of the van. The doors were wide open. Well, well. Decker could reach out and touch the currency paper Fort had given Nicolay. Four packages wrapped in heavy brown paper, each the size of a bed pillow and bound with steel strips. Each stamped—*Property of the U.S. Bureau of Engraving and Printing.* Straight from Fort's Aunt Lorraine.

Five suitcases rested near the bundles. Decker opened the nearest one. Cowabunga, dude. Stack after stack of new hundreds. Enough to keep a smile on Decker's face for years to come. He'd seen counterfeit before, but this stuff was outstanding. Laughing Boy certainly knew how to express himself.

Decker opened a second suitcase. More hundreds. A third suitcase revealed a different example of Song's handiwork. Decker was staring at a collection of counterfeit securities, bearer bonds and certificates of deposit issued by West German and Swiss banks.

Song had buyers in New York, Fort had told Decker. Laughing Boy needed to raise money; he was apparently in hock to somebody for large bucks. Fort didn't know who, but it had to be somebody heavy; Song was pressuring Dumas for a lot of paper in a hurry. In turn, Dumas was pressuring Fort. Decker concluded from the number of suitcases in the van that Song had to come up with a lot of money. Somebody had Laughing Boy by the balls.

Closing the van's doors Decker returned to the driver's window. Time to make it official. He showed his badge. "Detective Sergeant Manny Decker. You're under arrest for counterfeiting and for the theft of government property, namely the paper used in the making of United States currency. I'm also arresting you in connection with the kidnapping of Tawny DaSilva."

As the rain fell Decker Mirandized the Koreans from memory. Once or twice he let his eyes go to the house; if he was being watched there was nothing he could do about it. When he left the van and started up the stairs he'd be a target. The thought that Dumas might be waiting started his heartbeat racing again.

He said to Shin, "Dumas inside?"

The Koreans sat frozen.

"Does he have Tawny DaSilva?"

Shin fingered the tape on his nose.

"You're moving Laughing Boy's goods," Decker said. "This mean he's setting up a new meeting place for his customers?"

The Koreans sat frozen.

"Hard to get a word in edgewise with you guys," Decker said. Shifting the .38 to his left hand, he reached into the van with his right. Using thumb and forefinger he twisted Kim Shin's lower lip. The Korean's eyes bulged; he leaned away, his free hand pulling on Decker's wrist. Decker's grip held firm. No more Mr. Nice Guy.

"Where's Tawny DaSilva?"

Shin relaxed. Thinking the Korean was going to talk, Decker loosened his grip.

Shin spat in Decker's face. "Fuck you."

Decker felt no anger. Calm took over, the one cops felt when they knew they had life-and-death power over a perp. If there was one thing about being a cop it was having that power.

"Fuck me? I don't think so." He grabbed Shin's hair and yanked his head out into the rain. "I owe you for Buf and Ivan, for Gail and Max. If we have to do this all night, it's fine by me. Last time— where's Tawny?"

Kim Shin said, "Fuck your mother. That little girl, she get fucked too."

Decker felt calmer than ever. "Suit yourself," he said, and elbowed Shin in his damaged nose. The Korean gasped, head snapping back. The bodyguard reached across Shin's body and with his free hand flailed at Decker. Stick with the game plan, Decker told himself. Forget Muscles. Kim Shin was the man of the hour. Stay on him until he got with the program.

Shin held up one hand. Time out? Decker didn't have time. Shin's face was bloody but the fight hadn't left him. He inhaled through his mouth. "I tell you about the girl."

Decker was immediately on guard. He'd been in Nam and knew what hardasses Koreans could be; they had scared the shit out of Vietnamese, North and South. When it came to being cold-blooded, no unit, American or otherwise, could match them. Koreans killed anything that didn't kill them first. Kim Shin was no pussy. When he started being helpful, watch out.

"Dumas said he kept her downstairs in the cellar," Shin said.

Decker leaned forward, tried to keep his face blank, but inside a violent elation seized him. *Tawny was in the house.*

But there was more. The detective knew when somebody was holding back. "Dumas doesn't like girls. Why did he take Tawny?"

Shin looked straight ahead; in the night a half-smile on his bloodied, bandaged face made him look hideous. Decker thought, you're throwing shit in the game.

Go to Plan B. He grabbed a handful of the Korean's hair and yanked his head into the door frame. Shin's temple hit the metal with a bang. To get his point across, Decker did it again.

He was about to go for a third time when Shin held up his free hand in defense. "The girl is being held for . . ."

He hesitated. But Decker was ahead of him. He knew what Shin was going to say. Decker said, "Dumas plans to hand her over to Park Song."

Who else? Not Dumas and Yokoi, both of whom were fags. Not Nicolay, who could have snatched Tawny himself had he wanted her. Now Decker knew why Singular wanted him to stay away from Laughing Boy. An outsider's personal beef with Song could screw up a federal investigation.

Decker had traced the gun in the DaSilva killings to Dumas. Now he had a motive for the murders. Dumas had smoked the parents in order to pimp their daughter to Laughing Boy. So enraged was Decker that had he not looked away from Shin he would have killed the Korean on the spot. In Vietnam Laughing Boy was known to be hard on little girls. Very hard. Everybody knew it but nobody was concerned because in Nam life, a Vietnamese life especially, was cheap, and cheap at a time when there were no rules. While in Asia even Decker had stopped listening to his conscience.

He looked at Shin with contempt. For a few seconds he saw him as a dead man. The look wasn't lost on the Korean who blinked. Decker said, "Dumas told you she's downstairs, you said. Did you actually see her?"

Shin weakly raised his cuffed hand from the steering wheel. "No, I did not see her. Dumas said there was some problem and she might have to be moved to Queens. I don't know where. He just said Queens. You go inside and find out where she is."

Decker felt the fear return. If Dumas was watching this scene at the van, he'd be ready when Decker came to call. Decker would be walking into a confrontation with a headcase and on the psycho's turf. He suddenly felt burnt out. But it wasn't exhaustion or fatigue or nerves that had him ready to quit. It was fear.

He let the rain beat down on him for a few seconds. Then he thought of Gail and walked into the house.

Decker and Mrs. Esmeralda Moody, a meaty forty-two-year-old Jamaican nurse, stepped from a small elevator and into the basement of Yokoi's townhouse. It was Mrs. Moody who switched on the light then stood back to stare at Decker.

He had checked out the first floor, where he'd found Mrs. Moody in the kitchen eating dinner and watching a rerun of "Cheers." She'd told him there were just three people in the house—herself, Dumas and Yokoi. Some people were moving suitcases and bundles out of the house, but that had nothing to do with her. She hadn't liked having her dinner interrupted. Nor had she liked it when Decker, flashing his badge, ordered her to take him to the cellar.

In the cellar she said to Decker, "I wasn't hired to get involved in nothing funny. I'm a nurse, and that's all I am. I never been down here before. They told me stay out so I did."

"Just show me around," Decker said. He also had her with him because he didn't want her warning Dumas.

He stood near the elevator, letting his eyes adjust to the light. The cellar, a large low-ceiling room with concrete walls, was warm. Green metal filing cabinets lined one wall; a washing machine was operating loudly, and to his left there was a small wine cellar. At the far end of the cellar a short passage led to a green metal door. The cellar smelled of oil and mildew.

Mrs. Moody, arms folded across an enormous bosom, said to Decker, "Got a man sick upstairs. Supposed to be taking care of him."

Decker removed his hat and whacked it against his thigh to knock off the rain. "If you're talking about Mr. Yokoi, I don't think he's going anywhere. You sure there's nobody in the house besides you, Yokoi and Dumas?"

"I'm sure. Tomorrow morning woman comes in to clean. She'll be here four hours, then she leaves. Let me ask you something—if you're a detective how come I can't tell Mr. Dumas you're here?"

Decker looked along the passage at the green metal door. "You wouldn't know if anyone's in that room?"

"Got no way of knowing that. Seen some Korean men come down here, but it wasn't my business, I didn't bother with them. What you looking for?"

Decker walked to the front of the passage which was lit by a single bulb. He turned off the light, put on his hat and took his .38 from a coat pocket. He looked at Mrs. Moody. "When I start for the door, you go upstairs and dial 911. Don't tell Dumas you've called the police. You might get in trouble."

"Detective, I got me a patient to care for. What kind of trouble you mean?" Police had never did anything for black people and never would. White police, black police, all the same. No goddam good. If there was any shooting, she would be out of here so fast they wouldn't see her for dust.

Decker looked at the light coming from beneath the green door. His stomach tightened. For the first time he regretted not having called for backup. "Get out of here and dial 911. And if there's any shooting—"

Mrs. Moody went rigid. "Shooting? You mean bullets?"

Decker looked at her and decided not to say more; she was frightened enough. He couldn't stay with her and look for Tawny, too. He could only hope she'd take his advice and stay away from Dumas. Do that, fat lady.

He inched forward, his back against the concrete passage wall. His .38 was trained on the green door, his breathing deliberately shallow. He stopped once to wipe perspiration from his eyes. He had a tension headache; his stomach was in knots. A vein jutted out on his forehead. His attention remained on the pale yellow light coming from beneath the door. He heard the elevator doors open, then close. Goodbye, Mrs. Moody.

At the green door he crouched and listened, ear near the knob. Nothing. He felt for hinges and found none, meaning the door opened on the inside. Fear threatened to paralyze him. Decker fought it, willing his fear to turn into anger and fury, willing it to be the craziness a cop needed to deal with a crazy world. Hand on the knob he turned it slowly. *Showtime.*

He quickly shoved the door open and threw himself inside to the left, landing on a stone floor with his back against the wall. He tightened his finger on the trigger, afraid of dying and ready to kill.

The small concrete room was empty.

It had been occupied recently; he saw the unmade cot, the metal folding chair, the fast-food leftovers on a cheap card table. There were Korean newspapers on the floor. Also girlie magazines, cigarette butts in an ashtray, a pair of beat-up running shoes. A man's room. Nothing to indicate that a young girl had ever been here.

He got to his feet, eyes on a second metal door a few feet away.

Light could be seen through a glass panel. Decker could also hear heavy-metal music coming from the room.

Tawny.

He moved to the door, .38 shoulder-high. At the door he checked the .38. Safety off. He wiped perspiring hands on his topcoat then peered through the glass panel.

He saw a gray concrete room smaller than the one in which he stood. A wobbly card table stood directly beneath a flickering fluorescent light; on the table was a Mickey Mouse watch, a small backpack and a hair ribbon. A closed-circuit camera looked down from a corner of the ceiling. From a cassette deck resting on a metal folding chair came the sounds of Aerosmith singing "Walk This Way."

The room was empty. *Two empty rooms.*

Eyes closed, Decker leaned his head against the glass panel. His wet clothes suddenly felt colder and heavier. He was tired, bone fucking tired. He'd have given anything to lie down.

Defeat had left him exhausted.

In Ken Yokoi's bedroom Dumas sat beside the dying Japanese silently reading through one of the Rowena Dartigue notebooks stolen from the London depository. "The lady could have ruined us with this shit," Dumas said. "You, me and a host of the rich and famous. She's even got stuff in here on Song being one of South Korea's top agents. I should have put her on the payroll, she's that good. Let me read you this bit about Song and Youngsam, the Korean spy chief."

Yokoi smiled weakly. "Fire away, babe."

"Just in time for the good stuff," said Decker.

Dumas and Yokoi looked at him. Decker had quietly stepped into the bedroom and now stood inside the doorway. He held a book in one hand, his .38 in the other. He was unshaven and his clothes were rain-soaked. His eyes, bright in the half-light, were focused on Dumas.

An angry Dumas stood up slowly, jaw working as he quickly assessed the situation, seeing an unaccompanied Decker and wondering if this visit was personal. Personal could mean payback, depending on how much Decker knew. Dumas placed Rowena's notebook on the bed then took one step sideways toward a night table where he kept a .22 Magnum in a drawer with Ken's medicine.

Decker gently waved the .38. Dumas froze. Seconds later he returned to working his jaw as though chewing. "Fuck you doing here, Decker? You plan on shooting somebody with that thing?"

"It's your ass, you touch that table."

"Show me a search warrant duly signed by a judge or get the hell out of here."

"Talking probable, big guy. Police may enter a premises without a warrant if they suspect a crime is being committed. Your front door was open. Looked like a break-in to me. I also have cause to suspect you're holding Tawny DaSilva prisoner."

Dumas said, "Who's Tawny DaSilva?"

"Ran into Kim Shin outside. Bet you don't know him either. He says Tawny's been moved to Queens but he doesn't know where. Maybe you can tell me."

Yokoi coughed, drawing Dumas's attention. Dumas stroked Yokoi's forehead then looked at Decker. "Out or I'll make you use that gun."

"I'd be careful if I were you," Decker said. "I could miss you and hit your girlfriend. Speaking of poor aim, your people missed Fort and took out his old lady instead. Fort's pissed off. He's ready to roll over on you."

Decker saw Dumas's eyes close in thought then open slowly. The guy was good at playing laid-back. He didn't appear to have a nerve in his body. Decker thought, try this on for size.

He tossed the book across the room. It landed on a throw rag rug near the bed. "General Science textbook," he said. "Found it downstairs in the cellar. Has Tawny DaSilva's name inside."

Dumas eased into his wolfish grin. "Want to take that to court, hotshot? Be my guest. For all I know you planted it there."

Decker sat on a colonial hardwood chair, removed his hat and placed it on one knee. "I haven't slept more than six hours in two days. I'm tired, hungry and I need a bath. And I'm in a shit mood. Not finding Tawny makes me feel worse."

He looked at the ceiling. "Appears I just missed her and that's what I want to talk to you about. By the way, your Mrs. Moody's telephoned for the police. We'll be having company soon. Couple things I want to go over before they arrive."

He rubbed the back of his neck, thinking. Dumas and Yokoi waited in silence. Finally Decker said, "Where'd you move Tawny DaSilva?"

"Get fucked," Dumas said.

Decker stood up and dropped his hat on the chair. "The lab guys will dust the cellar and find her fingerprints. They'll find hairs and fibers belonging to her. You're toast and you don't even know it."

Yokoi coughed then whispered, "Like any overachiever, Sergeant Decker, you view the world from your perspective. And that perspective, as with all subjective views, contains built-in weaknesses. You're in this house without a search warrant. Any action initiated by you is unlawful if not criminal. A search warrant must specify exactly the area you wish to search. It must also list in detail what you hope to find. It has to be signed by a judge and we both know judges are very careful about signing search warrants. This has to do with the individual's civil rights, a concept obviously beyond your understanding. You're spinning your wheels, mister, and you damned well know it. Leave before you embarrass yourself."

Dumas smiled. A winner's smile. Decker, holding Dumas's gaze, couldn't argue. Yokoi was right; he had been running a bluff with the forensic remark. Search warrants didn't come easy in these days of the individual's rights. The attempt to rattle Dumas's cage had failed.

Dumas, sensing he'd won, widened his grin. And twisted the knife. "How's your partner, Decker?"

Decker held his breath. He squeezed the butt of the .38 now hanging at his side. His immediate impulse was to kill Dumas. Smoke him and drop a gun or a knife on him and claim self-defense because the man had as much as admitted he'd tried to waste Ellen. Decker felt his face grow hot with anger. He thought, chill out. Get your shit together before you destroy yourself.

The two men studied each other in silence. Outside the bedroom window, a driving rain pelted the glass. Inside, a Victorian clock chimed the half hour. Decker waited until he was calmer then said, "Wait till I tell Spice she nearly got iced by the faggot from hell."

"Faggot's an unacceptable term, sergeant," Yokoi said. "It's like nigger, kike, spic or cunt. Then again, you probably use these words constantly. Ben notwithstanding, cops are rather backward."

Decker said, "What can I tell you? There are times when I'm as disgusted with myself as you are. Backward, you say. I suppose I could stand to have my consciousness raised. If I hung out with you two scumbags and watched you pimp kids, would that make me politically correct?"

He pointed a finger at Dumas. "Speaking of backward, you're going to love this. My backward partner tied you to the DaSilva killings. She traced the gun you used to the LoCasio crew."

Yokoi said, "You're bluffing, sergeant. Where's the witnesses, where's the motive? You'll have to do better than that if you want to put Ben away."

Decker shook his head. "Mr. Yokoi, the trouble with you politically correct folks is that when you're not thinking of yourselves, you're not thinking at all. Did it ever occur to you how I got on to your little game? No, I guess it didn't. You heard me mention Russell Fort. Well, he tells me that Ben, here, admitted killing the DaSilvas. He said Tawny was being kept in this house. I don't have the complete story but I'm guessing it has to do with selling Tawny to Park Song. I say selling, since I don't think Ben would go to the trouble of killing the DaSilvas unless there was money in it. Those files downstairs say you're into flesh peddling. Hey, if I'm boring you ladies, just say so."

He watched Dumas blow into cupped hands then rub his palms together. Decker tensed as the ex-cop stopped smiling, and loosened his neck by circling his head left then right. Dumas's small eyes became even smaller until they nearly disappeared in the sockets. One thing was sure: Decker had just struck a nerve. Which made Dumas even more likely to go ballistic.

Decker said, "Fort's ready to admit he got you the currency paper for Park Song's counterfeiting operation. Whether we get you on kidnapping or murder or counterfeiting, the main thing is, we got you. You're going inside. And we know what happens when a cop goes inside."

Yokoi said, "You want him to die in prison, don't you?"

Decker scratched the back of his head with his gun hand. Yokoi did the thinking for these two queens, that much was certain. And if Decker wanted to keep Dumas off-balance, to get Tawny's whereabouts out of him, the best approach was to do a number on Yokoi. The Jap was the point of attack. Play with Dumas's head. But first, fuck over his favorite fagola.

Decker said, "You know, Mr. Yokoi, when your friend here goes inside, you're going to be all alone."

A tight-lipped Dumas eased towards the night table.

Decker shook his head. "Makes me nervous when you do that. Even if you could get past me where would you go? When Fort finishes talking the cops and feds are both going to want a piece of you. You can talk about search warrants all you want, but I'm wondering what the Treasury Department's going to make of all that currency paper downstairs. Three to one, they find a way to use it against you. Especially since they've already lost one of their agents to Laughing Boy."

He said to Yokoi, "Without Dumas you're going to be one fucked up little queen. I'm betting the minute he's dragged off, you'll go belly up two seconds later. You could end up lying in your shit and vomit. No Ben around to change your bedpans. Or pay the bills. I hear AIDS care is pretty expensive."

"You're a bastard," Yokoi said. "A fucking bastard."

Decker smiled. "You and me, my man. Two porcupines. One prick against another."

Dumas stopped chewing a thumbnail. "Got it all figured out, haven't you? Bust Ken's chops then maybe I'll wimp out. Ain't gonna happen, amigo."

But it was happening. Decker watched Dumas stare down at his lover, concern all over his big, flat face. Decker didn't need to be told; the lovers were visualizing the worst and for Yokoi, the worst meant dying even more horribly than he was now. Decker heard Yokoi whisper something and saw Dumas shake his head. Yokoi appeared to become more insistent. Finally Dumas turned to Decker. "He says to offer you money. I said he was wasting his time."

Decker said nothing.

Dumas turned back to Yokoi. "I told you so."

Yokoi said, "There's got to be a way."

"Forget it," Dumas said. "We got ourselves a real tough guy here. There's talk he might even be shoo-fly."

Dumas looked at Decker. "The day they prove you're with Internal Affairs is the day you get your fucking eyes gouged out. And I hope I'm there to hold you down while they do it."

Decker shifted his weight to one leg. "Mr. Yokoi is going to have to fend for herself. That's the part I like. You in the joint and Mr.

Yokoi flopping around on the floor like a wind-up toy. I mentioned I had a quick look at those files down in the basement. Juicy stuff.''

Dumas clenched his fists. "How'd you get by Kim Shin?''

"I said the magic word. So you shot Bags?''

Dumas grinned. "You asking or telling, hotshot? I heard you're supposed to be good with your hands. Why don't you put down that gun and you and I go a few rounds.''

Decker said, "It's a thought. But I prefer the idea of you in the joint worrying about your faggot friend. Want to tell me about this house in Queens where Shin says you moved Tawny? If it's in the files downstairs I'll find it eventually. I just thought you might save me a little time.''

Dumas said, "I'm not telling you shit.''

"Suit yourself. But take a good look at Mr. Yokoi because after tonight you're never seeing him again. You two have swapped spit for the last time. Where's Tawny DaSilva?''

Yokoi said, "Don't let him bluff you, Ben. We'll get the best lawyers. We'll fight him. He's not going to put you away if I can help it.''

Decker said, "I think you're missing the point, Mr. Yokoi. Ben's not worried about himself. He's worried about you.''

He watched Dumas look sadly at Yokoi. The look said it all: Decker's words were having an effect. With Dumas in prison, Yokoi might even die of a broken heart. Any way you sliced it, he was going to die sooner. Would Dumas allow that to happen? Decker could only wait and see.

Dumas said to Decker, "Fuck you where you breathe.''

And then the world exploded.

Carrying a tray containing hypodermic needles, a pot of tea and a steaming bowl of chicken broth, Mrs. Moody entered the bedroom. "I don't care about anything between you people," she said, "but I got a patient to take care of and that's just what I'm gonna do.''

Decker turned to face her. She mustn't step between him and Dumas. *Too late.*

Mrs. Moody stiff-armed Decker in the shoulder, pushing him off to one side. And then she was around him, heading for the bed, thinking, when it comes to nursing, I'm the queen bee in this house. This detective, whoever he was, had better get used to that. Besides, she had already called the police. Damned house be full of police soon.

She was between Decker and Dumas.

Decker yelled, "Goddam it, woman, move!"

Dumas's hand went into the night table drawer and came out with the .22 Magnum. At the sight of his gun, Mrs. Moody froze. Decker dropped to the parquet floor, .38 pointing at Dumas. The gun ended up aimed at Mrs. Moody. Decker held his fire. She turned to stare at him and that's when Dumas crouched and fired quickly, shooting her in the buttocks and the back of the head. She fell on top of Decker, pinning him face down to the floor.

On the verge of panic, he thrashed about wildly in a vain attempt to pull out from under the big woman. But Mrs. Moody was dead weight, heavier now than she'd been in life, and Decker remained pinned, his face and neck sticky with her blood. His gun hand, however, was clear of her. And pointing toward Dumas.

In desperation he fired three times, hitting Dumas in both legs and dropping him to his knees beside the bed. Dumas, in a kneeling position, now faced Yokoi. As Dumas struggled to stand, Decker pushed Mrs. Moody off his back. And onto his gun arm, painfully pressing it to the floor. The arm was immobile. It might as well have been nailed to the floor.

A terrified Decker saw his death. He saw Dumas look over his shoulder and catch Decker frantically attempting to pull his arm free. But Decker knew he'd never free himself in time. He was dead.

He saw Dumas again try to stand and then collapse on top of Yokoi and again look at Decker, and as Decker tensed to receive the bullets he saw Dumas shoot Yokoi in the head, then shove the .22 into his own mouth and pull the trigger.

A stunned Decker lay still. It was a few seconds before he could move. When he finally freed himself from Mrs. Moody, he sat on the floor, head down, listening to the ticking of the Victorian clock. His hands couldn't stop shaking. He touched his chest and felt his heart beating wildly. It was totally out of control and there was nothing to do but sit until it slowed down. When it did, he stood up.

Everything came down on him at once: confusion, shock, fear, and above all, relief at not having been shot. Dumas had escaped and taken his lover with him. No prison, no stinking public AIDS ward for them. And for Decker, no Tawny.

He checked Mrs. Moody's neck pulse. Nothing. Her family was about to go through hell. And all because she cared about her patient.

Decker had just witnessed an act of passion, one unlike anything he'd ever personally encountered before. It was going to stay with him a while, that's for sure. In time he'd know whether it was the most terrible or generous one he'd ever seen. At the moment he was too stunned and angry to decide either way.

He heard footsteps rushing up the stairs. Cops. Decker placed his gun on the floor and stepped to the bed. He had to work fast.

He picked up the notebooks Dumas had been reading and shoved them inside his overcoat. Then he pulled his badge from under his coat and let it hang from his neck in plain sight. He raised his hands and turned to face the doorway in time to see a thickly built Irish cop in an ankle-length black raincoat enter the room and immediately drop into a crouch, gun aimed at Decker's head. His toothy, long-faced black partner hung back in the doorway, gun aimed at Decker's balls.

The mick said, *"Freeze, asshole!"*

Decker froze.

At 11:42 that night Decker sat in the backseat of an unmarked Buick parked under an oak tree in Kew Gardens, Queens, and peered through a light drizzle at a two-story stucco house one block away. The house, which had a well-lit exterior, was one of four that formed a snug enclave on a tree-shaded street. It was guarded by two men who sat out front in a red Toyota.

In the front seat of the Buick Yale Singular stopped discussing college football with a slim black agent behind the wheel and shifted his bulk around to face Decker. "We having fun yet?"

Decker said, "What's keeping your guy?"

"Paperwork ain't that easy except when you decide to ignore it like you do. In case you forgot, this can make things sticky when you go to court. You tell me how long it takes to get a warrant. It helps if you get a judge who don't look too close at what he's signing. The judge we wanted was at the opera. We tracked him down and now we have to hope he's not too pissed that we disturbed his evening."

"Dumas's guys in the Toyota are ex-cops," Decker said. "Sooner or later they're going to make us."

"You distinguished yourself by finding the paper and Song's funny money," Singular said. "Now don't go getting hysterical on me. To enter that house and get your little girl we need a warrant. You braced Dumas without one. Not smart. As it turns out, he's not in any position to file a complaint. True we got Kim Shin with his hand in the cookie jar, but don't hang by your thumbs till he does time. He's a diplomat, and you didn't have a warrant. Now since you came to me to help find this little girl, this is how I choose to go about it. We wait for the warrant."

"If I didn't need backup I'd have gone in there alone."

"And gotten your head blown off. From what I hear you nearly got your gonads shot off."

"This address was all over Yokoi's records. Shin thinks Tawny's here. Dumas didn't confirm it, but it makes sense. Where else could they have taken her on such short notice?

"South Korean embassy, maybe," Singular said.

"Maybe. Except that Shin was also bringing the counterfeit and paper out here."

"If Song is on the premises it'll be like I died and went to heaven," Singular said. "Heads up, folks, I think this is the man we've been waiting on."

Blinking its headlights a yellow cab slowly approached the unmarked car. Singular said, "Let's get it on."

Decker, Singular and the other Treasury agent moved out into the rain. Singular spoke into a hand radio while the agent ran toward the cab as it braked to a stop. Moments later the agent was back to Singular and handed him an envelope with the warrant. The big man brought the radio to his mouth. "It's going down."

Secret Service agents and cops hidden in parked cars rushed into the wet streets, kicking up water as they sprinted toward the stucco house. Three cops, pump shotguns trained on the Toyota, stayed outside. Decker, gun drawn, stayed close to Singular, who moved his bulk quickly, even gracefully. Decker let him run interference; together they pushed through armed lawmen and reached the house first. *Tawny.* Decker's torment was about to end.

A small mounted television camera looked down on him and Singular as they raced through the doorway and into a pink-lit foyer. In front of them a young Cuban in a yellow leisure suit quickly touched his shoulder holster, then thought better of it and put up his hands. He'd been sitting on a metal desk, talking to a tall middle-aged Hispanic whose opened purple robe revealed nipple clamps and a studded dog collar.

The Hispanic asked Decker and Singular for ID, then spotted their guns. The sight of firearms and badges caused him to drop to the floor on all fours.

Anxious to reach Tawny, Decker now ran past Singular along a carpeted hallway lined with erotic prints, lit by pink light and smelling of incense and marijuana. At the end he stepped through a beaded curtain and into a large room decorated like a medieval dungeon. A sexual supermarket. The glitter ball in the ceiling and the sound of Vivaldi coming from hidden speakers was a mild counterpart to one of the sickest scenes Decker had seen in his life.

Two dozen well-dressed men of various races, with a handful of women, were examining naked youngsters shackled to the walls. The kids—black, white, Latin, Asian—were being inspected as though they were canned goods on a shelf. Decker looked frantically about for Tawny. She wasn't here.

At the sight of Decker's gun and the badge hanging from his neck on a chain, the buyers took off in all directions.

Decker grabbed one by the collar—a slick-haired, squat Arab with a spade-shaped face. Holding tight, Decker dragged the man over to the door. The Arab resisted, pushed hard. Decker elbowed him in the face and knocked him to the floor. He'd interrogate him later. Right now he had to find Tawny.

He entered a room just off the dungeon and found walls hung with chains, paddles, whips, nipple clamps, dildos, leather face masks. Also cages containing drugged, naked adolescents. And among the half-dozen thoroughly frightened customers was M. Jean-Louis Nicolay, all decked out in a white suit, dark glasses and sporting a beeper on his belt. The dyke maître d' from his restaurant was at his side with a clipboard. Jean-Louis, it seemed, was the auctioneer.

At the sight of Decker he began hyperventilating. His potential customers began looking for an exit. More cops and Secret Service men now blocked the door.

Decker grabbed Nicolay by his expensive tie. "Where's Tawny?"

"Tawny? I do not know what you are talking about."

Decker twisted the tie knot. Nicolay turned red and began coughing loudly. "Dumas and Yokoi are dead," Decker said. "According to Yokoi's files, this leaves you and Rowena to take the weight. Now tell me something good while I'm still in a mood to listen. Where's Tawny, and where's Park Song?''

A red-faced Nicolay croaked words Decker barely made out. "Louder," Decker said.

"Song and the girl are on their way to Korea. There's no way you will ever see them again.''

TWENTY-TWO

Forty-eight hours later, on the first day without rain, Decker and an uneasy Karen Drumman entered Yale Singular's office, carrying small suitcases. They remained standing, waiting for Singular, who was seated at his desk to acknowledge them. A formidable English secretary with throaty tones had been ordered to hold all calls.

The Texan sipped cranberry juice from a styrofoam cup as he examined pages photocopied from one of Rowena Dartigue's notebooks. Decker had sent similar duplicates to the Treasury Department, the South Korean embassy in Washington and the U.S. State Department. The pages were teasers, a taste of things to come. The notebooks were the real prize, and he had hidden them in a safe place.

The pages had gone out with an ultimatum; either South Korea turned Tawny over to the U.S. embassy in Seoul and extradited Park Song to America, or the notebooks would be handed to the media. Decker wanted an answer in forty-eight hours. After that the late Mrs. Dartigue's highly readable disclosures about counterfeiting, money-laundering and child prostitution would belong to the world. Which was to say they'd be given to everybody from "Sixty Minutes" to *Time* magazine. Decker expected to make enemies playing this kind of game and he had.

Under pressure from the feds, the police department started proceedings for Decker's trial on charges of suppressing evidence. Rumor had his pension going down the tubes. The State Department wanted him tried for assaulting Kim Shin and for being a threat to national security, though no details were offered as to how he had become so dangerous to the entire United States. He was also under FBI surveillance, which included wiretaps and a carload of Republican types parked across from his apartment building twenty-four hours a day. Decker was now playing politics, and if he hadn't known that politics was a blood sport before, he knew it now.

His courage came from the inability to forgive himself. He drew strength from guilt at not having saved Gail or rescued Tawny. There was nothing rational about this and he knew it; regret only twisted his reasoning and sent him racing down dark roads. But it also made him a man with a mission. Guilt reminded him that after all these years as a cop, he was still human.

Not everyone dumped on him. Some cops and feds secretly offered help, providing he didn't acknowledge where it came from. They tipped him about wiretaps, surveillance operations, record checks of his past cases and personal records, along with other forms of official harassment. They tipped him about battles between feds and cops over who had first crack at hanging Decker's ass out to dry. These were officers who weren't happy seeing a fellow officer get reamed for trying to save a thirteen-year-old girl. Yale Singular, with two daughters, was one of them. Singular also wanted Song's ass for killing a Treasury agent.

But he didn't have an upbeat view of Decker's future. Threat or no threat, the Koreans would hang tough, Singular said. Song was their boy; he knew too much to be hung out to dry. Count on South Korea to protect him. Which meant that Tawny DaSilva was expendable. South Korea and America were not about to trade a teenage girl for the billions of dollars involved in military and trade agreements. The kid was a goner.

But less than twenty-four hours after Singular's gloomy forecast he telephoned Decker at his apartment and said the South Koreans had caved in. Tawny would be returned to the United States and Park Song could be brought back for trial. As a bonus, the hundred-dollar plates would also be handed over to America. Decker had won.

He couldn't fucking believe it. In fact, he decided not to. As badly as he wanted Tawny back, something told him not to run out and party just yet. The Koreans were giving him everything he'd asked for. No threats, no hassles. There had to be a catch.

Singular told him what it was. "You have to go to Seoul to pick up Tawny. You can also bring back Song and the plates. But you have to go by yourself. And go unarmed."

Decker couldn't believe what he'd just heard. Singular was joking. He had to be. What Singular had said was so off the wall, Decker was sure he'd heard incorrectly. Singular was jerking him around. He had to be.

Decker said, "Run that by me again."

Singular did. There'd been no mistake. Decker had heard it right the first time.

"That's how it came down from the State Department," Singular said. "Either we do things the Koreans' way or there's no deal. They asked for you and specifically said you're to come alone."

A confused Decker flopped back on the bed, unable to make sense of what he'd been told, wondering if this was merely the Koreans way of saying, no deal. Eyes closed, he squeezed the bridge of his nose with a thumb and forefinger. This was some weird shit. How the hell could he go over there by himself without a piece? On the other hand, how could he *not* go? Talk about being between a rock and a hard place.

Somebody was running a game on him. Somebody in Seoul or Washington or maybe both places. Decker was being set up. But by who? *Decker in Seoul alone?* He said to Singular, "Are they serious or what?"

"You could refuse," Singular said.

"This whole thing sucks. Why me? A half-dozen marshals could go over there and bring back Song with no trouble. Tawny? All the Koreans have to do is turn her and the plates over to our embassy."

"That particular approach has been discussed. Matter of fact, I brought it up myself, hoping to save you a trip. Turns out the Koreans want to save face. Officially, they won't admit they've even heard of Tawny DaSilva. Nor are they willing to admit that one of their citizens is in possession of American hundred-dollar plates. All this is bad publicity, you see, and that's the last thing they want. From their standpoint, you can see why they don't want American police arriving en masse in Seoul. One American enters and leaves Seoul the same day. Short and sweet."

Decker did not want to go to South Korea alone and without a piece. He fucking did not want to go. Heart and mind revolted against the idea. But even as he looked for excuses not to go, he remembered that Tawny hadn't asked to go to South Korea either. And Gail hadn't wanted to die.

He said to Singular, "Short and sweet, you say. No way. Not with Asians, it isn't. The truth isn't important to them. And if that sounds racist, I don't care. Asians believe the truth is a waste of time. The Koreans aren't telling the truth. There's more to this than they're letting on."

"The martial arts didn't prepare you for this, I take it."

"It teaches you to be tricky, to never do the obvious. That's what's happening with this Seoul deal. Somebody's jerking me around. I wish I knew who and why."

Singular said, "We don't have time to find out. You've got to leave right away or forget it. The Koreans say the offer's only on the table for a couple of hours. We have to call them back right now and let them know if you're coming. And if you are, you're to leave immediately."

"I'll be on Song's turf. Christ. The bastard can kill and get away with it. Why drag me over there to do it?"

"I can also tell you you won't get any help from our embassy in Seoul. Ever been to Korea?"

"No. From what I hear I haven't missed much. Jesus, go to a strange country, pick up a psycho and do it without backup. Am I the only schmuck these people know?"

Singular said, "Here's another reason for making the trip. Bring back Song and the plates and your beloved federal government will forgive your past transgressions. They will also pressure the police department to be similarly forgiving. You've got everything to gain. On the other hand you have everything to lose. As sure as a fish drifts with the tide, Song won't go quiet. He'll try to kill you. And I think somebody here or over there knows it too."

Decker closed his eyes. "You think or you were told."

"Call it a country boy's educated hunch. You and Song are like Jews and Arabs, cats and dogs. Put you boys together and it's guaranteed somebody's bound to get hurt. By the way, in Seoul you've only got six hours to get Song and Tawny on a plane. After that the

Koreans say they'll stop cooperating. I guess it really comes down to that little girl, doesn't it? That's something only you can decide."

In Singular's office, the Texan was saying to Karen Drumman, "I already heard it from Sergeant Decker. Now I want to hear from you why you're going with him. Some folks don't want you to make the trip. I wouldn't put it past them to throw some last-minute interference in your way."

"Sergeant Decker did everything he could to discourage me," she said, "but I told him he was wasting his time. Police guidelines for dealing with abducted children *require* that a woman be present when a child is recovered. Men usually do the abducting, we all know that. So when a child sees a policeman it's really seeing another stranger. Just more danger. Women are less of a threat. I also have the advantage of being Tawny's godmother. She'll need to see a familiar face, especially with her mother dead."

"I tried talking her out of it," Decker said, "but she insisted on coming along. Thanks, by the way, for getting Korean approval on this.

"Why is everybody so uptight about me?" Karen asked.

"Miss Drumman, you're a new player," Singular said. "Nobody knows you. Besides, in government you keep your job by saying no. Some of the powers that be think you could be a loose cannon."

"I'm *going*," Karen said. "And if anybody tries to stop me I'll get a lawyer and make real trouble. Tawny means nothing to you but she means a lot to me. I'm scared to death about what could happen to her—and me too. But I'm still going and don't try to stop me."

Singular took up a white envelope from his desk and held it out to Decker. "This is for you. The extradition order. Signed, sealed and now delivered. Miss Drumman, I wouldn't think of stopping you. And if you ever decide that government work appeals to you, give me a call. I admire your persistence, if nothing else."

He leaned back, hands behind his head. "Park Song on trial in this country. A pleasurable thought. He's an argument for capital punishment, that boy. Can't forget that agent he killed."

Singular looked at Decker. "Don't suppose you'd care to tell me how you came by those notebooks. No, I guess not. Anybody ever tell you that stealing is wicked unprincipled behavior?"

He glanced at the pages on his desk. "They could bring down the Korean government and nobody here wants that. This sort of reading sets people to milling about in the streets and storming the palace."

"You get the complete notebooks when I get back."

"And if you don't get back?"

"I've left instructions to turn them over to you. Do what you think best."

"I thank you for your show of faith. But in my position I'll have no choice but to turn them over to my superiors."

Decker said, "Your call." He had left some of the notebooks with Gail's parents in Denver and some in the safe at Karen's office. One was with Bags, locked in the hospital safe with her valuables.

As for Kim Shin, he and his bodyguard were on the way back to South Korea. As part of the Decker-to-Seoul deal, no counterfeiting charges had been filed against Shin. The State Department had even written Shin a note of apology for any "disrespectful treatment" he might have received. Decker wondered if they'd offered to reconstruct Shin's nose too.

Singular said, "In Seoul it'll be you and Song. One on one. Some of us even talked about hiding a gun for you in a toilet at the Seoul airport. Like what they did for Michael Corleone in *The Godfather.* But we decided this is real life and if anything went wrong it might cause one hell of an international incident. The man who'll meet you at the airport is Colonel Youngsam, head of the Korean CIA. He'll be in charge of you while you're on his turf. Tough as cheap steak and smart as they come. He's been Song's rabbi, his protector. Strange, him giving up his boy without a fight."

"Unless he's not giving him up," Decker said. "Unless he's setting me up for stopping Song's counterfeiting sales."

Singular shrugged. "Anything's possible. It's a world of hidden agendas and dirty tricks, not to mention wily tactics."

Decker said, "We've got a plane to catch. Thanks for what you tried to do about the gun."

Singular placed his hands palms down on his desk. "Heard something interesting. Seems certain people wouldn't mind seeing you and Song kill each other."

When Singular saw the look on Karen's face he shook his head. "I have a mouth big enough to bite myself in the neck. Sorry, Miss Drumman. Sometimes I forget there's more than just us boys in the world."

"What if we come back with just Tawny and the plates?" Decker said.

Singular began twiddling his thumbs. He was in no hurry to answer. When he was sure he knew what Decker had meant, he picked up a pair of paperclips and hooked them together. He twirled the paperclips in his fingers then leaned back in his chair. He started to smile, stopped.

He said to Decker, "You telling me Song might meet with a serious accident and be unable to travel?"

Decker said nothing.

Singular held his gaze for a few seconds, then pulled his desk calendar closer and studied the day's entries. "Your call," he said. "Have a nice flight. Miss Drumman."

TWENTY-THREE

At noon on the day he was scheduled for extradition to America, Park Song danced in his living room to a video of *In Caliente*, his favorite Busby Berkeley movie musical.

Sitting rigid in an upholstered armchair, Tawny DaSilva listened to Song add his wobbly tenor to the song "Muchacha." *Muchacha, I've gotcha, and I'm hotcha for you.* He circled her chair, then danced over to the bronze Art Deco lions flanking the fireplace. A quick pat on the lions' heads then Song tapped his way back to the oversize television screen.

He was in an exuberant mood, cheery and lighthearted. He may have been down but he wasn't out. If others thought Park Song was dead and buried, that was their mistake. He was a survivor; he'd dance on his enemies' graves and that included Decker and Colonel Youngsam. Extradition or no extradition, Song had never felt so optimistic in his life.

He thought of Rowena Dartigue, that snobbish old bitch who'd been more interested in a man's dick than his brain, and hadn't she paid the price for that. Too bad he'd gotten carried away and cracked her skull. Better to have killed her slowly, dragging out her death and enjoying himself in the process.

He wished he could have interrogated her about those nasty little notebooks of hers. They were political dynamite. The American and Korean governments were losing sleep over what would happen if the notebooks ever fell into the hands of the American press. Heads would roll. And speaking of heads, Youngsam had to retrieve those notebooks or suffer the consequences.

The Razor's political survival, not to mention his life, depended on outwitting Decker and relieving him of the notebooks. Song wasn't exactly cheering Youngsam on, not after learning he'd been instrumental in approving his extradition. When it came to the double cross or selling-out, Colonel Youngsam was an absolute genius.

Song closed his eyes, visualizing himself dancing with Dolores del Rio, *In Caliente*'s beautiful Mexican star. How could she have sunk so low as to have appeared in an Elvis Presley movie? In her defense, she'd taken the role toward the end of her career when good parts were few and far between. *Live long enough and you'll see your victories turned into defeats.*

None of that victory-into-defeat shit for him. Decker had just landed at Kimpo Airport and was heading to his pavilion, but that didn't mean Song was whipped. He was not about to return to America with Decker or anyone else. And he wasn't giving up Tawny, his exquisite *kisaeng*. He was going to pull through because he knew the secret of surviving: there was no such thing as a thousand ways to fight. There was only one and that was to win.

In New York the Korean consulate had given him the bad news that the counterfeit money, securities and currency paper left with Dumas had been confiscated by Decker. The news had caused Song to weep and literally bang his head against a bathroom wall. He'd never wanted to kill anyone the way he'd wanted to kill Decker. Decker, who'd sabotaged his plans to repay Youngsam, thereby bringing about a catastrophe.

Nor had there been anything cheery in the news that Dumas had shot Yokoi to death before turning the gun on himself. Without Dumas, Song had no one to run proper background checks on customers or supply him with real currency paper. The unnatural and the unexpected had entered Song's life with a vengeance. His attempt to grasp the clouds had failed. His entire existence now appeared to be little more than an attempt to write numbers on water.

Since misfortunes never came singularly, he hadn't been surprised to learn Russell Fort was betraying him to the American police in hopes of getting leniency for himself. The man was so stupid he made a pig look brilliant. Unfortunately, he knew enough about the counterfeiting operation to get Park Song imprisoned until stars fell from the sky. Had Dumas been alive, he would have had him shut Fort's mouth permanently.

Forced to flee New York, Song had returned via Canada, where he'd hastily chartered a private flight to Asia. He was a dead man, an impending victim of the Razor's wild rage. He could no more raise the rest of Youngsam's thirty million dollars in time than he could empty the ocean with a sieve.

All he had taken with him from America had been little Tawny, who was every bit as beautiful as her photographs and who represented his one victory over Decker since Saigon. With Tawny and his bodyguards, he had headed toward Seoul, the only place he knew that offered him the chance to avoid extradition. Where else could he go to avoid American authorities who were closing in on him like hounds after a fox. Halfway over the Pacific he'd nearly come to blows with David Mitla over whether or not they should continue to Seoul or change course for somewhere else.

And then like a happy ending in an MGM musical he had received an unexpected reprieve from the hangman's noose. The Razor, via radio, had personally passed on the extraordinary news: Song's entire debt to him had been paid. *Paid.*

Unable to stop himself, Song had broken down and cried. Copilots and navigator had watched in disbelief as he broke into a time-step before rushing to the back of the plane to pick up a sleeping, drugged Tawny and spin her around.

His debt to Youngsam had been paid.

And how had this miracle come about? It seemed that KCIA agents in Tel Aviv had located an Englishman named Eddie Walkerdine who was there disposing of money and valuables plundered from a certain London depository. To get the details on this extraordinary crime the Korean agents had removed four fingers from Mr. Walkerdine's left hand. No further persuasion had been necessary. Walkerdine had told all then turned over the robbery proceeds, which were in excess of forty million dollars.

With no more use for Walkerdine, Youngsam's agents had buried him alive at the base of a sand dune north of Tel Aviv. Few mourned his passing. He had double-crossed his associates and murdered two, a depository guard and a black ex-convict. Walkerdine had always been ready to cut the throat of anyone who trusted him. His departure from this life was no great loss.

As Song heard the story, Walkerdine had smuggled the depository loot out of England through connections at Israel's El Al airline. What put Youngsam's men on to him had been Rowena Dartigue's jewelry, a bit of irony that had left Song laughing until he cried. Rowena had hidden the jewelry from her greedy husband, who'd then stolen it anyway, destroying Walkerdine in the process. Hilarious when you thought about it.

An hour after she had reported the jewelry missing to Scotland Yard its description was known to the KCIA. Youngsam then wired the description to his agents worldwide. Fate, apparently, had wanted Rowena's husband to die poor and Walkerdine to die painfully. Neither had been destined to enjoy their ill-gotten gains. Park Song and Colonel Youngsam, it seemed, were to be the lucky ones, proving again that this was indeed the Pacific Era and that Asia was to triumph over the West until further notice.

With Youngsam off his back, Song had assumed that life for him would go on as normal. For the first time in weeks he could breathe easy. He could sleep without being tormented by thoughts of his own death. He could eat without worrying about keeping his food down. The Razor was out of his life, out of it forever if Song had his way. From now on Song intended to stick to counterfeiting and the pleasure of his *kisaengs*.

But he had barely shown Tawny to her room when his world was shattered by a telephone call from his nemesis and savior. The Razor announced he could stay in Seoul for only thirty days. *Thirty days.* After that he would have to leave South Korea permanently. This decision was final, no appeal possible. When he protested, Youngsam hung up. *Thirty days?*

In desperation Song telephoned other government contacts but failed to uncover the reason for Youngsam's sudden cruelty. Some claimed they didn't know; others knew but were too frightened to say what they knew. Park Song had suddenly become an untouchable. And there was more shit to come. Two days after Youngsam's first phone call he telephoned with even worse news. *He had approved Song's immediate extradition to America.* Decker, of all people, would be coming to Seoul to take him and Tawny back to New York. Song was speechless.

He was trapped in a fucking nightmare. But it was no dream. Before the day was out a copy of the extradition order signed by Youngsam was hand-delivered to Song's pavilion. He'd been victimized by the same police treachery that had killed his parents. He now faced life imprisonment in America, an idea so terrifying it caused him to black out in front of Tawny.

His extradition, Song learned, could be blamed on Rowena's notebooks. Damn that whore. Decker had used the notebooks to force the South Korean government into submission. Because of these notebooks, which contained embarrassing data about Song's counterfeiting and KCIA relationship, Youngsam was turning over Song and Tawny to Decker. In the light of trade and defense arrangements with America, Song was small potatoes. Of course he blamed Rowena. Done in by a dead woman. An *old* dead woman, at that.

Noting that Song and Mrs. Dartigue had been business associates, Youngsam made a point of holding Song responsible for the notebooks' existence, a stinking thing to do, in Song's opinion. Unfortunately, it was Youngsam's opinion that carried the most weight. He noted that Song's obsession with adolescent girls, a fact given considerable space in the notebooks, had brought Detective Sergeant Decker into the picture, leading to the arrest of Kim Shin. In Youngsam's words, how many more agents would the KCIA have to lose because of a tap-dancing fool?

The Razor's treachery had sent Song to the medicine cabinet for sedatives. However, one aspect of this foul business had bolstered Song's spirits. His admirers in the KCIA, young agents who idolized him for his flair and cunning, had been angered by Youngsam's throwing him to the wolves. Why should Song, the most dedicated and conscientious of Koreans, be sold out merely to please the Americans? What kind of man was Youngsam if he would not defend his own agents?

The young Turks loathed the Razor, whom they considered imperial, stubborn and vicious, not to mention tightfisted and miserly for refusing to share his considerable monies from corruption, bribes and other graft. The rebellious agents had long sought a reason to knock the spymaster from his exalted perch. In Song they had found it. His forthcoming extradition was all the motivation they needed.

With Youngsam out of the way, the loot from his swindles and schemes would trickle down. He had to go.

The KCIA hotheads were being led by Kim Shin. Loyal to Song as always, he had relayed the young agents' pledge to help Song in any escape attempt. Song had welcomed the assistance. He was counting on it. He was delighted when Shin reported the rebels were truly worked up. The Razor had a special talent for stirring up evil passions and was now about to reap the whirlwind. According to Shin the rebels were also ready to dispose of Decker. But this came with a price tag. Song was not surprised. In their place he would have taken the same position. There was no free lunch.

He made initial payments to ringleaders, promising more when he was free. Money was no problem; he still had a few bank accounts, along with property in Hong Kong, Taiwan and the Philippines. His beautiful home, with its movie-star artifacts, was no longer his to sell. Youngsam had already claimed it for himself. He would be moving in after Song left for America, a piece of dismal news given Song yesterday when Youngsam had dropped by to confiscate the plates. Just another reason why Song was determined to see this so-called savior of the nation in his grave before the week was out.

If Song no longer had his beautiful home, he did have beautiful Tawny. And a plan to escape from Korea, which included killing Decker and Youngsam.

As Song tap-danced in his living room, Cha Youngsam prepared to leave his third-floor office, which overlooked the low two-story building that was the Republic of China's embassy. His departure had been interrupted by two men, high-ranking government officials who had shown up unannounced to discuss Song's extradition.

While unwanted and unwelcome, this pair of pen-pushers was too important to ignore. When it came to being devious and sly, Youngsam was their superior. These two, however, had the president's ear and could make trouble if they wanted to. Better to hear these idiots out even if he itched to slam the door in their faces.

The senior of the two was a small watery-eyed man named Rhee who had a talent for distancing himself from power struggles and who did most of the talking. It was Rhee who led off with what he saw as a tough question. Youngsam saw it as a waste of his time, an attempt to undo what could not be undone.

"Do you still feel you have made the correct decision to abandon Park Song?" Rhee asked.

Youngsam spoke to the ceiling. "Song's presence here threatens the stability of this government, which I am sworn to uphold and serve to the best of my ability. Furthermore, he has been identified as one of my agents, which makes his personal life and criminal pursuits a state matter. As you well know, this could affect our relations with the Americans. It might also encourage Western inquiries into our alleged government corruption and what Americans refer to as human-rights abuses. I prefer this not happen."

Fools, he thought. The kind who want to save a burning house by pissing on it. Still, they could very well be on Song's payroll. Youngsam made a mental note to keep a closer eye on them.

Rhee said, "Song has been a valuable servant of our government. There are those who feel you acted too hastily in approving his extradition. They say you want him out of the country to avoid being implicated in his so-called crimes. They say your own survival takes precedence over that of your country."

Youngsam's face didn't betray his anger. But his dark eyes nearly closed and his jaw tightened. To calm himself, he steepled his fingers under his chin and counted to ten. Then: "This matter has been cleared with your superiors, so with all due respect, any further discussion seems pointless. I protected Song for the good of our country. For this same reason I choose not to protect him any longer. I will not allow a scandal to bring down this administration. That is final."

Rhee gnawed at his lower lip. Youngsam thought, so the little penpusher isn't quite so sure of himself after all. Rhee whispered to his companion, a squat man named Paik whose moon face sported a natural scowl and whose government position had turned him into a strutting peacock, free of any sense of humor. Paik nodded but said nothing, letting Rhee continue to speak for him.

Rhee turned to Youngsam. "You have Song under guard, I assume."

"Around the clock. Three shifts, eight men a shift. He will be home when the American comes for him and the girl. I have also arrested Song's bodyguards. They will be released after this business is concluded. I'm sure you know that Sergeant Decker has just landed in Seoul. Song's extradition is proceeding on schedule."

Rhee said, "Over the years, in your service, Song has learned many government secrets. I would think you would want to keep him out of an American courtroom and away from Western journalists."

Rising from behind his desk, Youngsam walked over to his coat closet. These damn cretins had wasted enough of his time. They'd come here, probably on their own, hoping to bluff him into changing his mind. Well, they could all go piss up a rope. Youngsam's plan for dealing with Song had been approved by men who outranked these two fidgety imbeciles. Obviously, Rhee and Paik had not been told everything. Then again, who were they to be told everything? Perhaps he didn't have to be quite so polite to them after all. In any case it was time for him to leave and get on with his job.

His visitors were as feebleminded as those insolent young intelligence agents who had appointed themselves Song's protectors, who had dared imagine themselves as Colonel Youngsam's equal. Bureaucrats or would-be rebels, they were little more than self-destructive buffoons with a taste for high drama. They built their lives around outlandish dreams sure to fail. Youngsam saw them as eventual victims of their own confusion.

He slipped into a bear-fur coat, offering Rhee and Paik his iciest smile, and was pleased to see them flinch. "Song cannot stay in Korea and that is final," he said. "On the other hand, it is not to our benefit to have him appear in an American courtroom. It is my job to deal with this complication. It is up to me to do the impossible, to make the sun rise in the west and set in the east. And that is what I intend to do."

Youngsam reached into the closet for his fur hat. "Gentlemen, thank you for stopping by. Now if you will excuse me."

In his living room Song said to Tawny, "Do you like to dance?"

"Yes." Her voice was barely audible.

"I will teach you Korean dances," he said. "You will learn them perfectly. And you will dance only for me."

"I thought I was going home," Tawny said. "The man who came here yesterday said I was going home to my family. He said somebody from America was coming to pick me up."

In yesterday's appearance at Song's pavilion the Razor had promised Tawny her freedom. He had also warned Song that an escape attempt would be unwise; the guards had orders to shoot to kill. Song hardly needed to be told that. Youngsam also warned him not to have sex with Tawny. A doctor was to examine her at the airport before takeoff. Should her maidenhead be missing, Song would lose his balls. Fingers or testicles, the Razor couldn't resist menacing Song's extremities.

Youngsam had also ordered the arrest of Song's three printers, who worked in the pavilion basement. Throughout all this trickery Song had remained composed and seemingly detached, telling himself he'd soon be free of Youngsam *and* Decker. Knowing he would make Youngsam regret the day he ever thought he could screw Song and get away with it. He'd give anything to drink Youngsam's blood. Anything.

He pointed to the giant television screen. "Look," he said to Tawny, "see how Busby uses the camera? Look at those overhead shots and the way the girls' movements are synchronized. They don't make movies like that anymore. A shame, really."

Tawny's eyes shimmered behind tears. "I don't want to stay here, I want to go home—"

"This is the big number. Watch. Everybody sings 'The Lady In Red,' then the dancers do—"

He stopped talking and looked toward the front door. Horn sounding, a car had just entered the driveway. Song giggled. Now who could that be? The police patrol and their barking guard dogs could be heard converging on the vehicle. Welcome to Seoul, Sergeant Decker. May your stay be brief and unpleasant.

"I think your friends from America have arrived," he said to Tawny. "Time to begin upon our little adventure. It's cold out, so wear that lined denim jacket I bought for you during our stopover in Hong Kong. In the future I'll buy you whatever you wish. Just ask and it's yours. We'll have a wonderful time, you and I. Our next year together is going to be special."

In the large foyer of Song's pavilion Decker patted down the Korean for weapons.

He worked in silence, anxious to make the most of the three hours he had left in Seoul. Fuck the small talk, just get this shit over with, then leave for the airport. His motor was racing; he was charged, keyed up and trigger-happy. Trigger-happy, but without a gun. He could get blown out of the water any minute from now and he didn't have a gun. Decker was either stupid or the most snakebit, hard-luck, dick-in-the-dirt cop who ever lived.

Any chitchat with Laughing Boy would only be contrived. The two had hated each other's guts in Saigon; fifteen years later, nothing had changed. When they'd met today in Song's pavilion it was as if they were back in Vietnam, in that crummy, little *dojo* without windows and air conditioning, two young soldiers who had loathed each other on sight, not knowing or caring why. Yesterday and today, their mutual hostility came from the heart and was beyond either man's control.

Decker had another reason for avoiding small talk with Laughing Boy. Criminals didn't enjoy having their freedom taken away. Man or woman, put the cuffs on a perp and they could become agitated if not downright violent. Song was facing life in a federal prison like Atlanta or Joliet, homes to the most dangerous inmates in the government's penal system and where the death penalty existed unofficially because cons killed each other with a frightening regularity. Decker suddenly remembered that under a new federal law Song could be hit with the death penalty for having killed a Treasury agent. Common sense demanded he watch Laughing Boy like a hawk. Casual chitchat would only be a distraction.

The grueling flight from America had left Decker disoriented; he could have been in any one of a dozen Asian countries. He was ready to fall asleep standing up. He couldn't remember when he'd last slept eight consecutive hours. Or sat down to a hot meal.

Since Bags had gotten shot, he'd slept when he could and eaten on the run. On the flight to Seoul, his stomach had refused to hold down any food. He was getting by on coffee, toast, fruit and nuts, plus nervous energy. He felt as though he'd been born tired and suffered a relapse. If he hadn't worn out his health, he'd fucking come close.

In Song's pavilion Decker's every move was under the beady-eyed stare of three tough-looking Korean soldiers who reeked of garlic and body odor. They wore ratty fur coats and hats and carried Kalashnikov rifles, pistols, grenades and bayonets. What worried Decker the most were the Kalashnikovs.

Last April one of his informants, a Dominican named Marcos

DeJesus, had been killed by a Kalashnikov. DeJesus, a crack dealer, had decided to help a cousin peddle crack in a particular area of Brooklyn. Going in they knew it was Jamaican territory and that the Rastas played rough. They just didn't know how rough.

The Jamaicans gave no warning. Instead they brought it to DeJesus and Julio at their crib in Washington Heights, using Kalashnikovs to turn them into blood, bone and gristle. It was a picture Decker would remember for a long time. Which was why just looking at the Koreans' Kaslashnikovs made him break out in a sweat. He tried not to think that Laughing Boy might have bribed a guard to cap him.

Karen and Tawny clung tightly to each other as they stood against a wall painting of a windblown cherry tree with painted blossoms scattered over a second wall and the ceiling. Tawny had asked about her mother, and Karen had said, "We'll talk later, darling." Song watched this exchange with fascination. Decker, holding his breath, had waited for the counterfeiter to mention Gail's death.

Surprise. Song kept his lip buttoned. He hadn't even giggled. Decker couldn't believe it. He distrusted the bastard's silence but accepted it. Silence was an argument you couldn't contend with. Decker decided to take what he could get and consider himself lucky. Song was unpredictable; he might have said anything. Including ordering the guards to kill all three of them.

On meeting Tawny, Decker had instantly seen Gail in her face. That was the good news. The bad news: his memories of Gail were increasingly painful. Tawny would always be a reminder of his failure to keep her mother alive.

Laughing Boy. Decker had to admit the little prick had aged well. The counterfeiter of today and the young army officer Decker had known fifteen years ago looked almost the same. Song had added some weight, all muscle as far as Decker could see. His face was unlined and he had no gray hairs. Decker assumed he'd kept up his *taekwon do*, and if so, he now had fifteen years more experience. Making him that much more dangerous. Fifteen years. Had it been that long since Song had tried to waste him?

While being patted down Song indulged in his customary weird giggling. Decker thought, the fucker's too cheerful. Son of a bitch is facing life in the slammer yet he acts as though he's watching "The Simpsons."

But then, Laughing Boy knew something Decker didn't. He knew when the escape attempt would go down. And he knew when he would try to kill Decker. He had Decker under a death sentence. And only he knew when it would be carried out.

Decker's search of Song yielded five thousand dollars in counterfeit hundreds and credit cards under four different names. He pocketed the funny money and phony plastic, then waited for Song's reaction. The grin never left the Korean's face. Something was wrong with this picture.

Decker would have preferred a different reaction, something that would have forced him and Laughing Boy to get it on, to get their fight to the death over with. Nothing was worse than waiting. Instead, all the Korean did was give Decker a shit-eating grin that said, *I know and you don't.* Decker had to be careful; he didn't need Song woofing on him, messing with his head, making him foolish. Forget the bullshit and hang tough.

He examined a small valise Song was bringing with him, running his hands over the exterior and finding nothing out of the ordinary. Inside he found two shirts, a pair of jeans, sweatpants, tap shoes, toiletries, and video cassettes of old Hollywood musicals. He tossed every item, checking shirt pockets, the video case, the heels on the tap shoes. Clean. He closed the valise, looked at Song. *Bring it, asshole. Bring it to me now.*

On the flight from New York he had discussed Karen's options if anything happened to him. She really only had one: make her way to the American embassy and contact Yale Singular. Decker warned her against asking the embassy for help. Song's extradition was a political matter, which meant smoke and mirrors coated with bullshit. The United States didn't want to offend South Korea and South Korea didn't want to be offended. Singular was Karen's only chance. Providing he wasn't handcuffed by politicians and thrown into a closet.

They'd also discussed how best to tell Tawny about her parents. Decker saw no easy way. In the end they agreed that Karen would break the news. Tawny needed someone close and visibly moved by her sorrow. The cop in Decker had been trained to hold back tears. He could feel whatever he wanted to, but showing feelings on the street was weakness.

He finished tossing Song and said, "Let's go."

"Where are we going, sergeant?" Song pressed his nose to a white carnation in the lapel of a camel's-hair coat draped over his shoulders.

"To prison," Decker said.

"I see." Song threw up his hands in resignation. "Well, if I must, I must."

Decker tensed, thinking, here it comes. Laughing Boy's going to have a shit fit. Decker, ready, hoped Song would go nuts. *Bring it to me, asshole.*

But Song could not have been more laid-back, more down home. Decker watched him go to a wall mirror, put on a gray fedora and lean back to admire his reflection. "Nice," Song said. He adjusted the camel's-hair overcoat on one shoulder and smelled the carnation once more. A last look in the direction of his sumptuous living room, a smile for Tawny and he strolled toward the front door like a man without a care in the world. Decker, his teeth on edge, unclenched his fists.

Outside, he stood in the driveway and looked up at a gray, cloudless sky. He hadn't seen the sun in days. Not in Manhattan and certainly not in this ugly-ass country where there didn't seem to be anything but snow and freezing rain. It had been raining when he arrived in Seoul three hours earlier; now it was snowing and raining. Decker wore long underwear and gym socks, but they didn't stop him from shivering in the bone-numbing cold.

His bad knee had tightened, a sure sign the temperature had dropped below freezing. He cursed himself for not having worn a knee brace. If Laughing Boy didn't get him, the Korean weather would.

Decker ignored stares from Youngsam's guards, his mind on the bad weather, which could ground his plane. The one thing he didn't have was time. Would the Koreans extend his deadline? Don't bet on it.

He checked his watch. A little less than three hours until his plane took off for Guam. If the roads were fucked up, it could take that long just to get across town. Any delay in getting out of Seoul could be fatal as a kick in the head from Laughing Boy. The longer Song was on his own turf, the more likely he was to get ideas.

In Guam, Decker was to hand Song over to Singular, Secret Service agents and U.S. marshals. Singular's Guam appearance was strictly a career move, one that would boost him up the greasy pole of success in a hurry if he were lucky. A photo with the captured Laughing Boy could do for Singular what being photographed with the captured Manuel Noriega did for DEA agents. Nobody got ahead in law enforcement who was backward and shy. Successful cops were always in love with themselves.

If Song's extradition was not successful, Decker knew what to expect. The feds, quick to cut their losses, would deny they ever knew him. Look for their spin-doctors to paint him as another loose cannon in the tradition of Oliver North. Just another cowboy whose agenda blew up in his face. On the other hand, let things go smoothly and guess who would cop the credit. History was written by winners, and as Decker had learned, the feds were big on being seen as winners.

He ordered Song, Karen and Tawny to stay on the pavilion steps then walked across the driveway to their car, a green Hyundai with snow tires. He wasn't about to set foot inside without tossing it top to bottom. Directly behind the Hyundai was a black Toyota with four Koreans in leather coats, dark glasses and hats pulled way down to the tips of their noses. They were Korean intelligence, Colonel Youngsam's people. Decker would have them on his tail until he left Seoul. Or until Laughing Boy killed him.

He was tossing the Hyundai because he'd been in the pavilion long enough for a gun to be planted behind a seat. Or for the brakes to be tampered with. Or for dynamite to be wired to the engine block. He looked under the hood, checked the brakes, steering wheel and trunk. He looked behind the seats, on the floorboards, in the glove compartment. He found two condom wrappers, a broken shoelace, Korean coins and an empty Coca-Cola can. The car was clean.

He got out of the Hyundai to be greeted by a smiling Kang Jung Hee, the frog-faced, thirtyish Korean assigned as his driver.

"Everything okay?" Kang said.

Decker nodded. "Everything okay. Let's get this show on the road."

Everything was not okay. A hyped-up Decker was nervous as a dog shitting razor blades. Kang, whose eyebrows were so close they begged to be connected, was one of the few people in Seoul who had actually smiled at Decker. Give Kermit, Decker's name for froggy-looking Kang, points for congeniality. Still, Decker made him as Intelligence, on the set to insure he didn't stray from the game plan.

Decker and Karen had been met at Kimpo Airport by the jowly, bull-like Colonel Youngsam. Youngsam had not said much, but it was obvious he didn't like Decker blackmailing his country. He treated Decker as little more than a suspect, a fuck-up to be restrained and watched carefully. Forget professional courtesy; Decker was now on the wrong end of police power. He was at the mercy of the colonel's moods. He would leave Korea alive only if Youngsam wanted him to.

At the colonel's orders Decker and Karen had been searched for weapons, which had made Decker furious but he'd kept quiet. He had thought about wearing a bullet-proof vest but decided against it; if the Koreans wanted him dead, he was gone. He needed a run of luck to save his ass, nothing less. Luck was money in the bank.

The airport inspection ate up an hour of Decker's precious time. He had jerked around enough suspects in his time to know that Youngsam was deliberately fucking him over. For reasons known only to himself the colonel was tightening the screws. Decker figured he'd been tossed because Youngsam had been looking for something, *anything*, to indicate where the notebooks were. Give Curly credit for trying. *He* was willing to bring it to Decker.

Time to head to the airport. Karen and Tawny joined Kang in the front seat of the Hyundai. Song, a foot in the back, stopped and waved to the guards, who cheered, shoved rifles in the air and encouraged their Dobermans to bark. The theatrical scene made Decker even more jittery. He shoved Song into the car and quickly pushed in after him. Better to split before the guards decided to carry Laughing Boy around the driveway on their shoulders.

In the backseat Decker cuffed his left wrist to Song's right, then he turned to lock his door—and froze. The guards had surrounded the car.

Song giggled as the guards, chanting in Korean, pounded on the car with gloved hands and rifle butts. Decker couldn't understand a word; he didn't have to. The guards were telling Song to waste Decker then split. Song had the home field advantage and the guards were letting him know it. Decker reached inside his overcoat, anxious to feel the security of his gun. *Nothing.* Jesus.

"What's the matter, sergeant, you forget something?"

Decker wasn't as spooked by Song so much as by the howling guards and their snarling Dobermans. This was some scary shit. The dogs alone were enough to give Decker a brain hemorrhage. They stood on their hind legs, teeth glistening, eyes as bright as lasers, and clawed at the side of the car, determined to get at Decker. Tawny and Karen held each other tightly. Kang kept his hand on the horn. The uproar only aggravated Decker's migraine headache. He hoped it didn't leave him with gravy stains on his underwear.

A couple of guards peered in at him. He couldn't help it; he flinched. Their faces were primitive stone masks without pity, a remote look he'd seen on out of control killers. He forced himself to hold their stare. But he couldn't swallow. And he had a white-knuckled grip on the door handle.

Kang turned the ignition key and the motor roared to life. He switched on the heater then jammed his hand back on the horn. The guards refused to move. One took out his pistol and waved it at Decker who automatically leaned back as far as he could.

Song said, "Ask him nicely, sergeant, and maybe he'll let you hold it."

Decker thought, hold my dick, scumbag.

As Song threw his head back and laughed, Kang released the brake, letting the car roll forward. Guards leaped out of the way, yanking dogs with them. Decker exhaled in relief. He couldn't get away from here soon enough. Then the Hyundai stalled and he nearly fucking died. Song said, "That was a quick trip. Let's go back inside for tea."

Decker squeezed the armrest. He kept his eyes on the back of Kang's neck, willing the car to move, willing Kang to do something, and he was about to leap out of his seat and shove Kang when the motor kicked in. The Hyundai rolled out of the driveway, leaving guards and dogs behind.

Song looked at Decker. "Oh well, I don't much like tea anyway. What about you, sergeant? Do you like tea?"

Decker said his first words to Song since leaving the pavilion. "You're a funny man. They're going to love you in the joint." He felt good watching the smile fade from Song's face. Song then shrugged and stared out of the window. "Just trying to make conversation," he said. "Someone has to."

Decker said, "Yeah, right," and took a map from his overcoat pocket. He'd already marked his return route. They were heading southwest. With luck they should make Kimpo Airport in little over

an hour. Allowing for traffic and bad weather, add another thirty
minutes. Which should put them at the airport an hour and a half
before takeoff. Barely enough time for the required security check
on international flights. Decker was ready to get out and push if it
would help them get there faster.

He leaned forward and whispered to Karen, "How's Tawny?"

"Scared. And hungry. Tawny, did you know that Manny's a friend
of your mother's?"

Eyes red from weeping, the girl looked over her shoulder. "She
talks about you sometimes. You were in the Marines."

"That's right."

"How come my mother didn't pick me up?"

With the back of his free hand Song stroked the car window. "You
might as well know the truth, Tawny. Your mother—"

Decker twisted the handcuffs, painfully pinching Song's wrist.
Head back, Song inhaled through clenched teeth. "That wasn't very
nice, sergeant," he said with exaggerated calmness. "You hurt me."

"Is that right? Do us both a favor and shut up."

A tearful Karen took Tawny in her arms. "Your mother's dead,"
she said softly.

In the silence that followed Tawny looked at Karen then at
Decker. At the sight of their faces she buried her head against
Karen's chest and wept fiercely.

"I could have told her that," Song said.

"Say anything to Tawny," Decker said, "and I'll tie you to the rear
bumper and drag your butt to the airport."

Song grinned. "Sounds as though you're into S&M, sergeant. Perhaps we should compare notes." He began humming "The Lady In
Red," free hand patting his thigh in rhythm. Decker stared through
the window at a snow-covered Chinese temple, thinking it was going
to be a long trip if Song kept mind-fucking everybody. Like all tact-
less people, Song was never at a loss for words.

Seoul traffic, always bad, had worsened with the weather. Streets,
boulevards and roadways were slush-filled and congested; collisions
and pileups caused by drivers running red lights or refusing to signal
were commonplace. Decker found Korean drivers to be headstrong
and unrestrained, crazies who went wacko the minute they climbed
behind the wheel. He witnessed a fender-bender between two truck
drivers who ended up going at each other with tire irons. Kermit

wasn't above some wild driving himself. Any street pedlar who didn't get out of his way fast enough was in deep shit.

Trapped in a traffic jam, Decker stared at his watch, and shook his head in frustration. Suddenly he saw movement from the corner of his eye; several people were approaching the car. Adrenalin flowing, he leaned away from the window. Seconds later he saw—not Uzi-wielding Koreans, but several Buddhist nuns picking their way through the stalled traffic. Wiping perspiration from his lip, Decker went slack. Song continued to hum, the sound a direct attack on Decker's nerves. As it was meant to be.

The Hyundai crept through a huge open-air market where shoppers included dozens of uniformed American soldiers. Decker's window was closed but a strong smell of fish and powdered red pepper still found its way into the car, making his eyes water. His stomach grew queasy at the sight of wooden tubs of slithering squid. And you couldn't pour enough ketchup on a dead octopus to make Decker eat it.

He nearly barfed at the sight of a large pile of dog carcasses. Suddenly he remembered that Saigon restaurants had considered spicy dog soup a delicacy. No amount of persuasion could get him to try it; he'd sooner have eaten dog shit. He looked away from the market. Being a dog in South Korea was like being a judge in Colombia.

The sun popped out briefly, reflecting off high-rises lining water identified on Decker's map as the Han River. They were in southern Seoul now, where every other block appeared to be undergoing expansion. The sun didn't hang around long; within minutes it had vanished behind a darkening sky. As the car crossed the river, Decker wondered if maybe there was a chance of getting out of Seoul without serious incident—and then Song's off-key humming brought him down to earth. He had better stop thinking like a fucking visionary and start thinking like a cop.

Song was likely to make his move here in Seoul. America was out. Dumas was dead and Song hadn't had time to put together a new stateside crew. He might try some shit on the plane, but Decker couldn't see it. He'd have to kill Decker, take over the plane, then find somewhere to land a hijacked aircraft. Too big a hassle.

It would happen in Seoul, the only place where Song had the juice. It had to go down here. Where else could Laughing Boy put together an escape plan on such short notice? He'd try to cap Decker on the way to the airport. Or at the airport itself. Look for the shit to hit the fan sometime during the next two hours.

The Hyundai passed through the last of the city's crumbling medieval walls, then turned onto a nearly empty highway. Decker was glad to see the last of the heavy traffic. Goodbye to piles of dead dogs.

The car was immediately overtaken by a small blue bus filled with singing Korean men in alpine garb—windbreakers, backpacks, feathered caps, hiking boots. Decker saw their silly grins and relaxed; chalk up the smiles to booze being handed around. In weather like this getting half-bagged didn't seem like such a bad idea.

Honking twice, the bus driver passed the Hyundai, barreling through slush and across potholes as if they weren't there. Decker wasn't surprised to see the driver put the pedal to the metal. Koreans didn't believe in driving slow when you could go full blast. Kang tooted back, smiling at Decker in the rearview mirror as if to say, We're all one happy family over here. Decker looked at Song, thinking, That's what worrying me, pal.

He looked back at Kang to find him peering into the left-hand wing mirror. So Kermit wanted to check on the escort car. His wandering gaze simply confirmed Decker's suspicions; Kang was a spook, the guy Youngsam had on the inside, which was the sort of thing Intelligence people did. Decker had seen American Intelligence at work and come away unimpressed. Intelligence guys were so busy looking for people under the bed, they didn't have time to look in the bed itself.

He glanced through the back window, expecting to see the black Toyota with Youngsam's bird dogs. Instead he saw a pair of dusty GM vans some twenty yards behind them on a still bare highway. He also saw a long flat-bed truck stacked with small cars. What he didn't see was the black Toyota. He tried to ignore the warning coming from his gut. Forget it, he'd been a cop too long. To calm himself, he breathed deeply and tried to make his mind blank. To be aware of the danger was one thing; to brood on it was to weaken himself. Every sound in the car—flicking windshield wipers, Song's humming, Karen's whispers to Tawny—reached him as though coming from a distance. His mind tried playing games: it said he was imagining things, that he was presuming too much.

Karate, however, had taught him to be aware of the mind's weakness. He had learned that the mind always wanted to take the easy way out. The mind did not want to train when Decker was hurt or tired. It had wanted to quit when training became difficult. Decker had become good at karate only *after* he had learned to ignore the mind. He ignored it now, choosing to go with his gut. Song's people were in the vans and probably in the truck. Decker was in deep shit.

He looked to the front in time to see Kang make a sharp right, throwing Song into Decker's arms. Decker shoved Song away as the Hyundai left the highway and bounced along a snow-covered dirt road. They were in an empty park. They were not heading southwest anymore.

Decker shouted to Kang, "What the fuck are you *doing?*"

Dumb question. Kang was Song's man and he was bringing Decker to the killing ground. An angry Decker told himself he should have realized that Song, not Youngsam, needed the inside man. But if Decker had known about Kang an hour ago, what could he have done? Damn little. Even if he'd ripped Kang's lungs out, there was still the matter of the vans and truck behind them.

But he instinctively reached for Kang because the guy was puke and had it coming. That's when the Hyundai hit a king-sized pothole, hurling Decker and Song toward the car ceiling. They collided, falling back as the car raced past the park's low wooded hills, icy ponds and snow-covered temples. Decker looked over his shoulder to see the vans and truck closing in. Death was now about to cut off any hope he might have.

He started to reach inside his overcoat then stopped. *No gun.* Decker closed his eyes; his heartbeat was out of control and he felt exhausted. Choices: he could fight with his bare hands and die. Or he could refuse to fight and still die. Either way, he was finished. His life was about to come to a screaming halt in a cold, foreign land where people ate dogs and everybody was for sale.

Karen swiveled around, her eyes silently pleading with Decker to save them. Before he could say anything she saw the vans over his shoulder. She whispered, "Oh, my God," and took Tawny in her arms. Decker started to speak, but changed his mind. He could only offer false hope which would only hide the truth. He did feel sorry, however, for bringing Karen along. Maybe he should tell her that. Tell her he should never have brought her to Seoul.

Song's trap was airtight. Ahead the mountaineers' bus had blocked the road. *Mountaineers.* Sure. Mountaineers didn't wear steel helmets, cartridge belts or carry automatic weapons. The men rushing from the bus not only carried guns but moved with the professionalism of seasoned troops. They quickly took up defensive positions behind the bus, trees, rocks and aimed their guns at the Hyundai. The feathered Alpine hats and boozy good-naturedness of a few minutes ago were things of the past.

The sound of car horns behind the Hyundai drew Decker's attention. He looked over his shoulder; the vans and flat-bed truck were closing in fast. The game was over. If Decker thought he could beat this one he was sleepwalking. He was only minutes away from going belly up.

The Hyundai braked abruptly. Decker turned front to see that son of a bitch Kang fighting a skid. But despite his best efforts the Hyundai slid off the road and headed toward an icy foothill overlooking a frozen lake. Decker pressed both feet against the floorboard, free hand pulling hard on a window strap. If the car continued sliding, it would slip down the hill and end up in the lake. Decker didn't want a bullet in the head. He also didn't want to drown.

Song, too, recognized the danger. Face flushed, he screamed hysterically at Kang in Korean. Decker didn't understand a word but he sensed Kang was getting his ass chewed out. The driver got the point. Somehow he managed to bring the car to a shaky stop on top of the hill.

Decker, heart pounding, wiped sweat from his forehead with a coat sleeve. His mouth and nose were dry; he was dizzy with fear. He closed his eyes only to open them quickly when Karen shouted, "Manny, he's got a gun!"

Fucking Kang. He had his hand inside his coat and was turning to face Decker. Decker's brain said *do it.* Take away Kang's piece then tell Song he's meat unless his people back off. Upgrade Song from prisoner to hostage. And don't think about the difficulty of leaving Seoul with a hostage. Just snatch the gun from Kang before he starts wasting people.

The idea was risky; a thousand things could go wrong. Song might not sit still for being a hostage. He might just force Decker to kill him. Then what? Decker had also seen a police marksman with a high-powered rifle end a hostage situation with one shot in the hostage taker's forehead. Song's people had gone to a lot of trouble to free him. Let Decker get tricky with Song and those people would get tricky with him. On the other hand, what did he have to lose?

Leaping from the back seat Decker reached forward with his free arm, eager for Kang's gun, his only hope. Suddenly, he felt himself being pulled back into a sitting position. *Song.* For a split second Decker, in his excitement, had forgotten about Laughing Boy.

Song hadn't forgotten about him. As Decker tumbled back into his seat, Song lifted his cuffed hand and attempted to elbow him in the head. Decker brought up his cuffed left hand as a shield. Song adjusted quickly. He continued his motion but switched targets, driving his elbow into Decker's bicep.

The pain raced from Decker's shoulder to fingertips, leaving the arm nearly paralyzed. Arm throbbing, he drove his shoulder into Song, knocking him off balance. Then he started to reach for Kang but froze when he saw a PPK Walther in the driver's hand.

Karen saved him. Screaming, she raked her nails down the left side of Kang's face. Cursing, the driver pushed her and Tawny against the dashboard. Karen, however, had spoiled his aim. Kang's gun hand shifted unintentionally; the Walther went off twice, sending two shots through the car roof.

Looking down the gun barrel left Decker more psyched than ever. He jammed his left heel down onto Song's instep and when the Korean pulled away Decker went after Kang. Throwing himself across the front seat, he ended up nearly face to face with Kang. Then he quickly drove his gloved fist into Kang's throat, crushing the larynx.

Kang clutched his broken throat with both hands. Breathing was impossible; he opened his mouth to cry out against the awful pain but no sound emerged. He'd seen Decker leap across the front seat, seen the hatred in his face. What he hadn't seen was the American's hand; it had moved with the speed of a snake's tongue. He'd attacked before Kang could bring the gun to bear on him. And he'd punched with total commitment, with the spirit of a man determined to kill.

Kang's throat was in agony. He felt as though he'd been clawed by a bear. He lay against the steering wheel; the sound of the car horn grew fainter because he was dying, choking to death in his own blood. He couldn't stop his legs from twitching. He tried to swallow blood, to clear his throat so that he could breathe. He died just after wetting his pants.

Decker thought, *the gun.* The fucking gun. He reached across the seat, frantically pulling at Kang's corpse for the piece. *The handcuffs.* Song yanked him backwards. He was Decker's prisoner. But Decker was also his.

Decker yelled to Karen, "The gun! I need the gun!"

"No gun! No gun!" Song shouted. He threw himself on Decker, free hand grabbing for his balls. Decker seized the hand, thinking, break the pinky finger. Then break Song's neck. Kill the bastard and die happy. He heard Karen scream she couldn't find the gun, that she thought it was under Kang's body but she couldn't move the corpse because she wasn't strong enough. And through the windshield Decker could see some of the armed mountaineers creeping closer.

Song wanted his freedom but he was even more determined to kill Decker. The Korean had never allowed anyone to get the better of him. He'd always taken his revenge, always evened the score. Informers, rivals, traitors. He had annihilated them all, leaving no one to say they had triumphed over Park Song. Decker had ruined his plans to repay Youngsam then traveled to Asia to take his *kisaeng.* Even if the heavens fell on him, Song wanted his revenge.

He bit Decker's cheekbone, viciously digging his teeth into the detective's face, Song relishing the salty taste of blood and grunting as he willed himself to tear away all the flesh he could. He smelled Decker's coffee breath, felt his unshaven skin, sensed his panic at the unexpected attack. Decker tried to pull away. But in the cramped quarters of the car's backseat there was nowhere to go. Seized by a wild joy, Song bit down harder.

Decker nearly spooked. Being bitten in the face was a shock. The pain was fierce; only a freak like Song would pull this kind of shit. He reached for Song's throat only to have his hand knocked aside. Song immediately followed with a counterattack. Drawing back his head, he butted Decker in the face, cracking his left eye socket and cheekbone.

Pain ripped through Decker's skull; his head hit the window, leaving him stunned and confused. The blow also left him blind in his left eye. He grabbed Song and held on, thinking, I need time. Got to clear my head. Smother Song's attacks. That's all he could do for now. Song was killing him inside. Losing the sight in one eye was scary. It could also be fatal if Decker couldn't see well enough to defend himself.

Song sensed he was winning. The taste of Decker's blood was exciting, almost sexually arousing. Song became more agressive, clawing at Decker's eyes. The detective just managed to turn his head sideways in time.

Song tried to knee Decker in the groin. He missed; Decker was too close. But the knee managed to do damage. It hit Decker's hip, sending pain up his back. Song's infighting was taking Decker apart. He had to get out of the car. Get outside, where he'd have some room to maneuver.

Suddenly, the car door opened and Decker tumbled out into the snow, dragging Song with him. He caught a quick glimpse of Karen, who had left her seat to open the back door. Decker loved her, fucking loved her for what she'd done. He heard her cry out. The tone of her voice was a warning. But he couldn't stop fighting. Song wouldn't let him.

She was warning him about the lake. Warning him that they were too near it. But her alarm went unheeded. She stood helpless as Decker and Song slid down the icy foothill toward the weeds ringing the frozen lake.

Hauling Song behind him, Decker tobogganed downhill. Unable to slow down or stop himself, he felt his overcoat snag on ice chunks. Ahead wild ducks hiding in the weeds took to the sky, quacking and honking at the intruders threatening their sanctuary. Decker, counterfeit bills spilling from his coat pockets, reached the weeds first. He crashed through the ice and disappeared beneath the lake's surface. Song followed an instant later.

Decker rose first, soaking wet and coughing up water. And colder than he'd ever been in his life. He was in water up to his waist. Mud pulled at his feet and the taste of stagnant water was making him sick. His left eye was closed. And he was still handcuffed to Song.

Song, back to Decker, rose from the water. He spun around in time for Decker to hook a right to his head. Song, however, was quick. He ducked, and as the punch passed overhead, he drove a heel-palm at Decker's chin. Decker leaned away, missing the full force of the blow which stung the left side of his face. He was startled by Song's speed. He hadn't fought anyone that fast in years.

If fighting in handcuffs was a nightmare, fighting in waist-high water while wearing handcuffs was worse. Decker could hardly move; his speed and strength were useless. On the plus side, he didn't have to worry about Song's high kicks; he'd seen them in Saigon and knew they could be vicious.

But he did have to worry about the waterlogged clothes which hampered his every move. Did Decker have more stamina than Song? Why hang around long enough to find out. It was best to end the fight quickly. The longer a battle, the more chance of your getting hurt.

He yanked on the cuffs, pulling Song face down into the water. Song stayed underwater, surprising Decker who wondered why. Seconds later he got his answer. He felt Song's hands fumbling around his legs. Son of a bitch was going for his nuts again. Decker started backing up but Song tricked him. He attacked a different target.

He dug his fingers into Decker's right kneecap, ruthlessly attacking the nerves, sending stabbing pains racing foot to hip. Decker cried out. His leg trembled violently and threatened to collapse under him. He backed away from Song as fast as possible.

Song broke water, sucked in air, then shook his head to clear his eyes. Instinctively he yanked on the cuffs. With only one good leg, Decker stumbled forward and nearly went down. His left foot, now missing a shoe, sank deeper into the mud. He saw Karen on shore, waving and shouting at him. But his ears were clogged with water and he heard nothing.

The fight was a standoff, and Decker knew it. He also knew his strength would give out soon. Either he busted a move on Song or they'd both freeze to death. Both were experienced fighters, experienced enough to take advantage of each other's mistakes. First man to fuck up was dead.

Decker decided to make Song that man.

He tugged on the cuffs with both hands, pulling the Korean into deeper water. Song was strong, but Decker was stronger. The Korean resisted, digging his feet into the mud bottom and pulling back with everything he had. Still, Decker managed to move him. He had to weaken Laughing Boy's position. Weaken the son of a bitch before he figured out Decker's intentions.

Every step Decker took was agony. His left eye throbbed unmercifully. His right knee, screwed up by Song's fingers, could barely support his weight. Twice he nearly fell backwards into the lake.

When the water reached chest-level on him, Decker stopped pulling. He had Song where he wanted him. Had that headcase in water up to his chin, Song with the wild-eyed look of a gonzo as he shivered with cold and giggled, scaring the hell out of Decker. But then Laughing Boy always had been squirrely. Loose in the bean and a primo headcase. Decker never had a chance of taking him in alive. When you went against Song, you threw away the rules and concentrated on staying alive.

Song suddenly noticed the danger. He cursed himself for not having been alert, for getting caught up in a tug of war and not seeing that his arms were now underwater. He was also on tiptoe, off-balanced and weak. *Fucking Decker had tricked him.*

He'd lured Song into deep water to drown him. Song had been beating the great American detective; he'd drawn blood, nearly crippled one of his legs and forced him to run away. Decker was now admitting his defeat. Suddenly Song didn't mind the cold water. Winning took away the pain. He giggled. He was going to destroy this American piece of shit.

He yanked on the cuffs, intending to pull Decker toward shore. By twisting his wrist he pressed the steel painfully against Decker's wrist; every hurt inflicted on the enemy contributed to the final victory. Asian life was built on perseverance. Song was going to persevere until he'd won his freedom and killed Decker.

But his tugging and yanking failed to budge Decker. Strengthwise, the detective had the edge; he was digging his feet into the mud for all he was worth. Song hated him for that, for relying on brawn. As a proficient *karateka,* he had only contempt for those macho types who arrogantly relied on muscle to settle differences. He'd always made a point to demean these Arnold Schwarzenegger clods. Decker would be no exception.

Song saw the determination on Decker's face. Or was it desperation? Call it what you will, Song intended to put the great American detective to the test here and now. Bringing both the cuffs to his mouth, he sank his teeth into Decker's thumb. Sergeant Decker had traveled a long way to die. So let him die.

Decker moaned through clenched teeth. The pain in his thumb was unbearable; every muscle and nerve in his arm felt as if it were being scraped with broken glass. Song was a ravenous wolf, chewing through flesh and down to the bone. There was blood on his lips;

even the guttural noises he made sounded animalistic. Laughing Boy had freaked out. The little prick had gone around the bend.

Decker tried pulling his thumb out of Song's mouth. No way. Song, eyes bulging, bit down harder, then became even more vicious. Using his forefinger and thumb, he pressured a nerve inside Decker's left wrist. A stinging, burning hurt raced along the detective's arm and up his left side. He nearly dropped to his knees in the freezing water.

At the sight of Decker's agonized face, Song became jubilant. He shook his head wildly, teeth tearing at the detective's flesh and gouging an even deeper wound. His mind said, inflict more agony, more suffering, and he did. Sliding his fingers up Decker's wrist, he found a different nerve, then jammed his thumbnail into it.

An ache exploded from Decker's fingertip to shoulder. He could barely move the arm. But he willed himself to stand still. His plan called for being close. Face twisted in pain, he stood his ground.

Song saw Decker's pain and was ecstatic; he felt something close to sexual satisfaction. He'd always found violence to be erotic; he was incapable of having a relationship with a woman without violence. He wanted this excitement in the lake to last. Not to worry. His men were on shore. Decker would die now or he would die later.

Song's immediate formula for victory: work his way up Decker's arm, attacking nerves as he went, until he reached the face. Then gouge out Decker's eyes and drown him.

Through his pain Decker saw what he'd been looking for. Song had fallen into his trap. Laughing Boy had made *the* mistake and Decker had to capitalize on it before the bastard got wise. The mistake: in attacking Decker's thumb and wrist Song had committed both hands. For the moment he could do nothing else. He'd also placed his head within Decker's reach. Decker thought, it's now or never.

He threw himself on Song, wrapped both legs around the Korean's waist and squeezed hard. His free hand grabbed Song's coat. A deep breath, then Decker threw himself backwards, taking Song underwater with him. *Taking them both to their deaths???*

Gritty, frigid water trickled into Decker's nose, mouth, ears. Underwater vegetation and chunks of ice brushed his face. The meaning of what he'd just done hit him with full force. He'd submerged himself in a frozen lake while handcuffed to a psycho. Had Decker gone over the edge?

He saw bubbles rising from Song's mouth, saw him release the thumb. In the murky water, Song's face appeared ghostly white; his bulging eyes were full of terror. Decker had caught him off-guard, surprised the fucker and now had him shitting blue. Being held underwater could make anybody come unzipped.

The further they descended in the water, the colder it became. And the more difficult it was to see. Decker was a fair swimmer at best. He hadn't held his breath this long in years; doing it now was sheer agony. With each passing second his panic increased.

Five seconds underwater and he was scared shitless. Scared enough to think about freeing Song and saving himself. But karate had taught him to persist, to endure and outlast. He kept his legs wrapped around Song's waist, determined to drain him. To use that sucker up.

And then they landed on the muddy bottom.

Song's immediate reaction to going underwater had been to release Decker's thumb. He'd had no choice; either he closed his mouth or he'd end up swallowing this shitty water by the gallon. Decker's strategy had left him dumbfounded. Absolutely flabbergasted. It wasn't strategy, it was fucking suicidal. Was Decker mad? Was he trying to drown them both?

Mad or not, his legs were crushing Song's waist and ribs. Worse, being pinned like this prevented Song from surfacing and getting air. Unless he did something quickly this American fool would kill them both. If Decker wanted to die, that was his business. Lungs bursting, Song pulled Decker's hand from his lapels.

Decker thought, just a few seconds longer. Five seconds more. Five more fucking seconds to take the starch out of Laughing Boy. Five seconds more to sap his strength. After that, he goes.

He felt Song's hands brushing his legs. Decker tensed, remembering the pain from Song's earlier nerve attacks. He reached for Song's throat but the water encumbered his action. His movement was clumsy and heavy-handed, an endless, slow-motion gesture. But Song was forced to defend against it. Forced to take his hands away from Decker's knee.

But at the same time, Decker had started to take in water through his nose. *Fuck it.*

He dropped his legs from Song's waist. At once the Korean pushed off from the muddy bottom, frantically stretching overhead for the lake surface. He was suffering tremendous pain in his stomach and rib cage. He was, in fact, nearly helpless. Decker would pay for this. Oh, how he would pay. Just let Song get a breath of air.

Decker stayed with him and they broke water together, heads pushing through a layer of counterfeit hundreds, Song's mind consumed by one thought. *Air.*

Decker, however, had programmed himself to kill. He drew on all his self-control, willing himself to do without air one second longer. *One second.* As they emerged into the open, he blanked out his suffering and soreness and grabbed Song's head in both hands and snapped his neck, hearing it crack, feeling the head abruptly go loose in his hands.

Then Decker sucked in a mouthful of cold air, feeling it chill his lungs, enjoying its sweetness and life-giving force as never before. He had also enjoyed killing as never before.

Then the unthinkable happened. A dead Song began killing him.

The Korean's corpse now started dragging Decker below the water's surface. A groggy Decker fumbled in his coat pocket for the key to the handcuffs. *The pocket was empty.* He'd lost the key during the fight.

Decker now engaged in a tug of war with Song's corpse, Decker frantically pulling towards shore. A dead man was trying to drown him. Fucking unreal. Decker pulled harder.

But the fight had left him burnt out. He was a wreck, used up and dog-weary. His arms ached and his knee was just about blown out. He stopped to catch his breath for a few seconds only to have Song's corpse nearly yank him off his feet. Decker immediately resumed pulling. Either he dragged Laughing Boy's corpse onshore or they'd both go under.

He looked over his shoulder to see Karen wading toward him. Tawny also entered the lake, stopping in chest-high water. When a shivering Karen reached Decker she was in water up to her armpits. Without a word, she grabbed the back of Song's collar and began pulling toward the shore. A glance at her was enough. If she could try, so could Decker. He tugged at Song's lapel and the Korean floated toward them. Decker thought, pull this puke out of the lake or go home in a box.

But he wasn't going to die. Not in the lake, anyway. He reached Tawny who grabbed Song's sleeve and pulled. Tired as he was, Decker was nearly moved to tears by what the kid was doing for him. Gail had a very special daughter.

They dragged Song from the lake and onto the snowy bank. As Karen took Tawny in her arms, Decker collapsed on his hands and knees. Between his nerves and the cold, he couldn't stop shaking. He also couldn't stop coughing up lake water. But he was alive and Laughing Boy was dead. He looked down at Song. Nice try, assface.

What was it they said in Vietnam? Right. Everything happened in threes. Song had tried to kill Decker in Saigon, tried to waste him here in the park and after dying, had tried once more. Give the man an A for effort. Shit, give him three A's.

Decker's teeth were chattering audibly. His wet clothes weighed him down and he still had to find a way to free himself from Song's corpse. He sat down in the snow, wondering how you removed handcuffs without a key. Then he felt a tap on his shoulder and looked up to see Karen pointing toward the hill. Colonel Youngsam and a dozen uniformed soldiers were making their way down to the lake. Decker thought, I'm fucked. It was all over. He was about to buy the ranch.

Or was he? Something strange was going down. On the hilltop, the Koreans were divided into two groups. One half was holding the other half at gunpoint. Talk about some weird shit.

The so-called mountaineers and the Toyota spooks had their hands up. All were facing shotguns and automatic rifles in the hands of uniformed soldiers Decker reckoned had been in the vans and flat-bed truck. The uniforms belonged to Youngsam, Decker knew. What he didn't know was why Koreans had other Koreans under the gun. It didn't make sense. Or did it?

Decker stood up slowly, keeping his weight off his right leg. He rubbed his cuffed wrist, thinking, working it out in his head. And the longer he thought, the more he was inclined to believe that he and Song had been jerked around. Walking toward Decker was the man who'd pulled the strings. Say hello to Colonel Youngsam, the Wile E. Coyote of the Orient.

Decker tucked his hands under his armpits. Anything to warm them. Breathing wasn't all that easy either; the lake water had fucked up his stomach which wasn't all that healthy to begin with. The cold wind was turning his wet clothing into sheets of ice. His feet were numb. He hoped to hell they weren't frostbitten.

Youngsam glanced at a shivering Karen and Tawny but kept walking until he reached Decker. Was it Decker's imagination or did the intelligence chief smile briefly? Then it all came together in Decker's mind, Decker frozen stiff but still able to think. And thinking, schmuck, the colonel's smiling because you just did his dirty work.

Decker said through chattering teeth, "Son of a bitch, you used me."

Youngsam stared at him from behind dark glasses. "I was told you fought well. You did not disappoint me."

"You orchestrated Song's death. This extradition shit was a set-up. You wanted Song dead so that he wouldn't spill his guts in an American court. And you got me to kill him for you."

Youngsam permitted himself a half-smile. "You Americans like happy endings. So now you have one. Song is dead and you have recovered the girl. The show is over, so you can go home."

"What if Song had killed me?"

"Then I would have treated him as an escaped criminal. He would not have been allowed to evade justice, I assure you."

"You're saying if Song had killed me, you'd have killed him. You're fucking cute, you really are. Know something, colonel? I don't like being used. What happens if I decide not to give you the notebooks?"

He saw the contempt on Youngsam's face. He saw something else, too. This was a man used to having his way. Cross him and he spat out flames. Decker thought, I've gone too far with this dude. Too fucking far.

Youngsam said, "It is in your interest to surrender the notebooks, to take your government's offer of amnesty while that offer is still on the table and put this business behind you. You are in the middle, between my government and your own. People in the middle of the road get run over. Allow me to point out that with Song and Mrs. Dartigue dead it will be difficult to authenticate the notebooks."

He looked up at the falling snow. "You are concerned with morals, but this is not about morals. It is about politics and politics is about interests. You had a role to play and you have played it. I suggest you do not overstay your allotted time upon the stage. Return to your country, hand over the notebooks as agreed, and count yourself lucky that you defeated Park Song. One more thing."

Youngsam casually lifted a hand in a signal to the soldiers guarding the mountaineers and others. Karen seemed to know what was coming. Decker watched her quickly grab Tawny and turn away.

Youngsam said. "Are you watching, Sergeant Decker? This is what happens to those who don't keep faith with me."

He brought his hand down and the soldiers fired, killing the mountaineers. Killing the Toyota guys. Killing the Koreans who'd come from the vans, Kim Shin among them. Killing Song's would-be rescuers. Shotguns and AK-47's lifted the doomed men in the air, turning them into bloodied rags, sending them rolling and sliding down the hill.

Then as Decker stood with his heart in his mouth, wondering if he was next, Youngsam said, "I've ordered your plane held for you. We have an agreement, sergeant: Song for the notebooks. I strongly suggest you keep your part of the bargain. For your sake, I hope we never meet again."

TWENTY-FOUR

On Christmas Eve Decker, Karen Drumman and Tawny DaSilva were among thousands of patrons who entered the Grand Lobby of Manhattan's Radio City Music Hall for the noon show. Karen and Tawny marveled at the sixty-foot-high, gold-leaf ceiling from which a pair of chandeliers, each weighing two thousand pounds, hung like colossal twin earrings. Decker, dark glasses protecting his damaged eye, was remembering the last time he had seen the Christmas show. "I was fifteen," he said. "Our seats were so far back the horses looked like mice."

He thought, fifteen? What sort of dreams did he have then? It didn't matter. They hadn't lasted any longer than today's performance would. Even youthfulness of spirit was something he'd lost long ago. He could have lost it in Vietnam, on the cops or just growing up. He looked at Tawny, wondering how much of her youth had been lost during the past two weeks. Would she end up like Decker, carrying around things so deep and secret that she'd never be able to relax and unwind?

Outside, in front of the theater, an emaciated young-old black man had hit on Decker and Karen for a "contribution to the United Negro Pizza Fund." He'd been dressed in a plastic shower cap, mis-

320

matched running shoes and the sorriest-looking Army blanket since cloth was invented. Decker had slipped him a buck.

As Karen dug in her purse for change, Decker, ever the cop, had scoped the crowd. As a cop it was instinctive to distrust anyone you didn't know. The run-in with Colonel Youngsam had shaken him up; these days he was reluctant to trust even the people he knew. Decker smiled, remembering what he'd told his captain. "You could call what happened a kind of incident. Some people kind of fucked with Youngsam and he kind of killed them all."

He watched a Korean family, parents and three children, step up to the box office and attempt to buy tickets, only to be told the show was sold out. Koreans and the frigid weather reminded him of Youngsam. Decker shivered, and not just because of the cold.

As Karen handed the beggar a dollar, Tawny told Decker a joke. "What did the man say to the waiter in the restaurant? He said, 'Give me an alligator sandwich and make it snappy.'" Decker smiled, saying the joke was very funny. But his eyes were on the Korean family. Youngsam had made sure Decker was going to be antsy around all Koreans for some long time to come.

It had been Karen's idea to invite Tawny to New York for a couple of days, flying her from Baltimore, where she now lived with her grandparents. Gail had promised to take Tawny to the Christmas show, Karen said. And Tawny wanted to go because it would remind her of her mother. It was Tawny who had insisted that Manny Decker come along. He felt good about that. Very good.

In the lobby he unbuttoned his topcoat and wondered how Gail would have taken his trip to Bermuda with Karen next February. Then he decided, get real, crime fighter. Some things never come back, things like first loves and old good times. Enjoy yourself with Karen, because it won't last forever.

Tawny was finding it hard to adjust to the loss of her parents. Her suspicion of adults, males in particular, Decker could understand. Apparently he and her grandfather were the only men she felt comfortable around. Karen said Tawny cried at night and no longer made friends easily. All of which bothered Gail's parents, who were doing their best and not getting much response. Decker wasn't surprised. Tawny had been a victim, and many victims never totally recovered.

Sometimes Tawny didn't speak for days. She was doing poorly in school; her grades had never been worse. It was Decker who told Karen that Tawny might never lead a normal life again. She'd had it all taken away, what she'd known and would never know.

Karen had been more optimistic. "You don't know women. We're stronger than you are. Given the shit we take from you men, we have to be. She's a tough little one. There isn't enough darkness in the world to put out that little candle. You mark my words, there isn't."

In the lobby Karen said to Decker, "You bought the tickets, so I'm buying the popcorn. Tawny and I'll be right back. Wait here, unless you want to battle that mob at the concession stand."

Decker shook his head. "I'm staying put until you guys get back." When they'd disappeared into the crowd he positioned himself back to the wall. *Youngsam.* Try as he might, Decker couldn't get him out of his mind. Looking back, he decided that trying to blackmail him had been suicidal. In challenging Youngsam, he should have made sure that he, Decker, had a glass belly button. He'd had his head so far up his ass at the time, it would have been nice to look out and see where he was going.

Decker touched his face, feeling Song's teeth; Laughing Boy's vampire act on his body parts had called for a half-dozen tetanus shots. His aching wrist was healing but still bore cuff marks. Weight lifting had at least improved his knee to the point where he had stopped limping. Other than that and some bad memories, all he had to show for his December dip in the lake was a bad cold. But Decker was not about to forget his trip to Seoul any time soon. For sure, it would be a cold day in hell before he returned.

He'd been granted a week's leave by the department, which no longer regarded him as dogmeat. Why shouldn't they love him? He'd recovered the plates, plugged the leak in the undercover program and whacked Song. The whole world loved a winner.

But if he was a winner, why the hell couldn't he stop worrying? Because he was born to worry.

When Karen and Tawny returned with the popcorn the three entered the theater, which was the largest in the world and sat six thousand. As Decker waited for the show to begin, he found himself actually looking forward to the evening. The audience was in a good mood, so why shouldn't he be in a good mood? New York was a great town at Christmas. The rest of the year it was one big bug house. But Christmas? *Magic Time.*

The lights dimmed, the audience applauded, cheered, whistled. Singers in Dickensian apparel were suddenly targeted by spotlights that caught them arranged along the left and right side of the theater like living Christmas decorations. Another spotlight focused on a mammoth pipe organ, where a smiling, balding organist began playing "Deck The Halls." The organ was powerful, commanding; its vibrations surged through the floor, tickling Decker's feet. The singers joined in. "Strike the harp/And join the chorus." A hidden chord was touched in Decker's mind, bringing both joy and pain. He thought, Merry Christmas, Gail. Forgive me for everything.

Tawny, seated between Decker and Karen, bounced in her seat with excitement. Her eyes lit up. It was the first time Decker had seen her smile. Seeing Gail in her face, he smiled back.

SEOUL

At 9:10 A.M. on Christmas day Colonel Youngsam locked himself in his office, then returned to his desk, where he had been reading the contents of a file marked PERSONAL. Because of the holiday only a skeletal staff was on duty; most of the agency's workers were at home with their families. Youngsam wanted no interruptions. He wished to be alone while he inspected this file he kept in a floor safe in his closet.

He rubbed the back of his neck, his customary habit when thinking. When he'd warmed his neck he picked up a glass of snake's blood and took a sip. The snake's blood, a daily tonic, was the secret of his virility, or so he liked to believe. He felt healthy enough, but he'd be a fool if he didn't acknowledge that he wasn't getting any younger.

He regularly took his snake's blood, had the daily massage and kept up with his weight lifting. But he was growing increasingly fleshy and gray; his eyes were becoming a bother and he didn't hear as well as he once did. Like it or not, one had to obey the laws laid down by nature.

Professionally, his judgment had never been better. The recovery of the notebooks, coupled with the removal of Park Song, had lifted Youngsam's stature to an all-time high. If he still had enemies, they were lying low; for the moment no one dared speak against him publicly. He was the savior of the nation. South Korea's most powerful men were in his debt. When the time was right, Youngsam would collect on that debt.

He'd known about Song's planned escape from the beginning. He'd known who was involved, when they were to make their move, how they planned to go about it. Since Youngsam's foes were of his own household, he'd made a point of having spies in their camp. Had the young Turks defeated him, their actions would not have been called treason. It would have been called patriotism, courage, heroism or God knows what. Treason was the name winners gave to losers.

Youngsam had allowed Song's escape to proceed uninterrupted for three reasons: Song had to be kept out of an American courtroom, the notebooks had to be recovered and all challenges to Youngsam's control of the KCIA had to be eliminated. He lifted his glass. A toast to the arrogance of youth. Perhaps in their next lives they would have learned that to laugh at the elderly was to laugh too soon.

He'd long been aware of the Young Turks' admiration for Song's flashy life and it hadn't bothered him in the least. He wasn't surprised to see the Young Turks use Song's extradition as an occasion to rally around the counterfeiter. Youngsam, however, was infinitely smarter than all of them. He was crafty where they were inept, bold where they were hesitant, ruthless where they were infantile. They'd underestimated him and paid for this error with their stupid lives. The Razor had indeed cut swift and deep.

More than most men he was aware of life's changes and chances, aware that one had to be eternally vigilant to survive in a world where treachery lay around every corner. Youngsam saw life as a harsh reality. Either you conquered it or you went to the wall.

On to more enjoyable matters. He put down the report and picked up a color photograph of a young, blonde American girl. Her name was Anna Hendricksen and the file contained a complete background on her life, including an up-to-date medical history. She was twelve, lived in Portland, Oregon with her family, and had been selected by Youngsam from more than fifty photographs submitted by his agents. He knew everything about her.

He traced an outline of the girl's face with his pinky finger. Quite lovely. She would make a radiant *kisaeng*. Song had sent him the fingers of the last *kisaeng* he'd slaughtered, an insult Youngsam had avenged as promised. It was the notebooks with their details on Song's *kisaeng* fetish, plus Youngsam's own concern with growing old, that had set him to thinking about young girls in sexual terms.

The more he'd thought, the more curious he'd become until he'd finally decided to obtain a young American girl for his own sexual pleasure. Perhaps Song was right. Get them while they were young and unspoiled.

In seeking out his *kisaeng* Youngsam had decided to operate away from the irritating and vexatious Sergeant Decker. Should Decker learn of a kidnapping similar to that of the young Miss DaSilva, who knows how much mischief he might cause? Let sleeping dogs lie.

Lovely Anna was so young and unspoiled. Youngsam felt a stirring in his loins. A girl that age certainly made a man feel younger. He should have given some thought to untested girls before now.

How exciting to enjoy this little treasure before time and circumstances turned her into a lying mask of an old woman. How could a man meet his end without first having had his fill of all available pleasure? Without pleasure a man lived like a fool and died much too soon.

Youngsam would have his *kisaeng*. It was his reward for having outlived his enemies.